EVEN IF WE FIGHT

LOVE KILLS BOOK THREE

BRIANNA JEAN

Even if We Fight (Love Kills #3)
Copyright © 2021 Brianna Jean
All rights reserved.

This book is a work of fiction. Names, characters, organizations, places, events, and incidents are either products of the author's imagination or are used fictitiously. The author acknowledges the trademarked status and trademark owners of various products referenced in this work of fiction, which have been used without permission.
The publication/use of these trademarks is not authorized, associated with, or sponsored by the trademark owners. No part of this publication may be reproduced, distributed, or transmitted in any form or by any means, including photocopying, recording, or other electronic or mechanical methods, including information storage and retrieval system, without written permission from the author, except for the use of brief quotations embodied in reviews and certain other non-commercial uses permitted by copyright law.

EDITING: BOOKISH DREAMS EDITING
COVER DESIGN & FORMATTING: BLACK WIDOW DESIGNS

AUTHOR'S NOTE

OFFICIAL TRIGGER WARNING:
This is a work of fiction with mature themes such as emotional trauma, drug abuse, child abuse, neglect, strong language, infidelity, and suicide. It is not recommended for anyone under the age of 18.

This book in particular was heavily influenced by music.
SPOTIFY PLAYLIST: https://spoti.fi/3pBYeqF

To anyone that struggles with their mental health, whether it's anxiety, depression, addiction…I see you, I support you, I think about you daily.
You are not alone.
You are not broken.
You are human and you are worthy of being loved.
You're beautiful even when you're broken.
Keep fighting.

PART ONE

PROLOGUE
Phoenix

IN ONE SECOND, my entire life changed all over again.

One phone call was all it took to send my mind reeling down a path I was almost *too* familiar with, visiting old wounds and tearing open freshly sealed scars I thought would never reopen. The shittiest part about it was the sharp tang of remembrance.

Familiarity.

Gunshots. Blood. The death of one parent, then the next.

The distinct presence of shock racing through your system was something trauma victims never forgot, only wished to bury. That was damn near impossible when it has a taste, a smell, a specific look, and sported a sharp, pointed stinger than left you momentarily paralyzed.

I'd always pictured my personal version of shock holding hands with fear, making love to anxiety, only to eventually birth my nightmares and serve them to me on a silver platter made of electrical currents.

There wasn't a choice.

I couldn't refuse the offering. I couldn't push away the news that had just shattered my world all over again. All I could do was face it, stare at it, because if I didn't, it would still haunt me. It would follow me around everywhere I went and wreak havoc on my life until I eventually gave in.

I'd experienced this a few times in my life, but *this* time?

Twice as strong. Twice as brutal.

For myself. For Judah.

My soul screamed, given it was split directly in half, feeling not only my own emotions but his as well.

I always knew it, but over the last handful of months, I'd tried to tug the half that lived with him back into my body. I'd tried to fill the empty space, where the other half was supposed to be, with my new life, my new found family—the small, profound, modicum of happiness I'd managed to earn.

I spent all my time focusing on the other things and people I'd come to love, yet when it came down to it, when the tidal wave of tragedy came crashing down on me once again, the truth was the only thing left.

Judah's death had only been narrowly avoided thanks to the generous hands of the universe, and I should have been grateful. I should have felt relieved, but thanks to shock and her love affairs with various other negative emotions, this twisted miracle didn't feel miraculous at all.

Not yet, anyway.

* * *

"HEY." Frankie exhaled as I walked into our hotel room, quickly setting her laptop on the nightstand next to the king-sized bed before scanning me with those knowing blue eyes. "How did it go?"

Unable to answer right away, I simply held her stare, letting my agony speak for itself.

Surrounded by the luxury of the LUX resort, my best

friend's features were coated with remorse as she demanded gently, "Fuck, come here."

I listened, making my way toward the bed, but it felt like I was wading through choppy water in the middle of a hurricane. My body was too heavy, too exhausted, fucking terrified, as I lowered myself onto the white linen and fell onto my back.

All I could do was stare blankly at the ceiling, resentful of the sun shining outside, the waves playing on the sand, birds chirping in the sky.

This was my fault.

If I'd just answered the phone…

"What did Pharaoh say?" Frankie whispered the question as she lay down next to me, grabbing my hand and linking our fingers together as she settled in. "How is he?"

How *is* he?

I didn't know.

I knew his heart was beating, but beyond that and his near-failing organs, there was no other information.

"He's not awake yet," I mumbled.

"But…" She trailed off, sounding cautious, obviously trying not to trigger me into a meltdown. "He's gonna be…?"

Okay?

She wanted to know if Judah would be okay.

"Yeah, he, uh…" I paused, unable to finish the sentence, needing to clear my throat and will the tears threatening to engulf me to disappear before trying again. "He should wake up soon."

Would *I* be okay, though?

Ever since hearing the news, I'd been feeling too much all at once.

Numb. Confused. Guilty.

Nervous. Scared. Exhausted.

Pissed the fuck off…

I didn't know which emotion to focus on, which to

process first. I had no fucking idea how to layer my thoughts in a way I could understand, because they whipped through my mind like a cyclone on a constant rotation, too fast for me to catch.

Now, after the second phone call with Pharaoh, it felt like everything had just fallen from my mind, only to land painfully in my heart and soul, leaving me dragging my feet and stumbling through the pressure.

Frankie and I had made it to the resort somehow, though I didn't remember getting off the plane, leaving the airport, or even checking in. All I could think about was getting enough privacy to make the call to Pharaoh in the first place.

And when I did? My hands had shaken the entire time. I wore an invisible noose around my throat like an on trend necklace, tempting and dangerous.

My skyscraper overdosed.

And it's my fault.

"That's good. He's alive." Frankie sighed again, no doubt carrying a hefty amount of unwarranted guilt on her own slim shoulders for telling me to turn off my phone in the airport. "That's all that matters, right? That he's alive?"

"Sure, if you don't think about the fact that he's probably angry as all fuck and his stint in rehab might not stick," I ground out, voice raw, hating myself for being so goddamn negative, but *fucking hell*. "He may not even go."

Judah had overdosed.

He'd almost fucking *died*.

Two other girls *had* died.

"He has to," Frankie said as she shook her head, the blonde strands of her hair sliding on the expensive cotton beneath us. "He fucking has to go."

I hope he does.

"I had Pharaoh write him a letter," I admitted, needing to get it out there, out of my head, into the universe.

"You did?" There was surprise written all over her tone. "What did you say?"

Inhaling through my nose, I released the thick breath out of my mouth, not bothering to make it sound pretty. "I congratulated him on a solid effort to end his own fucking life, but then told him I won this round. He used fucking Percocet, Frankie, just like I almost did, and I know him well enough to see right through it. It was a message to me, one final fuck you for giving up on him, and if he'd succeeded? He knew I would've had to live with it for the rest of my life."

Everything hurts.

I squeezed Frankie's fingers, unable to hide the absolute hell I was experiencing.

Because if he'd died...

"I know," Frankie whispered, squeezing back. "But don't get caught up in that right now. What else did you say?"

Shakily, I continued, "I told him he needed to take this seriously, go to rehab, and do it right this time, and then I gave him a pep talk."

Because I couldn't fucking help it.

"Taking notes from me?" Franks sassed lightly.

I tried to smile but failed and simply replied, "Clearly."

"So? What else? What was the pep talk?"

"Honestly? I can't remember in full detail because I was trying to be strong, I guess. I wanted to sound firm, to the point, but I was blocking out the real emotion I was feeling. In my head, I was practically begging him, screaming at him that I needed him to get better, to learn about himself, to come back to me and let me love him the *right* way. I wanted to tell him so many things, get all my emotions out, but it felt like I would be rewarding him and giving him an excuse to make this recovery journey about me when it shouldn't be. So I hid all that, but I'm..." Heartbreak clogged my throat, and the organ in my chest was torn to shreds yet still beating so wildly, I knew I was heading into the danger zone, where panic waited to eat me alive. "I just…"

"You want him back," Frankie finished for me, already knowing, always too intuitive.

I hadn't let myself want it, hadn't even thought about it, before his overdose, because I hadn't believed it was possible, hadn't let myself consider this outcome.

Sniffing lightly, tears rolled down my temples, landing in my hair, as I admitted, "I want to know who he is outside of the manic, addicted version of him I fell for."

"What about Pharaoh?" she asked gently, and a part of me hated her for bringing it up. I knew I was going to be the monster in someone's story if I weren't careful, and I didn't want to be reminded of the moments I shared with Judah's best friend because they were real, tangible, they had fucking wings. At the same time, if Judah were sober, if he came back? If he were committed to living clean and taking his life seriously?

"I don't know," I answered honestly, stoically. "I don't know anything right now, aside from the fact that I want *my* Judah. I want the side of Judah I've never seen before but still know exists. Somehow, I know his soul, Frankie, even if he doesn't, but I have no fucking idea if I can have that. I don't know if he'll be able to show me what I see, because to get there? He has to see it for himself, and I know how much work it's going to take for him to get to that point." Rehab was no joke. It wasn't going to be easy for him, and if he didn't want to do it in the first place… "I hate this overdose, I hate this feeling, I hate what he did and how he did it, all the fucking heart ache he caused!"

My breathing was becoming erratic as those tears flew faster, soaking my hair now.

"But…" Frankie pushed, knowing I had way too many

things going on in my head and if I didn't get them out, I'd stay in this tortured state forever.

Choking out the words, I explained, "But there's also a miniscule part of me that feels like this could be a brand-new slate. It could be a new fucking life for him, Frankie. He could start all over. *We* could start all over. But what if he doesn't want to? What if I hate the man underneath the drugs? What if I fucked everything up by sleeping with Pharaoh? How am I going to navigate—"

"Okay, whoa there, princess," Frankie interrupted, her palm cupping the side of my face as she applied just enough pressure to force me to meet her eyes. "One day at a time, okay? You're going through it right now, so everything feels intense. That's okay, but if Judah does what he's supposed to do, he's going to be gone for a few months and you're on vacation for the next three weeks." The reminder worked to calm me down just enough to focus on her words. "Just like Judah gets the opportunity to start over, to have a new beginning, so do you. If he's your fucking person, you won't have to worry about loving the guy he is outside of the drugs. When he does come back, you will love him for exactly who he is, and if he isn't meant for you? If he doesn't do what he needs to do, or if he comes back and suddenly, he's not someone you want to love? Well, then you have your answer. For now, the rest is up to him."

She was right. I knew it, but I couldn't let go of the feeling I had in my soul—the awful, aching, desperation to be closer to him, to be with him, to hold his hand as he walked this path. No matter how pissed off I was, no matter how badly he treated me, no matter how toxic and completely fucked-up our relationship was, I still cared. I gave a shit about him. I loved him, for Christ's sake, and if his addiction hadn't taken total control of his world, who knew where we would be right now.

I couldn't help but notice that a new opportunity had been

presented, now that Judah had truly hit the bottom. He'd almost lost his goddamn life, and now the restart button had been pressed.

Selfishly, it was too much for me to handle all at once, reminding me of my parents and the unbelievable amount of change that had taken place after their blood was spilled. I couldn't turn back time, couldn't hold onto just one more moment. It was all over in the blink of an eye, and while this situation didn't end in death, that same amount of change was staring me in the face.

However, unlike the situation with my parents, this change wasn't up to me.

It was up to Judah.

Fear was an entity watching over me now, hope was a struggling child trapped inside my soul, faith was a faded white light way off in the distance I could barely see, while gratitude appeared black and grey. It was there—I was thankful Judah was alive, but a part of me wasn't sure if I might end up wishing he'd just died the first time.

I cried harder at the thought of going through it all over again if Judah couldn't get it together, if he didn't listen to what I'd had to say in that letter, but Frankie was right...

I had time. I needed to breathe, come up with a plan, and wait.

Pharaoh, tattooing, my friends, Trixie? I had plenty to keep me busy, plenty to keep my mind off of Judah's choices. I had a life I loved, dreams to chase, and in the current moment, a vacation to enjoy.

I just had to find a way to shut my brain off in the meantime.

* ❋ *

Judah

DETOX WAS THE WORST PART.

Nothing was more awful than enduring the absolute fucking hell that was cleansing my body of the poison that had failed to kill me. Throwing up until there was nothing but saliva and stomach acid in the bucket, shaking so badly I nearly fell off my hospital bed—not once but three times—the hallucinations, nightmares, episodes of shitting myself because I was too weak to walk.

They said third time's a charm, and sure as shit, it was true.

This was bottom.

This was the lowest I'd ever been in my life, and it was by far the worst withdrawal I'd experienced thus far.

At one point, I'd screamed at Pharaoh to leave my hospital room because the embarrassment was more than I could handle. I'd known he was still outside the room, though, fearful that my body wouldn't be able to handle the stress, that my organs would fail again, further breaking down what I'd already put them through.

ICU was bullshit, my life wasn't worth that much attention, but my doctors had insisted I was high risk and told me I needed to be watched for at least another seven days before I could be transferred to the rehabilitation facility Pharaoh had picked.

At that point, I wasn't sure I wanted to go at all.

Part of me wanted to break the fuck out of the hospital altogether and try it again.

Surely God couldn't save me twice in one week.

But it was *her* fucking words, that unwavering, bitter faith in me, that kept me crying, breathing, shouting my way through the process of cleaning out my system. It didn't stop me from dreading every step I'd have to take once the detox was over, though.

Daunting didn't even begin to describe it. Terrifying wasn't a strong enough word. Anxious didn't fit either.

Hatred was all I could taste.

I hated myself, the drugs, my choices. I hated Pharaoh, Phoenix, Hendrix, my friends.

The label and Brandon. My mother fucking *parents*.

I hated life in fucking general for giving me such a shitty hand, for wrapping me in barbed wire instead of blankets, for teaching me escapism rather than strength.

It was *bullshit*, every part of it.

But there was still this tiny little spark of faith, way off in the motherfucking distance, and while it was smaller than I'd have liked it to be, it was there and I could see it.

The spark didn't belong to me, though. It sat in the soul of another, but she shone brightly enough to make it known to me. All the way across the world, enjoying a long ass vacation, she somehow fed me strength. I still felt her, she never went away, and even through all my anger, through the horrid taste of failure on my tongue, she held me down, chained to that bed, where I knew I couldn't leave because it meant losing her.

If I gave up, I'd never know success. I'd never know if I was capable of obtaining peace.

Was all this worth it?

I couldn't help but question, knowing that I'd already done a solid job of ensuring she'd never forgive me. Yet the letter was somehow proof that all hope wasn't lost.

I just had to keep screaming, stay surrendered to the agony, rid my body of substances it couldn't handle, and face my inner truth, even though it all seemed impossible.

One impossible minute at a time, one tiny second, one moment to the next.

"...it's your last chance. You won't get another."

Yeah, thanks, Baby Bird. Part of me had been banking on that.

CHAPTER 1
JUDAH

FUCK THIS PLACE.

Fuck Phoenix.

Fuck Pharaoh.

Fuck my life.

I'd been at Cliffside less than twenty-four hours, and my skin was already crawling. The anger I'd become such close friends with stood front and center, never leaving my side and causing chaos in my mind, until all I could think was *fuck it.*

The aches, the shakes, the godawful cravings. The relentless guilt and torturous nightmares. It was too fucking much.

Don't even get me started on her goddamn letter.

P's words had become a crockpot full of bullshit. They wouldn't leave me the fuck alone.

Somehow, that goddamn piece of paper was now a living thing, screaming at me while I screamed back. Her words held me by the throat, squeezing until it felt like my head would pop off, because *come on*. Was she really going to forgive me? After all the shit I did?

Or did she just want to torment me?

That girl knew damn well how hard this was going to be for me, and it would be karmic fucking justice for her to give me false hope, making me think I stood a chance of getting her back after all the shit I did to her.

Did she really think I'd be able to put my life back together?

Bitch, please.

Stay sober?

Yeah, okay. Tried that twice.

Why bother going through rehab all over again? Why bother pretending like I'd be strong enough to resist my previous lifestyle while working in an industry that thrived off the very same vices I'd used on a daily basis?

I didn't want to party. It wasn't about the late nights and drunken escapades, it was about survival. I was merely trying to fucking survive and once again, WHAT WAS THE FUCKING POINT?!

It was three AM, and I found myself sitting on the cold floor of my new room, holding back a cry of bitter frustration, fearing that the night staff would hear me and barge in and pause my meltdown. I didn't want their help, didn't want *anyone's* help.

I just wanted all of this to *end.*

Her letter was clutched between my shaking fingers, and all I wanted to do was rip the thing to fucking *shreds*. Burn it. Erase its entire existence.

Because the whole thing, every goddamn word, was a sick joke.

A pretty little plan of revenge crafted by a brown-eyed bird.

She wouldn't forgive me.

She wouldn't take me back.

She was *laughing* at me out there.

On the way out of my system, the drugs told me I'd never make it alone. They scoffed at me, rolled their eyes, and claimed I'd never be able to live without them. They were positive that I'd be crawling back on bloody knees in no time, and I believed them because *why wouldn't I?*

What did I have to live for?

What was salvageable?

Court cases, investigations, no job, no friends, no Phoenix.

I had *nothing*.

"Fuck it," I snarled into the darkness.

I did exactly as I wanted to.

I tore her letter to pieces.

※ ❄ ※

2 weeks later

THE SOUND of clapping filled my ears, and I inwardly cringed, trying to tamp down the wave of anxiety that threatened to break free.

This place was full of bullshit.

Bullshit people, bullshit routines, a bullshit schedule, techniques, conversations, philosophies.

"Thank you so much for sharing that with us, Ricky." Tina's voice grated through my ears as I lifted my head to catch the look on her face. Our group therapy leader was smiling gracefully at the patient that had just finished telling a predictably sad story about how he didn't think he'd ever get over his incessant need to drink himself into a black hole.

Okay, so maybe it wasn't *all* bullshit.

The patients that were brave enough to speak up and tell their stories tended to speak honestly, but that was only because eventually, they were forced to. With ten of us sitting in a circle, closely watched and guided by addiction specialist, *someone* had to volunteer when the woman asked who'd like to go first. I hadn't been in this rehabilitation center for long, but I'd already gathered that after being here for an extended period of time, the pressure to tell the truth became insurmountable.

Which, in turn, left some poor sucker no other choice but to kick off the session and spill the beans about how they ended up in rehab. As far as honesty went…there couldn't *be* any bullshit from the patients because lying would be too hard.

Speaking to a room full of addicts? There was no point in making up fake stories about how your addictions weren't "that bad." That was shit you told your family when you got caught high as fuck, passed out under a bridge, or stealing money from your mother's purse.

Here, the gig was up.

Some form of tragedy had taken place as a result of your addiction, and now, your life had been interrupted by a three month stay in a facility with trained doctors and staff constantly taking your vitals and shoving antidepressants or antipsychotics down your throat, along with a handful of other medications to curb the horrid cravings that threatened to drive you mad.

It was what it was.

"Judah?" Tina called out my name as I stared at my hands folded in my lap.

"Hmm?" I questioned, dragging my head up again to meet her brown eyes, already knowing what she was going to ask.

"Would you like to share your story with us today?"

Did I want to tell a roomful of complete strangers that I was a royal fuckup? Did I want it to be widely known that I threw my entire life away for a backpack full of pills and killed two girls on my journey to attempted suicide?

"No." *I'm good.*

A look of pity flashed across her face before she regained

control. "No one here is going to judge you, Judah," she pushed gently.

Of course not, because we're all monsters.

"No," I repeated, looking back down at my fingers, unable to handle the similarities between her gaze and the one I missed the most.

Fucking brown eyes, all kind and empathetic.

"That's okay," Tina stated softly, as if already knowing she would fail in her attempt before even asking in the first place. "Maybe next time."

Not likely.

She called out another name.

Good.

I just wasn't there yet. The pressure had yet to wear me down.

It had only been two weeks since I'd checked into Cliffside, and I wasn't sure I was sold on the methods of this place. Couldn't see how any of the shit they made us do would help me want to stay clean, much less get me to dig into the root of the problem and open up to a bunch of strangers. Rehab hadn't done the trick the last two times I tried, and the only difference between this place and others was the amount of money I'd agreed to spend on my treatment.

Still, Pharaoh's voice drifted through my mind.

"Judah, come on. Cliffside Rehabilitation Center offers a luxury environment, so it doesn't feel so impersonal, and it won't make you feel like you're just a kid from the trailer park stuck in a hospital because you fucked up. You've got the money. They've got the most updated methods of addiction rehabilitation, and you get to live in a fucking resort while you clean up your life. It's perfect."

The memory of our conversation in my hospital room popped into head constantly, reminding me that I could be in a stuffy, low-budget, city run joint that didn't give a fuck about me, instead of here at Cliffside.

He wasn't wrong, of course, because Pharaoh had done his research.

The place looked everything like a resort. It was fucking beautiful, had the best amenities, and provided a seriously private space, away from the public eye. It still took my best friend two days to convince me to go for it, though, because all I could think was, *Is it seriously going to work?*

Cliffside was all about the luxury, with high-end, boutique hotel style rooms, sporting a giant flat screen TV, Wi-Fi, cable, and Netflix. Not to mention the thousand-thread-count Egyptian cotton sheets, spa treatments, acupuncture sessions, botanical gardens, incredible ocean views, and the fucking *maid service* that came in every morning to make the bed and clean the rooms.

I mean…really?

I deserved a jail sentence, a tiny room in the back of a shitty facility in the middle of nowhere, but because I'd already felt like a bag of useless shit and I'd known Pharaoh really wanted me to say yes…I did.

So here I was, a couple weeks in, fully detoxed, battling intense cravings, and drowning in guilt. I was also pissed at Phoenix for the pressure she'd put on me. It was the whole reason I hadn't left yet.

Somehow, without even speaking, we were still playing games. I could feel her presence haunting me, constantly hidden around every corner, telling me that sure, I could quit, I could check myself out, find the nearest dealer, and swallow my life away, but then I'd really be a failure. A waste of space, of breath.

Then she'd gloat, even in the afterlife, telling me she was better than I was because she survived while I was too pussy to do the same.

I couldn't get rid of her.

Then there was the fact that I had yet to look myself in the mirror, unable to face the soul deep failure in my eyes, and while I *could* have shared my story with the class and gained some insight regarding how to get out from underneath the weight of my situation, I still wasn't ready. Wasn't convinced. Wasn't sure I could pull this off.

Instead, as I had with all the previous group therapy sessions, I tuned everyone out and fell back into my mind, where a different version of Phoenix lived. Where she was smiling, happy, and laughing at something I'd said.

Even now, even with the resentment I carried around, she was my anchor, my reason.

I didn't give a shit if she didn't like it. I still believed Phoenix Royal would *always* be my reason for breathing, for fighting, for existing at all. She was stronger, she was a survivor, while I was obsessed and addicted to more than just the drugs, I was addicted to *her*, to picking away at her growth and challenging just how brave she really was.

Could she withstand my chaos and still stick around?

No, she couldn't. She'd left, and *fuck* her for that.

Yet she was still mine, because I wasn't going to just let her go. I couldn't. There was no way.

She was my muse, my dark little fighter. She had no problem biting back when I gave her my worst, and yet she knew she was the only thing I had that was mine, the only good thing I truly loved or wanted to live for, even if I was consistently high.

That right there was what she wanted me to change while I was in here.

She hated the pressure, hated knowing that without her, I didn't want to live.

But while I was on drugs, I didn't care. *Fuck* what she wanted.

Now, though, I had no choice but to face what I'd been so desperately trying to ignore. The overdose didn't kill me, and if I didn't leave this place with an entirely new mindset, I would lose Phoenix for good and have to survive the loss sober.

Like *that* was going to happen.

"I was a victim of rape as a child," I heard someone say from my left, and the feminine voice had me glancing up once again, searching for the person speaking. "My mother's boyfriend. He was a piece of shit, and I was only t-thir-t-teen."

A middle-aged woman was telling her story, playing with her fingers, much like me, while she spoke to the floor.

"I could never forget it, and it got to the point where I felt like I was living two lives—my current one, and the memories from my past. I did what I could, tried to block the whole event out, but when my own husband became abusive and started using sex as a weapon…our marriage fell apart. Then my nightmares got really bad, and rather than just walking away from the marriage and letting it crumble, I tried to save it by turning to a friend of mine and asking for help. I explained my situation and told her my anxiety was so bad, I could barely see straight, so she gave me some of her Xanax."

Fucking hell, I could use some of that right now.

This woman's story was the first I'd actively paid any attention to, and I didn't know why. Something about the way her stringy blonde hair fell against her slim shoulders felt familiar. The shape of her body, the bouncing of her left leg.

I narrowed my eyes, listening intently as she continued, "One thing led to another, and I found myself taking three times the average dose just to get through the day. My husband…he was a big name in the city and owned three successful businesses, one of which donated to a handful of charities. So there were galas, meetings, things I was required to attend, and because that was just the way our relationship was set up, I needed to play the part of the doting, supportive wife, but there were…consequences…if I didn't." I swallowed, fighting one of my own flashbacks, understanding her definition of *consequences* all too well. "But I was so uncomfortable and so pissed off at every event that I started mixing Xanax and liquor to help me lower my defenses and do my job. I smiled, acted like I was the happy wife, the proud mother of a perfect child, when the reality was—"

I stopped listening, already knowing how it ended.

The proud mother of a perfect child.

Fuck my whole life.

My mom.

Blood rushed through my ears, slamming into my brain with blunt force, sending me flipping backwards down memory lane as I put two and two together, as I recognized the similarities between this woman and my own mother.

Her personal story wasn't anything like ours, but…

I stood up, unable to sit in that fucking room for even a second longer, and abandoned my chair, leaving the circle entirely, even as Tina called out my name, asking me where I was going.

I didn't answer her, didn't turn around, didn't care.

I wanted *out*, away, desperate for fresh air as my breath came in too quickly, too choppy.

Crashing through the set of French doors that led to a patio area, I stumbled over a chair, barely able to keep myself upright as I hit the white railing of the balcony harder than expected.

My hands gripped the painted metal hard.

My mother.

"Son of a bitch," I cursed, clamping my eyes shut as I bent over and squeezed the tops of my knees, feeling helpless, like I'd never get away from all the damage she caused, the issues she left me with.

The only thing that women ever freely gave me was pain, confusion, self-hate, and doubt, and before now, I'd done a damn good job keeping those feelings far as fuck away.

I'd pop a pill to drown her memory out, mix that pill with as many substances as I needed to, and make *damn* sure I didn't feel a *thing* anymore.

That was how I survived. That was my excuse. That was my fucking life plan.

The only other times I didn't need to completely numb out where those initial few months with Phoenix. She might think I was high the entire time we were together, but I wasn't, I was *better* with her. Not entirely sober, not even close, but she lessened my addiction because she replaced it with herself, until I screwed it all up after "Fu*kUp" came out. I let the industry wear me down to the point where I blamed Phoenix instead of my own insecurities.

Except, I should have just told her, I should have opened up and admitted what my life had been like before she came into the picture. I could have explained where, why, and how I became the monster I was.

It wasn't my fault. My addiction could be blamed on my mother, on the myriad of shit she left me swimming in, on the deeply rooted questions and insecurities she inflicted on my confused, growing mind.

"Why?" I whispered, dropping my head as tears began to form, as Phoenix replaced the image of my mother, as her sweet face, her gentle touch, the memory of her soothing nature fell around me like a blanket. Then I started talking to a ghost. "Why did she leave? Why was my mother so fucking awful?"

What did I do to deserve it?

I wanted to ask P. I wanted to talk to *her* about this.

I didn't want to bare my soul to just fucking anyone. I wanted to tell my person—the *one* person on this planet that made me feel safe, even with the influence of drugs and high-functioning depression.

I was sure Phoenix thought that my love for her had been manufactured by the pills, but that wasn't true. I knew the difference between love and drugs, only because her love was a high I'd never felt before. My love for her was a form of distraction, sure, but more importantly, our love had taught me that I wasn't alone. Her energy spoke for her.

Underneath all that strength, Phoenix felt the same level of guilt, the same frequency of fear, and carried around the same number of unanswered questions. She understood.

Drugs had never done that for me. Only she could.

That didn't matter now, because Phoenix had grown into someone different than the girl I'd met on the rooftop last year. She was more sure of herself, more confident in what she wanted, and she wanted me. She just wanted me sober.

She wanted the *real* me, but the real me was falling apart. Ashamed. Broken.

An orphaned little boy who never knew how to stand on his own.

Deep down, I knew she didn't care that I was emotionally weak, that I was scared of my own shadow. No, Phoenix wanted *all* of my pain, she wanted to help me through my memories, wanted to hold my hand while I walked through hell to find myself again, but I was too much of a pussy to take her up on the offer.

Now I was here, wishing like fuck that I could take it all back and just talk to her, but *fuck my life*, I'd turned her down and lost it all.

I'd been too high, too deep in my addiction, and decided to block her out instead.

Now that I was sober, though, I was back to feeling completely alone and my past was bubbling up to the surface faster than I could've prepared for.

She was gone, I couldn't talk to her, I couldn't—

"Judah?" A voice sounded behind me, scaring me into a standing position as my breathing patterns remained broken, labored.

But when my vision cleared, I saw my therapist standing by the doors.

Dr. Blake Chapman.

Blonde. Sympathetic. Analytical. Understanding.

Not Phoenix.

"I'm fine," I stated and turned around quickly, swiping a hand down my face, hoping to hide the evidence of my emotional breakdown, even though I knew it wouldn't work.

It was only a matter of seconds before Dr. Blake would start an impromptu therapy session with me right there on the patio. Hell, she'd probably been waiting for this moment since I got here.

The woman wasn't one to give up, even if it meant talking to a wall. Which was what she'd been doing for the last two weeks while I sat in her office and stared blankly out the window.

"You know…" she started, proving my point as she made her way toward me. Her four-inch heels clicked on the concrete as she walked. "You remind me a lot of my very first patient in this facility."

Great, just another notch on her therapy belt.

I sucked my teeth as she stopped beside me and stared out toward the ocean, facing the same direction I was.

When I didn't respond, she kept talking, "He was an addict, like you, but he was also stubborn and crass. He typically jumped straight to anger when he felt cornered, and it was difficult to calm him down enough to talk things through."

Crass? Angry?

That wasn't me.

"I haven't said a damn word," I grumbled, not liking that

she was comparing me to some maniac that couldn't control his fucking emotions. I hadn't lashed out *once* since I'd gotten here, and I'd felt cornered on more than one occasion. I had almost *too* much control right now.

"I didn't say you were the same." She laughed a little, which only pissed me off even more. "I just said that you reminded me of him."

I didn't want to give in, didn't want to ask, but at the same time… "Why?"

"How about you answer a question for me, and I'll answer that question for you," she offered.

"Wow, you're good," I replied, mock praising her attempt to get me to open up, and added an eye roll for effect.

"Do we have a deal?"

Son of a bitch. "Fine."

"Why did you leave group therapy?" she asked gently.

I knew I had trust issues, but I didn't realize they went this deep.

I'd thought my inability to open up stemmed from being a musician in the industry. It was second nature when working in Hollywood, you learned quickly not to trust anyone you met, but this wasn't just about my career. This was about not trusting adults in general. Authority figures. People more powerful than me.

Dr. Blake was trained, this was her job. Hell, HIPAA was a thing. It wasn't like she could sell my secrets to the press, but still…I didn't trust her. I didn't want to give her all the gross parts of me.

What would she do with them? What if there was more wrong with me than just addiction? I mean, my recovery team suspected that I was bipolar, but I didn't want to give her any kind of indication, any additional reason to believe that I was. I didn't want to prove her right.

It was bad enough with the addiction, depression, and

anxiety—add bipolar to the mix, and they might as well just send me to a psych ward and call it a day. These people just wanted a diagnosis so they could prescribe more medication and make more money off my rapidly deteriorating mental health.

If I didn't open up, didn't tell my story, things couldn't get any more fucked up than they already were.

I wouldn't—

"Judah," Dr. Blake called, shocking me out of my spiraling thoughts and back to the fact that if I didn't start giving these people what they wanted, I'd never get out of here clean, steady, ready to put my life back together. "Why did you leave group therapy?"

So I spat out, "The woman sharing her story reminded me of my mother."

Silence rang between us for a few seconds before Dr. Blake asked, "But she wasn't, right? She wasn't your mother?"

"Obviously, that woman isn't my mom," I snapped, glaring down at her, given she was still shorter than me, even with the heels. "I'm not a fucking idiot."

"No." The woman shook her head. "You're not."

"So what was the point of asking then?"

"You jumped to negative conclusions when I said you reminded me of my first patient here," she explained, her tone remaining unbothered by my attitude. "It was a trigger for you to be compared to someone else, even though you had no idea what the connection was." She turned her body to face me then, giving me all of her attention while I refused to meet her eyes, looking back toward the ocean. "And that woman reminded you of your mother, even though she very clearly wasn't. It was enough to send you running. These are the things we can unpack, Judah. I can help you get a handle on your triggers."

I knew she was right, but instead of opening up, I bit the

inside of my cheek, clamping down on all my problems, refusing to give away any sign of agreement.

When I remained silent, she spoke again. "I think we got off on the wrong foot."

"How exactly could we get off on the wrong foot?" I scoffed. "You were assigned to be my therapist, it's your job, and I'm the sick patient that doesn't want to talk. It's kinda black and white."

"Actually" —she drew out the word, grating on my last nerve— "I chose you."

My blood pressure spiked.

"You *chose* me?" I glared in her direction, now willing to meet her bright green eyes. "What, you just picked me out of the crowd?"

Her lips lifted in a small knowing smile. "You came in alone, Judah."

I rolled my eyes. "Whatever."

Again, she was right—I did come in alone. We all did. This place was voluntary, so if she *wanted* to be assigned to me, there was a reason. Despite my reservations...

"Ask me why I picked you, Judah."

Fuck.

"No." I looked away.

It was her turn to scoff. "Try again."

"Fucking hell, you're annoying," I bit out.

"It's my job," she sassed back with pride all over her tone. Then, like she *wanted* to press every single one of my buttons, she repeated, "I picked you because you reminded me of my first client."

"Wow!" I exclaimed sarcastically, letting her see the warning in my gaze. "You just *love* the mind games, huh?"

"Mind games, therapy—it's all the same thing, isn't it?" She winked. "I'll tell you why, if you tell me why the woman inside reminded you of your mother. I think once we get through that, we'll have plenty to talk about."

Yeah, of course, because once she opened up the "what my mommy did to me" can of worms, I'd be in sitting on that leather couch in her office for hours on end.

Months. Years. Decades.

My gaze remained steady, heart closed, mind in a jail cell. "Not interested."

"Not yet," she replied, sounding as stubborn as myself. "But you will be by tomorrow."

"So sure of yourself, Doc," I crooned and clicked my tongue, hating her confidence.

She gave me that knowing grin once again before it faded into a form of seriousness I didn't like.

"You want to go home, right? Get back to your life? You want to get the hard part over with, but you're too scared to even start. I get it, trust me, but there really is no other way." *Thanks for pointing that out.* "I can help you, and you know it. So spend the rest of today thinking about what you'd like to start opening up about. It can be anything, we can stick to today's topic or you can pick a different one, but no more silence. Get ready for our session tomorrow, because I have a feeling it will be a good one for both of us."

With that, she turned around, leaving me alone on the patio, confused and feeling played.

She was right, of course, but what the fuck had just happened?

* * *

I SLEPT like shit that night, unable to erase the suffocating anxiety, thinking about all of the things I could say to my therapist that would incriminate me further. I had to be real with myself—I didn't have just one issue, I had a whole fucking truckload of bullshit I'd been pretending didn't exist. There was so much avoidance, so much masking, and all of it led to and fueled my addiction, but what if there was more?

What if I was so fucked-up, even Dr. Blake couldn't help me and I was sent to a mental hospital, where they made me live with a screaming psychopath or hooked me up to a machine for testing? What if I went home with a different backpack full of pills, ones that didn't get me high but rather kept me sane?

Was I truly broken? Could I be fixed?

I had no idea what was going to happen when I started to tell my story, but either way…

I. Didn't. Trust. Her.

"Hey, you're Judah, right? Judah Colt?" a female voice inquired from my right as I sat in an empty booth in the restaurant style dining room we ate every meal in.

Lifting my chin, I found a young girl with auburn hair and a freckled face standing with a nerdy-looking kid, glasses and all, right at the edge of my table. Both of them were looking at me like I was the popular kid in school, all bright-eyed and nervous, waiting for me to grace them with an answer.

"Mm-hm." I nodded slightly, then went back to pushing my breakfast around on my plate.

"I'm Cassie, and this is Brian," the girl introduced, speaking again and not taking the hint to fucking scram.

"Lovely," was I said, all I had to give, knowing that if they knew my real name, they probably listened to or actively made fun of my music.

Either way, their presence was unwelcome.

"Can we sit?" Brian asked, his voice sounding more timid than his female counterpart.

I didn't understand how anyone in here was stable enough to connect with another person, much less multiple. We weren't on vacation, we were in a fucking rehab facility because we all had fucking problems.

This wasn't social hour.

"If you must," I responded anyway, figuring that although the idea of people talking to me was annoying, it also provided a distraction from my personal bullshit.

"Great!" Cassie squealed a little, sliding into the other side of the booth with Brian hot on her heels.

The other tables around us were full, making the noise level decently loud with all the conversation going on, and it seemed that I was the only one who didn't understand why it was so important that we socialize.

When I was checked in, the staff encouraged me to make friends, to get to know the people in treatment alongside me, but I'd been very good at keeping to myself since that day.

Until now, of course.

"Soooo," Brian uneasily began, attempting to make conversation. "You've been here a little over a week now, right?"

Narrowing my eyes in his direction, I sneered, "Keeping tabs?"

Immediately, he retracted, blushing crimson and looking down at his omelet.

Aaaaaand, now I feel like shit.

"W-we didn't mean to bother you..." Cassie stammered, sounding more sheepish and less excited. "We just felt a little...well, we felt—"

Ah, I see.

"Bad for me?" I cut in, meeting her blue eyes, knowing that I looked pathetic spending all my time alone.

"Well, yeah..." She shrugged, only to immediately break eye contact and look down at the French toast on her plate. I watched as she picked up her fork and knife with slightly trembling hands. "Outside of this place, we listened to your music, so, we uh, well, when we saw you, we just…wanted to be your friend, I guess."

I laughed a little, sucking my teeth. "Wanted to kick it with the famous guy?"

"No," Brian spat, now looking a little angry. "We looked up to you."

He said it in past tense, as if I'd ruined their vision of me by acting like a complete jerk.

"That was a mistake," I replied honestly, pissed off at the pedestal I could never seem to stand on. "Look where we are right now. I'm no role model."

"You're not supposed to be. He didn't mean it like that," Cassie added, confusing me. It must have shown on my face because she explained a little more casually. "We didn't necessarily learn from you, we just understood you because we felt the same way and admired you for being able to put it into words for us."

Brian cut in. "The only reason we had to look *up* to you is because socially, you were more influential than us."

He was still pissed, but as he talked, he seemed to level out.

Wanting to forget the topic of my fame and switch the conversation back to them, I shot out, "If you can afford this place, you must be rich kids."

The two of them looked to be at least four or five years younger than me, so I was left to assume their money had to come from their parents, especially since they admitted that I was more socially influential. That meant they weren't living off Hollywood money.

"My mom won the lottery," Brian admitted with bitterness lacing his tone.

Okaaaaay. Not what I expected.

"What happened?" I asked in a low tone.

"She spent most of the money on drugs, gambling, and one

too many vacations," Brian stated simply. "She was forced kept her job at the strip club when it all vanished, while I took the chunk of money she gave me and invested it over the course of five years."

Interesting...

"Then what? You got into her pill stash?" I questioned, assuming it was drugs he was in here for.

Brian shrugged with a small nod. "Got sick of feeling alone, and she didn't care. Said it brought us closer."

He wanted to reconnect to his mommy.

"Sounds like your investments paid off if you can afford this place," I pointed out, glossing over the addiction part.

"I'm a closet millionaire," he replied with zero emotion, meeting me eye to eye.

"Good deal, kid." I smirked, warming up the little punk. "You checked yourself in?"

He blinked once, seeming to fall into a memory as his eyes glazed over, but he snapped out of it quicker than I ever could and nodded just a little. "Mom overdosed and died. I didn't want the same fate."

Fuck.

I choked on my own spit, feeling a brick hit the bottom of my stomach, causing nausea to explode. What was I supposed to say to that?

I overdosed.

I wasn't a fucking role model. *I could be a trigger for him.*

The table was silent as I reached for my water, sucking down the contents in the glass like it was full of lean while wishing like fuck that it was.

Thank god I don't have a kid of my own to disappoint or abandon.

Just a girlfriend I loved more than my own life.

Son of a bitch, I'm *the one that's triggered.*

"I'm the rich kid," Cassie threw in, cracking the silence in half, probably noticing my miniature freak-out. "Daddy owns a Fortune 500 company, left me to my own devices after my mom passed and his new girlfriend became top priority. Three credit cards made of metal, a trust fund, and my group of rich friends led me right to my own downfall."

The joys of being wealthy.

I didn't reply. I couldn't.

They wanted my story next, both of them staring at me expectantly, but they probably knew most of it, especially if they were fans of mine. My life was plastered all over the tabloids and social media outlets. They didn't need an update.

"So…" Cassie cleared her throat awkwardly when I didn't say anything. "How do you like it here?"

Oh, come on.

I gave her a *get real* look, which made her smile as she admitted, "Look, I'm just trying to make conversation."

"I'm not good at that," I replied with honesty. "Lone wolf."

"You weren't always a lone wolf," Brian supplied, reminding me that I had an entire life outside of this place. Friends, Phoenix, everything I was missing out on. "Why are you so…shut down?"

They really didn't know?

"How long have you guys been in here?" I asked, my eyes bouncing back and forth between the two of them.

Cassie answered first. "Three weeks."

Brian followed up with, "Four for me."

That's why.

They didn't know about my overdose.

I wasn't ready to share, wasn't ready to admit out loud that I'd fucked up so hard, two girls died in my fucking bed a full twenty-four hours before I tried to kill myself.

And I had no idea.

Scratching a nonexistent itch under my eye, I pretended like I wasn't affected by what happened to me and those girls.

"Let's just say my current social status in this place is what I think I deserve."

That was even more honest than I wanted to be, but I had to give them something. They'd just told me their own embarrassing fuckups, and I wasn't too proud to recognize how difficult it was to get to a place where you could actually admit your faults.

The two of them glanced at each other briefly before Brian whispered, "Fair enough."

From there, we all went back to eating, and I was fucking grateful for their silence, while still getting used to their presence. I could sense both of them watching me every once in a while, but I pretended like I didn't notice.

My upcoming therapy session was at the forefront of my mind, because as soon as I finished breakfast, I was headed straight to Dr. Blake's office, and I'd be stuck there for the next hour and a half.

I knew I was running out of time and staying silent wasn't helping my situation, especially given the fact that I was bursting at the seams. I needed to get out of my own head, out of my own way.

Finishing rehab and jumping right back on drugs wasn't an option, wasn't something I even *wanted*, if I were honest with myself. I wanted to get back to my life and hold on tightly, but I knew I couldn't go back with the same fucking problems. I'd fall right back into old patterns, and in order to avoid the temptation altogether, I knew I needed to learn how to face myself, no matter how horrifying the thought was.

Now, I had someone willing to talk me through it—a professional that could give me tips, provide insight. All I had to do was trust her enough to let her do her job.

Fuck my life. This'll be fun.

CHAPTER 2

JUDAH

WANDERING into Dr. Blake's office, I pretended like I wasn't nervous as all fuck, when in reality, my hands shook worse than normal.

The room was spacious, sporting floating black shelves that lined the bright white walls, stacked with plaques and green plants. Pictures of her husband and daughter were hung behind her desk, along with a few expensive looking pieces of art, and for her patients, there was a long black sofa placed perfectly in the center of the room, parallel to where she sat in a matching leather chair with her hands in her lap.

"Judah," she greeted, flashing me a smile as I rounded the couch and sat down, kicking my legs up and turning my body so that I could lie down. It was stereotypical of me, but I didn't want to look at her as I spoke.

"Dr. Blake," I said to the ceiling.

"How are we feeling today?"

Me and all the voices in my head?

Oh, we're good. My demons make every day super enjoyable.

I held back my eye roll. "I'm fine."

"Just fine?" she pushed.

Sighing, I cut right to the point. "Can we skip the part

where I don't tell you how I really feel and slide right into the nitty-gritty? Because I've been mentally preparing for the last twelve hours, and the more you stall, the more my balls shrivel up."

That earned me a laugh, bright and a little shocked. "Well, someone is spunky today."

"Who says spunky anymore?" I scoffed.

"I thought you want to skip the bullshit?" she threw back.

I snapped my head in her direction. "Damn, *that* gets a cuss word out of you?"

She smirked. "I'm a human being, Judah. Doctors swear too."

I lay back down. "A little unprofessional, don't you think?"

"Does unprofessional make you more comfortable?"

"Absolutely." My answer was immediate.

"Then I think I'm doing my job just fine."

She won that round.

"All right." I sighed heavily. "Go on then, before I lose my nerve."

I heard some light shuffling and figured she was grabbing her trusty notebook, getting ready to jot down all the evidence of my insanity, making my anxiety run wild. I breathed in and out the way they taught me to at the mediation sessions I was scheduled to attend on the daily.

Yeah, we were forced to meditate at seven AM every morning, either in the yoga room or outside in the gardens, and no, I didn't like it.

I was getting used to it, but I didn't like it.

Regardless of my feelings on the holistic hippy practice, the breathing technique somewhat worked to calm my jittery fears and soothe my overactive worrying as I waited for Dr. Blake to begin.

The key word being *somewhat*.

"So yesterday," she began, while I linked my fingers

together over my stomach and braced for impact. "I want to know why the woman from group therapy reminded you of your mother, but before you answer, focus your mind, calm your breathing, and get to a place where you feel comfortable enough to speak honestly." *I doubt I'll ever be comfortable.* "Start with the very first thing that comes to mind, and then just talk from there. Tell me how you felt when you first saw the woman, what it was about her that triggered you, and where you went in your mind that made you leave the room entirely." *Jesus fuck.* "Don't worry about sounding eloquent or keeping it short for my sake. Just talk and see where it goes, okay?"

My brain interpreted her instruction as "imagine you're talking to Phoenix."

Because plain and simple—that was what I'd have to do in order to get through this in the way Dr. Blake wanted me to. Speaking freely wasn't something I did unless I was writing music, and even then, I was so fucking insecure, I wasn't ever as honest as I could have been. I wrote what my demons wanted to say.

"Okay," I agreed softly as I closed my eyes.

Continuing to breathe in through my nose and out through my mouth, I called on another meditation technique but twisted it to fit my needs, imagining myself outdoors with my little bird. I pictured us sitting in the driveway of her house, like we did the night she told me that she thought we might be twin flames. The night she told me she almost killed herself.

The night that I should have been more honest with her.

The air was cool, the sky was dark, the stars were out.

Even though I knew it wasn't real, my daydream was enough to make me feel even a little more comfortable, because in some fashion, Phoenix was there with me, sitting next to me, waiting to hear about what happened to me the day before.

I swallowed once, then started. "The woman's voice was the first thing I noticed. It was what caught my attention, when normally, I'm able to tune everyone out. The tone of her voice was raspy, as if she were a smoker." I paused, squirming a little, feeling that anxiety making its way back in, but I needed to continue. I was *this* close to doing something right while I was in here. Something that set me forward, not back. "My mother was a smoker, and I'm talking two packs a day, not the occasional few. Except we didn't have the money to support her habit, because we were dead broke, but instead of cutting back on cigs, she cut back on food. Or clothes. Or money for the electric bill. Even the occasional haircut was out of the question, so I was left to use kitchen scissors most of the time. One time I, uh, used my father's razor to shave it all off."

Fuck, this sucks.

My skin was clammy, and my stomach churned uncomfortably.

Going from living in absolute filth to making millions of dollars in front of people who wanted to see you fail? It was no wonder I was fucked-up. I'd gone from one extreme to another.

"Anyway, it was the woman's voice that initially made me look at her, and immediately, I noticed her blonde hair. It wasn't full or thick, it was stringy and gross." I paused, realizing my mistake. "No…offense to that woman or anything."

"Don't worry about it, Judah," Dr. Blake said softly. "Keep going."

I cleared my throat. "My mom, she, uh…she didn't, um, take care of herself. Her hair looked like straw, and it was cut above her shoulders and super thin, like the woman from that group. But I still didn't fully recognize why she, uh, seemed so familiar until she…mentioned being the proud parent of a perfect child."

The last several words were whispered and a little hard to

get out. I had to pull in a few breaths, my body seeming to have a physical reaction to the event all over again.

While on the surface, I was telling a simple story, but that story triggered all the facts I was leaving out. The abuse, the part about how my mother genuinely loved pain, that she used me "getting in the way" as an excuse to get loud, piss off my father, and get him all riled up. There was so much to explain, so much to get off my chest, I needed to sort it all out in my mind before I could even say it out loud.

"Judah?" Dr. Blake called out my name when the silence dragged on too long.

"Yeah, sorry," I bit out, swallowing the anxious lump in my throat. Again, this was the beginning of my healing journey. The first of many steps I needed to take in order to get where I desperately needed to go, and the road ahead had me wanting to crawl in a hole and never come out. Still, I was already in the middle of my first attempt, so I kept going.

"The, uh, the word *parent* set me off. It was like my mom became a figure right in front of me, real enough to touch, but at the same time, I knew it wasn't her. That she was just a figment of my imagination. Except when I looked away from the woman in the group, I was still left with the feeling I always get when I think of my mom."

"And what feeling is that?" Dr. Blake asked.

Recognizing the emotional response already, I explained in a thick voice, "Tightness in my chest, anger so brutal I have to restrain myself from attacking whatever it is that set me off. If it's a person, I want to rip out their throat. If it's an object, it gets thrown. If I can't do anything about it…I get high. I do whatever the fuck I have to do to make her go away."

I was already losing it, grinding my teeth together, trying not to ball my hands into fists. The cravings I battled came back with a vengeance, inspiring thoughts of checking out early and finding a dealer up the coast just to try one more time.

This life wasn't worth it. Not when I had this woman stalking my every move, trying to drag me back to the hell I was raised in.

The heel of my Vans slid against the leather cushion as I bounced my foot, trying to release some of the malicious energy that seemed to be zinging through my body, lighting me up from the inside out.

Unable to stop myself, I blurted out, "I want to crawl out of my fucking *skin* when I think of her."

"Why, Judah?" Blake asked insistently.

"Because I have fucking questions!" I shouted, flying into a sitting position to glare at my therapist like *she* was the problem.

"Good," Blake stated in a matter-of-fact tone, setting her notebook on the desk behind her. "You *should* have questions. You *deserve* to have questions."

"Why bother?" I spat bitterly, looking off to the left and pulling my bottom lip in between my teeth to avoid screaming like I wanted to. "I won't get any fucking answers."

"Maybe not from her, no," Blake agreed. "But if you let yourself go back to your childhood and work your way through it, you might be able to get some answers all on your own. You're an adult now, you've matured, you can see her from a different perspective."

"*What* different perspective?" I exploded. "How would I see her any differently than I do right now!? And fuck, why would I even *want* to? She *deserves* to be remembered as the sick piece of shit that she was!"

Fuming didn't even begin to describe my current emotional state. Even physically, I was wound tighter than a jack-in-the-box.

"Your perception of how she treated you won't change,

Judah. You won't be wiping her slate clean, but you'll be giving yourself answers you can live with, even if they still hurt to think about." I rolled my eyes, not understanding how any of that would help, but Dr. Blake kept going. "You have such intense reactions whenever she comes up because you don't *want* to go back and think about any of it, and while I don't blame you, it's not a healthy way to live. Suppressing your pain only leads to more pain."

"Pain is all I know," I snarled bitterly.

"Is that really true?"

My eyes blazed towards hers. "What the fuck does *that* mean? Of course it is!"

"You don't have *anything* that brings you happiness? Your music? Friends?"

Please. "The music industry sucks, my career is another triggering topic, and sure, my friends made me happy occasionally, but all of us are fuckin' sad." I didn't want to tell Blake about Phoenix. She was my secret for so many reasons. "I've felt happiness, but it's fleeting. Real happiness doesn't last longer than a moment."

Dr. Blake shook her head sadly. "That's simply not true, Judah. It doesn't *have* to be like that."

"I simply don't believe you, Doc." I threw up my hands. "I don't get how dragging up my godawful childhood will bring me any happiness in the future."

"It's not about dragging it up," she insisted. "It's about facing your own personal feelings so you can tackle them. If you're angry at your mom, we yell at her in these sessions. We get it all out. We talk about how she hurt you, how it still affects you to this day, and then we learn how to manage the lasting effect she has on you going forward." *This is too much work.* "We forgive her, Judah, so you can move on. You have to grieve what you never had, and it's a process. Sometimes these things take years, but that doesn't mean you can't find happiness in the meantime. You just have to start somewhere."

Forgiveness? Grieving? *Is she fucking kidding?*

This was too much for one day, too much to think about, too much to process so early on in my recovery.

I changed the subject, switching lanes. "Why don't you tell me why I remind you of your first patient before I storm the fuck out of here and pace my room for the next six hours?"

Dr. Blake's eyes scanned my posture, reading my body language, confirming that I was about to walk the fuck out.

"Sure." She nodded before getting more comfortable in her seat. "Ryan was a lot like you in the way that he was feeling a lot of things all at once. He was constantly trying to escape, using drugs like you did, but where he was openly loud, actively angry, and always pushing people away in a literal sense, you do those things quietly unless provoked. If everyone left you alone, you'd just drown in your own head, whereas he couldn't be left alone because he'd destroy any room he was in. The underlying similarity between you and Ryan is that both of you were hurt as children, abandoned when you should have had a parental figure to love you unconditionally." I scoffed at that notion. "Neither of you felt safe enough to express, so you learned to suppress. You pretend nothing was wrong, like your trauma didn't exist, and while each of you project this air of brutality, under all of those memories and nightmares, you're both gentle souls. It was something I recognized immediately."

I blinked at her, thinking of when I broke P's iPad in a fight, of Paris, when broke her nose, and went to jail for assault. "You've got me all wrong."

I wasn't gentle.

I was a fucking natural disaster. I wasn't even gentle with Phoenix, I didn't think. I might have been soft a few times, but somehow, I always ended up yelling, with her yelling right back.

She'd *wanted* me to be gentle, to be vulnerable, but I never gave her what she wanted unless it was the middle of the night and I'd woken up from a nightmare. Little did she know, those were the moments I cherished the most.

In those moments, I'd learned to trust her.

"I don't, Judah. You just can't see what I see. But no matter what you believe, you're not meant to feel this way, to live with this pressure," Dr. Blake insisted again. "You weren't born to carry around questions with no answers, that's not how this works. You have the ability ask your mother the questions you have, and when you only hear silence, you can then come to your own conclusions and answer them as best you can, all on your own. Then you can close the chapter, but you can't do any of that without going back in time and reprocessing the triggering events." I was in hell. *Maybe I really did die that night.* "Drugs aren't an option for escapism anymore, not unless you want to continue down a path that would most definitely end in an early death this time. I think we both know that if you were promised a life free of this depression, of this need to run from your trauma, you wouldn't want to die."

"How do *you* know what I want?" I hated that this woman was doing a whole lot of assuming and somehow guessing right. I wanted to know how she knew what she knew.

What did she see that I couldn't?

"Because you're here right now sitting in my office, when you could leave at any time. You're not mandated to be here, not yet at least, but you still haven't left, so at least for right now…you haven't given up." She nodded her chin at me with pride glowing in her eyes. "That's all I need to know. I'm looking at a fighter."

I scoffed. "I'm good at fighting, but I'm not sure it's my life I'm fighting for."

She adjusted in her seat, getting more comfortable, "Okay, then what are you fighting for?"

Does she want the truth? "I'm not sure I want to tell you."

"Why's that?" she asked simply, patiently.

Fucking hell, I hate therapy.

The look on her face made me think she was capable of screwing with my mind, because despite my reservations, I felt compelled to tell her, pressured as hell.

"Because I'm fucked, okay?" I was getting angry again, feeling cornered. "Everything in my head is all turned around, and I have more than just mommy issues. I've got daddy, fame, girlfriend, best friend, and money issues too. The list goes on and on, and I'm still not even sure if I'm here because I want to live or because I survived my fucking overdose when the goal was to die. I've been forced to live another day, and now…"

I paused, not ready to tell her why I ended up checking myself into this place.

Sure, I would have ended up in rehab either way, thanks to Brandon's case against me and the two girls the police thought I killed, but I did actually choose to check myself in thanks to Phoenix's letter. The one I ripped up the day I got here, only to fall into a complete mental breakdown right after. I spent five hours sobbing on the floor of my bedroom as I tried to tape the stupid fucking thing back together, feeling like fucking shit for tearing it apart in the first place.

I hated her. I hated my life. I felt like an imposter.

I shouldn't have lived. I should have been dead and buried by now, just like the two women I spent those few days with.

Who was I to get another chance when I didn't even want it? Maybe those girls had. I doubted they'd *wanted* to overdose, not like I did.

And this process? The shit I'd have to relive if I actually wanted to see any results and heal the way I needed to? The pain I'd have to endure? Did this woman know what she was asking of me?

"That's a lot to unpack," Dr. Blake agreed. "But it can be done, Judah. I think I'm going to suggest adding an extra session with me to your day, if that's okay with you."

More time to pull up the shattered pieces of my childhood from the pit of my black soul, just to try and fit them back together and make a new, totally fucked-up picture, in case it helped me stay sober? *Yeah, that sounded like fun.*

"I have a question," Dr. Blake said when I didn't respond. "If you decided not to trust me with your past, what other choice would you have? What would your next move be?"

"I'd leave," I snarled and glanced away, trying to ignore the thought of my broken little bird, ruined because I couldn't get my shit together, disappointed in me, blaming herself and wondering if things could have been different.

"Sure," the Doc threw out. "You could do that. But what would you lose?"

What would I lose?

Silence descended and the walls closed in as blood rushed to my ears. Memories flew through my mind on a loop, displaying bright smiles and blunts. I could almost feel the weight of her curled up in my lap, scrolling on her phone or watching TV, laughing with our friends. The thought of her was more real than even my mother. More powerful. Inspiring.

"Phoenix," I whispered.

Her name slipped out of my mouth like a desperate prayer before I could stop it. An automatic reaction.

"Who is Phoenix?" Dr. Blake didn't miss a beat.

My answer was instant, quiet. "Everything."

Now that her name was out there, there was no going back.

I'd been caught.

But really, who was I kidding? I wasn't going to leave, because somehow, Blake was right—I was already sitting on the damn sofa, I had no plans to break out of here, and I'd already started opening up. If we were going to continue these sessions, this woman needed to know the truth. My relationship with Phoenix was the turning point in my life. She was my anchor, my biggest regret and brightest accomplishment. At the end of the day, there was nothing outside of this place that made me want to live.

Only her.

My career was a bust, I'd ruined that entirely. My band had broken up. My house sat empty in the Hills. Nothing inspired me anymore.

Nothing but her.

"Maybe we should start there, then," Blake suggested, gaining my full attention.

"You want to talk about *Phoenix* first?"

Hell no.

I didn't want to, didn't want to make my situation worse, because I knew what happened between her and me was a whole different kind of fucked-up and I didn't want to hear that I didn't deserve her. I didn't need it to be confirmed.

"I understand that trust is earned, Judah, and Phoenix is obviously the most important thing to you right now, so I think she may be easier to talk about. You can learn to trust me before we dive into your childhood, and we can build from there." Even though the thought made my heartrate skyrocket, it wasn't a horrible idea, just fucking terrifying. "This may be hard, Judah, and yes, sometimes it will be painful, but I won't let you leave this office without feeling like you've accomplished something too. It's time you learn to allow your successes to outweigh your failures. They're more important in the end."

Staring back at her, I let those words sink in before falling back on the couch and laying my head against the cushions.

I silently, reluctantly, agreed with her plan, only letting her know by admitting, "I don't know how to do that. My failures haunt me, and there are a fuck ton."

"That's what we'll be working through," she replied, trying to soothe. "You don't have to fix it all in one day because this is a process. We'll be taking it one step at a time."

I sighed, running my hands down my face, knowing that I was about to take a deep dive into the unknown. Once again, I was reminded of the fact that I had only one other choice. There was no going back to my old life the way I was, they wouldn't accept me. They shouldn't.

So I could either do what Dr. Blake suggested, or I could leave and kill myself.

Brutal, suicidal, but truthful realities were displayed before me, and I knew which one was the right move. I just hoped I didn't end up in a worse place than I already was.

Mumbling through my fingers, I asked, "Where do we start?"

I heard those same sounds of rustling, indicating that goddamn notebook was being utilized again, before Blake got down to business and suggested, "How about you tell me more about Phoenix. How did the two of you meet?"

Here we go...

CHAPTER 3
Phoenix

ST. Lucia was fucking *beautiful*.

The water was crystal clear, the mountains in the distance, standing proudly under bright blue skies, were covered in deep green foliage, and the weather was perfect. Frankie and I were spending our last day of vacation lounging in the infinity pool attached to our suite, sipping on margaritas and loading our bodies with more food than they could handle.

"I'm *so* not ready to go home," Frankie complained for the fortieth time that day. "Who would want to leave this?"

"Energy" by Tyla Jane was playing softly in the backroom, adding to the relaxed vibe but providing that tropical sass both Frankie and I embodied.

"No one," I said on a sigh, agreeing with her but still knowing that our time away from the real world was running out. "The *last* thing I want to go is go home and face all the shit I left behind."

"We've done a pretty successful job of ignoring all the bullshit we'll have to deal with when we get back," Frankie pointed out. "I'm proud of us."

"*Should* you be proud, though?" I chuckled, recognizing the twinge of sadness laced within the vibration. "We are masters of avoidance, but if we'd actually *talked* about some of this stuff, we'd probably have some fucking resolution right now."

"Please," she scoffed, waving a wet hand in my direction. "What is talking going to do for us? Your ex is in rehab, you fucked his best friend when you thought Judah would never clean his life up, while I'm one foot out of a completely healthy relationship and my guy has zero idea. Talking about it will only lead us into more confusion."

"That's a lie and you know it," I replied, laughing harder now, hoping she was being sarcastic. "You wanting to leave Silas *absolutely* could have been resolved by now if we'd talked about it."

"Yeah but…" She laid on the puppy dog eyes. "I don't *want* to talk about it."

"I know!" I splashed water her way. "That's the whole point—we didn't want to talk about anything, so we missed a perfectly good opportunity to get some clarity and help each other! Instead, like idiots, we buried it until now, when we have less than twenty-four hours until we're smack dab in the middle of it again."

"You make it sound awful when you say it in that loud, high-pitched tone you're using," Frankie muttered, stirring her drink with her finger. "You should stop talking about it so I can go back to blissful avoidance."

"Frankie Skyes!" I scolded. "You're the worst."

"Yeah? What about you, hmmm?" she sassed. "Would you like to discuss Pharaoh?"

I thought about it for a minute, considering telling her that no, in fact, I *didn't* want to talk about him, but… "Yes, actually, I would."

There was something to be said about time, space, and foreign air. Three weeks was the perfect amount of time for a vacation like this one, especially given everything that had happened in my life prior to leaving.

I spent the first few days locked in our hotel room, crying on and off, trying to control my intense reaction to Judah's overdose. Once I found a way to do that, I vowed to pretend none of it happened, which wasn't healthy, of course, but I was so fucking tired of feeling like shit.

I was absolutely done with the drama, the dread, and all the anxiety that came with Judah's addiction, so instead of focusing on the recent past, I'd pretended as if my life back home didn't exist at all.

Instead, Frankie and I had laughed, drunk, shopped, and eaten more incredible food in the last few weeks than we had in way too long.

The whole experience had cleared my mind, helped me hit the reset button on my emotions, and given me the chance to relax and feel good every chance I got. I'd forgotten what it was like to just enjoy the present, having spent all that time worrying about the future or heartbroken over the past.

It wasn't easy, of course, and I'd had to drink myself to sleep every night to avoid thinking about Judah and what his life was like back home—first in the hospital detoxing, then in some rehab facility continuing his sobriety journey—but I did what I could to keep my mind focused on the positives.

Now, though, it was time to go back and face my new reality, and hopefully figure out what the universe had in store for me next.

"Wait, seriously?" Frankie replied, stunned. "You're ready to talk about him?"

"*Ready?*" I laughed again, but it was slightly bitter this time. "I wouldn't say I'm *ready*, but I also have no other choice. We managed to get out of Pharaoh picking us up from the airport, but that doesn't mean he isn't going to show up at our house as soon as he gets the chance."

"Would he do that?" Frankie questioned, scrunching up her nose. "That feels desperate."

I gave her a *get real* look.

"My ex-boyfriend, who is basically Pharaoh's brother, overdosed and is now in rehab. I was halfway across the world when it happened, and we haven't spoken since they day I made him write that letter to Judah outside of my one text message, telling him Kavan and Ric would pick us up." I blinked at her once before splashing her again. "Of *course*, he's going to want to see me as soon as possible!"

She splashed me back. "Not to mention the fact that you fucked him and he's totally in love with you," she threw out.

"FRANKIE!"

"What?! I'm just sayin'. I see your point now." She shrugged, taking another sip of her drink.

"What the *hell* am I going to do?" I groaned loudly, not caring that I sounded pathetic. "How am I going to get through this without breaking hearts? My own included."

Frankie held up a hand. "All right, pause for a second. We need to get serious here, because I am still one hundred percent in avoidance mode and I'm going to be no help to you if I don't set this drink down and take a few deep breaths."

Just then, "Visualize" by SoMo began playing through the speakers set up around the suite, and once again, I groaned. "Why this song?"

"Because it's a fuckin' banger." Frankie laughed as she stepped off the underwater bench and swam her way to other side of the pool, setting her drink on the concrete edge. "It actually isn't bad advice for you."

"What? How?" I asked, following her lead to the other side.

"Listen to the lyrics. He's telling his girl to free her mind so she can think clearly. He wants to start over, celebrate, and do it right this time. Play one more game. The key for *you* is that you have two guys to choose from."

"Not really," I disagreed, feeling that awful sense of dread

I'd been trying to avoid. "We don't know that Judah is even going to get out of rehab with a plan to stay clean. And if by some miracle he is taking it seriously, we don't even know what he'll be like."

"You act like he's going to be some alien you've never met before," she said, brushing off my fear as she hoisted herself up onto the edge of the pool, turning around to let her feet dangle in the water. "He's Judah, Phoenix, and if you think for *one* second he's not going to get out of rehab and come right to you, you're fucking insane."

Was I, though?

"So much shit went down, Frankie." I shook my head, looking up at her from the water. "This situation isn't something you or I have ever dealt with before. I don't even know that I *want* to get back with him after all that."

"Now I'm starting to think the sun really did make you crazy!" She laughed, gaping at me. "Phoenix, get real."

"I am!" I protested, even though on the inside, I knew I was just being difficult, feeling like a love-sick puppy dog waiting for her master to come home. I *was* pathetic, but I was doing my fucking best to think rationally and not get too excited, dropping all my expectations and remembering that Judah totally obliterated my life.

"You're telling me that if Judah got out of rehab, knocked on our front door looking seriously remorseful, having learned his lessons, was committed to staying sober, and asked you to talk to him...you wouldn't?"

The look on her face had me rolling my eyes.

"Fuck off." I swatted her legs before using my arm strength to pull myself up next to her. "Fine, you're right, but we don't know that would happen."

She was only silent for a few seconds before she stating, "But you want it to."

More than anything.

In a perfect world, Judah wouldn't come back completely changed, because that was unrealistic, but he would come back different—different mindset, new attitude, with more hope for his own future. He'd open up to me, tell me what he learned about himself, about his addiction. He'd tell me that he understood his own insecurities, and even if they weren't gone, he'd be working on them. He wouldn't shut me out, but he'd prove to me that he was in this for the long haul, both in our relationship and his commitment to himself. He'd piece his life back together, apologize to our friends, our family, and start working again, without the pressure of his insecurities or any belittling outside opinions.

But that was a fantasy, something that could happen in perfect world, but in *this* world, it was much more complicated.

In this world, our love killed.

That was proven two times over. Nearly three.

If Judah and I had never met, those girls wouldn't be dead. If I'd never fallen for him, and him for me, I wouldn't have gotten into this confusing as fuck situation with his best friend. We wouldn't have to tell Judah that we slept together and risk fucking up his road to recovery.

I wouldn't have this weight on my chest.

Judah would have coasted through life, and even if he'd eventually have ended up in a similar position regarding the drugs…it wouldn't have been my fault he overdosed.

But we were here now, and I was fucking *rocked*.

I didn't know what to do, couldn't figure out what step to take next.

Frankie was right though.

"Of course I want it to," I admitted. "But that seems foolish after everything he did to me, Frankie. Part of me wants to walk away, wishing him the best, and the other half wants to wait like a lost pet for him to come home. At the end of the day, rehab doesn't change the past, it's only an opportunity to change the future."

"I know, but, Phoenix, you can still hope for it to all work out and just leave it at that for now," Frankie stated softly, sliding back into my super spiritual, wise as hell best friend, who believed your thoughts created your reality. "It's not foolish for you to hope that Judah gets through this part of his journey or hope that he listens to what you wrote in that letter, because if he does? He is *absolutely* coming back to you."

I hadn't thought about it that way. If Judah took what I'd said seriously and did everything I'd encouraged him to do… he *would* come back sober and committed. He would reintroduce himself. We could start over.

Hoping that would happen, though?

That seemed risky. It felt like I would be setting myself up for another round of heartbreak if he decided to say fuck it and ruin his life all over again.

"And Pharaoh?" I asked, glancing at her.

She tilted her head and asked, "Well, is Pharaoh a real option in your eyes?"

The question sent an invisible rock plummeting into the pit of my stomach.

"Yes," I answered honestly. "If Judah weren't in the picture and I met Pharaoh on a random day, there would be no question, but this situation is just not that simple. I feel like if Judah and I didn't work, it wouldn't work for Pharaoh and me either."

"Why not?"

"Because it would always be a sore spot for Judah," I explained, having already thought about this. "I mean, really, even if they stopped being friends? I know Judah, and in his eyes, it would feel like his best friend took his girl, and that's a whole lot of negative pressure to put on a recovering addict. I can't do that to him just because Pharaoh and I have chemistry.

We only slept together because the situation was so stressful that we needed a release, and I only got as close to him as I did because we were trying to survive Judah's bullshit." The more I dove into the possibility of Pharaoh and me, the more clear it became. "We're wound-mates, Franks. We were in survival mode. Is that really a solid foundation for a relationship?"

"For Pharaoh, it's more though, and you know that," Frankie pointed out, making me feel sick.

"I know." I sighed. "And that's the shittiest part. I don't want him to get hurt. It feels like I'd be choosing Judah over him, and it's not like that for me. Pharaoh wasn't supposed to be an option, and sleeping with him seriously fucked this up."

"Yeah…" Frankie drew out the word. "Taking my advice that night might not have been your best idea."

I shot her a bland look. "You think?"

"I'm sorry!" Franks threw up her hands. "I just wanted you to have a break, and we all knew Pharaoh was into you. The last thing I expected was Judah to end up in rehab before the week was fucking over. It was an impossible situation to predict."

I didn't blame her, not really, not when I was the one that made the final decision. Either way, it was selfish of me to lean on Pharaoh like that, knowing his feelings for me, because if I were honest with myself, I didn't feel as deeply for him as he did for me.

Was there chemistry? Fuck yes. Could I have fallen hard for him? Absolutely. But was I in the same place he was as far as feelings went? No.

I was still heartbroken, still confused and hurting and one hundred percent in love with Judah. That last fact had never changed, still hadn't.

"Looking at it from Pharaoh's perspective isn't a good idea," Frankie surmised. "You'll always want to protect him from any bad feelings. It's Pharaoh. He's like a wounded dog

—you just want to bring him home and take care of him, even if you don't have the space or proper time to do so."

Son of a bitch.

"I know. I have to think about it from all perspectives," I agreed sadly, shaking my head as dread bled through my veins. "It wouldn't work with Pharaoh, even if Judah came back totally fucked-up. I, personally, couldn't put Judah through that, and it was stupid of me to even agree to trying when Pharaoh suggested it."

Hindsight was a bitch, and no matter how badly I wanted to be that person for Pharaoh, I had to admit that my feelings for Pharaoh stemmed from my hatred of him never getting what he wanted. I knew he wanted me, and I hated that when he lost control of Judah, when everything went to hell, Pharaoh was alone. I wanted to fill that space for him, but I might have done more damage than good in this scenario.

My head was a landmine of feelings. I wasn't thinking clearly, and while I wasn't even sure I was fully ready to make any decisions now, I was in a better place than I had been back then.

"Damn," Frankie said on an exhale. "This is all twisted the fuck up."

Worse than I could have imagined. "It sure is."

We'd gotten ourselves into a mess, but even if I got everything I wanted and I somehow managed to keep a friendship with Pharaoh, taking Judah back on right away wasn't an option.

He and I had a lot of shit to work out, a whole fucking lot of things to talk through.

The two of us had been toxic as hell *before* I found out about Judah's addiction, and I couldn't forget that. Not to mention, he wasn't the only one with issues either.

I had a nice backpack full of bullshit too.

Basically, our journey wasn't over yet, not by any stretch

of the imagination, but when all was said and done, I would have my resolution. I couldn't live like this, couldn't stay in limbo, always wondering when the next bomb would fall from the sky. It wasn't fair to me after all the work I'd done, and Pharaoh deserved to be happy as well. He deserved that freedom and appreciation, to be loved equally and fully.

I just didn't want to lose him while trying to explain all of this to him, because while my feelings didn't match his, I still had them. I loved him in a different way, but it was no less impactful than the way he loved me. It might have been selfish of me, but I didn't want him to erase me from his life if I told him this wouldn't work in a romantic sense.

And that right there was my biggest fear.

Losing Pharaoh would be just another person I no longer had by my side, and I wasn't sure that I could handle that kind of loss. It gave me just as much anxiety as losing Judah had.

They'd both become integral in my life—Judah first, and Pharaoh right after, helping me pick up the pieces.

"Okay, one last serious question," Frankie started, interrupting my thoughts. "And it's a heavy one, so I apologize in advance."

My eyes found hers as I picked up on the gravity of her question.

"Okaaay…"

"Don't hate me for this," Frankie prefaced her question, making me even more nervous. "But do you…do you really *want* to be with a recovering addict?" *Whoa, she wasn't kidding.* "Because, Phoenix, it's *always* going to be a struggle for Judah. For the rest of his life, he will be a recovering addict. He could relapse and hurt you all over again, even if it's unintentional. I know that his relapse wouldn't truly have anything to do with you or how much he loves you. I believe he loves you the only way he knows how, even right now, but while he's in rehab, he's simply breaking up with his addiction, and there's always a chance that even after they split, he'll go back to her." *Ouch.* "It's like another woman, a third party in your relationship. Is that something you want to live with for the rest of your life? The possibility of him relapsing hanging over your head?"

The world seemed to spin around me as I stared at the water, thinking through her questions.

But before I could answer, Frankie spoke again. "And before you think I'm judging you, or trying to convince you not to take him back, I'm not," she rushed out. "I'm honestly not even sure what *I* would do in your shoes, but I had to pose the question just in case you hadn't thought about it like that."

"I haven't," I whispered, fighting that nausea in my stomach. "Not like that. Probably because when we got here, I tried to shut it off completely. This is what I meant by if we'd talked about this shit from the beginning of the vacation, we might have some clarity by now."

After running a hand down my face, I blew out a frustrated breath, thankful that I hadn't put anything but moisturizer on this morning. I'd look like a rabid raccoon right now.

"Yeah, that wasn't very smart of us." She chuckled softly.

Despite not having asked myself the question before she did, it didn't take me long to come up with an answer.

"If I'm being one hundred percent honest, the thought makes me nervous," I admitted, trying to walk down that road mentally, allowing myself to think about the possibility of a future with Judah. "You're right—there would always be a possibility of J relapsing. But if Judah really is as incredible as I think he is underneath his addiction and outside of all his issues? I just…"

Pausing, I took my time, continuing to imagine a life where Judah was sober, even if he struggled some days.

"The anxiety may never go away," I started again. "For him *or* for me. We can't forget that I have issues too, Franks.

My father killed my mother, and it haunts me to this day. The situation with Judah only made it worse, honestly. Because of his overdose, I'm left to think about the fact that my love is destructive every minute of every day. He almost killed himself because I didn't answer, and while that was fucking shitty to think about, it's the truth. It's brought back all of those fears, but I still don't *want* to live like this, because the fear surrounding what my father did and the fact that it could happen to me really does feel like a death sentence."

I wanted to be free from the worry, even if there was risk involved.

"I could snap at any moment, and I even said that to Judah when we first met. Back then, he didn't care, but I never realized that was only because he was dealing with his own shit that he hadn't told me about. He figured we were just going to explode together."

I took another deep breath, feeling like I was getting ahead of myself, but it was all pouring out as my thoughts tried to untangle themselves.

"Fact is, Judah and I are two sides of the same coin. He's insecure, angry, terrified of his own reflection, and a pro at burying his past, where I'm almost the opposite. I don't give a shit about how I look, don't bother with being angry. I'm too confident about something that may or may not happen because I spend too much time looking at the possibility of my biggest fears coming true. Either way, growing, living, succeeding—it's all complicated and foreign to both of us. Difference is, I found a way to endure it, to work past it, and he never even tried."

I took a deep breath. "So, basically, in a perfect world, if Judah really did put the work in like I've been trying to do, I don't think I could hold his past over his head. I couldn't fear him relapsing, just because it could creep back up on us, because my issues could too. If we wanted to make this work, we would both be taking a risk on each other."

Silence followed my monologue, but I knew Frankie was just digesting what I'd said, trying to understand my situation, even though it was harder for her because there were really no similarities between her and me. She didn't have to deal with the things that constantly lingered in my mind, and she'd never been in love like I was.

But then she spoke. "That makes sense, I think. I just wonder...shouldn't you both be with partners stronger than you? Partners that aren't as...traumatized?"

The thought stung, but I knew she wasn't trying to be an asshole. She was just genuinely trying to help me figure out what would make me the happiest.

"I don't know," I admitted. "I don't know that I would want to take that same risk on someone perfectly healthy. Maybe that's fucked-up, but it's the truth. Being with someone that has issues like I do, makes me feel...safe, I guess. All I know is that if Judah comes back and turns out to be seriously working on himself, I wouldn't hold his addiction over his head because I was afraid of the future. I'm *already* afraid of the future. Either of us could snap, and while you could argue that my situation is significantly less worrisome than his...it isn't to me."

Memories from that day came in hot and fast, causing chills to race down my spine.

"My father, who loved my mother deeply, fucking *shot* her, Frankie. Out of nowhere. And no one could tell me why. I have to think about that—I don't know how *not* to. I don't know how to be normal and just hope for the best."

Somewhere along the line, I began to grow past that debilitating fear of my future, and I was still holding onto that growth with white knuckles. But in moments like these, when I had to think about it in such a realistic light...it was harder to find that strength.

For some reason, though, I knew that even stone-cold sober, Judah would shut that fear down in a second, just like I would do for him if he were able to open up to me in the same way. If he thought he might relapse and he told me about it, I wouldn't freak out, I wouldn't judge him, I would help him.

It was all I ever wanted to do.

Continuing to explain my thoughts, I said to Frankie, "I know firsthand what childhood trauma does to a person's mind—even yours now that I've taken the time to put myself in your shoes—and we both know it's easier to live happily as an adult if you have someone you trust to talk to and be open with. If Judah can learn to talk about his shit instead of burying it, we have a chance at making it. He could truly live a sober life, and I could feel safe in a relationship, knowing that my partner took the same chance on me that I did on him."

But in the end, it all came down to Judah and the work he was willing to put in.

"Lord have mercy, this shit is fuckin' heavy," Frankie exclaimed on a groan. "I'm not qualified to help you make this decision."

I chuckled a little. "I'm not sure I'm qualified to make it in the first place, but I'm following my heart, which wouldn't even have woken up if it weren't for Judah."

Without his presence in my life, I wouldn't be who I was, and that was almost scary to think about. How would I have grown? Who would I be friends with? What would my life look like without Ricco and Kav? Trixie? Pharaoh, Silas, even the guys in Judah's band? My life felt so fucking full, all because Judah had refused to let me go.

"See," Frankie started, clicking her tongue and leaning back on her palms. "This conversation is how I know what you and Judah have is some deep kind of love I've never felt before. That motherfucker screwed absolutely *everything* up for you, on more than one occasion, and yet here you are, able to explain it away because you know what it's like to be totally out of your own control. You see past his bullshit and love him unconditionally. I honestly don't think I'm capable of loving someone like that."

Eyes wide, I stared at her with my heart beginning to ache in my chest. "Franks, why would you say that?"

"Phoenix, you *feel* lost, you *think* you're lost or broken or whatever, but you're not," Frankie replied, sounding sure of herself. "You are so fucking self-aware, you know *exactly* why you are the way you are, and now that you've done that for yourself, you see the same shit in Judah. You can see where he stops, and his childhood trauma takes over. That's a fucking gift. It's why you can love him unconditionally, but still know when to walk away. I don't know myself like that. I can't love like that."

"Frankie," I said on a sigh, hating the dejected tone of her voice, even with the confidence she normally carried.

"I'm serious," she muttered. "I've never seen it until now, but I shouldn't be with Silas. I don't even know what it is I *like* about him, other than the fact that he's fuckin' great in bed and he treats me like gold. I know don't…love him. I don't even really *know* him, but that's only because I'm terrified of emotional intimacy, and I don't know why."

"Because you didn't grow up with it," I explained, now understanding a little more of what she was talking about. Frankie's problems were very obvious to me, but not in a bad way, rather in a way that made me sympathize with her. "Your parents didn't teach you the value of emotions, and if you compare that to my parents—who very much did—that's why I'm so fucked-up over what happened to them. I knew love. I saw it, felt it, experienced what it was like to be loved by two people, and yet it still ended in tragedy. Whereas you…your parents are cold as stone. They assume love is currency. They look at love as something that can be bought, which is why you love the finest of things, but that leaves you fighting with yourself when it comes to emotional love. It's foreign to you." My last words were whispered.

"Fuck my liiiife." Frankie groaned, running two hands down her face. "Self-love isn't about buying nice things and treating yourself to a mani-pedi once a week. And let me tell you…I am learning that the hard way."

I cringed a little, knowing this was fucking hard on her. It would be hard on anyone.

"It's understandable, Franks," I said, trying to make it easier for her. "It's not easy to work through. How can you be comfortable with someone else loving you, if you don't even know your own heart? If you've never known what it's like to be loved in a genuine way, it's bound to freak you out."

Frankie scoffed. "My heart is hidden from even myself. I've got walls higher than the Empire State Building around that bitch, but it's not on purpose because you're right—my parents didn't show me what love was. The only person who's ever loved me is you, P."

Fuck.

The top of my nose began to burn with the threat of oncoming tears.

"And I hurt you too," I whispered, feeling like fucking shit.

At that, she looked away, but she still reached over to grab my hand, so I knew she was just trying to hide her emotions, as she always did. I could see that my best friend was truly about to embark on a new journey, one that would teach her a lot about herself, and the situation with Silas was just the beginning. I'd failed her before when I left. I'd made a choice to save her in one way, but screwed her in another.

Not this time.

"Franks, look at me," I demanded softly.

When she did, my chest cracked under the weight of the pain swimming in her eyes.

Reaching forward, I caught the single tear that slipped over her bottom eyelash and down her cheek. It fell onto my finger like a runaway train as my palm settled against her face.

Even though emotion clogged my throat, I whispered with conviction, "I know I've said it before, but I'll say it as many times as I have to—I'm sorry for leaving you in California when I went to college. I'm sorry that I didn't open up to you and bring you with me. I'm sorry that your parents left you to fend for yourself, and I'm sorry that they haven't loved you the way you deserve to be loved, but my love for you hasn't ever extinguished, Frankie Skyes. I'm going to be here, loving you, until your dying breath. And even past that."

More tears fell as she watched me, and her left hand shook when she lifted it to grip my wrist. Her eyes closed, and so did mine, leaving us in a bubble of affectionate, painful silence.

Yet I couldn't help but feel grateful, because after all this time, I was finally in a place where I could give her the apology she deserved—something she needed, wanted.

Though it was scary, it seemed that I was somehow growing past her, beyond the typical Frankie and Phoenix dynamic, where she held me up. I was strong enough to hold my own, for the most part, where she was just starting to realize where she was lacking, what was missing, and what she needed to focus on in order achieve her own happiness.

"Thank you," she whispered, sniffing, as she leaned into my touch. "I don't let myself think about this shit, because the more I think about it, the more lost I get and the more alone I feel."

"But you're not alone, now, okay?" I pushed gently. "You have me, and we're both in a new territory here. We're getting older, trying to navigate the bullshit we've had to deal with for our entire lives."

She shook her head, pulling my hand from her face but remained holding it in her lap. "You're going to have enough on your plate with Judah."

"Well, yeah, you're not wrong. I'm headed back to a clusterfuck, but I need you just as much as you need me, especially now," I insisted. "Dealing with Judah is bound to be a whole *thing*, one way or another, so you can watch me make mistakes or we celebrate the win. Either way, step by step, you and I are both learning how to love and we're doing it together. Which is sad, of course, because we're grown ass adults, but both of us are a little fucked and that's okay, right? It is what it is." I smirked, catching her smile in return. "Hell, you think you're bad, but if I were normal, I wouldn't have abandoned you and we wouldn't even be having this conversation."

"So what you're saying is, I should've just found a *normal* best friend while you were gone," she joked, shoving her shoulder into mine, trying to shake off the heaviness of the conversation. "That girl might have been able to help me through this a whole lot sooner than you did."

I barked out a laugh. "Don't you even think about it. There's no room in this family for another best friend, then or now. It's me and only me, got it?"

"Wait…" Frankie paused, meeting my eyes in mock seriousness. "Are you *my* Judah?"

"Fuck off." I busted out laughing, pushing her into the pool.

She fell under the surface of the water, popping back up a few seconds later. "Yup, definitely Judah—causing all kinds of destruction when cornered."

"You're the worst," I yelled, just as she gripped my ankle and tugged hard, pulling me into the water too.

As my body fell through the surface, I closed my eyes and held my breath, letting my limbs go weightless.

Living life knowing that Judah could relapse would be

hard, sure, but the love I had for him? It was unmatched. I didn't think I'd ever love anyone the way I loved him, and if he did this right, if I somehow ended up with everything I wanted, we'd be too close, too honest with each other, for him to turn to drugs to escape.

If he wanted to drown again, he'd have a support system to keep him floating. He'd open up, let me in, tell me his fears and explain his memories, and we'd tackle them together. He'd have Pharaoh to call, Kav and Ricco to confide in, or even Frankie, if they were able to gain a level of trust.

We wouldn't let him drown again.

But first, he had to choose himself. He had to *want* to live that life. He had to begin that healing *before* I became an option again. He needed to be his own reason for living, and that had been what he was missing this entire time.

Judah had thought I would be willing to die with him, give up with him.

But that simply wasn't an option for me.

Still, no matter what I said out loud, deep down, I *was* hoping he would turn this around. I hoped he was working on himself, facing himself, and telling the damn truth for once. I hoped he was searching for his internal sunshine and recognizing the potential hidden within himself.

But until I saw that change reflected in his eyes, hope was all I had.

JUDAH

2 weeks 2 days in rehab

"HOW ARE YOU TODAY, JUDAH?" Blake asked as I sat down on the couch in her office two days later, exhausted from another shitty night's sleep.

My tone was bland as I closed my eyes and lowered my head onto one of the black decorative pillows resting against the arm of the couch. "I feel like hell."

"Another nightmare?" she asked sympathetically.

"Mhm," I mumbled, having already given up on the whole vow of silence thing. It wasn't so much that Dr. Blake was growing on me, but more that the restless anxiety, consistent cravings, headaches, nightmares, and lack of physical strength was getting the best of me. Plain and simple, I was too damn fucking tired to fight this process anymore.

"Would you like to talk about it?"

No, not one bit.

Except I was so fucking lonely, so desperate for someone to tell me that my fears were normal, that I would get better eventually…it was becoming harder and harder to keep my thoughts inside my head.

This right here was the whole point of getting high. The

drugs took away *this* feeling, and now that I didn't have them to rely on, all I could do was either drown in my failing mental health or fucking talk about it.

I'd officially reached the point of no return, the one I'd noticed early on. Thanks to the fact that there was nothing else to do in rehab, I had eventually worn down to the point where the pressure to talk openly became insurmountable. No drugs to rely on, no parties to attend, no friends to bitch to. I was in no-man's-land, and it felt like I'd been thrown in the middle of the ocean and my only lifeline had been thrown by a complete stranger on a boat, heading to an unknown destination. I could either get in the boat, or die alone in shark infested waters.

After sighing heavily, I recounted my dream for the Doc to psychoanalyze. "I relived my overdose—which was fucking awful—but in the dream, Pharaoh told me it was Phoenix and Frankie that died in my bed, not Sarah and Rachele."

There was more, of course, but I wasn't about to explain the rest. Not when I was already feeling the crushing panic and irreparable guilt I'd felt in the dream.

It had been horrific. The words Pharaoh used, the resentment, anger, and tears in his eyes…

And to top it all off, once he was done telling me what I'd done, he left me, refused to show me any amount of understanding or forgiveness like he did in real life.

No, he left me in my hospital room alone where I had no choice but to grieve over my own mistake. My own screams haunted me even now.

"Wow," Dr. Blake whispered. "So they're becoming more personal."

"You could say that," I scoffed choppily.

"Do you have an idea of why? Or would you like my help?"

She was a master at doing that—getting me to *ask* for the help myself, rather than shoving it down my throat free of charge. Problem was, it was just as annoying as it would've been if she'd gone full psychology on me right away.

"You know damn well I have no idea why this is happening, so just tell me."

My chest tightened, despite my uncaring tone.

This whole process fucking sucked, and it wasn't making staying sober any easier.

"Sure," Blake replied, calm as ever. "Over the last couple of days, we've been breaking down your relationship with Phoenix, right? We started from the beginning and worked our way into the present, so all of those feelings were brought back to the surface, but this time, you have a clear mind."

She wasn't kidding.

It was part of the reason I was willing to admit to her that I was having nightmares in the first place. We'd gone deep into my past with Phoenix, and Blake hadn't once made me feel like a basket case. Instead, she saw our relationship from a genuinely caring place. There was no judgement, which was nice, but that didn't erase the internal hell I was in, recounting all of the things I did wrong from the moment I met my little bird.

"Because of that," Dr. Blake continued, "you're feeling those initial emotions stronger and more accurately than you did when you were high. Your guilt from the overdose is mixing with the guilt over the things you did in your relationship with Phoenix. This happens when we start the healing process—all of those subconscious or forgotten emotions become conscious and remembered. However, they continue to appear in your dreams because you've gotten so good at suppressing in your waking state, even now that you're sober."

I couldn't help it, I chuckled, and it sounded disgustingly sad. "Fucking fantastic."

She gave a small laugh herself. "Why don't you tell me how you feel about what you saw in the dream?"

And here was the part I *really* hated. The part where I had to actually *speak* about the pain, rather than just the experience of it.

That required a whole new level of vulnerability.

It felt like I was strung to a fence, being tormented by everything I wished to forget. My mind never really took a break, no matter how good I was at suppressing. Even if I never pinned down an exact memory, I still felt the phantom pain. And all the guilt I carried from the things I'd done in the last few months? It was tearing at my fucking insides, making it hard to eat, hard to talk to the two people who had attached themselves to me after our first breakfast together.

But I had to admit that with every conversation I had with Blake since I started opening up, I felt some form of relief. It was almost as if once every shitty thing I did was out in the open, some of the weight was lifted off my shoulders, even if it only lasted an hour.

Because of that, I quietly admitted, "When I dream like that, I just feel…alone."

Instantly, moisture built behind my eyelids.

Fucking hell, I hate this.

"In the dream, I was crying, screaming at my dead ex-girlfriend, asking her why she didn't take me with her. I still *wanted* to be dead, even in the dream state. It's like she abandoned me all over again, then I wake up and have to face how fucking dark my soul is, how screwed up I really am."

Sniffing, I wiped angerly at my tears, pissed off that I was so messed up I had to say that shit out loud just to figure out how to fix it.

But I was already in, already firmly planted in my own bullshit again, so I continued, "I woke up and realized that I fucked everything up with Phoenix because I was hoping someone would prove that I was worth dying with. Not *for*. I never wanted Phoenix to die *for* me, I wanted her to die *with* me. It's why I asked her if she ever thought about killing herself that first night on the rooftop."

Since opening up to Blake, I thought about that night often, remembering it in a whole new way, now that I was sober enough to see it at all.

"If Phoenix hated this life as much as I did, I wouldn't have been alone anymore. I was sick of feeling like an alien because everyone else found reasons to be happy, even if they were fake. I couldn't seem to do the same." *I can't believe I'm saying this shit out loud.* "When Phoenix came around, I knew she was in the exact same place I was, knew she did hate life, and on top of that, she hated herself, but because I'm a sick piece of shit, I wanted her to stay there in the mental space because I refused to leave. Hell, I asked her if she'd ever done hard drugs instead of telling her I did them on the daily, just to see if she would fit into my world even a little."

"You're not a sick piece of shit, Judah," Dr. Blake chastised as I took a deep breath. "You were in a manic depressive state, and it's completely normal to have thoughts like that when you mix in downer drugs or alcohol. You'd be surprised how many times I've heard something like that."

I ignored her, breathing in through my mouth now that my nose was stuffed up from all the liquid emotion I was expelling.

Blake said shit like that often, forgetting that I didn't give a flying fuck about the other people out there struggling like I was. Knowing that other people were just as fucked-up as I was didn't make me feel any better.

I wasn't done though. "When I met Phoenix, I thought she would be it. I thought we'd fall down the rabbit hole together and end it all as a giant fuck you to everyone that ever hurt us, but it backfired because she never wanted that. I read her wrong. *I'm* the mess. I hurt *everyone* over and over again because *I* hate myself, and these dreams..." I cleared my throat, wiping the tears that wouldn't stop falling, trying to erase my vulnerability. "The dreams just alienate me even more. They make me feel like if my thoughts are that dark, if I was capable of getting so high, I had no fucking idea that Sarah and Rachele were fucking *dead*? I'm worse off than I thought."

What I wanted to say was that I thought I might never get better, because really? How was I going to come back from that?

"I don't think you give yourself enough credit," Blake announced, countering my admission in a soft, understanding voice. "You just told me the reason you did the things you did with perfect clarity, and you were right. To take it a step further—the reason you pulled Phoenix into your world without telling her about your addiction was because you were hoping that by the time she found out, she'd already be six feet deep with you and think the two of you had done it together. You recognized in her what you saw in yourself—someone that was barely hanging on, someone needing to be loved and understood. What your addiction hid from you is that she was already on the healing path."

"She was never willing to drown with me," I muttered shakily, running my hands down my face, smearing salt water.

"Right," Blake agreed. "A part of you hated it, while the other part thought you could change her mind by fighting with her or pushing her boundaries." *Jesus Christ*, she was right. "You were never going to get in her way, though, Judah. She tried to avoid you from the beginning because she'd already made that commitment to herself. She thought she wasn't strong enough to be in your world and not drown, but when you eventually got her to cave, she switched plans and thought she could help you see what she saw in you. She thought you could heal together, except…she had no idea that you were already an addict."

"She said that to me once, I think." Some of my memories were more foggy than I'd like to admit, but this conversation had me remembering. "She told me she wanted to live, while I didn't. At the time, I still thought she was lying. I…I th-thought her love for me would be enough to bring her—"

I couldn't finish, didn't want to finish that disgusting sentence out loud.

"What did you think, Judah?" Blake pushed, tone inquisitive, yet somehow, all knowing.

"I can't," I whispered, voice shaking as the words left my mouth. "I'm a fucking *monster*."

"You're not a monster," she corrected easily, as if all of this was no big fucking deal, while I was biting my lip hard enough to make it bleed in order to keep myself from screaming. "You're uncovering the truth. Sometimes, that can be hard to process, and even harder to forgive."

Ha. *Forgive?* She was out of her fucking mind.

I said nothing, couldn't see past the blinding rage swimming beneath the surface of my skin. The part of me that loved Phoenix unconditionally, completely, was sickened by what I'd done, and it genuinely felt like I was two people in that moment.

When I was high, anything was possible. I was able to rationalize my actions, but my logic was skewed. The fact that I'd put Phoenix in that position? That I genuinely cared so little about her life? Her wish to keep living it?

I didn't deserve her.

"Fucking hell." I moaned softly, completely humiliated, as those damn tears rolled down my temples, my jaw, onto my neck. The embarrassment had nothing to do with my showcase of emotion, but rather everything to do with how I must look in P's eyes.

Right there on the couch, I choked on my own repulsive nature.

Dr. Blake remained silent, allowing me to sob my way through the memories rushing in.

I was reexperiencing moments in time, but without the haze of opioids, I got to witness the magnitude of my own damnation. I destroyed P and Frankie's house, I fucked another girl in front of Phoenix just to try and get a rise out of her. Yet she *still* told me she loved me.

Standing in the middle of a kitchen full of broken glass, Phoenix had screamed her feelings for me, *at* me, begging me to listen, begging me to save myself.

"I can't fucking do this." My voice was foreign, cracked, clogged with liquid failure.

"Can't do what, Judah?" Blake coaxed, though she sounded far away.

"Remember!" I screamed, ready to claw my own eyes out.

"Breathe for me, please," Dr. Blake instructed. "Breathe your way through it."

Is she fucking kidding?!

I flew from the couch into a standing position and glared at my therapist. "There *is* no way to breathe through this! I lost *everything*!"

"You didn't, though, Judah." Dr. Blake sat forward in her chair, meeting me eye for eye as that stupid notebook of hers sat in her lap, forgotten.

"What do I have left, exactly?" I sneered, tears racing down my cheeks. "The only family I had hates me, I don't even deserve to *look* at Phoenix much less apologize, my band is nonexistent, I have an *assault* charge to deal with when I get out of here, and the police think I killed the two girls I spent three days on a bender with. I have *nothing* left!"

"Judah," Blake called out, trying to gain my full attention, given that halfway through my rant, I'd begun pacing.

"What?!" I snapped, done with this conversation, with this whole goddamn experience.

But I met her green eyes, and everything stilled as we stared at each other. When she was sure she had me in a headspace to hear her clearly, she stated, "You have your life."

I blinked.

Once, twice.

"That's all I have," I whispered, bottom lip trembling. "There's nothing else."

"But that is enough," Blake stated.

"Enough?" I scoffed, laughing without humor.

"Enough to rebuild," she continued, sitting back now that I was calm enough to entertain a conversation. "You're right when you say you have nothing tangible right now as far as relationships are concerned. However, you can only go up from here…if that's what you choose to do."

"They'll never forgive me," I threw back immediately, understanding where she was going with this. "Not a chance in hell."

"Somehow, I doubt that," Blake disagreed. "Pharaoh is your best friend, your brother, and he's smart enough to know the difference between your addiction and your heart. If you spoke from your heart, I'd be willing to bet that you never lost his love for you. And Phoenix? Well, she fell in love with you, regardless of the toxicity, Judah. The love she had for you wasn't fake, and no matter what you may think…it was earned. In her eyes, you brought her back to life, which is why the various betrayals hurt so much worse, yet she never truly gave up on you. All she wanted was for you do exactly what you're doing right now—getting the help you need."

"And my dream?" I spat, deflecting, still unable to believe I deserved forgiveness from anyone I'd hurt. "What about the fact that I was still dreaming about wanting to die? Doesn't that mean I still want to die? You said the truth is in the subconscious, isn't it?"

The way I posed the question made it sound like I wanted

her to tell me I was correct, that suicidal thoughts would haunt me forever, but I desperately needed to hear the opposite.

I was fighting mania, trying to distinguish fact from fiction, but one thing was for sure—I wanted to get better, not worse.

"If you're questioning whether or not you want to end your life right now, I'd say you're making progress." She smiled a little in my direction. "But sure, dreams are the subconscious mind coming to life, so your dream tells me there's still work to do regarding your suicidal thoughts. However no, it doesn't mean you're still in that place you were when you overdosed."

I let go of the breath I was holding, stepping back sloppily until I hit the couch, where I slumped backwards, sitting down and resting my head in my hands.

"This is another side effect of the detox, Judah," Blake explained. "Unfortunately, the first few weeks can be messy as you remember more and more of what's happened over the last year, but you will get through it. Reliving what you experienced, the things you did, and discovering why you did those things, it all helps you prevent making the same mistakes again."

"I need a break," I muttered into my hands. "Can we cut this session short for today?"

Dr. Blake took a few seconds to respond, but when she did, she agreed. "Sure, but I'll see you for our second session after lunch."

Great. Lookin' forward to it.

* ❋ *

MY LITTLE BREAK served me well.

I spent the next four hours prepping myself for my afternoon session, and after wasting the first two pissed the fuck off and hating my entire situation, I was left realizing there was legitimately nothing else to do. If I wasn't going to kill myself, if I wasn't going to throw it all away, then I had to get the help I needed, and in order to do that, I wanted to just rip the fucking Band-Aid off.

Playing both sides of the fence, picking and choosing which topics were allowed and which weren't, was only wasting precious time. Three months in rehab felt like a long time, until I realized I was already down to two and a half months and my list of issues hadn't gotten smaller. If anything, it had grown now that I was starting to remember all the things I'd done. Despite the awful feelings that came when I took a stroll down memory lane, I'd found a new molecule of hope in my back pocket, because as much as I hated it, Dr. Blake was…right.

If I looked at everything, from beginning to end, including my childhood and all the shitty things my parents did, if I faced the pain once and for all? There was a slim chance I could quite literally start with a blank slate.

There was no guarantee that I'd regain Pharaoh's trust and his friendship. I had no goddamn idea how I'd convince Pierce and Vale to hear me out, and I'd kissed Hendrix—as well as Mammoth Sound—goodbye, but I still had a chance.

If I learned how not to screw it up.

And Phoenix? Well…

There was more I needed to figure out when it came to her.

Our downfall happened slowly in some ways, but faster in others, and there was a mixed bag of issues outside of my drug use. I needed to just dive in and deal with the facts if I was ever going to get back to a place where I felt comfortable enough to face her again.

"All right, this is going to suck, but it already fucking sucks, so whatever," I announced, walking into Dr. Blake's office after pushing food around my plate in the dining room. "I'm ready to… Well, I don't even know what I'm ready to do, but I know it's going to hurt, and the only thing I know for sure is that I want to go back to Phoenix. Except there's still shit I need to work out when it comes to her, and then we can get into the absolute disaster zone that was my childhood and my eventual friendship with Pharaoh."

"Wow, you're...*excited* right now." Dr. Blake stared at me, a little wide-eyed. "What's happening here?"

"I'm *sick* of this," I growled, feeling that anger bubbling again. "That's what's happening. I'm sick of the guilt, I'm sick of running, only to hit another brick wall, but I want to do it fast, because I know it won't be fun. So, get to it. Ask me anything, and I'll tell the truth."

"Whoa." Dr. Blake chuckled a little. "While I appreciate the enthusiasm, we need to just take a few deep breaths and sit down for a second, so I can catch up."

I made a motion with my hand signaling that she do whatever she needed to do. "Fine."

Once I was seated, legs bouncing, she started. "So, you're ready to talk about your parents?"

"Yes," I replied, nodding. "Among other things."

"Okay." She grabbed her trusty notebook. "Can you tell me what the difference is between now and a few hours ago?"

"*That* is what you want to ask me?" I narrowed my gaze on her face. "I'm willing to talk about *anything*, and you want to talk about how I got here instead of just taking advantage of the opportunity you've been waiting for this whole time?"

"Humor me, Judah," she pushed blandly.

"Fine," I grumbled. "Two weeks ago—hell, two days ago, I didn't want to look at anything because I was afraid of what I'd feel. You forced my hand with your voodoo mind therapy tricks, and we spilled out the Phoenix can of worms. Then this morning, I remembered some shit that I really didn't like reliving, but hell, I survived it, and I learned I'm a shitty as fuck human being but I can still, technically, turn it around. I know I can't do shit until I've gone through all my baggage and looked at everything. So here we are."

"So what you're saying is, you want that blank slate?"

I paused and looked left, feeling the longing in my chest expand like a balloon, imagining what it would be like to gain back everything I'd lost. "Yes."

"Great," was all Dr. Blake said, but I heard the satisfied pride in her tone. "What would you like to talk about?"

Staying true to my word, I answered instantly. "My abandonment issues."

"Interesting, okay. What about them?"

Feeling better now that we were on our way to getting into the nitty-gritty, I sat back on the couch and crossed my arms, swallowing down my anxiety in favor of taking a leap of faith into the dark.

"I know they stem from my mother leaving me, but I'm also trying to work through how that situation followed me into adulthood, and how it affects me now. Even though I know she doesn't deserve it, I still...resent Phoenix. And I'll be honest, it doesn't make much sense to me."

I hated that part of myself—the bitter, desperate, bitchy part that hoped she was suffering without me, all because it would make *me* feel better. Deep down, I was still the douchebag who felt like shit all the fucking time and hated when others managed to thrive in a world I couldn't stand.

"You're so much more self-aware than you think you are, Judah," Dr. Blake said with a chuckle. "All right, let's start with this... Do you think that your drug use worsened when Phoenix left you at the airport because you wanted to escape the feeling of losing her, or because you wanted to get *back* at her for leaving you alone on tour?"

Yikes.

Going back to that moment, I experienced it all over again—what it had felt like when I realized she wasn't getting on that plane with me. I hadn't wanted to show her, didn't want her to know what she'd just done to me, but there had been this overwhelming sense of absolute panic. What if she found someone else? Why was I alone again? How dare she grow past me? She wasn't supposed to be able to *breathe* without me, much less survive living in a completely different country while I was gone for months on end. How was I the only one panicking over the thought of living without her?

Instead of just explaining to her how I felt, I'd turned it into a sickening game, wanting to fight, threaten, push every one of her buttons, just so she would hurt as much as I had.

Swallowing was a little difficult, but I responded as soon as I had the answer. "I wanted to get back at her. In my mind, I was offering her the chance to leave her entire life behind and run away with me. We could have gotten lost together. Different countries, unlimited partying, on-stage appearances, drugs, sex… She would have been my fucking queen."

"But from her perspective…" Blake prompted, steering me toward that growth mindset, helping me see what I refused to before.

Except now that I was back in the past, I wasn't feeling nearly as confident as I had when I walked in.

But I refused to stop, knowing the longer I delayed the inevitable, the less likely I was to achieve anything while in this godforsaken place.

"She, uh, she was afraid of losing herself in my l-lifestyle. Sh-she knew it wasn't healthy, especially for her. And I, uh…" I coughed, hating myself. "I-I hurt her pretty bad during the two weeks leading up to leaving, but I…did it on purpose."

Fuck my life.

"I ruined her trust, and well, I guess I confused her more than anything, because my attitude changed so quickly, thanks to my drug use. So coming on tour with me was a risk she wwasn't willing to take, especially since she was in the middle of her apprenticeship."

"And why do you think that was so hard for you to understand back then?" Blake asked, while writing in her notebook.

"I didn't even try to understand it," I admitted softly as my eyes glazed over and my thoughts drifted back to those few weeks. "In the back of my mind, I knew what was going on, I knew that I'd been a royal dick to her, but that voice was so small and all I could see was that she was leaving me. That meant I wasn't…worth it for her." It still hurt. The fact that she chose herself over me hurt in a way I knew was my own problem and not hers, but I couldn't erase the truth. "I truly believed that even though I treated her like shit, she was supposed to love me anyways."

"*Love* you?" Blake asked. "Or excuse your behavior and physically *be* with you, no matter the cost?"

Fuck. "I see your point."

Blake nodded. "Phoenix chose to stay in LA because while yes, you hurt her, mainly, you confused her—did a complete one eighty—but in my eyes, it had nothing to do with not loving you. She just didn't love who you became."

"Because I was fucking high," I spat out, frustrated with myself.

"Right," Dr. Blake agreed. "Your perspective was skewed, but Phoenix sounds like a very intuitive, yet very communicative person. Those types of people only speak when they feel their words matter to the person they're talking to, and you didn't want to hear her. Especially after you pushed her away by blaming her for the criticism when your single came out—which is another trigger we'll get to."

I had so much shit to unpack, it was nauseating.

"When you started to party again, you left Phoenix in the dust and triggered *her* abandonment issues, but where you masked yours with drugs, she went inward. Phoenix went back to the beginning and reminded herself of the reason she moved back to LA in the first place—she chose herself. She knew that if she got on that plane with you when she was angry at you for how you treated her, she might have turned to drugs in order to tolerate you, to forget the negative and focus on lust rather than love, but she'd already walked away from that way of coping in New York. She—"

"Wasn't going to do that again," I concluded for Blake, understanding with more clarity than I liked. "Phoenix *could* have drowned with me. I didn't completely misunderstand her in the beginning, I just never thought she'd be able to leave me like that. It made me feel like an idiot, so I wanted to get back at her, but—"

"Hold on," Dr. Blake interrupted, sounding curious. "Did she really leave you though?"

Now I was confused. "What do you mean?"

"Did Phoenix ever *really* leave you? Or did you leave her first?"

Jesus Christ.

I bit my lip, unable to say it out loud.

Blake stayed silent, knowing that I was going to eventually admit it, but it was going to take me time, because the shit I was feeling right now?

Everything was my fault. Phoenix had done virtually nothing wrong and I hated her a little for it, but now that I'd started down this road, the wish to fix my life outweighed my comfortability.

Still, I glared at Blake for pointing this shit out. "You fucking suck, you know that?"

"I'm sorry," Blake replied, not sounding sorry at all.

"Fucking hell," I whispered aloud, shaking my head. "*I* left *her*. There—I abandoned Phoenix, and she had every right not to come on tour with me."

My leg bounced fervently as I tapped my fingers on my

knees, feeling anxious, embarrassed, and like a total fucking asshole.

Blake nodded once. "But she did come to Paris as soon as Pharaoh called her, hoping she could fix things, because she most likely feared that her not coming with you was the reason your behavior was so erratic in the first place. Again, not realizing that you had a problem long before her," she pointed out.

"This is so much worse than I thought," I said on a groan, wanting to crawl out of my skin.

"Judah, try and listen to the underlying positive here," Blake suggested. "Phoenix pushed you away, and rightfully so, but she never *left* you. Even when she did find out about your addiction, she was still fighting for you, telling you she loved you, she just wanted you to get better. *Love* was never the issue. She just wasn't the person you and your addiction wanted her to be."

I was beginning to understand why everyone in my circle thought Phoenix was so fucking amazing—because she was. But even now, recognizing that she truly had done nothing wrong, I still had a bitter taste on my tongue.

She was better at everything—surviving, showing love, growing, changing to fit her circumstances, despite how hard I knew it was for her. Even though I'd known it in some form or another, it was startling to face the fact that I was so far behind. I felt like a fucking child, and it was humiliating to realize how long I'd let myself believe it was the other way around.

As soon as the realization clicked, it was as if the last year of my life played on a time loop.

Fast as hell, memories whipped through my mind, but I was standing in Phoenix's shoes this time, watching myself spin out, feeling just as abandoned, just as hurt, just as lonely, because I didn't want her when she was healthy.

The entire time I'd known her, I wanted to be worth it in

her eyes, but never once did I show her she was worth it in *my* eyes. In her shoes, from her point of view, it was clear as fucking day that my little bird really was the Phoenix. She rose from the ashes of her past and she'd wanted to take me with her, but I'd refused.

Except nothing, not even my bullshit, got in her way.

Sure, she'd cried over my addiction, showed true fear that I would end up dead, but still, every time I disappointed her, she'd gone back to living her life. She'd picked up her shattered pieces and kept living.

Everyone else celebrated her growth, everyone made it seem like she was the queen of all queens, and now…

"I, uh…" I cleared my throat again, blinking up at the ceiling to make the tears go away as I whispered, "I'm a fucking asshole."

Blake must have known I was going to keep talking, because she remained silent while I gathered my thoughts and swallowed my self-loathing, because now that I'd somewhat come to terms with her strength, I was able to see Phoenix in a different light—as a child. I could remain in her shoes, go back to a darker moment in her life, before she even met me, and feel the same crushing sense of abandonment I carried around.

My heart ached, my soul screamed, realizing that Phoenix was at one point just a thirteen-year-old girl that had needed to be loved genuinely, fiercely, and she deserved to be protected and cherished after her parent's tragedy took place. I'd never allowed myself to think about it, hadn't had the emotional maturity or foresight, given my issues, but now I recognized that the *last* thing I would have wanted was for that poor girl to grow up suicidal and addicted.

Then I couldn't help but think…was that how she'd seen *me* this entire time?

Just a broken boy from the trailer park that had gotten so used to abuse, he became an abuser?

What in the fuck had I done?

"Phoenix came back to Los Angeles to grow." I sighed shakily, beginning to think out loud. "She wanted to escape the party scene and learn how to live without the destructive tendencies, right? And then I came along and made her focus on me, feel me, fall for me, but my lifestyle was still dangerous in her eyes. All I did was frequently dangle that life in front of her and prove all her fears correct."

"The difference is," Blake cut in, seeing where I was going with it. "She wasn't in love with her life in New York, but she *was* in love with you, so you were worth the risk when she initially decided to take it. As your relationship unfolded, she excused a lot of your behavior because she hoped that her love for you would transform you, make you want to live a better life with her. The same way you hoped her love for you would pull her into your destructive tendencies."

The guilt was bone crushing.

On drugs, I tried to make everyone else the problem, and the substances let me. They made me a king in my own section of hell, while everyone else walked away. Now everyone was gone and it was just me, standing in the ashes of all the things I used to love.

And for what?

Why did I do that? Why did I listen?

How did I fucking get here?

Unwilling to get lost, feeling panic rising higher, I asked, "Where do I go from here? Because now I see what Phoenix meant when she said I needed to figure out what I wanted and who I am... but I can't help but feel like there's so much shit to dig up, and while I guess I'm willing to do it, I still don't see how I'll pull this off. How do I put my life back together after accepting the fact that I willingly, openly, destroyed it all on my own?"

Dr. Blake shifted in her seat, her grey skirt sliding against the leather of her chair. "You take it one step, one day, one thought at a time. Your world, the *real* world, is coming back to you, little by little, and it's frightening because you're realizing how much you missed or messed up, but that's why you're here—to talk through your thoughts, your emotions, your past, and answer those unanswered questions so you can keep going."

It felt like too much, like I'd never tackle it all in the two and a half months I had left here.

"You've still got a while before you have to go back home and fix what's broken, so don't worry about putting it all back together," Dr. Blake said, trying to ease some of my fears. "This is about realizing what went wrong, facing it, and learning from it. From there, you can decide what you want to work on rebuilding and what you want to build from scratch, but that comes with time, Judah. It doesn't have to be rushed."

It had only been a couple days since I'd started talking, after two weeks of silence, and now I was mad at myself for wasting that time, but that dread was still very much present. Those cravings lurked in the shadows, preparing to attack as soon as the lights went out, because the grip I had on my growth wasn't tight at all. It was limp and weak, just like my mindset.

While Blake was correct, I wasn't going home anytime soon, I still didn't feel like I could just sit with these realizations and not say something. How was I supposed to sleep at night, knowing how much I'd fucked up with Phoenix? It would be impossible to keep my mouth shut, but at the same time, I didn't want to talk to anyone directly...

"Wait," I mused out loud, "I know what you said about talking to people, but we're allowed to send letters, right? To people outside?"

Momentarily surprised, she nodded. "Yes, absolutely, you

can send letters anytime you want. You passed the two-week period."

"Good to know." I nodded as an idea formed in my head. "Is it a bad idea to write a letter to someone, not asking anything of them, but just…getting some things off my chest?"

"Not at all," she replied, shaking her head. "It's a great idea. You just have to be prepared for their responses. Not everyone will be as quick to forgive you, as you are to forgive yourself, and that's okay. You're going to get sick of me saying this, but these things really do take time."

"Right," I muttered, swallowing the lump of guilt in my throat.

The thought of not being forgiven dropped a hardened chunk of sin right into the pit of my fucking stomach, but I was also too desperate to get my thoughts onto paper to let it stop me. I couldn't spend my time in here pretending like all of my friends weren't out there living their lives, while I sat in countless therapy sessions, realizing how shitty I was to them, and not say anything.

The sober version of me wasn't a monster. In fact, he was an emotional wreck.

"I'll see you tomorrow, Judah," Blake said, interrupting my thoughts, her smile full and knowing. "I'm proud of you."

I gave her a small nod, not understanding what she could be proud of. "Thanks."

Little by little, I was starting to understand that there really was a difference in who I was sober and who I was as an addict.

My demons disguised themselves in tiny little pills and told me their venom was better than the truth, and while that was true in *some* cases…in the aspects that mattered the most? It was bullshit.

This would be hard. It would be fucking awful, and I doubted I'd sleep peacefully for the entirety of my stay at

Cliffside, but if I took it seriously and used Phoenix as an example rather than a crutch... I was beginning to believe I could do this.

She was the strongest person I knew, and for the first time, I could see that rather than trying to destroy that strength, I could use it as a model for my own. Not only was she the light at the end of my tunnel, she was in the tunnel with me. She had been from the start, I'd just been too blind to see it.

It was time I opened my eyes.

CHAPTER 5
Phoenix

"MY FUCKIN' BAAAABIES!" Kavan shouted as he rounded the front of his Aston Martin and bolted to where Frankie and I stood on the platform outside of baggage claim.

We had very little time to prepare as his body crashed in between us, forcefully pulling us both into a near suffocating embrace.

"Ow, Jesus," I muttered, laughing as my forehead slammed into his shoulder.

"Ricco, get the fuck over here," he yelled over our heads, ignoring my protest completely. "Family hug! *Now!*"

"I'm comin', I'm comin'," Ric called back. "But we've got a dog in the fuckin' car, and she almost jumped through damn window because you left it open!"

"Trix!!!" Frankie screamed into Kavan's shirt, trying to push him away. "Let me see my girl!"

"No way in hell, blondie," Kavan shot back, squeezing us tighter against his body. "You can have doggie snuggles the whole ride home. *This* snuggle is for me."

"This snuggle is very public, and people are starting to stare," I pointed out, chuckling as I peeked over his shoulder to see a family of five smiling at us, along with a single paparazzi on the other side of the busy airport road.

"Screw 'em," Ricco chimed in, joining the hug by wrapping his big ass body around the back of us. "Let the whole world know you're home and your boys are too happy about it."

"Geez!" Frankie exclaimed, laughing along with me. "It's like you guys missed us or something."

At that, Kav stepped back, just enough to look down at her. "Missed you? Bitch, that word ain't enough to describe how we felt while you were gone."

"Empty, abandoned, dejected, misplaced, bored as all fuck," Ricco threw in. "Those are just a few."

"You guys are so dramatic." I snickered but didn't try to move. Instead, I tipped my head back, leaning it against Ric's chest in order to catch his eye. "But I'm also not mad about it because we missed you too."

"Way more than I thought we would," Frankie added. "Who knew you assholes had grown on us like that?"

"You two are awful," Ricco responded with a bright ass smile on his face. "We give you the warmest welcome home, and you're like 'eh, we kinda sorta missed you a little bit too. Shocking, right?' I mean, *what?* Y'all suck."

"Can't let your egos get too big," I sassed as Frankie and I smirked at each other.

"Okay, but really," Franks started, wiggling in the center of our group hug. "There's a lot of body heat happening here, and my makeup is most definitely smeared all over Kav's shirt. So kindly get the fuck off."

Kav backed away, immediately looking down at his black T-shirt. "Yeaaaaah, there's a whole bottle of foundation goin' on here."

Frankie turned in my direction with a slightly panicked look on her face. "Shit, do I have an empty patch now?"

"You sure do," I replied, laughing at the difference in color on her right cheek. "It's fine, though. We're only going home."

She rolled her eyes, then shrugged. "I'm fucking stoked that we don't have to worry about social media content for the next month. I can rock the no makeup look and turn down all of Julia's events." She did an excited little jig. "Our followers are going to freak out now that we're home."

While I'm sure my followers would be excited to see where I'd been, I didn't make any actual money off my social media account, so Frankie was the only one cashing in on the outrageous number of photos we took on our vacation.

"Lucky you," I said on a groan. "I head back into the shop tomorrow."

As the group split apart, Ricco kept his arm draped over my shoulder. "Don't act like that wasn't your choice. I'm willing to bet that Kenji told you to take an extra day off to unpack and relax."

I gave him the side-eye as Kav started loading our bags into the trunk of his car. "You be quiet."

He barked a smooth chuckle. "That's what I thought."

"Oh, my little giiiirl!" Frankie's voice floated toward me from the passenger side of Kav's car.

Realizing what was happening, I flew into action, running toward her, where she was kissing Trixie's sweet face, hugging the tiny ball of fur to her chest as she swayed back and forth.

"Hey, let me in there too!" I pulled on Frankie's shoulder, turning her and Trixie toward me so I could at least pet the damn dog as my best friend held her hostage. While I inspected her, I called out, "Did Trixie get bigger?!"

"Nah," Ricco stated. "You've just been gone a while."

"Give her to me," I demanded, wrapping my hands around the dog's body.

Franks let her go but kept a hand on the dog's back as I buried my face in her soft fur, letting the animal try her hardest to lick my ear off. Trixie was more than excited, her little tail running wild as we gave her the attention she missed from us for the past three weeks.

"All right, my ladies," Ricco started, coming up behind me. "Get your cute butts in the car. We're about to hit some serious traffic on the way home, so settle in."

It was nearing five PM, one of the worst times to land if you were flying into LAX, because not only was there traffic in the airport to begin with, but the bumper-to-bumper bullshit started before you even *left* the airport, given that it was rush hour. The highway was backed up long before you even hit the on-ramp.

"Ugh, I hate it here," Frankie said, groaning, as she got in the car. "We should have stayed in Thailand."

"Yeah, right," Kavan muttered, closing the driver side door behind him. "You two alone together in a foreign country, permanently? I'd give it one extra week before we got a phone call, asking us to fly out because one of you did something stupid."

"Hey!" I called out. "I'll have you know that we had *three* stupid moments on this trip and not once did we think about calling either of you."

"Is that a lie?" Ricco turned around to ask Frankie, and because she loved to embarrass me, she caved.

"Absolutely. We almost called twice."

"Ha!" Kav smacked the steering wheel. "I should have bet money on that statement, man. I lost a serious cash opportunity with that one."

"Okay, fine," I said, sulking. "But it was only because I got bit by something and we didn't want to go to a hospital because…foreign country and all…so we *thought* about calling you guys to see if you knew what it was, since you've been there before. But we didn't. And I ended up being fine."

"Did you panic for two days instead?" Ricco asked, flashing me a knowing smirk over the seat between us.

"She sure did," Frankie replied, laughing. "I googled it, told her it was fine, but she didn't believe me until the swelling started to go down."

"What was the other incident?" Kav asked.

I glared at Frankie, pointing a sharp finger in her direction. "Don't you fucking dare."

She bit her lip, cringing like she wanted to tell them. "Come on, it's not that bad."

"It's humiliating," I snarled. "Do *not*."

"Can we guess?" Ricco asked.

"No," Frankie and I responded at the same time.

A smile bloomed on my face. She had my back.

It wasn't bad, it was just…well, stupid. I was banking on us taking the whole experience to the grave.

"Wants and Needs" by Drake and Lil Baby came on as soon as Kav hit the road, so of course, Ricco turned that shit up, and I couldn't help bobbing my head to the beat. The production on the track was so sick, and Drake's voice always put me in a fucking trance.

"Yo, we have to do this one," Ricco yelled over the music, slapping Kav on the shoulder. "And now that our baddies are back, they can film us."

"Film for what?" Frankie called out.

"We started a TikTok while you were gone." Kav smirked at us in the rearview mirror. "We went viral with 'GREECE' from DJ Khaled and wanted to keep up the content, but it ain't easy to film ourselves and time the music correctly."

"WHAT?!" I shouted, picking up my phone. "What's your username?"

From there, Frankie and I spent the drive watching their videos, while Trixie went from lap to lap, getting spoiled with belly rubs and behind the ear scratches. Soon, the four of us began creating a new playlist, picking out songs for the guys to dance to now that they had a huge following.

It was hella fun, and even though I'd been nervous to come home, being back with our little self-made family was an incredible feeling. I was surrounded by excitement and love, creativity and art. I'd found peace, best friends, and solidarity in our group of four. It was a far cry from what I'd thought would happen when I came back from New York last year, but it was exactly what I never knew I needed.

Now, I just had to endure the Judah and Pharaoh situation and hope to god my life wouldn't be blown to bits again.

※ ✱ ※

LATER THAT NIGHT, after Ricco and Kav left, Frankie and I were chilling in the living room, avoiding our still packed bags, drinking wine, and watching an episode of *New Girl*, when my phone pinged.

I grabbed it without thinking, my eyes still glued to the scene playing out on the TV, but when I glanced down at the screen, my stomach dropped to the floor.

"Fuck," I barked, flipping the device over so the screen hit the couch cushion, shielding me from having to read the text that had come through.

"What?" Frankie asked, distracted.

"Pharaoh texted me," I stated a little breathlessly.

Anxiety swam in my stomach as Frankie turned her head slowly, wide-eyed as she chewed not so gracefully. Her mouth was still full when she shouted loudly, "What did he say?!"

"I didn't read it!" I exclaimed. "Why am I so fucking nervous?!"

She swallowed her snack before taking a sip of wine, then laughed a little. "Damn, you were right—it's been less than three hours since we got home, and he's reaching out. You better check that text, just in case he was letting you know he's on his way here."

"Shit shit shit," I picked up my phone, waiting for Face ID to unlock the message.

Pharaoh: Hey you, get home safe?

"Okay." I breathed out a sigh of relief. "He just asked if I got home safe."

"Oh, you Gucci then." Frankie shrugged, going back to watching TV.

I barked out an incredulous laugh. "Um, no I'm not! We're gonna have to talk. He's going to want to *talk*, Frankie!"

"So talk, babe!" She laughed, as if it were that easy. "Tell him that you're confused and worried and not in any kind of mindset to be in a relationship. He'll understand if you tell him you need to see what happens with Judah first."

"Bro, no!" I shook my head. "That is so not fair to him. 'Hey, just wait around for the next two months while I see if your best friend is going to get his shit together. If he doesn't, I'll hit you up.' That's awful, and we already talked about the fact that it won't work regardless."

"Ew, yeah, okay you're right," my best friend agreed. "Well, what do you *want* to say? If you had no filter whatsoever and there was a guaranteed positive outcome at the end of this, what would you tell him?"

I thought about it, unsure of what the right move was. Even when someone asked me what I *wanted* to do, I had to run it through the filter of right and wrong.

It was ridiculous.

"I don't know," I said on a groan. "Pharaoh is one of my best friends now and I miss him, but fact is, Judah's overdose kicked my ass. That's all I know. My head is a mess and I don't want anyone to get hurt, but I'm afraid it's going to happen anyways."

Frankie just stared at me before suggesting, "Uhhh, just say that."

"You're kidding."

"I'm not." She smirked. "That's the best response you can give him right now, because it's fucking true! You're trying to keep this easy on everyone and you're entitled to that. It's Pharaoh we're talking about here, babe. He loves Judah just as much as you do, and he's probably thinking the same thing you are right now. You need to stop overthinking this."

She was right—it *was* Pharaoh.

And thanks to Judah, I knew him so much better than I had before. I could be honest with him. I *had* to be honest with him, but...

"I don't want to lose his friendship," I stated, feeling the truth of those words. "Fucking him was a horrible idea, in hindsight, but I found genuine friendship with him, Franks. What if I lose it?"

"You won't." Her tone was full of confidence I couldn't find. "Pharaoh is one of the most kindhearted men I've ever met, and he seriously cares about you. He wouldn't end a friendship with you just because he couldn't have you romantically. There's no way."

I hoped she was right, because he'd become a huge part of my life over the last few months. The heartache would be ten times worse if I lost him because we slept together and I didn't follow through.

I was afraid of his reaction more than anything, but the less logical side of me needed to see him, *wanted* to see him. I had grown attached to him, and that was just another thing Judah had done by letting his addiction run wild. He'd shoved Pharaoh and me together, forcing us to lean on each other to get through the fucking awful things Judah put us through.

I couldn't feel bad about that, not if I wanted to keep my sanity over the next couple of months.

"Fine. I'll just...see what happens, I guess."

Frankie gave my shoulder a squeeze as I opened the text and began to type.

Phoenix: Hey, yeah I'm home. Got in around 5 tonight. Just watching TV with Frankie now.
Pharaoh: Good, I'm glad to have you back in town.

Seeing the three dots again, I chewed on my thumbnail, waiting for his next reply.

Pharaoh: Are you working tomorrow?

Fuck.

Phoenix: Yup. I'm at the shop until 8.
Pharaoh: All right, I'm gonna come by the house after, if that's cool with you. I have updates on J.

Just like that, the world fell out from underneath me, causing me to stand and throw my phone on the couch, only to shove my hands in my hair right after.

"What? What happened?" Frankie asked, sitting up on the couch, too aware of my panic.

"Fuck my life," I whispered, looking to the ceiling as bats took flight in my chest and my breathing became labored. "He has updates on Judah."

"Oh...shit," Frankie stated slowly. "That's, uh, not what we were expecting."

I didn't fucking prepare myself, didn't even think about the fact that Pharaoh would have information on Judah's progress, because there was something triggering about the thought of Judah sitting in a facility, away from all of us, away from me, where I couldn't get to him if I wanted to. I hated it as much as I loved it.

Getting an update, hearing how he was doing? I wasn't ready.

"Frankie, I didn't even think about the fact that Pharaoh probably went with Judah when he checked in." I sighed, running my hands over my face. "Judah has no fucking family. If the facility is going to update anyone, it's going to be Pharaoh."

Jesus Christ.

"What about HIPAA?" Frankie asked with confusion written all over her tone. "What could they possibly tell him?"

I met her eyes. "If Pharaoh is on Judah's list of contacts, he probably signed a form allowing him to know about his medical treatment. Someone has to know how Judah is doing in there. I just didn't..." I trailed off, pissed at myself for not preparing for this possibility. "I didn't fucking think about that."

"Okay, I know you're freaking out, but you *need* these updates, P," Frankie pushed gently. "This is a good thing."

"I know, I know," I grumbled, frustrated. "I just wasn't ready to dive back in so fucking soon. I'm nervous and anxious, and the fact that Judah is even *in* rehab is still a fucking shock, Frankie. It's Judah! *My* Judah! I never expected my relationship with him to end up here. I haven't processed this properly!"

"That's because neither of us process anything the way we should," Frankie unhelpfully pointed out. "Look, I know you didn't expect information this fast, but it *has* been three weeks since he overdosed..."

"Fuck my life," I said again, trying to shake off the anxiety. "All right, well, at least I have the next twenty-four hours to prep myself for this conversation."

"Or you could just ask Pharaoh right now?" Franks suggested. "You're already texting. Just get it over with—ask him now."

"No," I said, pushing that idea away instantly. "I need to see Pharaoh in person. I may not know how what I'm going to do about the whole sleeping together thing, but I know him, I care about him, and he's been dealing with all of this alone. He needs someone to talk to, and the only way I'll know what the truth is, is if I see him in person. I don't want him to be on an island, handling all of this by himself."

I was protective of Pharaoh, worried about him, because in a sense…he was me.

We both loved Judah enough to sacrifice our own happiness, we would do whatever we could to keep him alive, but we also had a breaking point, and together, we'd hit it. Then we'd lost him.

Judah had become the nightmare we'd tried to avoid.

Now? Knowing Pharaoh had had to endure Judah's recovery alone, as his only family?

No, I needed to see him. I needed to help him, be there for him.

Even if I didn't feel ready.

"What if the news is bad?" Frankie asked, sounding worried.

Don't say that. Please for the love of god.

But I knew it was a possibility, so my response was whispered, stressed, "Then it's bad, I guess. Either way, I still want to be there for Pharaoh."

Frankie clicked her tongue and grabbed my thigh as I sat back down, but when I looked at her, there was pride shining in her eyes. "You've got a ginormous heart, you know that?"

"Yeah." I laughed humorlessly. "Too big sometimes."

Nothing had changed, apparently. I was about to start right

back up where I'd left off, supporting Pharaoh in order to fill a need inside myself. When I made sure Pharaoh was okay, I felt like I was okay. It gave me something to do, something to focus on, but I couldn't lie…I was fucking sick of this feeling.

All I could do was hope that it wouldn't last much longer.

Welcome home, Phoenix.

CHAPTER 6

PHARAOH

HOPPING INTO THE G-WAGON, I swallowed the nervous ball of energy lodged in my throat, trying to shove it down as far as it would go.

I was going to see Phoenix again, after three weeks and one overdose apart.

Half of me was dreading it, while the other half was starving for it.

Since she left, everything had changed—for Judah, for P and I. It was all different. Everything that Phoenix and I had feared would happen, happened, and with it had come a tsunami that washed away any hope I'd had for a relationship between the two of us.

I didn't know what was going to happen now. I'd had weeks to think about my future, the possibilities, my feelings for Phoenix, my friendship with Judah, and while knew what I *wanted* with every fiber of my fucking being, I also knew I never got what I wanted.

I was used to it by now, and given how much was at stake, my only choice was to change courses, switch directions, and settle in for what I was sure would be internal hell for me.

Even still, I told myself that simply being around Phoenix was enough, standing in her presence, holding her hand through Judah's recovery, utilizing her wisdom and subtle strength to stay afloat. She was a fantastic fucking friend, and I needed that. I needed her.

But I'd be lying if I said a part of me didn't hope she wouldn't take him back.

A miniscule part of me wanted to stay optimistic, especially when my mind wandered into memories of what it felt like to hold her, kiss her, to feel her skin against mine. That little spark of hope wanted me to believe that what I made her feel was stronger than what she felt for Judah.

Bur I wasn't an idiot.

While she was gone, I'd tried to kill that spark and save myself the heartache.

Because Kavan and Ricco had gotten me hooked on Chase Atlantic, "EVEN THOUGH I'M DEPRESSED" blared through the speakers as I sped down the highway toward P and Frankie's place, watching the sun set in the sky ahead of me. Light blue bled into brilliant orange with just a hint of pink mixed in, painting a beautiful picture that worked to warm my battered, disappointed soul.

I was tired, my heart hurt, and my mind was a mess of what-ifs.

Dropping Judah off at rehab? It was different this time. More painful, more worrisome. Yet I wasn't sure why the ache hadn't lessened after so much time had passed, especially given that Judah had a real chance of turning his life around this time because he had a fucking reason to.

The last two times I'd done the very same thing—drove in complete silence with Judah in my passenger seat, heading to a facility that would hopefully help him get his shit together—he'd had no reason to change, nothing to live for aside from his music. The previous problem had been that even his career tore him to bits, so what was the point of committing to getting better?

This time, though…

I'd witnessed firsthand what he was going to lose if he didn't get his shit together. I'd felt her love, tasted her essence, and three weeks ago, as I held the phone to my ear with one hand, and a pen in the other, I'd listened to Phoenix dictate her letter to him. In that moment, I'd known I was handing over my relationship with her. I was giving it right back to Judah, because her words were too powerful for him to ignore. They'd haunt him like they haunted me.

All alone at Cliffside, having to make temporary friends just to get through the days, countless therapy sessions, the detox, cravings, sleeping alone…

Phoenix would be on his mind constantly, her words spinning in his head on a never-ending rotation, and with that melody on the brain? Forget about it.

I'd make it through, I'd remain standing, but there'd be no one standing next to me.

Still, though, I had that stupid fucking tiny spark lighting up my heart, just enough to keep it beating for her, unwilling to put to be out until it needed to be. When that time came, I'd do it willingly, because my core belief hadn't changed.

Phoenix Royal deserved the best. She deserved to be happy, to be in love, to be cherished and worshipped, and I knew my best friend. I knew his heart, and underneath all the bullshit, under the sharpened claws of his addiction, I knew his soul was made of gold.

Judah could be everything she needed and more if he let himself, if he did what she told him to do in that letter.

Those were my last thoughts as I pulled into the driveway of P's house, recognizing Kav's Aston Martin parked next to Frankie's Porsche.

I rolled my eyes.

Of course those two are fuckin' here.

Instantly annoyed, I blew out a breath.

I needed to get Phoenix alone, and they were going to keep their damn mouths shut about it, or I'd lose control of the fragile hold I had on my temper.

To say I'd been wound tightly these last few weeks would be an understatement.

Slamming the door behind me, I steadied my breathing and steeled myself, wanting the first moment I saw her to be a happy one, if only because I'd missed her. If she had any feelings for me at all, there was no doubt she'd missed me too. I needed this reconciliation. I needed the comfort she consistently provided.

Lifting my hand, I went to knock on the front door, but before I could, it swung open to reveal Phoenix—tan as fuck, wearing a green hoodie with shorts that disappeared under the length of the sweatshirt. She was smiling, but it was uneasy, nervous, as her eyes roamed my face.

Fuck, she's so beautiful.

I smirked back at her, hiding the dread in my chest, and broke the silence. "Hello, Little P."

With those three words, her smile slipped and that seemingly never-ending sadness took over as she flew forward and jumped to wrap her arms around my neck.

I exhaled thickly as her small body crashed against mine, instantly cocooning me in her scent.

God, she feels so good.

All on their own, my arms wound their way around her waist, just as she asked, "Are you okay?" But before I could reply, she grumbled into my shoulder, "And don't fucking lie to me."

I chuckled sadly, burying my head in her neck, not giving a fuck that she would eventually reject me. "No, baby, I'm not okay. But I'm getting there," I replied.

"I shouldn't have left you alone," she mumbled, face still buried in my shoulder. "You had to walk in on him that night, you had to handle all the hard stuff, you had to live *alone* afterwards and sit with your thoughts. I should have come back, I shou—"

"Hey," I shushed her, palming the back of her head to calm her down, wondering why she was so worked up all of a sudden. She'd been fine over text yesterday. "Don't go there right now, all right? We're good. Judah is where he needs to be, and he made it. He's alive. That's all that matters."

"Fuck." She pushed back, setting her feet back on the ground as she wiped underneath her watery eyes. "I don't know what the hell is happening to me."

I did.

She was sliding back into reality after taking the vacation she'd so desperately needed, and I was a reminder of everything she'd lost, everything that had hurt her.

After swallowing what felt like chalk, I cleared my throat and changed the subject. "Did you have a good vacation?"

"Yeah." She laughed sadly, meeting my eyes again, and those brown orbs were muted, sad. "That's the problem. I tried to forget everything happening here, and now that I'm back, I feel like I have to relive it all over again."

I knew it.

"Come on, little miss." I put two hands on her shoulders and spun her around, pushing her gently over the threshold and into the house. "We need a drink and a breather."

Despite the pain I knew was coming, I already felt better, just from having my hands on her, even in a platonic way, in *any* way. But she definitely wasn't the only one struggling.

We both needed some liquid courage.

CHAPTER 7
Phoenix

PHARAOH'S HANDS on my shoulders did very little to settle the myriad of emotions whipping through my body. On the one hand, I felt grounded and secure with him at my back, while on the other, I was fucking terrified of what was to come.

As soon as I'd laid eyes on him again, all rationality went out the window and all I cared about was the fact that he was standing in front of me, in need of support. I felt bonded to him in some way, and having him so close again both settled and scared me.

Romantically, my feelings didn't go deep enough to truly pursue him, but our friendship? The relationship we'd built on a foundation of grief? *That* felt permanent, and I was deeply dreading the conversation I needed to have with him about our future as a couple.

Regardless of what happened with Judah, losing Pharaoh felt like the equivalent to losing a limb. He'd become a part of me. Important. Necessary.

I didn't want to lose him because of the choices we made when it all became too much, and I hated the fact that I'd led him to believe we could be more than friends, when in reality, it wasn't truly possible. I'd been out of my mind, and I couldn't help but think so was he.

Still, he was here, and there was no way out of it now. It was time to set the record straight and see what we still had left afterwards.

"Phar! My dude," Ricco shouted, smiling from his place on the couch next to Frankie. "How you been?"

"Since the last time I saw you two days ago?" Pharaoh chuckled, and I stopped at the response, turning around to quirk an eyebrow at him. The guys had been talking while we were gone? He met my stare and smirked. "What? You think we only hang out when you two girls are around? We were friends long before you came into the picture, little one."

I wasn't sure why I was so surprised, because he was totally right, but the fact that he spent time with Kav and Ricco actually calmed my spirit a little more, something about knowing Pharaoh wasn't truly alone this whole time.

"Don't 'little one' me," I sassed back with a small smile on my face. "I'm just surprised."

"Because I'm anti-social?" he threw back.

"I'm not walking into *that* trap," I replied, letting out a loose laugh before turning to everyone else. "We're getting drinks, anyone need a refill?"

"Grab me a Truly," Kav requested from the chair, where he was playing a super intense game on his phone. His forehead was creased in concentration, eyes laser focused on the screen. "A mango one though, I'm done with the other flavors."

"What's wrong with the other flavors?" Frankie asked, smirking as she shoved Ricco's legs off her thighs and got up to follow us.

"They taste too artificial," Kav muttered, distracted, before letting out a loud, "Son of a bitch!"

Watching him drop his phone in his lap with a huff had me covering up my smile, which only became more difficult to hide as he pulled off his hat and threw his head back, using the black cap to cover his face.

"Drama king in the hoooouse," Ricco exclaimed, chuckling loudly. "I'll take a Truly too, P, but I don't give a fuck what kind."

"You got it." I snickered.

The three of us made our way into the kitchen, but Frankie took care of the guys while Pharaoh went straight for the cabinet where we put our liquor and grabbed the bottle of Patrón.

"Frankie, how was your vacation?" Pharaoh asked, making conversation as he pulled two glasses down and set to work on making our drinks.

"Fan-fuckin-tastic, thanks for asking," Frankie replied, winking at me from across the island. "How was it here?"

"Oh, you know," Phar started, turning around to head toward the freezer. "Picking up the pieces of my shattered career while trying to live a semi-normal life. It's been all right. Same shit, different day."

Inwardly, I cringed, hating that he was able to be so casual with everyone about his pain, while knowing damn well he was feeling anything *but* casual on the inside.

"Yo, these last few months have been hell," Frankie responded. "I'm sorry you've had to deal with it. Both you and P. It's horrific."

Pharaoh shrugged as he put a few ice cubes in each glass. "It is what it is. There's nothing we can do to change it, so it's more about following the tide."

As I jumped on the counter, sadness leaked into my bloodstream, and I began to wonder if the news Pharaoh had to tell me about Judah really *was* bad. His casualness could have been a mask, or he was genuinely just resigned to the situation, but either way, I was having a hard time figuring it out.

Just then, Ric called from the living room, "You and P gonna go talk? We were planning on watching a movie, but we'll wait for you if you want."

"Nah, you go ahead," I told him, making an executive decision. "Phar and I are going to hang on the patio, I think. We do need to order food, because I'm starving and at this point, it'll take at least an hour to get here."

Pharaoh had arrived only a few minutes after I got home from the shop.

It was nice being back to work and getting reacquainted with my art after so many weeks without creative expression. My machine felt strange in my hand, but I'd only had two clients—both of which were very nice—and thankfully, their designs were simple enough that I could get back into my job rather easily.

I was also glad neither girl asked any questions about Judah, even though paparazzi were camped outside the shop all day. It seemed the girls were able to read my energy, which was very guarded, but once I knew they weren't going to pry for details, I loosened up and ended up enjoying the conversations we'd had.

"Sushi?" Frankie asked the group. "Chinese? Pizza?"

"Wings?" Kav suggested, no longer sulking. "Oooo, we should get chicken wings!"

"Fine," Frankie agreed. "Only if you guys promise not to eat like fucking cavemen and get wing sauce all over my furniture like the last time."

"Ehhh, I should probably eat at the table because that's just not possible for me," Kav admitted, making me snort. "Phoenix, Phar? You guys good with that? What kind do you want?"

"Honey garlic," I called out and looked at Pharaoh, who was busy cutting up a lime for our drinks. He was distracted, not paying a lick of attention, so I gently kicked him in the side. When he glanced at me, I noticed how far away he was but didn't question it, instead asking, "What kind of wings do you want?"

"Sorry." He gave me a small smile, then called out, "Barbeque. Get a side of onion rings while you're at it."

My stomach growled at the thought.

"All right, you," Pharaoh addressed me, tapping my thigh with one hand and holding out my drink in the other. "Let's go. Patio time. We can roll a blunt."

"Let's do it." I nodded, grateful for cannabis and its ability to settle my frayed nerves.

I was low-key grateful Ricco and Kav were here and the night was turning out to be pretty chill, but as we walked toward the glass doors, my stomach began to knot up again. I knew I was about to hear about Judah and his progress, along with having the discussion about my and Pharaoh's very fragile, very new relationship.

Pharaoh must have noticed because once we were outside, he put a hand on my shoulder and whispered, "Relax, Phoenix. It's just me."

I tried my best to smile, but I was sure it came off looking more like a cringe.

When we sat down at the small table in the back, I agreed to roll the blunt, needing something to do with my hands. The silence ate up the seconds as he watched me break apart the weed and place it in the grinder. My anxiety peaked around minute two, but luckily, Pharaoh found some courage before I did and spoke first.

"So," he stated, but then cleared his throat and shifted a little in his seat.

"So," I echoed, glancing up briefly to see that his body language appeared relaxed, but I couldn't take that as a positive sign because he was so fucking good at hiding what he really felt. I'd have to actually take my time and study him if I wanted to figure it out, but I was too chicken to dig that deep.

When I caught his dark stare, he gave me a lopsided smile

and asked, "Should we just get it out of the way and say this is weird?"

"Uh." My laugh sounded as awkward as his question. "Yeah, it's weird, but it's only weird because this situation sucks and neither of us knows what to do now."

"Basically," he agreed, tapping his fingers on the table before deciding to light up a cigarette. "I'll just start simple… How are you?"

There was that pit again, floating in my stomach, taking up way too much room.

"I'm okay," I responded, knowing full well it wouldn't be enough.

"Phoenix." Pharaoh said my name like an accusation, like he knew better.

Which, of course, he did.

I sighed, giving up, but looked back down at my hands, giving my attention to the blunt. "Fine. I'm not sure *how* I feel, because I feel a whole lot of things," I admitted.

A tick of silence.

Then a whispered, "Me too."

I bit my lip, tearing at the flesh as I thought of a response, because again, what the hell was I supposed to say?

But after a full minute of crickets chirping in the background, Pharaoh rushed out, "Is it bad that I feel relieved?"

"Relieved about what?" I murmured, unsure of what he meant.

"About Judah, you know, his overdose…" Pharaoh clarified in a voice full of shame. "It's awful, I know, but for a while there, it felt like there would never be a pause in the chaos and we'd have to run away completely if we wanted to get out from under it."

I scoffed, sprinkling weed into the blunt wrap. "I had the same thought when I was on vacation. Hell, maybe it *is* fucking horrible that we think this way, but at least it's over now. Judah will finally be sober, and that's either going to last...or it isn't."

The last part of my sentence was quiet, less confident.

After pulling on his cigarette and releasing the smoke, Pharaoh cleared his throat again. "About that... I talked to J's counselor a few days ago—the one overseeing his schedule."

I murmured nonsensically as my leg began to bounce underneath the table and breathing became more difficult. "And?" I bit out.

"She said that for the first two weeks, he wouldn't speak to anyone." Phar sighed, sounding more tired now. "Apparently, his therapist couldn't get him to talk, neither could his group therapy leader. He would barely even make eye contact with anyone, but she said that changed recently."

Nausea curled in my stomach, thinking about Judah all alone, drowning in his head, not wanting to talk to anyone.

"Did she tell you if he has any friends?" I tried to sound as nonchalant as possible, even though my chest started to rattle with unshed tears.

"I asked the same question." Pharaoh let out a small laugh. "I guess his counselor saw him sitting with two people at breakfast just a few days before she called me. She said it was around the same time he began opening up in therapy as well."

My only response was a small nod as I licked the edge of the blunt wrap, preparing to close it. Questions started to stack in the forefront of my mind, causing a headache to form in between my eyes.

"And his detox? How was that?" I inquired, trying to keep my voice even.

At that, Phar let go of a heavy breath, reminding me that I wasn't alone in my stress over Judah's situation.

"I was there for most of it," Pharaoh informed me. "After his medical team was able to stabilize him, they started the detox process and...it wasn't pretty. He was sick for a while, which made him really fucking angry, probably because he was embarrassed, so he sent me out of the room for the last couple of days. When most of the drugs were out of his system, we started talking about rehab facilities, and a few days after that, I dropped him off."

I couldn't even imagine what it must have been like for Pharaoh to witness Judah in such a state, but I figured it might not have been his first time, given the other two instances Judah overdosed.

"From there, once he checked in, the woman I spoke to said he said he mainly kept to himself," Pharaoh explained. "They continued to give him the drug that helped to wean him off the ones still lingering in his system, then they switched him to one that would help reduce the cravings, though it doesn't work one hundred percent of the time. Overall, it sounded to me like he just stayed in his own head and dealt with it."

I leaned back, examining the blunt before meeting Phar's eyes. "That's pretty surprising."

He nodded. "Especially because during his last two stints in rehab, he fought it the whole way."

I wanted to ask about more about Judah's previous experiences, but I honestly didn't think I could handle any more information that would paint a brighter picture than the one that was already in my head. Instead, I focused on putting the remaining weed back in its jar and cleaning up the table.

Once I was finished, Phar tipped his chin in my direction and asked, "Need a light?"

"Yeah." I nodded, putting the blunt to my lips as he handed over his Zippo. Once the cherry was lit, I took a minute to myself, pulling in a few thick hits to calm my mind, ease my worries, but then passed the blunt to Pharaoh. "So, Judah's at least talking now?" I inquired.

"Yup." He nodded, again with that casual energy. "Which is a good thing, I guess."

"Yeah, it's good," I agreed, only to pause for a few heavy seconds. "It just doesn't mean anything yet."

"No." Pharaoh sighed, scratching his temple. "It doesn't."

With that, the mood tanked further, now coated in worry, doubt, and a lethal amount of fear over Judah's recovery. Both Pharaoh and I knew that Judah's journey would dictate how life would be for us when he got out.

"How often will you hear from the counselor?" I asked after a moment, curious about how much information we could really obtain while he was in there.

"He had to get through the first two weeks before they would tell me anything, and now I think they update me every few weeks? I'm not really sure."

Knowing about Judah's history, I figured Pharaoh would have this routine down pat by now. "Is this place different than the others he's been in?"

"Yeah, completely," he informed me. "Cliffside handles addiction differently than the other state-run facilities he's been in. I just fucking hate not knowing what's actually going on in there, because while the phone calls are great, we don't actually get any real information. The counselor that calls me doesn't even work with Judah directly. She works with the therapists and nurses that work with him, so it's all secondhand information. None of it's directly from the source."

"That's what I wondered about," I replied, feeling a little better now that I was getting a glimpse of Pharaoh's feelings. "I wasn't sure that we'd actually get any info that would tell us how he's really doing or what to expect when he gets out."

"Nah." He shook his head. "I believe he can write letters to us now, if he wants, but that's up to him. It's a vulnerable process, so they try to keep as much of it inside the organization as they can. All I know for sure is that he's following a pretty strict schedule, getting to a place where he's used to living sober, and talking through what led him to his addition. Then I think once the three months are up, they transfer him to an outpatient therapist, get him an addiction sponsor, and then set him free. He'll have groups he can go to when he's out as well, but other than that? The rest is up to him."

So much was going to be up in the air as we waited for him to get out, and it left me feeling bitter all over again, frustrated with the circumstances.

"You know what? I don't think I want to hear what the counselor says," I stated honestly. "I mean, if all were getting is 'he's talking to his therapist and eating meals with two people,' what's the point?"

"For you?" Pharaoh asked. "There isn't one, but I'm written down as his family, so it's just about letting me know he's alive and cooperating. He didn't do so well at the last two places until the very end, so I'm actually grateful to know he's adjusting this early. He hated the previous places, which is why I picked Cliffside this time around."

"What do you mean?" I questioned, leaning forward to take the blunt from his extended hand.

"This facility is considered a luxury rehabilitation center," he explained. "It's fucking gorgeous and basically looks like an all-inclusive resort, but they use different methods of therapy—meditation, yoga, acupuncture… Basically, all the holistic practices that Judah's never tried before."

In a shocked rush, I blew out a thick cloud of smoke and tried not to choke.

"Hold on. Judah is *meditating*?" I couldn't help it—I laughed a little. "Bullshit! He'd never do it."

"He kinda has to." Pharaoh smirked. "That's why I picked it—it's a part of their morning routine. There's a schedule he has to follow every day, and meditation is the first thing they do."

For some reason, I snickered at the thought of him being forced to meditate.

Payback is a bitch.

"I mean, I started meditating last year, and it one hundred percent helps. I just can't believe you got him to agree to that place."

The smile slipped off Pharaoh's face as he admitted, "I think he only agreed because he felt guilty. He was very quiet after he found out you'd gone on vacation, and even more so after his initial detox. Plus, the news of the Sarah and Rachele passing away? He was…I don't know, lost in his head, I guess."

The girls.

Fucking hell. I'd done everything I could to stop myself from thinking about them, but now I had their names. Somehow, it was my first time hearing them, and it made it all worse.

They were people. They'd had lives, family, friends, and now they were just gone.

And their lives had ended in Judah's fucking bed.

Without him even realizing it.

The whole thing painted an extremely dark, extremely sad picture in my head, and I *hated* it.

What must have happened to get them *all* to the point of overdose?

I just…

"I can't even imagine how he's dealing with that," I whispered, feeling sick all over again.

The blunt wasn't helping like it normally would, only serving to elevate my feelings rather than mellow them out. I felt like I was floating in a bubble of questions, taking on Judah's energy, full of worry and guilt that wasn't mine.

As much as I hated Judah for what he put us through, I couldn't forget the love I had for him, the way we'd been together before I knew the truth. Memories of him bursting into my life, unwilling to let me walk away, haunted me.

Judah's love laced with a passion I'd never experienced before. He was just so sure of me, and it fucking sucked that all that passion was wasted because he wanted to drown instead of fight to get *away* from our pain.

Judah sank our ship before we ever had a chance to find dry land.

All I got was a fucking *taste* of what we could have been, and that taste was so miniscule, it made me wonder if we really had anything at all.

Then I always circled back to my birthday, the friends he brought into my life, the nights we shared playing games and watching movies, and I got so confused. I just wanted *that* life back, the fantasy one I'd thought I had, not the one where the man I loved nearly died along with two other women.

I wanted the guy I fell for, the skyscraper I imagined, the illusion I clung to.

"He'll have survivor's guilt," Pharaoh said, interrupting my thoughts, speaking in a voice full of layered sadness. "There's no way he could avoid it. Judah isn't heartless."

"No, he isn't," I whispered. "His heart is huge."

"Too big," Pharaoh agreed, sounding just as lost in memories as I was. Both of us were speaking on autopilot. "And that heart was broken before it had a chance to be loved properly."

"It's no fucking wonder he ended up like this," I spat out, instantly angry. "He's still a fucking child, Phar. He's been trying to mend a severed heart with drugs, because he was too scared, not to mention stubborn, to let anyone help him. But who could blame him? No one was there to help him or even guide him as a child, so he's not used to it as an adult."

"We better hope he lets his therapist do her job," Pharaoh muttered. "With this overdose, he lost more than he ever has—

the girls, you, the label, the shit with Brandon. His problems are bigger now."

"Are *you* okay?" I asked, suddenly overcome with the need to check, because it wasn't just Judah going through this. They were brothers in all the ways that counted, and anyone who thought Pharaoh wouldn't be affected was ignorant as all fuck.

"I'm struggling," Pharaoh admitted finally. "I just wonder, especially when you talk about him as a child, if there was something I could have done to avoid this. I did that shit *with* him, P. It's not like I've never used before. I was with him through every step, and lately, I've been feeling like I didn't do enough."

"Phar, you're only human." I sighed, hating the guilt, the shame. "You didn't know any better than he did, because if you're honest, you've been in survival mode for your entire life too. You just didn't *need* drugs to get through it."

He met my eyes, and in those dark pools there was a sea of pain, reflecting years of neglect, secrets, and memories I'd probably never get to hear about. "You're right."

It was during moments like these that I felt a love so instinctive, so primal, I wanted to wrap Pharaoh in bubble wrap and take him everywhere with me, just to make sure no one ever hurt him again.

So in the softest voice I could manage, I stated, "It was the blind leading the blind back then, Pharaoh. Neither of you knew any better. The only thing you, personally, can do now is learn from this, just like Judah is, and ask for help when you need it."

"Like I'm attempting to do now?" The corner of his mouth lifted in a small smirk, and those black eyes of his seemed to quietly blaze in my direction.

I doubted he even realized the way he looked at me. It was just who he was—guarded until that guard came down.

"Yeah, even though you're really bad at saying it out loud."

I smirked back before my lips went down as I sighed. "But really, I'm not sure I'm the one who should be giving you advice, given the fact that I have my own pile of shit I need to deal with. We *all* need fucking therapy."

At that, he chuckled a little. "Maybe we should go."

"Maybe we should." I shrugged, seriously thinking about it.

Hitting the blunt again, I let the silence descend on us again and drew smoke deep into my lungs, holding it as long as I could. The air between Pharaoh and me might have been clouded, but there was a giant elephant planted in our little bubble, reminding us that we hadn't even begun to discuss everything we needed to.

Yet it seemed that both of us were too pussy to bring it up.

Until a few seconds later, of course, when Pharaoh found the courage to call out, "Phoenix."

I swallowed as I met his gaze and read the question in his eyes, which caused me to let go of a weighted breath. "I don't know, Pharaoh."

"Yes, you do," was his only reply.

Our eyes stayed glued, linked with one another as time slowed down and the truth settled on the table between us.

Yes, you do.

I didn't know shit.

I didn't know *what* the right move was, didn't know how not to hurt him or myself, because the thought of losing Pharaoh was like a jagged, rusted, knife to my soul. It was too much to even think about.

"You and I both know that we can't hurt Judah," Pharaoh said, filling the gap when I couldn't. "*I* can't hurt Judah, not when he's this vulnerable. Even if you decided right now that you're done with him for good, what happens when he gets out of rehab and you and I are together? It would only make things worse."

Shock blasted through my system.

Not because he was right—it was what I'd been thinking the entire plane ride back to LA and I'd said as much to Frankie—but because I hadn't been expecting Pharaoh to be the one to point it out. I should have known.

Pharaoh Roman was the king of self-sacrificing for the people around him.

Especially Judah.

"And if you're honest with yourself," he continued, grilling me with a gentle sort of understanding, "you know you're not done with him."

There it was.

The truth that had haunted me relentlessly for the last few weeks.

I *wasn't* done with Judah. We had unfinished business, and my feelings for Pharaoh came in right at the end, making it all the more complicated.

Still, I didn't want to hurt Pharaoh, but I couldn't lie to him either.

"I agree," I whispered, even though that pit in my stomach had grown big enough to crush my rib cage.

I was uncomfortable and antsy, wanting to crawl out of my skin as I sat up straighter in my chair and planted my elbows on the table. Running my fingers through my hair, I closed my eyes and tried to count my breaths, attempting to even out my anxiety.

When nothing worked and the pressure became too much, I laid out my fears. "Pharaoh, I don't want you thinking this is easy for me, that I'm just dropping you because Judah may get better. I also don't want you thinking you're the second option. But you're right—even if Judah gets out of rehab and nothing has changed...I think us being together would blow everything up and make it worse all over again."

There would be no "us."

There was no room for Pharaoh and me to live happily ever after, unless we left the fucking city.

We couldn't showcase our relationship in front of Judah, even if his choices in the past were shitty. Our love for him was unconditional, and it seemed that love was stronger than our wish to be together.

"He's my best friend," Pharaoh stated calmly. "But he's also the love of your life, and in my mind, there is only a slim chance that he'll come back unchanged."

I couldn't believe what I was hearing. "You are way more confident about that statement than I am."

Pharaoh dipped his chin sadly. "I know, but after he woke up…when he figured out what happened and realized you weren't even there? On top of hearing about the girls, and then reading your letter? I don't know, Phoenix, if you honestly think Judah won't try to be everything you need him to be after all that…" Phar shook his head, rubbing his eyes quickly before he met my watery stare. "No way. Phoenix, he's going to try."

"I want to believe that," I admitted, feeling the weighted hope in my chest, the ache in my soul. "But you and I—"

"Are friends," Pharaoh cut in, stating it as if it was a done deal. "We can still be friends, P. I'm man enough to put my feelings aside because you are not replaceable. This friendship is not replaceable. If it turns out Judah isn't deserving of you when he gets out and he decides to blow up our lives again, then you can bet your motherfucking ass I'm coming for you. For now, it's not worth getting our hearts tangled any further, only for you to have to make a choice in two months when he gets out, because let's be real—you wouldn't choose me."

Ouuuuuch.

My fucking *heart.*

What made it all worse was that he wasn't even fucking mad. He wasn't resentful of my feelings for Judah, and he didn't even appear *sad*. Yet tears stung my own eyes as I stared at him, unable to ignore the utter agony I knew he was experiencing under the surface.

I could see clearly what he thought he was so good at hiding.

Pharaoh couldn't fool me with all that masculine decision-making energy he was putting out, making it seem like this wasn't extremely difficult for him, like this conversation wasn't another hit to his pride. It was *bullshit*. He'd cared for me long before I developed any feelings for him, and then I gave him my time, false hope, hell, I slept with him and led him to believe there was a chance for us, only for that chance to be ripped away in less than a month.

He deserved to be pissed at me.

As I struggled to keep it together, my head fell into my hands. It was all I could do to shield my eyes, trying to hold back the sobs, unable to think of what to say.

This is torture.

Pharaoh was so fucking pure. He was born kind, gentle, loyal. He provided everyone around him with love, light, talent, peace. He could give *me* all of that and more, but he deserved the same *from* me, and I wasn't in a position to be what he truly deserved.

My heart was with his best friend, and I didn't know how to change that.

Fuck, I hate this.

But there was only one thing I knew for sure, so I lifted my head, wiped my nose, and stated shakily, "I'm sorry, Pharaoh."

As my heart cracked in two, his eyes softened. "This is not your fault, Phoenix."

His hand reached out to grab mine, and while the statement insisted that I believe him, it made me want to scream. How was he so accepting of this ending? How was he still so kind to me? I would hate me if I were him.

"I knew what I was getting into that night," he said, his fingers squeezing mine. "I was hopeful, but well aware of what could happen."

I laughed a wet sound and pulled my hand back, taking a hit of the nearly forgotten blunt, as that bitterness came back with a vengeance.

When shit hit the fan with Judah, *I* hadn't known what the fuck I'd gotten myself into. I hadn't known that meeting Judah Colt would lead to this. I'd had no motherfucking idea what would happen throughout the next year and if I had, I certainly wouldn't have chosen to continue down this road...

Or would I have?

Without Judah, I wouldn't have met Ricco or Kav, Frankie wouldn't have met Silas, I wouldn't have this connection with Pharaoh...

"God, I'm just...I-I'm so fucking sorry," I whispered, my voice trembling, then the dam broke and out came the sob I'd been trying to hold back. "None of this is *fair* to you, Phar! I-I could have chosen someone e-else to lose myself in for a night. It didn't have to be *y-you*." I waved a hand in his direction. "I didn't have to hurt you more than you already were. You weren't supposed to get hurt, you weren't—"

"Hold the fuck up, Phoenix. Look at me," Pharaoh demanded, his tone harsh, once again insistent. It was only out of shock that I looked up, but those black orbs were lit up, full of indignation. "You think that night *hurt* me? You think I would take it back just because, in the end, you wouldn't be mine?"

Feeling confused, nervous, guilty, I remained quiet, unsure of what to say or how to explain myself.

"Come here," he requested, pushing his chair back to make room for me.

I raised a silent, bewildered eyebrow.

He rolled his eyes. "Just do it—get over here."

Because I was a masochist and I needed to see this through, I stood, setting the limp blunt in the ashtray as I walked around the table to stand in front of him.

His gaze tracked my every move, only intensifying as he patted his lap and demanded, "Sit down."

Fuck me sideways.

If he was trying to remind me how fucking hot he was, it was working. His energy was intoxicating. The way he spoke to me with such a gentle form of confidence, so full of control, there was no way I wasn't going to listen.

I straddled him, feeling small and sheltered by the expanse of his shoulders, the height of his upper body compared to mine.

I didn't know what to do with my hands, so I left them in my lap and stared down at my fingers as he leaned forward to pick up the blunt behind me. Casually, with one hand on my thigh, he pulled in the last two hits, one right after the other in rapid succession, and blew out the smoke over my shoulder.

When he sat back, he got right to it, taking my face between his hands, forcing me to meet his eyes. His palms were rough, calloused from the drumsticks he swung around on the daily, but his stare was sincere, his gaze explorative and serious.

"There isn't a single thing that I regret, Phoenix Royal," he began, and that voice of his was full of gravel, sexy and deep, causing my heart to further splinter. "I spent too many months wondering, wishing I knew what it was like to have you in my arms, feel my hands on your body, thinking of what you might taste like, but what I wanted most was to know what it would be like to be *loved* by you."

Fucking hell.

"The way you loved Judah? I've seen it only one other time, and it was gone before I had a chance to fully experience it. But here's the thing…" His thumb ran over my bottom lip, bringing back a fresh wave of tears as I felt the sharp sting of this breakup, as I braced for the loss of Pharaoh's tender affection. "As we got closer, as I became a staple in your world, I realized I didn't even need to have sex with you to find out what that was like to be loved by you. Because you, Phoenix Royal, love with every fiber of your being."

Stunned, I felt tears race each other as they tumbled down my checks, pooling against Pharaoh's fingers. "Ricco and Kav, Frankie, Trix... Once you connect to someone, you give your whole heart. You love unconditionally, completely, and you already loved me in all the ways that mattered the most before we slept together. That night was a product of our circumstances, and I refuse to regret it. Of course, I hoped for a different outcome, because you're you and who wouldn't? But, Phoenix, if we do this the right way, I won't actually lose anything here."

As his words settled into my heart, saving it before it shattered completely, he finished with, "All I ask is that even if you end up with my best friend, you don't take that love away from me."

Jesus Christ.

Once again, I let go of the emotion I was trying to hold back and closed my eyes, silently sobbing as Pharaoh wiped the streams of salt water away, one by one.

"Hey," he whispered. "Remember when I said we can start over? Have that friends-to-lovers situation goin' on?"

Unable to help it, I laughed through my tears, nodding in his hands.

"Good, we're going to keep that plan, just minus the lovers part. We'll switch it to friends to *best* friends," he suggested, seeming to already have a plan. I opened my eyes and studied his, trying to gauge his level of pain, trying to decide if I was a monster or if he was seriously okay with our situation. Knowing I was looking for reasons to hate myself, he pushed,

"Be my best friend, P. Be the girl my future girlfriends are jealous over. Make it so that every girl I date, I'll be forced to explain over and over again that you're *just a friend*. Make me explain that you're also not going anywhere, so if they can't accept you, they can't have me. And then, of course, they'll leave me, and I'll have to date around forever…until I find the *one* girl that accepts you and thanks you for loving me while she wasn't around."

My chest was on fire, my soul screaming over the idea of getting to keep Pharaoh in one way or another, while rejecting the idea of accepting it because I feared I didn't deserve his friendship.

He was so fucking good to me, when all I did was ruin his best friend and fuck him over in the end, but that was *my* guilt to work through. As I looked at Pharaoh, it was clear as fucking day he was serious about this. He wasn't resentful, wasn't angry, and in fact, he appeared grateful.

"Phoenix, don't carry the weight of my pain too." Pharaoh sighed, planting his forehead against mine. "I know in my heart you were never meant to fall for me, but you *are* meant to love me, so just do it. Take this opportunity and pray that in the end, we both get everything we ever wanted."

Overwhelmed and unable to keep even the small amount of distance between us, I broke free of his hold and flew forward, wrapping my arms around his neck and molding my small frame to his larger one. I relaxed into the feel of his hands on my body, one sliding underneath my hair to circle the back of my neck, while the other pressed against my lower back, pulling me closer.

"I'm okay, baby," Pharaoh promised into my temple. "All this time, I wanted you to be mine in some way, and *this* way, you still can be. Judah can't take this connection away from us, because you bet your ass I'm gonna be the best fuckin' friend you've ever had. Kav and Ricco better watch out. Frankie too."

My laugh was wet, my heart hurt so bad I could barely see straight, but it fucking sang at the same time. I was both elated and devastated, knowing that whoever Pharaoh *did* end up with...she'd be a lucky fucking girl.

And fact was? I was in love with Judah, and it wasn't fair of me to even act like my feelings for Pharaoh compared to the magnitude of my connection to his best friend.

Pharaoh and I weren't meant for each other, but best friends?

We sure as fuck could do that.

"Okay but, wait," I exclaimed, speaking for the first time in a while, and sniffed as I pulled back to meet his eyes again. "You can't go trying to be Frankie's best friend too. This time, it isn't a package deal."

He made a *pfft* sound as he pushed my hair away from my face and wiped the remaining moisture from underneath my eyes. "Girl, please. I only have one slot available, and it was made for you."

"Good." I chuckled softly, but then it slipped, falling back into sadness as my bottom lip quivered. I ran my finger along the curve of Pharaoh's eyebrow. "Why does this still hurt?" I whispered.

For the first time since we'd started this conversation, his voice came out choked as he stated, "Because even if it's not as strong as it is with Judah, you still love me."

"I do," I whispered as more tears fell.

And I did. Somewhere along the line, grief, worry, and downright fear had brought Pharaoh and me together, and I did fall. Maybe I wasn't meant to, but I did, and though what I felt in my heart was less intense than what I felt for Judah, the emotion was still the same, just on a different frequency.

"And I love you," Pharaoh whispered as his arms wound around my back and pulled me in again. "No one saw me, P. They always saw Judah first, and I was forever the accessory, but not with you. You care for me genuinely, loudly. You showed up, over and over, time and time again, and without you, I wouldn't have made it through round three with him. I would have given up. So now I'll be *damned* if anyone tries to take you away from me."

"They won't," I insisted softly, internally vowing to always be by his side. Even when I'm with someone else, when I'm in love, happy, soaring, it'll be because Pharaoh is with me too. I'll be surrounded by love on all sides, which is something a girl could only dream of.

"Without you, I would have been dust," I admitted in a soft tone, feeling the truth in my soul. "Without you and this connection we found, I would have given up, shriveled up, and screwed up all of my progress. We did this together, and from now on, we'll face *any* hardship together, but we'll also make hella memories, have a fuck ton of fun, and we'll do what we can to live our best lives."

When we broke apart, there was a new light shining in Pharaoh's eyes, a subtle confidence that wasn't there before. "That's a damn good plan, little P."

My smile was small as I stated, "Glad you agree."

He smirked, looking over toward the house for a second, before glancing back at me. "This conversation was heavy, yeah?"

I chuckled, running my hands down my face, no doubt continuing to smear makeup everywhere. "Uh, *everything* is heavy right now."

"True. But somehow, I feel better," he admitted, running a big hand down the back of my head. "You?"

I nodded in hesitant agreement, feeling that same sense of lightness, but there was still the ache of what could've been a missed opportunity. At least the pressure was gone, and this particular unknown had become known. "Yeah, I feel better."

"All right good, because I'm fucking starving and that

blunt hit me right in the stomach." Pharaoh laughed softly, but before either of us stood up, he made sure he had my attention by gripping my chin. Those black eyes bored into mine as he said, "You're a goddamn queen, Phoenix Royal. You got that?"

I don't deserve him.

"You're one of a kind, Pharaoh Roman," I shakily whispered back, tapping his nose with my finger to hide my pain.

"I'll try not to let that go to my head." He winked, but I saw the same feelings reflected back at me.

Attempting to shake off the negative vibes, I climbed off his lap and grabbed the weed supplies, along with my still full glass of tequila. "You need a bigger ego, I think. You're not nearly as egotistical as you could be," I said.

"Geez, she's gassin' me up already." Phar chuckled, whistling at the end. "I knew you'd be a great best friend."

"Just wait," I sassed, walking backward toward the door. "I'll be the best fuckin' friend you've ever had."

His eyes smoldered, lighting up again as he stated, "I have no doubt about that."

Phew.

As I walked inside, I thought about Judah and what his reaction might be when he got out. What he would do when he found out Pharaoh and I had slept together.

I had to tell him. I wasn't going to keep it a secret, and after, he would either understand my relationship with his best friend and be grateful for the fact that we got each other through, or he'd be pissed. In the end, it wouldn't matter how he felt, because I wasn't letting Pharaoh go.

It was enough that I remained open for Judah to come back and try again. It was enough that I was willing to forgive him. But I wouldn't settle for anything less than I deserved, either.

Pharaoh was right—I *was* a queen. I *did* love with my entire heart, even though a part of me struggled to believe my love wasn't destructive.

Judah would have to earn my love back, even with my forgiveness. He'd have to prove his dedication to himself first, and me as a runner-up.

If he did that?

There really was a chance that I could have everything I ever wanted.

And if he didn't?

I'd still get everything I ever wanted. It just wouldn't be with him.

CHAPTER 8
JUDAH

"JUDAH!" *My mother screamed my name from her bedroom.*

Startled, my head shot up from where I'd hidden it in between the pages of my book—a children's book, which was far below my reading level, but I found it too comforting to give up—and immediately, I began thinking of all the reasons she could be calling for me.

I braced myself, counting to five, knowing that she always had an ulterior motive and it never ended well for me.

"Yes, Mom?" I called out once I was sure my voice wouldn't shake.

Momentarily, I hoped she was just making sure I was in the house, rather than about to ask me to abandon the loving world I was pretending I lived in for the shitty one I actually *lived in.*

"Get your fuckin' ass in here!" she bellowed.

Crap.

My pulse skyrocketed and my ears began to burn, which spread red heat straight into my cheeks, thanks to the panic shooting through my body as I wondered what I could have done wrong.

Did I say something? Did I leave something out on the

counter that could piss my father off? Did she see the action figure Pharaoh let me borrow?

She hated when I got gifts from other people, so I made sure to hide it under my pillow when she got home from work. But did she find it?

Despite not knowing, I had to answer her call. If I didn't... there would be hell to pay.

So, unsteadily, I stood from the couch and began to make my way through the living room, counting my footsteps as I went, if only to keep my mind busy.

"Yes?" I asked meekly as I pushed the door open.

There were clothes strewn across the floors, along with cobwebs and dust caked in all four corners of the ceiling. The sheets on her bed hadn't been washed in months, but still, she sat nearly naked in the center, wearing just her bra and underwear.

My mother eyed me for just a second before rolling her eyes dramatically like she was pissed she even had to be in my presence...even though she was the one that had asked for me in the first place.

"Go get me the orange bottle in the bathroom. It's on the counter," she instructed in an annoyed, snarky tone.

I didn't know what she meant, what orange bottle she was referring to, but I went anyway, pausing for only a moment to watch as she did her makeup, holding a tiny hand mirror in front of her face. It was always in moments like these that I wondered why she hated me so much, why I was such a bother, but I could never come up with an answer so I shook off the train of thought and did as she'd asked.

My parents' bathroom counter was disgusting, full of all kinds of stuff, covered in toothpaste stains and general grime from lack of cleaning. I was used to it and knew that it was rare for anyone in this trailer to actually clean up after themselves.

As I scanned the area, I located the orange bottle she was referring to all the way in the back, leaving me to stand on my tippy-toes to reached for it. As I did, I accidentally knocked a bottle of shaving cream into the sink and cringed at the loud sound of metal clinking around.

Fearing the worst, I quickly snagged the bottle from the far left corner and lowered myself to the ground. Before I left the bathroom, I tried to read the bottle, studying it for just a few seconds, but failed to understand what it was, which caused me to frown.

I could read and I was very smart, but the words on the bottle were too advanced for me to sound out. I kept trying but still hadn't figured it out by the time I entered the bedroom again.

Extending a trembling hand, I whispered, "Here you go, Mom."

"Good." She nodded, not bothering to look away from the mirror. "Leave it on the bed and get the fuck out. Better make yourself invisible. Your father will be home soon."

Instantly, I clammed up. I dropped the bottle on her sheets and ran out of the room, going straight for the couch where my book was, and pulled a dirty blanket over my body to try and make myself just that—invisible.

My dad rarely left the house, and when he did, he always came back pissed off because people didn't treat him the way he wanted to be treated while he was out.

I didn't particularly understand why or how he was treated differently, but I knew I didn't like who he was when he came home from any outing.

Forty-five minutes later, I'd gotten comfortable in my spot, so when the front door slammed open, it made me jump under my covering and sent my book flying over the side of the couch and onto the floor.

Shit, shit, shit.

"What the fuck is this!?" my father shouted immediately, ripping the blanket from my body, leaving me vulnerable and terrified and...cold.

"I-I'm sorry...you...you s-scared me," I stammered, glancing up at the man in fear, knowing I'd already fucked up.

I should have just gone to my room. Why didn't I go to my room?!

"Scared you?" He laughed, but it sounded all wrong—menacing, terrifying, sarcastic, and bitter. Leaning down, my father met my eyes with an intensity I was never prepared for but should have expected by now. *"Awww, you're such a fucking* pussy.*"*

I was paralyzed, had no time to prepare myself for when he gripped the front of my T-shirt in his brutal fist and yanked me off the couch, dragging my body toward him so fast, it sent my head backward with the gravity and speed of the movement. I cried out softly, petrified of what would come next.

"You're such a little bitch, *you know that?!"* he bellowed, forever disappointed in my ability to handle the pure rage wafting off him. *"You're a man, you're supposed to be stronger than this!"*

He dropped me without warning, and I hit the side of the coffee table in my descent to the floor. On the way down, my tailbone slammed into the corner, sending lightning bolts of sharp pain up my spine, rattling my teeth in the process.

I bit straight through my lip in order to clamp down on the scream that threatened to escape, swallowing the burst of blood that flowed into my mouth. Now on the floor, I did everything I could to hold in any sounds.

"Roxanne!" my father shouted, calling out for my mom as he left me there on the carpet, curled up in a ball and trying not to cry. *"Where the fuck are you?"*

"Shut the hell up!" she yelled back, baiting him to head in her direction.

That pain I felt? The ache in my bones, the fire in my chest? She craved it. My mother seemed to like the wounds my father inflicted—on her, on me.

"Shut the—*You did NOT just fucking say that to me!*" my father boomed, pounding his way into their bedroom just before I heard the door slam shut.

My mother's cry came only two seconds later, along with the sound of various other things being thrown around the room, until all I heard was the distinct chorus of flesh hitting flesh.

The noise raped my ears, encouraging me to stay where I was, to not make a peep as my mother screamed in the background, as my father's grunts could be heard through the fake wooden door, giving me a front row seat to the shit show that was my parent's relationship.

Faintly, I wondered if my backside was bleeding or if the throbbing was just the start of a nasty bruise.

Tears streamed down my face as I began to crawl toward my room, moving slowly enough to avoid making noise.

Why was it that the other kids in my school could show up happy, without any marks left behind by their parents? How come their clothes looked fresh, their lunch bags packed with snacks and love notes, while I showed up empty-handed?

How come Pharaoh was all I had?

Without him, I'd be starving, but even with his sacrifice, the two of us were never satisfied because his family was just as fucked as mine. He couldn't afford to feed the two of us, and yet he never let me go completely hungry. His lunch kept both of us only semi-full.

Just enough to get by.

Still, though, as I grabbed Pharaoh's action figure from under my pillow and hugged it to my chest, I couldn't wait to get to school tomorrow.

At least there, nobody would hurt me.

"Son of a bitch!" I cried out, sitting up in bed only to shove my hands into my hair as my breath came out in choppy, unorganized waves just before a sob escaped my throat. "I can't *do* this anymore."

In the dead of night, I was surrounded by shadows—shadows that held unknown threats, pulling up memories of a childhood I'd so much rather forget.

The LED clock set up on my nightstand provided the only light in the room, flashing the time, telling me it was just past three AM. I groaned out a harsh whimper at the thought of making it through another three hours before the sun started my day.

I swore my demons mocked me from the corners of my room as a frozen fist held my windpipe tightly, making it damn near impossible to catch my breath. Gasping, I dropped my head into my hands, trying to *process* the emotions like Dr. Blake had instructed, but just like every other night, the only conclusion I came to was tha it would have been far easier just to block it the fuck out.

As I tried to breathe, sweat began to coat my face, and my stomach made a deep rumbling noise, as if starved. I did my best to swallow away the craving, but it wasn't fucking easy, given I could still taste the memory of liquor flowing down my throat, could still feel the tangy, bitter sting of Oxy crumbling in my mouth.

It could all vanish if I had just one pill. At this point, one pill and I would be just fine. Or fuck it, a couple swigs of vodka. A shot or two of bourbon. It didn't even matter what the substance was, all that mattered was with a little toxic help, I wouldn't have to sit shaking in the middle of my bed, in a strange place with strange people, fighting age-old demons that only wanted me dead while reliving memories that made me desire that same fate.

My nightmares had gotten worse, bringing me to a point

where sleeping wasn't worth it. I'd rather spend my days awake and exhausted, walking around like a zombie, if only to avoid the fucking chaos that exploded in my sleeping state.

It had been three weeks since I'd started opening up about my past, since I'd begun writing and throwing out letters to the people I hurt the most, and in those three weeks, my therapy sessions with Dr. Blake had gotten more and more intense.

Despite my initial reservations, I'd thrown myself into the process of healing, desperate to just get it over with, and opened up about what happened to me as a child, asking questions and crying through the lack of answers. Even with the small amount of clarity I'd gained, the effort seemed to backfire, making my nights fucking unbearable as memories of my mother, my father, my life in general, came back with a vengeance.

It was horrific, going back in time to reexperience the childhood version of me, the one who'd felt so alone, he didn't even know how to handle it. I'd realized very quickly that my coping mechanisms as a child had followed me into adulthood, only they'd gotten more dramatic, more desperate. I was a shell of a person, even at the ripe age of nine, walking around the halls of my school like a ghost, hiding under blankets when I got home.

It reminded me that without Pharaoh, without his friendship, his constant support, or his presence in my life in general, I'd be no one. Except with those memories came the guilt, forcing me to look at the fact that because I was a coward, I'd fucked everything up. Now I struggled to believe I even *deserved* any type of forgiveness, which in turn, made every letter I wrote not good enough.

As a kid, I'd been quiet, reserved, until I'd finally understood what my mother had been taking all those years.

My father's painkillers from an accident he'd been in when

I was four or five, one that had left him with chronic pain and an excuse to call in refills every month for years on end.

Two years before I'd started stealing those same pills, given my mother wasn't around anymore to figure out what I was doing, I'd found the power of music. That had ignited my passion for rapping, which in turn, helped me find my voice, but the need to escape was still there, especially since I was still living with that monster.

His pills granted that wish.

It took me nearly ten years to take the plunge, but once I'd popped that first Vicodin, it was over—I was free. But when that one type of drug wasn't enough to rid myself of the flashbacks, I moved on to another, fell in with the wrong crowd, and started mixing potions until *boom,* my childhood was buried six feet deep.

Only, I was now discovering that while it had been buried, it certainly wasn't dead.

All these years later, it felt like everything I tried to say, every apology I attempted to express wasn't good enough, wasn't sincere enough, wasn't deep enough. At the same time, I didn't know how much deeper I could get.

That thought alone brought a knife to my throat, and my guilt pressed the blade firmly against my skin so that with every movement, I bled. Once again, I was left wiping my tears, tasting my mistakes, and trembling under the weight of all I'd done wrong.

Fuck my life.

Every day, I felt myself losing years of maturity I'd pretended I had. Now, stuck in rehab, I was weak, sad, and lost in the excruciating reality of having been abandoned, neglected, thrown to the side by the two people who were meant to care for me.

And Dr. Blake talked about how I needed to forgive myself for how I'd chosen to cope.

Sure, in the daylight, I saw the benefits of that forgiveness and tried as best I could to give myself a break, but at night? When I was completely alone, left to my own devices? Forget about it. I wished I had a gun just to take myself out of the equation all together. I could leave all my discarded letters behind as a suicide note. Everyone would get the fucking point.

I had to remind myself every night that I was only halfway through the program, I still had time, and things were already looking up. In the waking hours, I didn't necessarily blame myself anymore, I just didn't know how to truly let go of the guilt.

Yet I understood now that when I chose to pick up the drugs when I was a teenager, it had been out of desperation, at an age where logic meant nothing. I'd been avoiding very real abuse, very harsh, unrelenting, and visceral emotions that without the help of opioids, would have killed me.

I'd been trying to save myself from the torture, but I ended up torturing everyone around me by asking them to just deal with it because I couldn't figure out any other way.

As a kid, I'd done my best not to cry because, according to my father, crying was weak, and it made me more vulnerable to his attention. Tears seemed to be his green light to get physical, and every time he saw me emote, he'd put his filthy fucking hands on me.

But really, *any* emotion triggered him, and it wasn't until I was sobbing in Blake's office, unable to breathe, that I realized my father and I were the same. His attitude, his anger—my mother's too—it was all a result of the drugs, the demons that had haunted both of them, and years of suppression they'd subjected themselves to and then passed down to me. Add my father's constant consumption of alcohol and my mother's disgusting need to feel pain?

My parents had painstakingly made the fucked-up cocktail that was me.

TheColt. The screw up. The sick boy.

The toxic, insecure catastrophe.

The addict.

I'd *hit* Phoenix. I'd broken her fucking nose and hadn't even realized it happened because I'd been lost in the haze of side effects. Fighting was natural, anger was the only emotion I genuinely understood, and it was all beginning to make sense. It was in my blood. My parents had done nothing but give me the tools to ensure my family's legacy would continue.

For so long, I'd hidden my parents' addiction from the people in my life out of pure self-preservation, but it cost me in more ways than I could count. I could have opened up, especially to Phoenix. I could have had *her* to talk to, to help me walk through this bullshit, because if anyone was trustworthy with this kind of pain, with the darkness that lived in my childhood, it was her. But without her, *before* her, I could have talked more openly to Pharaoh, even back then, before I dragged him into my world and convinced him to stay a while.

If I'd known *how* to lean on someone and trust that they'd catch me, Pharaoh might have held me to a higher standard. I might have shaped up, but he was just as broken as I was. His bloodline was just as tainted, only not in the same way. His demons were of a different species, from a different corner of hell.

His coping mechanisms were different.

And I just…

Shouldn't have buried this shit for so long.

It was too much to handle now, and honestly, I didn't know how the fuck I was going to make it through.

❄ ❇ ❄

FIVE HOURS LATER, as I walked out of my morning meditation session, I still felt like shit. Which only pissed me off because wasn't that the whole point of meditation? To make you feel better? Get you…*grounded* or whatever?

Yeah, well, it didn't work.

Thanks to the mountain of nightmares I couldn't seem to avoid, I'd refused to go back to sleep and pulled out my notebook instead, trying once again to write a letter to Phoenix. When that didn't work and the words just wouldn't come out right, I'd tried to write one to Pharaoh. When *that* didn't work, I gave up entirely and started jotting down chunks of lyrics, if only to try and unclog my mind. Nothing I wrote made any sense, just a bunch of words—jagged, brutal, mind-bending twists on typical definitions, all strung together. I found it fitting, given how I'd been feeling at the time.

As I continued down the hallway toward the dining room, I heard the distinct sound of Cassie's voice calling my name and interrupting my thoughts. "Hey, Judah! Wait up!"

Instantly, I bit down on a groan.

I also didn't turn around.

"Catch up, short stuff," I yelled back.

She ran, of course, doing exactly as I'd said, and slid up next to me. When I looked down, I came face-to-face with her bright smile and couldn't help but scoff, hating that her eyes reflected happiness and appeared so much less haunted than my own.

"What's up, Mr. Grump?" she sassed cheerily. "Brian is meeting us in the dining room."

My eyes rolled all on their own. "Fantastic."

"Rough night?" she inquired, seemingly unfazed by my attitude.

And that was the part where I heard Dr. Blake chastising me in the back of my head, pushing me to tell the truth, urging me to get used to opening up to people that I knew were worthy of being trusted. Blake frequently told me that in situations like these, I should answer questions honestly, even though the very thought had me wanting to rip out my own vocal cords and shove them down Cassie's throat.

But I was growing, or *trying* to, so I explained stonily, "Nightmares. Slept like shit."

"Ohhhh, yeah…" Cas sighed as her energy turned down a few notches. "Mine were fucking *awful* at first, but they do start to turn around. I mean…eventually."

That didn't sound promising.

"*Eventually* is not soon enough," I bitched. "How am I expected to get better when all I feel is worse? It doesn't make any sense."

"Well," she started, "I don't really know how it works in a literal sense, but I do know that time changes everything. I'm only a couple weeks ahead of you, and I only have nightmares a few times a week now."

"Oh good, only a few times," I muttered sarcastically.

When she responded, her voice was whispered, almost hurt. "Progress is progress, Judah."

Fuck, now I feel bad.

My resentment and self-hatred were clearly still issues, but I was starting to see that rather than keeping that shit to myself, I really *did* project it onto others. I didn't have to belittle her successes because I wasn't having any. That wasn't fair, and this new eyes wide open frame of mind was clearly working, even though it also seemed to be backfiring on me as I was forced to realize how much of an asshole I tended to be.

In order to try and make her feel better, I said, "I know,

I'm…s-sorry. I'm just struggling with the whole process, I guess."

She nodded. "I get it."

Fuck, now she's in a bad mood.

"Do you still get cravings?" I blurted out, knowing damn well she did, but not knowing what else to say.

"Those never go away," she replied blandly, glancing up at me. "You know that."

"Yeah," I said on a sigh. "I do."

I had accepted the fact that I was always going to crave any form of escape, wishing I could numb out, but apparently—according to Blake—my wish to stay sober would get stronger than the urge to fade myself to black.

With Cassie silent next to me, pressure wrapped itself around my throat and squeezed until I stated, "All right, seriously, I'm sorry for acting like a dick. I'm in a horrible mood, and you're always so chipper and happy. I don't understand how you can be so goddamn positive in a place like this. It makes me jealous and angry, and then I feel like a failure."

There, I fucking said it.

"And yet you apologized, and now you're telling me the truth. You've never really cared if you were a dick to me or Brian before today," she pointed out, sounding less hurt and more impressed. There was even a small smile on her face. "That's progress. That's *good* progress, Judah."

Anger bubbled beneath the surface of my skin again, because I was irritable and hated being so goddamn vulnerable and on display.

"Whatever." I trained my eyes ahead, toward the door leading to the dining room.

"Hold on," she requested with a sigh as she grabbed my arm. "Slow down. I wasn't trying to make you mad."

Frustrated, feeling guilty for causing yet another problem, I paused to rub my closed eyelids with my fingers. "I know.

Today is just not a good fucking day, and I hate that half the people here seem so goddamn put together."

It was a repetitive statement, but she hadn't given me any answers so I was left with the same feeling.

"Judah." She sighed again, but deeper this time. "I am *not* put together."

Opening my eyes, I studied her, taking in the lines of her face, which still held onto those baby-like features. Despite being young, she was pretty, well taken care of.

I never would have guessed she was an addict if I hadn't met her in fucking rehab.

"My damage is just different than yours," she murmured, meeting my stare with new intensity, revealing *her* hidden demons. They flashed before me, biting at the air between us. She sounded mature, wise, as she kept on with her explanation. "As a famous musician, you were living in a high-pressure situation on a daily basis, and from what I already know about you, from what I can tell, you've been hiding from your past. Quite frankly, I'm the exact opposite. I had too much freedom and no one paying attention to me. I talked about my life to anyone who would listen, and I did it with a smile. I just never let myself *feel* any of the things I was talking about." Sarcasm dripped from her tone as she went on, "Lonely? *Nah*, I wasn't lonely, I was surrounded by forty people on a yacht! How could I be lonely?" She rolled her eyes, laughing softly, bitterly. "It was bullshit. I was completely alone. I have the same issue as you, just planted in a different garden. My addiction came from me *wanting* to feel something, where yours helped you numb out. It's easy for me to pretend like everything is okay, when on the inside, I feel like dying. That's my coping mechanism. In here, I'm learning to feel again without the drugs."

Listening to her speak, she reminded me a little of Frankie.

All sunshine and rainbows, but under the surface lurked a dark monster made of pain she refused to address.

Cassie was right—I felt too much all the time.

I didn't want to feel at all, that was where my addiction took control.

Lock 'em up, boys.

But then I couldn't figure out how to respond or what to say, even though I appreciated her honesty. It gave me a new perspective on our situation, made me feel less *broken* and more understood.

So I did what I could to let go of the anger, feeling it simmer down to a lukewarm pool of restraint as I reminded myself she was trying to be my friend and I deserved that friendship.

"Gotta love the art of addiction," I finally mumbled before coughing a little to clear my throat. Then, not wanting to participate in such depressing conversation anymore, I quickly changed the subject and nodded toward the dining room doors. "Come on, pipsqueak, we've got breakfast to eat."

I wasn't hungry, but I'd need the energy to get through the day, so as Cassie led the way, I followed her through the doors. It wasn't hard to find Brian, given he was seated at the table I used to occupy alone.

"There you guys are!" he stated, smiling widely we sat down. "I ordered a round of orange juices for all three of us."

The dining room was set up like a restaurant, serving breakfast, lunch, and dinner, with an extensive menu we got to choose from at each meal. All the food was cooked fresh by a gourmet chef in the kitchen, and I was low-key grateful as fuck because the last two rehab facilities I'd been to had served the equivalent of hospital food...which was unfortunate for everyone involved.

"Thanks, man." I gave him a half-hearted grin in return, still trying to get used to people wanting me around.

I'd never realized how much I didn't believe I was worthy of true friends or family until I ended up in rehab this time around and all this shit started coming up. I loved my group of friends, but I felt like the only reason we got along was because we were all in survival mode. Without my coping mechanisms, those suffocating insecurities clouded all of my thoughts and fear came back, screaming at me, making me believe my life would be like elementary school all over again. Anxiety constantly had me believing that if I was sober in the industry, I'd have to repeat the absolute embarrassment that was my childhood, never fitting in, always the weird kid in the back wearing clothes that didn't fit, hiding bruises I didn't want anyone to see.

If I was sober, would anyone fucking like me?

I didn't even like me.

But Cassie and Brian seemed to prove my insecurities wrong by showing up on the daily, remaining constant, consistent, and practically begging me to give them any morsel of attention I was willing to hand over.

Cassie spoke next, as her eyes scanned the menu in her hands. "If I don't stop ordering the French toast for breakfast, I'm going to gain some serious weight. I *have* to pick something else, but I think I have a new addiction."

"It's the real maple syrup." Brian shrugged. "That shit changes the game."

"I've had real maple syrup my entire life!" She dramatically huffed, looking up to glance between the two of us. "I don't understand why I'm so in love with it."

The mention of French toast had me spiraling down memory lane, and for some reason, I couldn't keep my thoughts to myself.

"It's actually the kind of bread they use," I explained in a soft voice, looking down at my menu, unable to meet their eyes. "It's, uh, challah bread. They use heavy cream, vanilla, and brown sugar in the egg mixture, too. Makes the best French toast, no matter what kind of syrup you use."

Pretending to be unaffected was nearly impossible. My stomach bunched up into a fucking knot, and tears pressed against the back of my eyes.

Why was I such a fucking baby?

Get it the fuck together.

Brian coughed a shocked sound. "Sorry, how the fuck do you know *that*, master chef?" he asked.

"Yeah, what the hell?" Cassie echoed in a voice made of stunned curiosity.

I had to remind myself to breathe before I could respond, fearing that I'd show too much emotion or break down right there at the fucking table.

Which was the last thing I wanted.

"My, uh…" I nearly choked. "My girl—my *ex*-girlfriend used to make it the same way." There were tiny bits of concrete in my throat, I was sure of it. "Best French toast I've ever had."

Such a fucking sap.

It was something so goddamn small, and yet the tiniest fucking memory felt worse than all the others I'd encountered. Still, I was catapulted back to the mornings I'd spend posted up at the island in Phoenix's kitchen, drinking coffee as I watched her put together a masterpiece meal. Sometimes Frankie helped. The girls said it was a family recipe, but they'd shared it with us anyway. Me, Ricco, Kav, and on occasion, Pharaoh, whenever he was around.

It was only a short period of time that we spent in that suspended state of bliss, not long at all, but we'd formed a routine, made a new kind of family.

And Phoenix? She was *mine*.

She was *my* masterpiece.

The girl made me feel like I really could love, like I could *be* loved, but instead of believing I'd found my happily ever after and running with it, I saw her as a person I could meet in the afterlife. She was supposed to be someone that I could walk through hell with, whistling the whole way.

Except when I looked back now, when I remembered those mornings, I saw the sun shining behind her, through the window above the sink in her kitchen. There was so much light, so much laughter and flirting and genuine happiness…so why did I do it?

Why couldn't I have seen what was right in front of me?

I'd had a motherfucking family back home and I'd ruined it, destroyed it with my own hands. I spat on the on the gift I'd been given and thought ending my life, cutting it all short, was easier.

It wasn't. I was just a fucking coward.

I'm so sorry, Baby Bird.

"Judah, come back," Cassie whispered, her hand meeting my forearm.

I cleared my throat, nearly gagging on emotion, on the guilt raging in my rib cage. "Sorry, what did you say?" I eventually I ground out.

"She's your ex?" Cassie asked with eyes full of sympathy and confusion. "Your… The girl…the one you're talking about? Is she Baby Bird?"

Fucking hell.

I kept forgetting they were fans of mine. They knew whom I was talking about.

Dr. Blake's words slammed through my eardrums once again as I looked down at Cassie's hand on my arm.

"When you get the opportunity to share your story, when you trust the person asking you a question, answer it honestly. It will give you the chance to breathe and get some of those thoughts out of your head, but it will also give that person a chance to prove themselves as your friend. You need to make

genuine connections from here on out, Judah. You'll need people in your corner to help you through this."

Brian eyed me with the same expression Cassie wore, but his was somehow more intense—empathetic rather than sympathetic.

"Fuck," I whispered, dropping my head, but immediately looked back up and answered only semi sharply. "You know the story, or some of it, if you've read the tabloids. But yes, she's technically my ex."

"Technically?" Cassie pushed again, and hope lingered in her voice.

When I cut her a glare, she held up two hands. "I'm sorry, I'm sorry. I'm just… I… Fucking hell, I was *obsessed* with the two of you, and I guess I hoped all that shit in the media was wrong. I know how Hollywood works, and I know half of the magazines are fucking wrong about what they write about. The pap photos make the situation look bad, sure, but I saw the videos of Phoenix surprising you on your birthday while you were on tour, so I just thought…"

Her voice trailed off, leaving me with the concentrated stinging sensation of *that* particular memory.

"We figured you guys were still together," Brian finished for her. "You just seemed so…right for each other."

We are. We're written in the goddamn stars.

"I fucked it up," was all I said before picking up my menu again, done with the conversation.

"You can fix it. I'm sure of it," Cassie insisted softly.

I couldn't respond, and they didn't push me any further.

Fact was, I was going to do everything in my goddamn fucking power to fix it. I just didn't believe I deserved Phoenix anymore.

The things I did? What I put her through? The *agony* I caused?

I destroyed her fucking house looking for *drugs*.

I wouldn't forgive me if I were her.

"You have to forgive yourself, Judah. If you can't forgive yourself, if you can't understand why you did what you did, why you made the choices you made, you'll shatter completely when someone else doesn't forgive you. They have a right to feel the way they feel, but they key is...another person's opinion of yourself shouldn't carry more weight than your own."

Again, Dr. Blake took over my mind, but I wasn't sure how I was going to pull that one off. I could forgive myself all I wanted to, I could spend all this time figuring out *why* I was the way I was, why I did what I did or made the mistakes I made, but if Phoenix couldn't see it?

If she didn't forgive me?

If I didn't get my girl back?

I just...

The thought was still too much to handle, still brought me right back to a place where the sun didn't matter, my dreams didn't matter, my career, my life... *None of it* mattered if I didn't have her.

She *was* the sun, she was a part of my dream, integral to my career, and I still desperately wanted every experience to be dripping in Phoenix Royal.

How could I simply move on with my life without her in it?

How would I recover from that?

I didn't have that answer.

Guess I know what today's therapy topic will be about.

CHAPTER 9
Phoenix

Six weeks in rehab

TODAY WAS UNUSUALLY HARD.

Something in me felt *off*, like I was treading water in the middle of the ocean with no land in sight, no boats around, and not a single person floating around me. The day was sunny, the temperature inching toward being too hot, and while I should have been downright terrified, all by myself, wading in the expansive blue sea, all I felt was a strange sense of restlessness.

If I were honest with myself, I knew what it was.

Judah had been in rehab for a month and a half, and I was…feeling it.

For the last few weeks, I hadn't been exactly living my best life, but I wasn't depressed either. I simply felt like a vital part of me was missing, sort of like when he was gone on tour. Somehow, this time, the feeling was both better and worse—better because there wasn't the constant worry that he was driving himself into a hole he couldn't get out of, but worse because I couldn't find him anywhere. His face wasn't taunting me on social media or on the front page of the tabloids. His presence was just *gone*.

On top of that, I knew how hard it was to face your own demons, to face yourself.

It was awful for the average person, for someone like Frankie or me, but for Judah? It would be hell on earth for him after spending so much time avoiding the task. As the days came and went, as I continued to think about it, picturing him talking to a therapist or sitting in group therapy sessions, my anxiety got worse.

I wanted to ask him if he was okay, see his face, check for myself what state of mind he was in. Even after all the bullshit in Paris and the signs I didn't pick up on, I still believed I could read him better than anyone because we were one in the same. I knew when he was drowning, when he was floating, when he was happy or sad. I just wanted to know where he was at right now, how he was doing, and I hated that he wasn't available to me in that way anymore.

"Phoenix," Frankie called through the speakers of my car. "Dude, where are you right now?"

"Sorry." I shook my head, flipping on my blinker at the last minute before switching lanes in order to get off the highway, feeling grateful that she'd yanked me out of my head before I missed my exit entirely. "I'm almost home."

"You good?" she questioned, not missing a thing.

"Weird day," was all I could say, not wanting to admit my struggles, fearing she'd judge me after everything Judah did, the chaos he caused. "I had three back-to-back clients today. I'm just exhausted."

And I was.

I wasn't sleeping well.

But rather than bad dreams causing my shitty rest, I found it hard to sleep at all. Instead, I spent most nights with my eyes closed, lingering on the fine edge of dreaming but unable to cross over. The darkness sat with me, and I with it. Hours and hours passed as my mind slow danced with the unknown.

"All right, well, I made a massive pork roast for dinner because the guys are back from their trip and Ricco called me saying he was 'aching for a home-cooked meal.'" She laughed a little, sounding like she hadn't believed a word I said but didn't want to push me.

"Good, I'm starving," I replied, trying to make my voice seem lighter to soothe her worry.

I really was fine. I wasn't depressed, wasn't suffering any panic attacks, I was just…

Missing him.

When Judah was actively destroying my life as well as his own, I did everything I could to shut down my love for him. I locked my feelings in a box and nailed it shut for good measure, but that box had blown open all on its own when he nearly died, leaving the scattered pieces of my love for him out in the open and all over the place.

As the time passed, I found myself looking at each individual piece. Lately, it felt like I was putting them back together, but it was hard to figure out, like a puzzle without a picture to guide me.

Plain and simple, everything was different now.

The man I'd known was gone, almost dead but saved by destiny, and all I had left was the invisible link that connected us. Except it felt like that link was void of electricity, like the power had been shut off, but I still remembered what it had felt like when the wire was live and too hot to handle, too dangerous to touch.

It was both bitter and sweet to walk down memory lane, recalling only the good parts of our relationship and the dreams I'd once had for our future.

"Okay, well, I'll see you soon," Frankie muttered distantly.

After repeating the statement, I hung up but felt like shit for not being honest with her. I simply didn't know what to say.

Today was just a particularly hard day, and by the time I pulled into the driveway, I'd steeled myself, hoping I'd done enough mental preparation to be able to put on a good face in front of everyone. But seeing the guy's car in the driveway, I was hit with a small wave of excitement now they were back in town after a week in New York, working with a dance crew that was trying out for a competition and needed some fresh choreography. I'd missed their energetic presence around the house, and I hoped it would help me bring my spirits up.

As I made my way up to the front door, I stopped at the mailbox and absentmindedly pulled out the contents, putting the stack of mail under my arm in order to bring it inside, but then paused before entering the house, frowning when I spotted a big ass Amazon package. Knowing it was probably for Frankie, I bent to pick it up, trying to juggle my bag, the mail, and my water bottle at the same time.

Grunting the whole way through, I was somehow able to open the door with three fingers, but wasn't able to make it farther than just over the threshold before I dropped everything in a huff.

"Frankie Skyes, come help me!" I whined, yelling out for my best friend.

"Help with what?" she called back, but before I could respond, she came around the corner, saw the pile of shit at my feet, and ran toward me with a smile, bending immediately to snatch up her package. "Fuck yes, it came early!"

I watched with eyebrows raised as she tried to tear the box open with her fingers but failed.

"You're gonna need scissors," I pointed out, smirking at her.

She rolled her eyes. "Son of a bitch."

Then she was gone, running back into the kitchen and leaving me standing there in the doorway with the rest of my shit scattered on the floor.

My smirk remained as I shook my head and began to pick up the mail I'd dropped, going through each piece and sorting them into two piles—one for the envelopes addressed to myself, and one for the mail sent to Frankie. She had quite a few pieces, while I only had two. One was a statement from my bank, and the other...

Holy shit.

My skin grew cold as I stared at the paper.

All the blood in my body rushed to my head, pounding in my ears, drowning out any outside noise as my stomach hit the floor.

It was a letter.

The room spun around me as I read the return address over and over and over.

Cliffside Rehabilitation Center.

Oh my god... Judah.

I couldn't move, couldn't breathe as I stared at the heavy, expensive-looking envelope.

It was his handwriting on the front. I knew it intimately, recognizing the pattern, remembering the times I'd watched my skyscraper haphazardly scribble lyrics onto the pages of his notebook.

It was familiar, intense.

Judah.

I closed my eyes.

Breathe. Count to ten.

I listened to my own inner voice, the guiding light I'd been working on building, calling on that strength I'd stacked over the last few months.

On the last exhale, I lifted my eyelids and glanced down the hallway as sound floated my way again, as the world seemed to right itself after it had nearly fallen out from under me.

Dark, joyful laughter registered in my ears as Ricco and

Kavan bickered, sounding as if they were playing a video game in the living room. Frankie squealed my name, beckoning me into the kitchen, wanting to show me what she'd ordered.

But I was rooted in place, hands shaking, heart slamming against my ribcage.

I glanced down at the letter again.

Not here. Not now.

I needed to wait.

Still, tears hit the back of my eyes and the top of my nose began to sting with emotion as I stared at it.

Was this why I was feeling so off today?

Did he know I needed to hear from him?

Did our connection spread that wide? That far?

"Whenever we aren't together, it feels like my soul is being stretched across the city…"

Just like that, with only the memory of Judah's voice, I was transported back to the night we sat in my driveway, when I googled the signs of meeting your twin flame. Remembering how he asked me to read them out loud to him, it was almost too much. As we went through each one, Judah had been enthusiastic and insistent, where I'd been hesitant, confused, terrified of what it all meant.

Judah had never questioned our connection. Seemingly able to believe instantly that we shared a soul, he'd agreed with and had been able to justify every warning sign, and now…

"*Judah,*" I whispered, lifting a shaking hand to cover my mouth in order to muffle the whimper that escaped.

All day, I'd felt lost, lonely, vacant, and I came home to *this*?

Without even knowing what was in the letter, a thick tear fell from my eye and slid down my hand, only to land with a small splash on the front of the envelope.

I hadn't seen his face in six weeks.

There was a giant fucking wall between his energy and mine, and I…hated it.

"Wherever you are, I can still feel you."

He'd said those words so easily that night, with meaning, confidence.

Was it still true?

"Phoenix Royal, what the fuck are you doing over there?" Frankie called, getting impatient.

Jesus Christ, I needed to pull it together.

As I wiped my eyes and sniffed my emotions back into place, an idea formed in the back of my mind. A crazy one, but it felt…too real to ignore.

In the depths of my soul, I wanted to speak to Judah, to see him, even just for a moment, so I followed the small, out of the box prompt lingering in my heart and closed my eyes. Taking a deep breath, I mentally pictured my skyscraper, scanning those blue eyes, that arrogant, beautiful, shit-eating grin, and I let myself love him. Let myself hope that when all was said and done, he'd come back to me. I gathered every ounce of my affection, my desire, and slowly, those feelings formed into three little words written in the air between us.

In my mind's eye, I imagined Judah standing in front of me and scanned his body, stopping at his chest, and watched as each letter of my statement was delicately written in neon pink font, right over his heart. Without speaking out loud, I prayed a silent prayer, asking God, the universe, whoever the fuck was out there controlling what happened down here, to send this message to him. To deliver my statement safely.

The three words glowed, shining brightly as I stared for only a moment longer.

I miss you.

And when I opened my eyes again, my whole body tingled, like it did after a long, successful meditation session, and although it only took a handful of seconds, something told me it worked.

I had no proof, no way of knowing if Judah and I were truly two halves of one soul, but I hoped he felt my words nonetheless. No matter what was in the letter, he'd given me a gift.

※ ✿ ※

RICCO AND KAVAN left around midnight, leaving Trixie behind to stay with us.

The little ball of fluff pranced around our feet as Frankie and I cleaned up the kitchen, while I tried to stay calm, knowing I had a tiny bomb waiting to go off in my room.

The unread letter was eating at my insides, but I knew I had to save it.

Something told me I needed to be alone, away from other people's opinions and the greedy hands that might want to read it too. I just couldn't…do that to him. Couldn't risk someone else reading what was most likely meant for my eyes only.

I had a feeling whatever was in there would be personal, too personal to share with just anyone else.

"Okay, bitch, the gig is up," Frankie stated with a sigh, shutting the dishwasher with her hip as she turned to face me. "What's happening with you?"

I knew she'd notice I was all up in my head.

Even though I wouldn't let Frankie read the letter, I had to at least tell her it existed. I didn't want to be in a position where I had to tell her about it after I'd already opened the damn thing and find her pissed off at me. Keeping that many secrets wasn't allowed in this friendship anymore.

"I need a drink for this one," I muttered, exhaling thickly

as I pulled down a shot glass from the cabinet before reaching for the bottle of Tito's on the counter to my left.

As I poured, I admitted, "Judah sent me a letter today."

For three whole seconds, there was total silence.

Then, "WHAT?!" The girl smacked my arm, scolding, "Why the *fuck* didn't you tell me?"

"Ow, you bitch." I threw her a look before downing the liquor. "I didn't want Ricco and Kavan to know!" I explained after swallowing the burn.

"Why the hell not?" she asked, yanking the glass out of my hand.

"What Judah is going through..." *How can I explain this?* "I don't know, Franks. *I* haven't even read it yet. I saved it for when everyone was gone so I could be alone. If I'd told the guys, they would have wanted me to open it right away and tell them what Judah said, and that's just not something I would want Judah to do if it were me. Whatever is in there could be either good news or bad, but it's something. He's vulnerable right now, and I want to respect his privacy."

If he sent a letter to me, his recovery team at Cliffside most definitely knew about it. It was probably a part of his healing process, and the last thing I wanted to do was disrespect that.

"Jesus Christ," Frankie muttered, pouring herself a shot and sucking down the liquor like a champ before not so gently setting it on the counter. "It *better* be good, or I swear to all fuck..."

She tilted her head, looking like she was capable of committing murder.

"I know," I agreed softly. I was so nervous, it felt like there were tendrils of snow dancing in my belly, despite the heat the vodka provided.

"Okay, well, I say we take one more shot for the road and then you can get to it," she offered, but I shook my head.

"I'm good. I'm gonna take a blunt to the patio with me

after I get ready for bed," I explained. "I need to read it outside. I feel like the fresh air will help. The letter is…thick."

"My stomach just dropped." Frankie's blue eyes were wide and full of secondhand anxiety.

All I could do was nod. "Now you get why I was weird tonight."

"You were weird on the phone too," she pointed out with a knowing eyebrow raised.

I sighed, too exhausted to explain. "I'll tell you why tomorrow. I need to just get this over with.-

She continued to eye me, no doubt reading my energy, taking in my facial expression and body language to double check that I was truly all right. She must have found what she was looking for, because she graced me with a small nod, but then her dainty hand grabbed mine and I was yanked forward, straight into a crushing hug.

Startled but thankful for the affection, I wrapped my arms around Frankie's slim waist.

"Don't shut me out, okay?" she whispered in my ear. "We can do this together. Whatever is in there, good, bad, or ugly, just don't get lost."

Aka, don't leave me alone again.

"I won't." I squeezed her with both of my hands splayed on her back, my head on her shoulder. "I promise."

When she pulled away, her eyes bounced between mine, checking one more time before she kissed my nose and said, "Okay, go."

Warmth ignited in my chest, warming my heart and reminding me of the conversation Frankie and I had the day before we came home from vacation. We were supposed to have each other's backs. I'd promised her that, and I needed to stick to it. She was living up to her end of the bargain.

"There's no one like you, Frankie Skyes," I told her as I walked backwards toward my room.

"There's no one like *you*, Phoenix Royal." She winked as she placed the shot glass in the sink.

With that, I turned, heading through the living room where Trixie was ripping apart a new stuffed toy that Ricco had bought her. As I passed, I kissed the top of her head and shut off the TV, then padded across the carpet, down the short hallway, and into my room, where Judah's letter sat on my nightstand.

Knowing that no matter what was in there, I'd be crying, I went straight into the bathroom, washed off my makeup, and completed my nighttime routine before grabbing a pre-rolled blunt from my weed stash.

As I made my way to the patio, the letter seemed to burn between my fingers. Possibilities whipped through my mind, turning those tendrils of snow into a full-blown blizzard in my tummy, shining a light on all the hopes I'd been hesitant to think about, the daydreams I'd tried to shove away.

Don't get your fucking hopes up, Phoenix. You don't know anything yet.

Biting the inside of my cheek the whole way into the backyard, I found myself damn near dizzy as I sat down at the table. Unable to hold onto it any longer, I set the letter on the table and focused on the blunt in my hands. My fingers traced the paper, back and forth, flipping it around and around until I couldn't take it anymore and placed one end in between my lips and lit the other end with one of Pharaoh's lighters I'd stolen a few days ago.

My heart galloped as I stared at the envelope.

Please don't let there be anything bad in there.

One hit after another, I held the smoke in my lungs, counted to five, and then let go, breathing it into a cloud before me, and watched the letter like it was a living thing, like it might sprout legs and attack me with a knife.

Open it. Just get it over with.

I couldn't.

Instead of listening to my own impatience, I stalled for so long that I smoked the entire fucking blunt as I stared and stared, eyes wandering over the scrawl of Judah's handwriting…

Then, once I was as high as I could get, as the world twisted and turned around me, I did it.

I reached forward with an unsteady arm and grabbed the envelope, opening it with the tip of my index finger, careful not to rip it haphazardly. Once I'd achieved that part, I pulled out the thick stack of folded papers on the inside and straightened the crinkled edges.

Before I read a word, I squeezed my eyes shut, trying to calm my nerves.

Fear, worry, grief—the emotions I felt danced around me like a cyclone until I couldn't stand it anymore. My eyes flew open, and with my heart in my throat, I began to read.

Phoenix,
Hi.
It's, uh…me.
Judah. Obviously.
Fucking hell, if you could see me right now…
I've written this goddamn letter so many times, I don't even care how I sound anymore. I've thrown out so many versions because I wanted the words to be just right, I wanted you to feel me physically, mentally, and spiritually as you read it, but it's starting to drive me to damn near insanity so I'm just going to get this out.
Forgive me if it comes out wrong.
Listen, I'm not going to start by saying I fucked up. You know that and so do I, but I am going to say that I'm sorry. Before you get angry, before that little nose of yours scrunches up and you close your fists and get all pissed off,

please know that it's okay if you don't believe me. I know that I've said those two words one too many times.
Here's the thing though… This time?
<u>*I mean it.*</u>
And I can admit now that I didn't mean it before.

I glanced up, feeling like I could barely breathe, seeing those words written so plainly, as tears tumbled down my cheeks.

I kept going once I'd cleared my vision enough to even see the words.

I'm sorry if that's a hard pill to swallow, even though I'm pretty sure you already know it. Back then, I didn't even know what I was apologizing for. I didn't understand that every word out of my mouth before now was a farce. If I were actually sorry back then, I wouldn't have done half of the shit I did, and the point of writing you is to say to you that you didn't deserve it.
Any of it.
You, my baby bird, my little light, you didn't fucking deserve it.
You know, all of this kind of reminds me of how before you came into my life, I couldn't write at all. I'd been burning lyrics and telling myself I was a useless piece of shit for months. Songs were too hard to pull together, my personal truth was lost in the wind, my insecurities were eating me alive, but then you came along.
You pushed me.
You told me that the world, my fans, even my haters, needed my music. You told me I deserved to tell my story, and fuck anyone that had anything shitty to say about my art.
You were right, of course. I don't think I ever told you that, but you were.

There are a lot of things you were right about that I didn't want to admit before because if I'd said it out loud, I'd have no more excuses. I would have been out of room to make the stupid decisions I made.
Decisions that hurt you. Decisions that ruined us.
Now it's really fucking hard for me to put myself in your position, because when I do, I want to kill myself all over again. The pain I caused? The shit I did to you?
Phoenix...
I'm just fucking sorry.
I'm sorry I couldn't be what you needed me to be. I'm sorry I didn't take the time to learn with you, to grow with you. I'm sorry I tried to rip that progress apart because I wasn't in a frame of mind to understand why you would choose yourself over me.
And I'll be honest, I'm a shell of a man right now. I'm not doing so hot.
The shit I have to face, the nightmares that walk through my mind, even in the daylight hours? Hell is on Earth right now, but no matter where I am, no matter what I'm going through, no matter how I'm feeling...
You remain.
All the strength I hated to see before, it's what's holding me up right now. It's what's continuing to push me forward, even though I feel like I take one step forward and two steps back. Either way, no matter what I'm experiencing, you remain.
Even after saying that, I need you to know that you deserve better than me.
That's not a pity line. I'm not talking down on myself, and I'm not saying you should move on while I stay rooted in all my bullshit. I'm saying it because it's true.
The guy you knew, the version of me that you fell in love with? That guy didn't fucking deserve your love. He didn't

even know what to do with it, how to reciprocate it properly, and in the end, I made you doubt how incredible, how rare, and how special you really are.
I'm not saying I'm brand-new, I'm not even sure who I am right now, but all that remains a fact. You deserved better.
Another fact? I miss you.
Desperately.
But that's not the point of this letter, I just needed to say it. The point of this letter is to tell you that I see now how much damage I did, how much pain I caused you, and now that I see it…it's caused me pain too. Pain that I deserve, of course, but pain that is almost too hard to handle.
My nightmares aren't always about my childhood anymore. Now they're laced with how I made you feel, what I did to Pharaoh, my career, how I disappointed my fans. It's all in ruins because of my own selfish choices, and there's so much to unpack that I'm drowning over here.
But I'm also trying.
Every day, I take your advice, because after going through the phases of hating you, hating your strength, and ripping up the letter you wrote me, I started to take it seriously, and the more I do it, the more I use your words as further motivation to keep going. The shitty reality is that half of the time, I want to give up, get high, say fuck it all. Many times, I've thought about running so far from this place that no one will ever find me again.
Surely the universe can't bring me back from the dead a fourth time, right?

"Fucking stop it," I whispered, sobbing into my hand, feeling the sharp vibration of his pain radiating all over my skin. I wanted to drop everything and drive to Cliffside, just to be sure he was still alive, because that one sentence had my heart cracking all over again as panic raced through my veins.

But I kept going, hoping he wasn't done, hoping he wouldn't give up like that.

It just feels like it's all too much sometimes.
I still want to rip my face off when my therapist asks me leading questions. I want to burn the place to the ground when those memories of my parents come to haunt me, but I'm here.
I'm still trying. I'm still fighting.
And no, I'm not doing it for you.
Though I do fall back into those tendencies sometimes.
I can admit that without knowing you're out there in the world somewhere, I wouldn't be doing this, but as I keep going, as I sit with my therapist everyday…well, I find myself cooperating because quite frankly, I'm exhausted.
Now that I've started digging into this shit, it feels like no matter what I do—whether I jump right back into drugs or if I stay the course and continue my healing sober—the pain won't go away…until it does.
And I believe at some point, it will.
The choice is and always has been, life or death.
In a way, you taught me that the pain either dies with me and all my demons, decades too soon, or it dies with my choice to live. One is easier than the other—just ending it all and not giving a single fuck—while the other takes courage.
I'm not sure how much courage I have in me, but I'm trying to find out.
I'm learning who I am, but I still don't love my own reflection. My therapist says it takes time, and I want to believe her, I really do, but I'm impatient to see the results, because while I'm trying to become a better man, I'm afraid I'll never get there.
I want a guarantee that one day, I'll be someone I can be proud of, someone who doesn't let his friends down.

Someone that can recognize what he has before he cuts it into pieces.
I'm striving to become that someone, and while I'm not sure if I'll make it there, I'm still so fucking sorry, Phoenix, for all the things I put you through.
The guilt is very clearly eating me alive, but I'm not giving up. I'll keep going until that courage runs out, and when it runs out, I'll do my best to find more.
Don't know how…but you can bet that sweet ass, I'm going to figure it out.
Finally, with all that being said, here comes the warning…
I'm coming back.
To you, to Pharaoh, my bandmates, and fans.
I will be reintroducing myself, just like you said.
I don't know who I'll be in another six weeks, because it feels like so much has already changed, and even though it feels like I'm just as depressed as I was before, my therapist says it gets worse before it gets better, so I'm banking on that.
I probably won't be fully fixed. I'll definitely need more therapy, more bullshit group sessions that I still can't stand, but I'll be sober and asking for forgiveness…in person.
I don't know if you'll want me, or even if you'll love me like you did before, but I can promise that my feelings for you, my love for you, will not have changed.
I still feel you, Phoenix Royal, down to the marrow in my fucking bones, and I don't know what will happen if you reject me after all is said and done. I'm still figuring that part out, but that's for me to work on, not you to worry about.
You owe me nothing.
If you've moved on, you're entitled to that.
The only thing I ask of you now is that you don't respond to this letter.

    What?

My heart crashed into the concrete under my chair.

It hurts to write. I'm choking on sobs as my pen slides across this paper, but I'm just not ready to hear from you.
I need to do this on my own, and if I hear from you, I will heal **for** *you. If you respond, I'll know there's still hope for us, and I'll want to escape and rush the process. I wouldn't be able to think clearly until I saw you again.*
Without knowing if you'll take me back, without hearing about your life out there, I'm alone, and while I'm struggling and I hate every motherfucking second of it, it's working.
By the time I get out of here, I will be well on my way to being the man you deserve.
That's my goal, at least.
I won't send another letter. I won't torture you like that. I just had to get this one out so I can finally breathe again.
I needed to tell you that I'm sorry, for real this time.
If you let me, when I get out of here, I'll prove it.

I hope you're okay. I hope you're <u>more</u> than okay.
I hope you're thriving.
I love you, Phoenix Royal.
I'll see you soon.
Xo,
J.

I was fucking *sobbing*.

My entire face was covered in moisture as a waterfall of emotion streamed down my cheeks, into my mouth, and I struggled to breathe, to even read the words.

I had to reread the letter four times before I was able to finally put it down, and when I did, my crying only accelerated.

Skyscraper.

The letter was everything I wanted, and yet all I could feel was his pain.

What nightmares? What memories of his parents?

What was it like in there?

Why did he tell me not to *fucking respond*?

The logical side of my brain understood, but the rest was pissed, heartbroken, and desperate to talk to him, to tell him I was proud, tell him I had his back and that he'd get through this. I wanted to let him know that when he got out, I'd be there, but that wasn't what he wanted. It wasn't what he needed.

He was doing what I'd told him to, and yet…

I felt rejected. Alone.

But I was also elated and proud, full of awe and…hope.

I'd never admit it out loud, but a part of me loved that Judah lived for me. A part of me craved his passionate devotion that rode that toxic line because it was pure fire when we were together. I loved our flames, but only when we weren't in a third-party situation with his addiction.

Me, him, and his many bottles of pills.

So something had to give, and this was the moment that happened.

He was breaking up with the addiction that nearly killed him, but in order to do that, he needed the space from me too, and I wanted that for him. I really did.

But at the same time…

I wanted to be a fly on the wall of his therapist's office, a dark angel standing at his back, a light in his dreams, shooing away all the bad things, killing anything that tried to hurt him. I wanted it to be *me* that he talked to. I wanted all of his darkness, wanted to know what he'd seen, felt, and experienced as a child. I wanted to be closer to him.

It was all I'd ever wanted.

But he was right—I deserved better than how he'd treated me. I deserved to be loved. Happy. At peace.

And Judah did too.

So, after reading it one more time, when my tears started to slow and my weary heart began to ache from all the pounding it had done, I allowed myself to greet that peace.

I'd felt every word of that letter, read between every line.

Judah wanted to know if I was going to be there when he got out, but he was more concerned about being who *he* wanted to be when that day came, and if I reached out, I would get in the way of that progress.

I understood with perfect clarity that Judah *did* need to be alone, even though I hated the thought. While he believed I could move on, while he thought I might not love the man he became while he was in there…I knew now that couldn't be further from the truth.

Just like he'd said, I felt Judah Colt in the marrow of my bones, even when he was double fucked and always faded. But now? With a clear mind, a humble heart…

He was coming back.

That was all that mattered.

CHAPTER 10

PHARAOH

I WAS FUCKING around on my drum set, working on a new project I had planned with an up-and-coming band, when my phone began ringing in my pocket.

After setting my sticks on the snare drum, I pulled it out, thinking it was one of the guys, but instead saw the number for Cliffside blinking at me.

Hmm. Is it time for another update already?

It had been six full weeks since Judah had been admitted, but I'd just heard from his counselor last week...

"Hello?" I answered, holding my breath, now concerned that something might have happened to Judah.

"Hey, man."

Holy fuck.

I stood, abandoning the drum set entirely as my stomach hit the floor.

"Judah?" I nearly whispered, feeling like a ten-pound brick had crashed against my chest. "Wh—I mean, h-hey. Uh, how are you? Is everything okay?"

With a hand on my forehead, I began to pace, feeling the weight of worry on my shoulders.

"It's good to hear your voice," was all he said, but I couldn't miss the emotion in his tone.

"J, you good?" I pushed, feeling my blood heat with fear.

There was only silence for a few seconds before he cleared his throat and replied, "Yeah, yeah, I'm, uh, I'm fine. I just called to let you know that I sent Phoenix a letter."

That brick in my chest hit my heart like a bullet.

"Okay…" I drew out softly.

"Can you just, uh, check on her for me?" he requested. "I don't know what's going on over there or how any of you feel about me, but I don't want her to be alone right now."

"She's not alone, Judah." I sighed. "I promise."

More silence.

Until finally, he whispered, "Good."

"How are *you*, J? How you doin' in there?" I needed to know why his energy was so low, why he was so…reserved.

I heard a bit of shuffling in the background before he responded. "I'm getting better, that's all that matters."

Why was he being so fucking cryptic? Why wouldn't he talk to me?

It gave me anxiety to feel this far away from him, and yet I didn't want to nag him or push him too far, fearing that if I did, it would make things worse.

"Good," I echoed. "That's good, brother."

"Yeah." His tone was so fucking sad. "All right, well, I've gotta go. I just wanted to check in and let you know I reached out, just in case Phoenix kept it to herself. I didn't want her to feel like she couldn't tell anyone."

"Judah, wait," I said, attempting to stop him from hanging up. "Listen, we're all worried about you, man. We're not… mad at you."

That wasn't necessarily true. Kavan and Ricco were defensive as all fuck, but that had everything to do with their fear of Phoenix getting hurt and their protective nature when it came to her. I wasn't mad, and I didn't think Phoenix was either.

Judah sighed. "Thanks. I'll talk to you soon."

"Wai—" I tried again, but it was too late. He'd already hung up. "Son of a bitch."

Too worked up to keep practicing, I abandoned the small room in my apartment and grabbed my keys from the kitchen counter, deciding to pay Phoenix a visit. It was Tuesday, so the shop was closed. I just had to find out where she was and if she was free to talk.

I shot her a text.

Pharaoh: Hey, you busy?

If Phoenix had heard from Judah, she probably had more information than I did at the moment and I needed to know that my best friend was all right, especially after that call.

Phoenix: Nah, what's up?
Pharaoh: I'm on my way over.

✳

LETTING myself in to P's house, I found the kitchen and living room empty, so I headed straight down the hall and stopped at the door of her room, where I knocked and waited for her response.

"Come on in," she called out, sounding like her normal self.

I found her sitting in the middle of her bed with her iPad in her lap, wearing ripped black jeans and a House of Drew hoodie.

"You drawing?" I asked casually, kicking off my shoes and placing them by the door before joining her on the bed. I laid myself horizontally across the end of the mattress, watching as she set the device down.

Those brown eyes met mine as she said, "Yeah, I have this big ass back piece to do tomorrow and I'm still not done with the design. It's driving me insane."

I smirked, knowing she hated when the inspiration wasn't flowing like she wanted it to. "You need help?"

The question earned me a grin in return. "From you? No."

Laughing, I grabbed her bare foot and yanked, forcing her to lose her balance and fall back onto the bed. "Hey now, what's wrong with my help?"

"You're a shit artist!" She giggled and pulled her foot back. "You couldn't help me even if I wanted you to."

"Whatever," I replied as I crawled toward her pillows and mimicked her position so both of us were lying down, staring at the ceiling. "I'm not that bad."

Not bothering to entertain my bullshit, she cut right to the chase. "What's with the drop by? You okay?"

I sighed as worries attacked my stomach all over again. Judah's phone call had me all twisted up. "I'm here to ask you that exact question," I stated.

Phoenix turned her head to face me on the pillow, and I felt rather than saw her studying my profile. "What? why?"

She was pretending to be unaffected, obviously didn't want to tell me about the letter, and I wasn't sure why, but it didn't make me feel good.

Hoping to crack her code, I faced her and admitted, "Judah called me."

Instantly, her features fell and her normally sun-kissed skin paled quickly. "He w-what?" she whispered.

I nodded against the pillow, then looked toward the ceiling again. "He wanted me to check on you. Told me he sent you a letter."

Thick silence fell as she swallowed, no doubt taking the

time to collect her thoughts. Then, rather than responding, Phoenix got off the bed entirely, leaving me to push myself onto my elbows with confusion written all over my face as I watched her disappear into her closet. Eventually, it became clear what she was doing, because she returned holding a chunk of folded paper in her left hand.

Phoenix said nothing as she sat back down, but I straightened into a sitting position, knowing she was about to let me read what J had sent her. I wasn't even sure I wanted to, given that my feelings for Phoenix hadn't exactly up and vanished, but I knew she wouldn't hurt me in that way on purpose. Whatever was in the letter was important enough to have her handing it to me.

P didn't utter a word as I took the papers from her grasp, but instead lay down again, this time falling sideways and placing her head in my lap.

Despite the heaviness of the energy around us, gratitude slid through my veins as she got comfortable, reminding me that while I didn't get to keep her in a romantic sense, Phoenix was still mine in *this* way. She still trusted me to carry her through the darkest parts of her journey, still relied on me and remained affectionate, even in a platonic way.

Once she was all set and I began to read…the world fell away, and all I was left with was the weight of Judah's recovery and the chaotic mess of emotions he'd inked onto the pages of his notebook.

CHAPTER 11
Phoenix

KNOWING that Judah was able to pick up the phone and call Pharaoh was both a punch to the gut and a welcome piece of information. The fact that he'd called and asked his best friend to check on me had my skin clammy, my tummy in a knot.

He still cares.

I knew it, given what Judah had said in his letter, but it something completely different now that J had involved Pharaoh and I wasn't left alone to deal with what was written inside. The whole exchange felt more real, more important, and all I could do was hold my breath as Pharaoh read.

I only felt comfortable giving the letter to him because if Judah told Pharaoh about it in the first place, then assigned him with the task of making sure I was okay, it was up to me what I was willing to share.

Was I okay?

I wasn't sure.

"Fuck," Pharaoh whispered after a good twenty minutes of silence.

"Exactly," I muttered, still lying in his lap, staring at the blank, turned off TV.

Another full minute passed before Pharaoh concluded, "So that explains why J was so cryptic with me."

My blood pressure spiked. "He was cryptic?"

Pharaoh let out a heavy sigh. "Yeah. It didn't even seem like he wanted to talk to me. It felt like he literally called just to have me check on you and that was it."

That hit me straight in the soul.

Judah's first time reaching out to either of us, and all he cared about was making sure I was okay. Pharaoh had to feel some type of way about that.

"I'm sorry," I whispered, feeling guilty for some reason. "He should have…I don't know…talked to you, I guess. He could have given you some peace of mind."

That wasn't Judah's job, and we both knew it. It was a selfish way of thinking, but this situation fucking sucked for everyone.

Pharaoh's hand found its way into my hair as he admitted, "I wish he would have."

Neither of us spoke for a few moments.

"Maybe he knew I was going to show you what he sent me," I said, finally. "Or at the very least tell you what was in it. Maybe he couldn't tell you how he felt out loud, so he figured the letter was enough."

Pharaoh made a non-committal sound. "Maybe."

Judah had chosen *me* to be the one he talked to first, and while I was both happy and torn about that, I was seeing the effect it had on his best friend and I didn't like it. Pharaoh deserved his own moment with Judah, not just a secondhand experience with secondhand information from me.

"What do we do?" I asked, wanting Pharaoh's opinion, needing his help to sort out my thoughts.

Except he seemed to be in the same place I was, though for him, there were no tears after reading what Judah had to say. I'd sat up most of the night in various states of disaster.

"Not much we *can* do, little P," Phar replied. "Judah wants to do this alone."

As he should.

In my heart, I knew how important it was for Judah to walk this road by himself, but it would be a fucking lie if I said I liked it.

In fact, I hated all of it. I resented Judah for putting us in this position in the first place.

When I failed to respond, Pharoah asked, "Did you get much sleep?"

I scoffed. "Like three hours."

"That's what I thought," he stated, then began to shift, forcing me to lift my head. "Take a nap with me?"

I swallowed, suddenly fighting tears as I whispered, "Yes, please."

We had no real way of knowing what our future held, so we couldn't deny that no matter what Judah said, he was still in the thick of his recovery and his situation could change at any given moment.

Daunting, worrisome, the whole experience had our hearts splintered and cracked, but we had each other. It was the one thing I held onto with both hands, knowing that no matter what happened, Pharoah had me and I had him.

So from there, I cuddled up with Phar and used his steady presence as an anchor. Then I closed my eyes and fell into a blank, restless sleep.

CHAPTER 12
Phoenix

Eleven weeks in rehab

THE NEXT FIVE weeks flew by in a blur.

My schedule was packed, Frankie had started working with Julia again, and in turn, time both flew by and dragged on.

We were now one week out from Judah's discharge date, and while Pharaoh had gotten updates from Judah's counselor, it was still very superficial information. According to Cliffside, Judah was fine, he was talking openly with his therapist, he'd made friends, he was showing up to all of his scheduled events, and taking his medication.

But that was all the information we got.

Judah hadn't written or called again, so Pharaoh and I were left to assume that he was doing well enough, which of course, was both concerning and surprising.

"All right, kiddos, great job today!" I called out, smiling at the group of ten kids I'd been teaching over the last month. "I'll see you next week."

"Thanks, Miss Royal!" Aiden, a ten-year-old boy with sharp grey eyes and pretty blond hair, called out to me. "I had so much fun!"

Chuckling, I waved back. "I'm so glad, buddy."

After receiving Judah's letter, I'd needed something to fill my free time, so I reached back out to Carmine, the head of a low-income outreach program in Northridge that Pharaoh had tried to hook me up with at the end of last year. Since Frankie and I had chosen to leave for an impromptu three-week vacation, I'd had to cancel the meeting, but when I contacted her again and asked to set up another one, she was super sweet, very receptive, and got me in the next week.

When we met, I was able to pitch my idea for a new class, where I would be teaching kids how to draw, with a curriculum surrounding the art of tattooing.

Carmine had loved the idea and began marketing the class in her other, already established classes. Before I knew it, I had enough kids to begin teaching for the remainder of the winter season.

And to my surprise, I fucking loved it.

It had given me a new sense of purpose and helped me channel all of my extra energy into something productive, something other than overthinking and tattooing.

"Bye, Lexie." I smiled down at a little black girl that attended my classes, loving how happy she looked. "You did great today. I love the rose you drew," I complimented.

"I'm going to draw an elephant next time!" she informed me enthusiastically. "With more flowers!"

"I think that is a fantastic idea," I told her. "You can start drawing the piece at home this week if you want. Come in next time with what you already have, and I'll help you polish it up."

Her eyes lit up. "Thank you, Miss Royal!"

My chest squeezed at the thought of her drawing in her room, like I used to at her age. "Anytime, sweet girl."

After Lexie met up with her mom, I held the door open as the rest of my class—a mixture of boys and girls—ran out of the building and toward the line of cars out front, where their parents waited to pick them up. Milo's mother, Arya, waved at me from the front seat of her beat-up GMC, and I happily returned the gesture, thinking of ways I could help these families, even just to lighten the load a little bit.

My family had never hurt for money, but Judah and Pharaoh had a very different past, and ever since learning more about their childhood, it had been on my mind to find a way to help kids like them.

"God, they love you, girl." Carmine's voice floated toward me as the last kid got in their parent's car. I turned, finding her walking in my direction from the other side of the gymnasium I held my class in. "I made a good choice bringing you on board."

Smiling, I let the door fall shut behind me. "I'm certainly glad you did. I love them too."

"Are you sure you can't stay on for the spring session?"

This was the fourth time she'd asked me, but my answer hadn't changed.

"I really wish I could," I explained again, hating that I didn't have a better response, "but my schedule at the tattoo shop is packed until the end of June. When I looked into trying to fit these classes in, I just felt like I'd be taking on too much. But I did look into my summer schedule, and I haven't fully filled my books yet, so if you'll have me, I'll make time to teach here again."

The kids had brought so much joy into my life, and I regretted not making time for the spring session. When I initially agreed, I wasn't sure how I would like it, given I'd never spent any time around children before.

"Of course we'll have you," Carmine replied, waving me off like I should have known. "I'm just giving you shit because even *I* like having you around."

"You sound like you're surprised by that." I chuckled as

she pulled back her long, thick black hair and tied it into a ponytail.

The woman was beautiful.

"Well, when Pharaoh brought up that he had a female teacher for me to check out, I stereotyped and wasn't sure what to expect from a famous drummer recommending a female. He could have been offering up a random girl he was sleeping with or something."

A grin spread across my mouth. "Can't blame you there, but Pharaoh has good taste."

"He sure does," Carmine agreed and threw me a wink. "Hey, how have you been handling the media lately? They've been relentless the last couple of weeks."

Swallowing, I pushed the resentment away as best I could and held onto my most positive tone of voice. "I'm…dealing with it. They know Judah is getting out of rehab soon, and since I wasn't in town for the overdose, they're stalking for any information they can get on my feelings where he's concerned."

Carmine barked out a sarcastic laugh. "And they think they'll get it by stalking you around the city? How does that make any sense?"

She knew all about Judah, since she knew both Pharaoh and me, but she never judged and, quite frankly, didn't give a shit about the drama.

"Right?" I scoffed. "But those bastards can find a way to make money off body language or even lip-reading. If they catch me on a phone call, they'll try to figure out who I'm talking to. Hell, even catching a glimpse of my phone and the picture on my lock screen would be enough to sell. It's insanity."

"It's fucking bullshit is what it is," she spat out.

Shocked, I couldn't help but laugh. "Geez, I never thought I'd hear you swear."

"Please," she said, waving me off. "We just haven't spent enough time together yet."

I could see myself being friends with Carmine if I had any free time to spare. She was kind and gentle with the children but had a fierce soul when speaking to adults. It was a fine balance, something I admired.

From there, we fell into easy conversation about random things as we finished cleaning up the gym and putting all the tables back in the storage closet, completing our tasks just in time for Pharaoh to make his way through the entrance of the gym.

"There he is!" Carmine called out. "The man of the hour."

"Man of the hour?" Pharaoh questioned, smirking at me. "What did I do?"

"Ah, nothing." Carmine shrugged cheekily. "We were just talking about how you charm all the little girls in class with your fancy bad boy vibes."

"Oh, shut up." He laughed, waving her off.

"You're their first crush," I threw in, wiggling my eyebrows playfully. "It reminds me of when I was a little girl. I was fucking *obsessed* with Justin Timberlake. I had like ten posters of him in my bedroom, but I specifically taped one to my ceiling so I could stare at him as I fell asleep every night."

Pharaoh's eyes went wide.

"Mm-hm," Carmine agreed, giving Pharaoh a once-over. "You're definitely on at least two of those girls' walls. Maybe even a few of the boys. We don't discriminate."

"Ew." Phar scrunched his nose, trying not to smile. "I don't wanna think of *any* of them like that, thank you very much." Quickly cutting off the conversation, Phar made his way to me. "You ready? Frankie texted about that event we have tonight. Reminded us not to be late getting back to your place."

"Fuck, I forgot," I said on a groan, letting my upper body sag in defeat.

It felt like I had very little time to myself lately, given how busy my life had gotten over the last month. I'd been booked solid at the shop and spent one night a week teaching for Carmine, plus now that Frankie had begun booking promotional events with Julia again, I was back to playing wing woman too.

I was exhausted.

"You two head out, I'll lock up," Carmine told us both. "Thanks for everything!"

"Thank you," I replied as happily as I could before glancing at Pharaoh and nodding in the direction of the door. I let out a whiny, "Let's go."

We both taught a class on the same night, so Pharaoh typically drove, given the fact that we'd spent so much time together lately. After we were finished, he would usually come over for dinner, along with Ricco and Kav, but tonight, Frankie had charmed all four of us, plus Silas, into attending some sort of launch event for a makeup company. I probably would have tried to find a way to get out of it, but even Julia suggested I make an appearance because the brand was launching a new type of concealer that was supposed to be pigmented enough to cover tattoos.

She said they might want to team up with Death's Door to sell their products in our shop.

Kenji would lose his mind.

"Okay, I am *beat*," I complained once we were outside, but made sure to keep my head down in order to avoid making eye contact with the two paps I'd spotted across the street. I also made sure not to physically touch Pharaoh, knowing that if I did, we'd have tabloid articles talking about the two of us having an affair behind Judah's back.

It had already happened once.

"Me fuckin' too," Phar replied as we reached the G-Wagon.

Both of us hopped inside, and once we were seated, he continued with, "I could sleep for a week straight. I don't understand why I have to go tonight."

"I don't know," I said, shrugging as I grabbed my seatbelt. "But if I am going, so are you."

We were about forty minutes from my house, so I hooked my phone up to the Bluetooth in the G-Dog so I could sync my music. Before I hit play, I saw the date on the digital display and recognition dawned, leaving me a bit anxious, but more curious than anything.

"Hey, have you heard from Cliffside about Judah's discharge yet?" I asked Pharaoh right away.

He shook his head.

"Not since the last check-in a couple of weeks ago," Phar explained. "Even then, Judah's counselor just told me he was doing great and getting better every day."

Somehow, I doubted Judah was doing *great*, but in the grand scheme of things, I figured that was good news.

"Hmm, all right," I replied, ignoring the nervous buzzing in my veins. "Well, let me know when you find out what the plan is."

Pharaoh's hand came over the center console and squeezed my thigh. "You know I will."

I nodded, giving him a small smile, before pressing shuffle on my playlist.

"You Know Wassup" by Kehlani was the first song to play, making me scoff and shake my head.

I had *thousands* of songs in my library, yet somehow, every time I hit shuffle, the song that played first always fit my situation almost too perfectly.

The week after hearing from Judah, I did my best to settle back into my own energy again, trying not to worry about what was happening with him, what he was going through, and focused on my own life, my normal routine. But the next month seemed to race by and the closer we got to him coming home, the more I felt his presence.

His energy creeped closer with each passing hour and seemed to slither around me like a not so quiet reminder of all the questions I had about our future together.

I had absolutely no fucking idea what was about to happen, but I had mixed feelings about the whole thing. Half of me was excited and hopeful, ready to see him again, while the other half dreaded the whole thing. I was triggered by the past, fearful of the future, and uncomfortable in the present moment.

Could I trust myself to do the right thing?

Would I be able to read between the lines and protect myself from further heartbreak if the situation presented itself? Or would I fall back into his ozone and lose all sense of reason again?

It was terrifying to think about, and yet there was the side of me that just knew he was going to do the right thing, that believed what he spoke about in that letter. Still, though, I had no idea what the sober version of Judah would be like or how our first meeting would go.

Would it feel the same when I touched him?

Would he look at me like he used to?

Was there anything to save or had too much damage been done?

I had no clue what to expect, but the more I thought about it, the more anxious I became.

"It's gonna be all right, P," Pharaoh said after the song ended, seemingly able to read me as well as Frankie could, now that we'd spent so much time together. "I know you're all up in your head about it, and I'm…nervous too, but I really do think it's going to be different this time."

For Pharaoh to say that? It had to be the truth. He'd gone

through too much with Judah, been hurt one too many times. If Pharaoh still had hope, it made me think I could hold on tighter to mine.

I just hoped he was right.

CHAPTER 13
JUDAH

Eleven weeks in rehab

"HOW ARE you feeling now that Brian and Cassie are gone?" Dr. Blake asked a few minutes before our session was supposed to end, closing out the session with a question that was a whole lot easier to answer than the few she'd asked before.

"Surprisingly?" I laughed a little. "I miss the annoying little assholes."

Blake smirked back at me. "I'm not surprised," she admitted. "The three of you formed a pretty solid bond. Do you think you'll reach out to them when you leave next week?"

The thought of getting out of there kicked my blood pressure up a few notches.

"Uh…" I scratched my forehead, my mind a little out of sorts. "I don't know, honestly. I have both of their information, but I'm more concerned about fixing what I broke back home. I'm not sure I have the space in my life right now to worry about continuing new friendships."

"Makes sense." Blake nodded, though I knew she hoped I would remain in contact with them, despite my reservations. "Have you spoken to Pharaoh about what you want to do when you get out? You're going to need his help getting home and settled in."

I shook my head, once again feeling like the ground beneath me could give out at any moment, especially when I thought about my old house in the Hills, untouched and dark.

Not wanting Blake to know how bad my anxiety was about getting back to real life, I had to clear my throat in order to assure my voice was steady. "Not yet. I'm planning to call him tomorrow."

Maybe.

I just had no idea what the hell I was going to say to him, given I wasn't sure how to set myself up for success once I got out of Cliffside. I had plans for my apologies, I knew who I needed to talk to, but the one thing had yet to figure out was Phoenix. I couldn't handle her being involved right away, given the unknowns surrounding our relationship. I could barely handle not knowing how she was going to react to me, and thanks to my behavior, I'd basically shoved Phoenix and Pharaoh together. I was well aware of the fact that they'd grown close, and I knew my best friend would tell her anything I told him unless I specifically asked him not to.

Which would look suspicious…

But I needed to save myself, think about myself, and keep Phoenix as far away as possible until I knew for sure that I was ready to handle her rejection, should that be the case.

"Good idea," she replied before an idea lit up her eyes. "I haven't asked in a few days, but what's the update on your project? How's writing going?"

Finally, a question I could handle.

A sense of calm excitement washed over me.

"I'm almost finished," I supplied, feeling more confident as I met her stare. "And I actually think it's…good."

"I'm sure it is." Blake grinned, and there was pride swimming in her eyes, making me feel warm, like I'd done something right for once. "And you plan to reach out to your former bandmates when you get out?"

"Mm-hm," I replied. "It's part of what I need to talk to Pharaoh about. He has no idea I've been working on anything in here, obviously, and we don't exactly have a label or a manager anymore, so I have a lot of stuff to figure out and a fuck ton of work ahead of me."

There was so much to think about when it came to leaving this place, and it had me in avoidance mode, fearing that if I took on too much or got too excited and ended up hitting a roadblock…I'd be shattered.

Thankfully, I'd gotten word from my lawyer a few weeks back, telling me that I'd been cleared in the investigation of Rachele and Sarah's deaths, but I still needed to speak to him about Brandon's case against me.

As far as Brandon went… Fuck that guy. But those girls? A part of me believed I should have gone to jail and wanted to drop my lawyer all together and let Brandon run me over, just so I could end up serving time either way. I didn't remember enough about those three days, had never once spoken to those girls sober so I had no idea if they were chasing death like I was, but either way, it felt wrong. I felt responsible, and the guilt was overwhelming, damn near debilitating.

However, when I spoke to Blake about it, she'd had me write letters to both girls, telling them how I felt, getting my thoughts onto paper, and then had me read those fears and apologies out loud in front of her. It was cathartic, sure, and it helped lessen the load just a little, especially when Blake reminded me that those girls had choices, just like I did. If they had been willing to risk overdose, they had to have known what could have happened.

Still, it didn't completely erase the triggering memories.

It did, however, remind me that I could do better now that I was sober. What I was working on had serious potential, and because of Phoenix, I had learned to dream. Then, just like she'd said, I began to dream bigger.

Something good could come out of the damage that had been done in the last year, and I spent many nights thinking of the possibilities, but still, I wasn't sure how Pharaoh was going to feel about working with me again. I wasn't sure if I could make those dreams come true, if he would even be willing to take another risk on me, and I was even *less* sure of how Pierce and Vale would react.

It was discouraging to think about, truthfully, but it was also all I had to hold onto.

"You could go independent," Blake suggested. "Do everything yourself versus worrying about working for a label."

I nodded, having already thought about that. "It would be harder but worth it, if we got to do whatever the fuck we wanted to."

With that little nugget of positivity, I got lost, thinking of how I'd gotten here.

The last five weeks had been full of nightmares, memories, daydreams, and tears. I'd screamed at my mother in front of Blake, sobbed into the black pillows on her couch every day like I lived in her office. At one point, our sessions had been so intense that Blake had gotten emotional right along with me.

I'd only recently begun to truly see the light at the end of this goddamn tunnel, and I feared it all crashing down again, landing me right back at square one.

But I'd done too much work to back out now. I'd gone back in time in order to remind myself of the moment I fell in love with music and the expression of rapping. I'd found my sound again, developed my voice, but it was still just me in my own head. While I thought it was fantastic, I wasn't sure how the outside world would perceive my truth.

Again, it was daunting, and yet I wasn't going to let my fear stop me because I had absolutely nothing to lose.

That was the other thing I'd had come to terms with.

I was already completely alone, sitting firmly in rock bottom, sleeping in the ashes of my old life, so really, there was nothing standing in my way. I could either crawl my way up and into daylight again, or I could die there on the floor of my self-made prison cell and rot for the rest of my life.

I wasn't comfortable with option two anymore, not with the amount of shit I'd worked through, the fears I'd faced, the demons I'd beaten to a bloody fucking pulp all because I was sick of feeling like shit. I wanted to make my way to the top again, but once I got there, I wasn't sure who would be with me and who wouldn't. I didn't know which friendships had survived my chaos and which hadn't made it. All I knew was whoever was waiting out there for me, whoever would find it in themselves to forgive me, truly believed in me, and those were the people I needed in my life.

In order to figure all of that out, though, I had a lot of apologizing to do. I had time to make up for, promises to—

"Judah," Blake called out, interrupting my thoughts in an attempt to regain my attention.

I blinked back to reality, where I was still in rehab with a week left to get my shit together, and adjusted in my seat. "Sorry."

"It's okay," Blake replied, sounding a bit concerned. "Where did you go?"

"I, uh..." I cleared my throat again, fearing that with one too many haunted confessions, she'd tell me I should stay longer, that I wasn't ready to leave Cliffside yet. But over the course of the last few months, I really had learned to trust Dr. Blake, so I leaned into that. "I was just thinking about what it will be like to go home," I admitted.

Understanding fell over her features. "And? What do you imagine happening?"

"I don't know," I replied honestly. "That's kinda the point,

I guess. It could either go really well once I get all my apologies out, or I could be left with no one."

Yikes, saying it out loud makes it worse.

"Do you honestly believe that no one will forgive you?" Her tone was neutral.

"No," I stated, shaking my head only a little. "I mean, I hope not. But Phoenix…"

It wasn't that she was the most important person to me right now, it was the terrifying notion of getting everyone else back and not her. I knew even now that I would genuinely struggle with the amount of regret I'd have to live with if that were to be the case, and it wasn't the first time I found myself hating my decision to ask her to refrain from responding to my letter. If I had just allowed her to reply, the suffocating fear might have gone away by now, soothed by her forgiveness, or at the very least, I would have learned to live with the opposite result in the safety net Cliffside provided.

By taking that option away, I was gambling with my sobriety.

"Her rejection would be the hardest to accept," I concluded, feeling the pressure of Blake's eyes as she watched me work through my fears.

"But you'd move on, Judah," Blake insisted in return. "It would be hard to lose her, there's no doubt about that, but you would still have that fresh slate to build on. If she can't find it in herself to forgive you, if too much damage was done, then maybe she isn't your person. Either way, you still have the opportunity to start over. You'll figure out who your person is, fall in love again, and still get to live the life you dreamed about."

Except I didn't dream of a life without Phoenix. In fact, most of the time, I daydreamed about all the things that would happen once she did forgive me. Once I proved myself to her and showed her that I was taking my life seriously, just like she'd always wanted me to.

"It's just a lot to think about," I replied briskly, wanting it to end, feeling buried by the negatives. "The good news is, if I can convince the guys that I'm ready to get back to work, for real this time, I think I have something solid to show them."

When Blake looked at me this time, there was finality in her eyes and a sense of closure in the air, which was only confirmed by the way she stated, "I'm proud of you, Judah. I think this is exactly what you need to keep you inspired when you leave here."

"Thanks," I muttered, glancing at the time on the clock above her head. "Well. Guess it's time for group therapy."

It was one session after another in this place.

"You going to tell your story today?" she asked, smirking at me.

"Nope," I answered immediately, but tacked on a grin of my own because she damn well already knew that.

"One of these days..." She trailed off, even as that knowing smile grew.

"There are only seven left." I winked, walking backwards toward the exit.

What Dr. Blake didn't know was that I already had a plan.

Thanks to the seriousness of my situation, and the fact that I was determined to make good on my promise to Phoenix, I'd taken the last six weeks more seriously than I'd taken the first. Because of that, I actually *did* find that courage I needed, and I held on to it tightly. I coveted it.

In Cliffside, I learned what it was like to be courageous for the first time in my life, but I still wasn't totally positive that it would stick around, so I charged that courage like a battery, hoping it would carry me through the next part of my journey.

Now that Cassie and Brian were both gone, I was alone all day, with plenty of time to formulate a plan of action for when

I got out next week. I needed that time desperately, given how nervous I was, how undeserving I felt, and while I still missed the drugs, while I still struggled with nightmares, I felt strong enough to stay sober upon leaving. As long as Phoenix was able to at least talk to me, to hear me out. As long as I wasn't left totally alone when all was said and done…

T minus seven days until freedom.

Now I just had to figure out what the hell I was going to say to Pharaoh tomorrow.

CHAPTER 14

PHARAOH

"JESUS FUCK," I said on a groan, squinting as I endured an absolutely *awful* sound coming from the kitchen of the girls' house. "Frankie, what the hell are you *doing*?"

"Trying to squash this fucking hangover," she called back, shouting over the blender in a determined, damn near angry tone of voice.

"Well can you stop and just suffer like the rest of us?" I yelled back, ending my question with a tortured moan.

The blades stopped spinning long enough for her to say, "Nope. I have a meeting in three hours, and I absolutely will *not* make it through if I don't fix this."

The event last night had thrown all of us for a loop, so much so that I ended up crashing on the girls' couch because I couldn't even make it home. None of us had partied since Judah went into rehab, but we'd all found ourselves drinking way too much champagne at dinner the night before. Which on the one hand was a good thing, because the alcohol had us loosening up and relaxing more than we had in quite some time, but on the other, the amount of alcohol we'd consumed in order to achieve said relaxation had backfired in a brutal way.

Silas and Frankie had gone the hardest, while Phoenix and

I had come in at a close second, but I still managed to wake up with a pounding headache and a too sensitive stomach. I couldn't imagine Phoenix was feeling any better.

"Where's P?" I asked groggily, trying to sit up as slowly as possible. "Is she awake yet?"

"Nope. Still asleep," was all Frankie said before turning on that fucking blender again, making it feel like there were a bunch of tiny men throwing knives against my temples.

"Come onnnnn," I snarled and covered my ears.

"Frankie!" Phoenix shouted less than a minute later, storming into the living room looking like she'd been hit by a truck. "Can you fucking *not* right now?"

"Do you want to survive the day?" Franks shot back as she shut off the noise. "Or would you like to spend the next twelve hours in the goddamn bathroom of Death's Door, having to explain to your clients that you can't keep it together because you decided to throw caution to the wind last night?"

"Ughhhhhh," P growled in return. "I'm never drinking again."

I actually believed her because I was thinking the same thing.

Since coming back from tour, my alcohol tolerance had completely tanked. I hadn't consumed more than a drink or two in one night since Judah's overdose, so the three bottles of champagne we'd demolished at the event reminded me exactly why two was my new limit.

"This day will be torture," I told the room.

"Fuck my life," Phoenix muttered, then announced, "I'm going to sit in the shower for an hour."

When she disappeared around the corner, I mumbled to myself, "She doesn't have an hour."

I had her schedule basically memorized and knew she needed to leave in forty-five minutes or she'd be late for her first client.

"She'll figure that out eventually," Frankie muttered just before that goddamn blender started up once again.

* * *

AFTER FRANKIE MADE Phoenix and me drink her horrible hangover concoction made of God only knows what, I felt slightly better but ended up waiting for Phoenix to finish getting ready before leaving the house. I needed a shower and wasn't willing to risk driving before I gave my body more time to recover. I had nothing to do until later in the evening, when I had plans to meet up with the manager of another up-and-coming band who was seeking me out to feature on a track. I still had to make it home without throwing up on the side of the road, though, and that required time and patience.

Once I was clean and dressed, my phone began to ring from P's nightstand, where I'd had it plugged into the charger.

Grumbling about wanting to be left alone, I made my way over to the device and picked it up, fully intending to ignore the call, until I saw that someone from Cliffside was calling.

Holy fuck. Finally.

"Hello?" I answered quickly enough to leave me wincing against the throbbing in my brain.

But then... "Hey."

Shit. I perked up, trying to forget about my headache as Judah's voice hit my ear, reminding me that I was only a handful of days away from picking my best friend up from rehab once again.

"It's me," he clarified, sounding a bit apprehensive.

"Yeah, I know." I exhaled, rubbing my forehead. "Thank fuck, man. How are you? I was nervous you weren't going to call me before the day of your discharge, and I'd be left to stress about it until then."

His responding laugh was small, nervous. "Nah, I wouldn't do that to you. Mainly because I, uh, I need your help."

A twenty-pound brick dropped into my sour stomach. "Okay...with what?"

There was only a short pause before Judah started talking a mile a minute.

"All right, it's going to sound a little crazy, but I'm just trying to figure out how to do this in the best way possible," he began, but because I'd been through this before, I immediately jumped to the worst-case scenario, thinking he was going to ask me to try and score him drugs or link him back up with one of his many dealers. My heart thundered in my chest as he continued, "I know you and I haven't had a chance to talk, and we will, I promise, but before I get out of here, I need you to try and arrange a meeting with you, me, and the guys." *Wait, what?* "Pierce and Vale, I mean. I'll deal with Ricco and Kavan after them. Then Silas, of course, but for now, I need to talk to the band."

I coughed through my shock and had no choice but to sit down on the edge of P's bed in order to steady the dizziness creeping in. I wasn't sure if my body's reaction was due to Judah's request or the fact that I was hungover, but the room was definitely spinning.

"Okaaay," I drew out, "but they're going to want to know why, J. I haven't exactly...reached out to them in a while."

There was a heavy pause, then a quiet, "You haven't?"

I shook my head, even though he couldn't see me. "No, I haven't."

Hell, I couldn't.

"Why not?" His voice was clipped but missing its usual anger.

It felt like I'd chosen a side by sticking with Judah after everything he'd done.

Pierce and Vale had seen Judah spiral before, but his mess

had never left the two of them jobless. This time around, Judah's choices had ruined their reputation and gotten them dropped from the label, and even still, I'd helped him. I'd waited for him to come back, and because of that, I felt like just as much of an outcast as Judah did.

I needed to phrase that as nicely as possible, but without sugarcoating the truth either. I wasn't about to baby-step around Judah's disaster. I would help where I could, but in the end, Judah would have to clean up the mess himself.

"Because they don't know you like I do, and I wanted to give them a chance to simmer down," I explained. "They're pissed, J, and they have a right to be. I wasn't… I just wasn't sure if we'd ever have a chance to play together again anyway, so I was waiting until I heard from you to decide if I was going to try and link back up with them."

This time, when Judah spoke, there was a new level of determination in his tone. "Okay, well, it's time."

That isn't what I expected.
Why isn't he lashing out?
Why isn't he more defensive or pissed off?

"What's going on, J?" I asked, curiosity taking over.

Silence was the only sound until he stated simply, "I wrote an album."

It was a damn good thing I was sitting down, because I was one hundred percent sure the floor fell out from underneath me as I tried to process what he'd just said. "You…*what?*"

"Don't sound so fucking surprised, asshole," he bit back, but I could hear the pride in his voice.

He…wrote…

"Judah, you wrote an entire *album*?" I had to get clarification, just to be sure I'd heard him correctly.

"Yeah, man, and I need you guys," he replied with a sigh. "I fucked up. I know I did. And I know I've spent my entire adult life fucking up, but I'm done, okay? I'm done running,

I'm done bitching, I'm done making everyone else pay for the shit this life has handed me, and I wrote a whole goddamn album about it, so can you please just make the fuckin' phone call?"

Without my permission, tears pricked my eyelids.

He wrote a fucking *album.*

He was done.

He knew he fucked up, and for once, he sounded like he meant it. Like he really was…done.

"Judah," I croaked out, unable to hide the emotion from him, feeling way too many things all at once.

"Please don't," he whispered back, sounding just as choked up as I was. "I'm so fucking tired of crying."

That statement only made it worse, causing moisture to leak down my cheek and land on my thigh before I could erase the evidence.

God, an album…

With a quick shake of my head, I sniffed, trying to pull it together, and cleared my throat, knowing that if he was serious about this, there was work to be done—work I needed and wanted to do. "All right, all right, I'll make a phone call and see what I can do, but what else do you got for me? What's the deal with discharge?"

"Hell if I know." He chuckled a little, and the sound made me feel so fucking good, a smile bloomed on my face. "All I know right now is that you can pick me up on Sunday, and I'm free to go. I don't have my schedule yet, regarding outpatient therapy appointments, but I'm sure they'll give that to me over the next few days."

"Cool, man." I nodded, even though he couldn't see me. "Okay, well, I'll call the guys and see if they'd be willing to meet up when you get out. How soon after you get home do you want me to make this meeting happen?"

"As soon as possible, please," he stated like he was conducting a business call. "Oh, and one more thing…"

"Sure, what's up?"

"Don't tell Phoenix."

Everything stopped, my heart included.

I glared at the wall in front of me as if it were Judah I was looking at. "W-what do you mean, don't tell Phoenix?"

"I don't want her knowing about the album."

He was being cryptic again, but this time, the topic terrified me. "Okay, I guess, but she knows when you're coming home, dude. Aren't you going to see her?"

"Not until I'm done with the things I need to do."

Is he joking?

"What things?"

"I'll explain when I see you on Sunday," was all he said in response.

"Hold on, hold on, no," I exclaimed as I stood from the bed, ignoring the intense rolling of my stomach, hoping he was just trying to save himself from a rejection that wouldn't come. "You are getting out of *rehab* after three *months*, Judah. This is Phoenix we're talking about. She's expecting me to give her updates, bro, and she's going to be expecting to *see* you. What am I supposed to tell her?"

He didn't even hesitate. "That I'll reach out when I'm ready."

What in the mother of all fuck?

Anger blew through my veins, but I held it in, trying to remind myself that Judah was a recovering addict and if he wanted more time away from Phoenix, there had to be a reason for it.

Right?

"Fine," I said apprehensively, rubbing my forehead to try and soothe the headache that had now come back to bite me. "I don't get it, but I'll do what I can."

"Thank you," he stated firmly, ignoring my very obvious confusion. "All right, so I'll see you Sunday. I'm sure my counselor will call you with a time to pick me up."

"Yeah, okay," I muttered, distracted by the questions in my head.

"And please," Judah threw in, "make sure the guys agree to come."

"I'll do what I can," I reassured again, feeling fucking suspicious.

Then the phone went dead and I was alone, left to replay the conversation over and over again, wondering why the hell Judah wouldn't want to see Phoenix as soon as fucking possible.

This was his girl we were talking about. Hell, *my* girl.

Why the hell was he asking me to keep this secret? Not only that, but he was asking me to basically ignore the fact that he would be getting out of rehab, yet had no interest in seeing her...

Instead, all he wanted was a meeting with the band.

Which wasn't a bad thing, not by any stretch of the imagination, given that Judah's career was the only way he could make money, but aside from his drug habit, Phoenix was always more important than anything to him. I knew that, Phoenix knew that, and I couldn't understand what the hell had changed, especially since his letter had said he was coming back for her.

But that was six weeks ago.

My body went cold as Phoenix's fears popped up in my mind.

She'd confessed multiple times that she wondered if Judah would want her when he got out, and she'd gone as far as to wonder if he'd even be the same guy she fell in love with. While she knew Judah's sobriety would have to change certain aspects of his personality, she was more concerned about him not acting the same toward *her*.

Despite all the promises I'd made during those conversations, despite the assurances I'd given her…it seemed like her fears might have been valid.

And I had no fucking idea what to do with it.

CHAPTER 15
Phoenix

AFTER THE DISASTROUS event we'd all suffered hangovers from, Frankie and I stayed low-key for the next week. We spent our time hanging out with Kavan and Ricco, since Frankie was attempting to gain some space from Silas and Pharaoh had been...avoiding me.

Now, it was Saturday, the day before Judah was scheduled to be released from Cliffside, and I was nearing the end of my day at the shop, working on finishing Frankie's latest ink. My best friend had requested two moths with floral wings, one above each of her knee caps. The design had turned out sick, and I was stoked to see the final product, not to mention how grateful I was for the distraction she provided.

Until, of course, the questions started.

"So what's the plan for tomorrow?" Frankie asked while scrolling through her phone, completely unbothered by the pain thanks to a new brand of numbing crème that Kenji had ordered for us to try out.

Immediately, my anxiety peaked.

"Oh shit," Kenji called out from behind the counter, where he was drawing on his iPad. "Judah gets out tomorrow, doesn't he?"

"Yup," Frankie responded, popping the P for emphasis,

then I felt her eyes hit the top of my head. "But our girl here hasn't given me an update on what happens when he gets out."

My emotions were all knotted up, but I tried to hide my struggle as I answered Frankie's question as neutrally as I could. "I'm not sure what happens."

"Sorry?" Frankie's voice was high-pitched. "What do you mean you're not sure?"

After shrugging as casually as I could, I turned around to dip my needle in the black ink, even though I didn't need to top it off yet. "I just don't. Pharaoh hasn't told me anything."

Correction, Pharaoh hadn't even *talked* to me in the last three days, and before that, our conversations had been short as hell. Honestly, it had me freaking the fuck out, but I also didn't want to come across as desperate or needy, so I'd kept my confusion to myself and waited restlessly for him to come to me.

"Didn't you see him for your monthly meeting with Carmine yesterday?" Kenji asked, knowing my schedule.

"No," I responded as calmly as I could. "He didn't show up."

"What the fuck? Why didn't you tell me?" Frankie asked, calling me out. "I wondered why he didn't come for dinner, but I just assumed he had shit to do to get ready for Judah."

Yeah, that's what I'd thought too, but I had no way of being sure since he didn't return my call last night.

All I could think to reply was, "I didn't think about it. I had shit to do."

She's gonna kill me.

"You didn't *think* about it?" Frankie laughed sarcastically. "Bullshit, Phoenix. You're in avoidance mode!"

Glancing up from her leg, I met her suspicious stare. "Can we not right now? I'm working. Do you want me to fuck up your tattoo?"

"You're not going to fuck it up by answering a question,

Phoenix." She clicked her tongue and crossed her arms. "What's happening right now?"

With the needle still hovering over her skin, I sighed, knowing she wasn't going to let this go. "I don't fucking know, okay? Pharaoh said he would let me know the plan when he found out what it was, and now it's Saturday night and I haven't heard from him in days. Is it weird? Yes. Do I want to overthink it? No, I don't. So just drop it."

At my fast, straight to the point response, Kenji whistled from his place behind the counter, causing me to roll my eyes and bite my tongue to refrain from lashing out.

"You could have told me, but fine," Frankie agreed, then added for good measure, "I still think it's fucking sketchy."

Yeah, I did too, but it was also Pharaoh. The guy never did anything shitty.

I couldn't imagine him keeping information from me on purpose, especially where Judah was concerned. There had to be a reason for his silence.

Maybe Judah doesn't want to see you.

The thought had been floating in my mind all week, and with every minute that ticked by, I was starting to believe it to be true.

Fact was, Judah didn't *have* to want to see me. It wasn't required, and it could be considered selfish of me to expect it, especially since I'd put up such a fight about Judah revolving his whole life around me in the first place.

If he really didn't want to talk to me, he had good reason. Once he got out, he needed to get acclimated again, needed to spend time at his own house, sleep in his own bed. He probably had a fuck ton on his mind, and if he didn't want to see me right away, that was fine.

Except if I allowed my heart to have an opinion, she'd say it *wasn't* fine.

She'd say it fucking hurt.

"I'm sure Pharaoh will call you tonight," Frankie decided a few minutes later. "There's no way he won't."

"We'll see," was all I said.

I hope so, was what I left out.

* * *

YEAH.

Pharaoh didn't call me.

In fact, he didn't even respond to my text.

It was around ten PM later that night when I caved and shot him a message, asking what time he was picking Judah up the next day, and there I was, five hours later, with no response.

The whole thing was a brutal blow to my ego and gave me very little hope that this homecoming would be a good one.

Pharaoh and I had been solid as fuck for the last three months, and up until a handful of days ago, nothing had changed. There was no way he hadn't spoken to Judah or his counselor yet, so I was left to assume that whatever he'd been told had caused him to go silent on me.

So, in order to protect myself, I knew I needed to drop all expectations and remember that Judah had a lot going on. It was selfish of me to expect Pharaoh to keep me in the loop, given Judah was going to need him quite a bit for the foreseeable future, and if either of them wanted to reach out to me tomorrow, they could.

I blamed my disappointment over the amount of time I spent thinking about what Judah had written me in that letter, and I had to constantly remind myself that Judah wrote to me at the halfway point in his journey. His plan might have changed, his feelings could have changed, and even if they didn't, Judah was allowed to do this in whatever way he wanted to, and I needed to calm down.

Judah had said he was coming back to me, to Pharaoh, to the people he'd left behind, and in order to keep my head on straight, I needed to hold on to that.

I'd gone this long without speaking to him.

I could wait a little longer.

I just hoped I wasn't waiting for nothing.

CHAPTER 16

JUDAH

WAKING up on my last day of rehab was surprisingly bittersweet. The room I'd occupied had become a sanctuary of sorts, and for the rest of my life, I'd remember it as the place I wrote my third album.

That thought alone was fucking wild, but as I walked out of my last meditation session that morning, I'd smiled to myself, because hell, I'd done it.

I survived rehab and did it for real this time. To top it all off, I finished an entire album, and I'd read through it so many times, I was pretty goddamn positive that the lyrics were as good as they were going to get without the fine-tuning of the rest of the band.

There was a lot of work to do in pretty much all areas of my life, but I was excited to get back into the swing of things and figure out how we were going to relaunch ourselves, how I was going to reintroduce myself as TheColt.

It was intimidating, especially since no one had even agreed to work with me yet, but after pumping myself up for the last week, I was determined to do whatever I had to in order to regain their trust.

This album was being released one way or another, no matter how long it took or who helped me produce it.

"You ready for your last group therapy session?" Dr. Blake asked as we sat in her office after our final inpatient session.

"Yes." I smirked at her once again, knowing full well she had figured out my plan over the last week.

She nodded a chin in my direction. "You're cheeky, you know that?"

My smile grew bigger as I stated, "It's an essential part of my charm."

I'd decided to continue seeing Dr. Blake after being discharged, and together, we came up with a schedule that included a couple of phone calls during the week and one in person therapy session, while we searched for an addiction sponsor. I could either choose someone who was once an addict and had stayed sober, or I could put the job in the hands of someone I trusted to keep me on the straight and narrow. Given I hated strangers and wasn't keen on the idea of some random asshole calling me all the time, I was leaning more toward the idea of my sponsor being someone I already knew. However, the only people I trusted that much were Pharaoh and Phoenix.

I didn't want to interrupt Pharaoh's life like that, given how much he'd already done for me, but Phoenix had once stated that she was willing to sponsor me. She'd mentioned it during a fight of course, and I'd told Blake that, so neither of us were confident that the offer still stood. We made a deal and planned to search for another sponsor until I was ready to ask Phoenix if she was still willing to assume the role.

Once that was settled and I was officially sponsored, I would then attend one in person session with Dr. Blake, as well as one phone call per week, and I'd have the option of attending a group session if I'd like to. Both Blake and I already knew I would most likely skip the group therapy thing.

Groups weren't my thing.

"Get to it then," she said, waving me off. "I'll see you after you're done so I can say goodbye."

I gave her a casual salute before standing, feeling more emotional than I'd ever admit, and made my way out of her office.

Once I hit the hallway, I slowed my steps, taking my time as I headed toward the room where everyone sat in a circle and spoke about their individual struggles, knowing this would be the last chance I'd have to walk the halls of Cliffside in peace.

Glancing around, I found myself suspended in gratitude for the facility Pharaoh had chosen for me this time around. In some ways, Cliffside had been a house of horrors, but now that I was about to leave, it felt like I was strolling down memory lane with a whole new perspective, and the blessings were visible in every corner.

I'd been sober for three months, and for the first time in my life, I had no plans to throw all my progress in the trash the second I got out.

Instead, this time, I planned to take advantage of the latest lifeline I'd been thrown, knowing it was most likely my last. Meditation still only worked half the time, I would be leaving with three different medications I was required to take daily, and I had a mental health diagnosis I still couldn't stand, but I held onto hope that eventually, at some point, I would come to terms with the way my life had shaken out.

I hoped that in another three months, I'd find myself surrounded by the people I loved, knowing they forgave me, even though a part of me felt like I didn't deserve it. I hoped I would be able to prove to those very same people that I was a risk worth taking and that this time, I would be able to make good on the promises I planned to make.

Those were the things I thought about until I sat down in the group therapy circle twenty minutes later. It seemed that everyone was already there, even Tina, who was busy chatting with the older man that was seated to her left.

I kept my head up this time, rather than staring at the floor, and allowed myself to study the group of people around me without coming off as creepy. I found myself recognizing the different stages of the recovery journey written all over our group. It was obvious who had just arrived verses those that had become accustomed to the rehabilitation setting. Previously, I hadn't wanted to compare myself to anyone else, but if I'd paid attention, I would've seen that no one gave a shit about the people around them.

It wasn't just me that stared at my hands. Other did too. Some people stared blankly ahead, appearing lost in their own heads, sporting deep bags under their eyes, showcasing the intense exhaustion of the first few weeks. Others were very obviously nervous, knowing that soon, they'd have to speak up in front of the group and tell their story.

A couple of people held a certain level of comfortability in their posture, but I assumed they'd already spoken about their addictions and were long past the embarrassing first time jitters.

"Hello, everyone." Tina's soft, bright voice lit up the group, interrupting my perusal. "How are we today?"

A lackluster response of answers floated between the group, but I remained silent, too busy watching everyone else as Tina explained to the two newer members what to expect from today's session.

I didn't see the woman who'd reminded me of my mother back when I first got here, which led me to believe she'd been released back into the real world.

Hopefully, she was still sober.

There was a foreign kind of optimism swimming in my veins, along with empathy for the people in the room that were brand new, and while it was strange to feel like I'd grown past most of the people in attendance, I couldn't deny that it felt good.

Felt right.

I'm almost done.

"Who would like to go first today?" Tina asked, addressing the group.

Here goes nothing.

"I would," I announced confidently with a small raise of my left hand.

If the situation weren't so serious, I would have laughed my ass off.

Tina was fucking *shocked.*

I couldn't blame her, given how many times I'd turned her down over the last ninety days.

"Ar-are you sure, Judah?" she asked with a slight stumble of her words.

She'd never asked another patient if they were sure.

I couldn't help the small smile that formed on my lips as I adjusted in my seat. "Yes, ma'am, I'm sure."

I held her brown eyes as she sat back in her chair and nodded, still obviously stunned by my willingness to open up. "Then by all means, go right ahead," she stated, her voice full of subtle curiosity and the slightest hint of pride.

A handful of heads turned my way, forcing me to take a deep, cleansing breath, but for the first time, I wasn't nervous. I wasn't ashamed.

I still felt that harrowing guilt, but it wasn't an insurmountable feeling.

It was quiet, almost supportive, providing a rare form of determination that motivated me to do better, *be* better.

"My name is Judah Colt," I started, looking around at the people watching me, meeting those who were willing eye to eye, "and three months ago, I tried to kill myself."

No one in the circle was shocked, since plenty of other

stories started just like mine, but once again, I found myself feeling grateful that Cliffside didn't teach the normal twelve steps or encourage you to announce to the room that you're an addict, because…duh. Instead, they let you talk freely and tell your story however you wanted to.

So I did just that.

"I grew up in a very toxic, very abusive household, run by two very broken people," I admitted, recalling all of the things I'd talked about with Dr. Blake. "I still believe they shouldn't have had a child in the first place, but they did, and because of it…they made my life hell. I was constantly in the way, forever told to shut up or else. My parents hated me in every sense of the word, and even when I hadn't said anything at all, even when I hid in my room and tried to never come out, they found an excuse to beat me for my presence in their lives, no matter how insignificant."

The memories surged again, and while they stung, while they threatened to wipe me out completely, I didn't let them. Instead, I swallowed my fear and reminded myself that I was *here* now, and not *there*. I had made something of myself, even if I'd soiled it all with the help of my addiction.

"My mother was physically abused by her father for the entirety of her adolescent life, and in turn, developed some form of Stockholm syndrome, mixed with a little bit of battered woman syndrome. So in turn, and because it was all she knew, she married a man just like her father. Rather than rejecting the pain of the abuse, she craved it, thought it was normal. She believed she deserved it."

Dr. Blake had helped me walk through my mother's past by piecing together my memories, along with the stories I'd overheard as a child. I'd had to recall things I'd heard about my grandmother and her relationship with my grandfather, who had died in a car accident when my mother turned nineteen. My grandmother never left her abuser willingly, but had been miraculously set free when he died behind the wheel.

Except at that point, my mother was too far gone to be saved.

At nineteen, she jumped into prostitution, which explained why my grandmother had frequently called her a whore during my childhood, forever putting my mother down for her choices. Somewhere along the way, my mother had found my father.

Who was an exact replica of *her* father.

"As a child, I never really knew what a mother's job was—mainly because mine was so fucking bad at it—but deep down, I knew I wanted her to love me, to protect me, and give me a healthy home life. She was never capable of that because she, herself, had never experienced it. I was as much of a victim as she was, except I was too young to understand it at the time." I could still feel the texture of my father's palms against my skin, the way his fingers had felt when he wrapped them around my arm, my ankles, my throat. I could hear my mother screaming in the background as my body hit the wall of our trailer. "My father was an alcoholic, which was most likely how the addictive gene was passed down to me, but when I was seven, by a twist of fate, he also got into a car accident. Rather than death greeting him, he was left with a serious number of broken bones that would leave him with chronic pain. The doctors gave him painkillers, and due to the severity of his injuries, it was an ongoing prescription. My mother almost immediately got ahold of them, and after five years of abusing my father's pills, she left us entirely."

This was normally the part where I lost control, wanting to shut down and push away the memories, but thanks to Dr. Blake's patience, I'd walked this path many times, trying to pick up on stray details that would help me understand what had happened to my mother.

"I was thirteen at the time," I continued, leaning forward to place my elbows on my knees. "My father was a drinker, so he was good with the mixture of Percocet and beer, but my mother? She was lost. As an adult, I'm left to assume she left because she wanted more than what those pills could offer, so she went searching for more. But as a teenager? I couldn't understand why she'd leave me behind like that, I didn't understand the twisted art of addiction. Even though I knew she never really loved me in the first place, she was still my mother. One minute, she was there, and the next, she was gone and I was stuck in that stupid motherfucking trailer with an absolute monster."

Anger surged, causing my ears to pop and ring, but I took a deep breath and closed my eyes to try and bring myself back to the center.

This time, I spoke to the floor. "My father turned all of his anger toward me, and the beatings became so frequent, I would sleep with a bat. By fourteen years old, I started to fight back, even though I was young and weak and I knew it would only make him angrier. I didn't care, because it was all I could do and I was sick of feeling so helpless. As I got older, I got more desperate to make the pain go away, given how many fights we'd gotten into on a weekly basis. I was known as trailer trash in school, so showing up with black eyes and busted fists was normal. No one thought to ask me if I was okay, and to this day, I wonder why. I wonder how many other kids are out there suffering at the hands of their abusers while no one questions the bruises on their skin."

It was something I'd talked to Blake about frequently.

When I was in elementary school, my father seemed to know where to hit and I knew how to hide the evidence, but really, it wasn't uncommon for young boys to have bruises on their legs or arms. Boys played hard, right?

Well I didn't. Never wanted to. I struggled to even open

my eyes every morning, much less have the energy to roll around in the dirt after school or play sports for fun. So how come no one noticed? Why did my father's abuse turn me into stereotypical trailer trash? How was that fair? What would my life had been like if someone had called child protective services and gotten me out of there?

It was a question I asked myself often.

Opening my eyes, I blinked toward the floor and then sat back and extended my legs out before me but kept my head down and focused on my hands folded in my lap.

"But anyway…after a few years of enduring the endless shit with my dad, it all became too much and I was faced with a choice. I remember looking in the mirror, at seventeen years old, and asking myself if I could survive one more year living at home without killing the man I called 'Dad.'"

This was where that forgiveness came into play, where Dr. Blake had coaxed me into seeing the truth behind how my addiction started and how I ended up where I did.

One disastrous repercussion after another.

"I knew the answer was no. I knew I was angry enough to take him out right then and there, but I was also stunted emotionally. One side of me wanted to commit murder and run away, but the other side of me didn't want to lose another parent. I could have turned him in, I could have called child protective services, but despite how angry I was and how much I hated him, I also didn't want to lose him."

That was the most fucked-up part of my story, the part I rejected the most.

I still loved my parents, even though they never, ever showed me love. I held onto the desperate hope that one day my mom would come back or my father would treat me right. I was more like my mother than I wanted to admit.

"So instead of doing any of those things, I chose to numb the pain entirely," I admitted to the room. "I picked up my father's pills, just like my mother had done all those years ago, and that was the start of my addiction."

It was that simple. A choice between losing my father to jail, killing him myself, or letting him live and enduring the pain until it was time for me to graduate.

"It's been eleven years since that initial choice," I stated, lifting my head to glance around the room. More people were watching than before, and one woman was crying, staring at me like she couldn't believe I was real.

I didn't know why, of course, but I kept going, because maybe she had a similar story. Maybe I was helping her.

"Up until three months ago—when I'd hit a point in my life where I couldn't run anymore—I spent every moment trying to forget my childhood. With the help of drugs and alcohol, I thought I could bury my past while it was still alive and live a normal life. I thought I could skate past my nightmares, my questions, my insecurities, and this isn't my first time in rehab, but it is my first time telling the truth. Because of my desperate need to make it all go away, I clung to my pink backpack full of pills and ruined every one my friendships, lost the love of my life, slaughtered my career, earned myself an assault charge, and when I could no longer see any other way out, I attempted to take my own life."

I couldn't believe I was telling this story with a straight face, couldn't believe that I was opening up in this way, this loudly, this honestly, but it felt good. It felt liberating.

Because fucking hell, Dr. Blake was right.

I'd gotten answers.

"But the universe had other plans for me that night," I told the room. "My best friend found me on the floor of my bedroom and got me the help I needed before it was too late. But, uh...there were two other casualties that night."

And here was the part of my story I didn't think I'd ever get over.

The survivor's guilt. The responsibility I'd taken on. The nightmares.

It was…excruciating.

I coughed a little, finally getting hit with the emotion I'd been able to avoid this entire time. "I'd been on a-a bender for three days, along with two other women. We were all fucked up, but it wasn't until I woke up in the hospital that I found out they had overdosed and passed away the night before I did."

An audible sob rang throughout the room, causing me to wince as guilt shot me in the chest.

I sniffed and ran a hand under my nose to wipe the moisture gathered there. "Today is my last day at Cliffside," I admitted. "I'm about to go home to a whole list of unknowns, but I am sober now, and I'm left to live with knowing those women never got the chance to feel what I feel today. It's a wound I'm not sure I'll ever be able to close, because no matter how I look at it, I still feel responsible, I feel at fault, I feel confused about why I was saved and they weren't, but I am here, and so are all of you."

I didn't know what I was saying anymore, but the words were tumbling from my mouth all on their own.

"You're alive, you're in a rehab facility surrounded by people that can help you, and it's embarrassing and terrifying and you may be thinking there's no way you have the strength to stay sober, but let me tell you…I am no better than any of you. In fact, the man I was when I walked in here would tell you that I deserved to die that night for all the shitty things I've done. He had absolutely no hope, but I know a little better now. I've come to terms with the fact that I've made more mistakes than I can count. I know I've royally fucked up my life and it's going to take some serious work to rebuild, but I can see the light now. I see the truth—I know that my childhood didn't set me up for success. I know that I was a wounded, broken child when I made that initial choice to choose drugs over losing another parent, and while it ended up biting me in the ass and I ended up leaving my father behind the first chance I got anyways…at least it's over. I got out, and I know that if I try hard enough, I can live a happy, sober life going forward. I hope all of you can get to the same place."

I wasn't perfect, I wasn't completely healed, and I wasn't brand fucking new.

I was still *me*—damaged, broken, abandoned, and addicted—but for the first time in my life, when clapping roared to life around me, I felt deserving of the recognition. I felt like I'd done something worthy of congratulating.

I chose myself. I chose to fight. I chose sobriety.

And I'd continue to do so.

One day at a time.

PART TWO

CHAPTER 17

PHARAOH

SITTING in the parking lot of Cliffside, I reread Phoenix's text message from the night before for the hundredth time.

I still hadn't responded. Didn't know what to say.

When I talked to Judah again on Friday night, he'd insisted I keep Phoenix out of this part of the process. He'd also refused to tell me why, saying instead that he would handle it himself when he was ready to talk to her, but fucking hell, I was torn.

Judah didn't know the full extent of my relationship with Phoenix. He assumed we were tight, but he had no idea just how close we were. Not mention the fact that he had no clue we'd slept together once upon a time because he'd driven us to near insanity.

I was genuinely struggling to keep this from her.

I felt like shit, knowing that I'd completely abandoned her at a time like this. She was probably spinning out. I knew she would fear the worst, but I didn't know what the fuck to tell her either. I didn't want to hurt her by saying Judah didn't want to talk to her, yet I knew I had to tell her *something*.

However, despite my anxiety over the whole thing, I'd decided to wait until Judah was officially out of Cliffside and I was with him in person, so I could talk to him one more time, just to make sure he meant what he said.

It was finally that time—Judah was getting out.

I was five minutes early, but too impatient to wait any longer to go inside, so I hopped out of G-Dog after closing out my message thread and locked the wagon behind me. It was six in the evening, but the sun had yet to start setting, and while I'd been relatively chill on the way over here, I was nervous as all fuck now.

I hadn't seen my best friend in months, and while I'd gone through this before, everything was different this time around.

"Hello," the receptionist greeted me with a wide smile as soon as I stepped into the lobby. "You here to pick up Judah Colt?"

Too worked up to smile, I simply nodded and confirmed, "I am, yes."

"Perfect, he should be—"

She was cut off by the sound of a door opening over on the far side of the room.

I held my breath as I laid eyes on my best friend for the first time in way too long. He stared right at me, seeming more aware than I'd ever seen him before. Those bright blue eyes were no longer enclosed in dark shadows and heavy blue bags, but instead, surrounded by fresh, healthy light.

Holy fuck.

Even his posture was different. No longer hunched, even as he carried his Louis Vuitton duffle bag over his shoulder, he held himself higher and appeared taller as he sauntered toward me. I couldn't find air anywhere as I scanned Judah from head to toe, checking for any signs of abuse, pain, or fear, but came up empty, aside from the intensity of my own warring feelings.

"Phar." J grinned in my direction, nodding his head just slightly in greeting.

I prayed my voice didn't shake as I responded with a watery, "Jude."

"Damn, it's been a long fuckin' time since you've called me that," he replied, chuckling a little, then moved quickly to close the distance between us. His body hit mine before he wrapped two arms around my shoulders and squeezed tightly.

Without hesitation, I returned the gesture, giving his back a hard slap, trying to choke down the emotion threatening to make itself known.

"You good?" I whispered for only him to hear.

"Yeah, man," he responded into my shoulder. "I'm good."

"Good," was all I could say, now unable to hide the tremble in my voice. "That's really good."

When we broke apart, I sniffed, turning so that I could wipe my face without looking like a little bitch in front of the receptionist. When I finished, I saw that she was smiling sweetly at the two of us, no doubt used to these kinds of reunions.

"So I'm all set?" Judah addressed the woman, clutching the strap of his bag on his shoulder.

"Yes, you are." She nodded. "Dr. Blake said you scheduled a call with her tomorrow morning, and the rest of your outpatient paperwork will be sent to your primary doctor. You have an appointment with him in a week."

I had an email from Cliffside that I still needed to read, outlining Judah's outpatient recovery plan, but I was too stressed about the whole Phoenix situation to care. I planned to go through it once I got Judah settled at his place.

"Sounds good." Judah nodded as if he already knew. "Thank you."

"Absolutely," the woman replied with a wave of her hand. "Congratulations. Call us if you need anything at all."

"Thanks," Judah responded. "Will do."

And with that, the two of us headed toward the exit. Judah

walked quickly and confidently ahead of me, but strangely, I felt like throwing up. Every step we took forward, my mind swirled, trying to piece together what felt...off.

Judah looked better, that much was for sure. His skin tone had returned to a healthy color, no longer pale and malnourished. His dark jeans and Chucks were clean and he needed a haircut pretty badly, but it wasn't the superficial shit that was grating on my anxiety. It was the energy wafting from him. He appeared to be excited to leave, and yet every warning bell in my body was going off all at once.

I couldn't put my finger on what it was, but it was something.

His energy was...foreign. New. Strange.

"There she is," Judah called out, looking at G-Dog. "Missed this old girl."

I tried to smile. "She's not old."

"She is to me," he replied and nudged my arm.

I was doing my best to act normal, but I couldn't get over the difference in how he was acting compared to the previous two times I'd picked him up from rehab. In past experiences, Judah had left the facility sullen, annoyed, and resentful. He'd hated me initially because I wasn't the one with a problem, he was. This time, Judah seemed content in his own energy. He wasn't locked in his head or trying to shut me out. In fact, he was casual.

Too casual.

I knew I was being overly critical of his behavior, especially since it had only been less than five minutes since we'd been in the same space again, but I couldn't help it.

I wasn't sure what to expect, but this definitely wasn't it.

Judah slid into the passenger seat as I opened the driver side door, and as soon as I was buckled in, he asked, "How did it go with Pierce and Vale?"

Right down to business, huh?

"They, uh, they agreed to meet tomorrow, if you were up for it..." I told him, glancing his way to check his reaction. "If not, they aren't free again until Wednesday."

"I'm good for tomorrow," he responded as he lifted his hip and reached into his back pocket to pull out his phone. "I don't want to wait."

Interesting.

"What time is the call with your therapist?" I asked, turning on the car while watching him stare at the black screen of his device from my peripheral vision.

"Eight in the morning," he replied, and this time, for the first time since he'd walked out of Cliffside, I witnessed a glimpse of the old Judah.

His tone had finally fell to a muted level, and it had something to do with the dead phone in his hand. He'd gotten lost in his head, and it wasn't until that moment that I realized why I was so confused. He'd been blocking me out, pretending like everything was fine, like he was fine, when I knew he had to have a lot going on internally.

He was trying to appear strong, and while he might have been stronger than he was three months ago, no one expected him to be a superhero after what he'd been through.

"What's up, J?" I asked gently, hoping he'd take off the mask just long enough to let me in.

To my surprise, he did.

"I don't want to turn it on," he admitted softly, as if shocked by his own reaction.

Again, this was new territory, but it was a damn good sign.

"Then don't," I answered, glancing his way. "Leave it off until you're ready."

"I have to be ready by eight a.m. tomorrow," he reminded me with a roll of his eyes.

"Right." I nodded, still carrying around the awkwardness of our situation. I was quiet for a moment before an idea hit me, one that would potentially bring us closer, offer up an opportunity for us to regain some of the friendship we'd once had. "What if we charge it when we get home and then I could turn it on for you? I'll get rid of all the bullshit notifications, then I can sift through your texts and delete the ones that aren't important, and you can start fresh."

It was something I'd thought about doing the last time he got out of rehab, but back then, Judah was so fucking eager to turn the damn thing on so he could link back up with his dealers, the opportunity never came up.

"Dude, that's going to take forever," Judah replied with a sigh and shook his head. "I don't want to make you do that just because I'm too much of a pussy to handle it myself."

There's the Judah I know.

"Don't start this shit now," I threw out, feeling more confident now that I could see through the farce he was putting on. "I'm here to help you, J. So *let* me."

He met my eyes and began to search. I felt those blue orbs going straight for my soul, where I knew he'd find my sincerity, my love for him, and the fact that even after all his bullshit, I still wasn't going anywhere. I didn't need him to put on a mask and act like everything was A-okay. I needed him to be my Judah, my best friend, my brother. He must have seen at least of glimpse of that truth, because rather than agreeing to my suggestion, he simply stated, "I'm so sorry, Pharaoh."

Holy fuck.

My heartbeat raged in my chest.

Are we doing this right now?

"I have so much to say to you, and the last thing I wanted was to do was say it in the damn car, but I still needed to get that out," he admitted with a heavy exhale before looking up toward the roof of the wagon. He stared for only a moment before meeting my gaze again. "This is the third time we've done this, but it's the first time I'm humiliated. While I have a plan, while I know what I want and I know how to get it, none of that erases the fact that I am so fucking sorry for all the shit I've put you through over the last twenty years. It goes way beyond the tour last year and what happened in the months after. Fact is, if you were anyone else, you would have left my ass in the dust a long time ago. I just need you to know that I see that and I'm fucking grateful for it."

I remembered telling Phoenix that I always felt like Judah never really had my back. I had him, but he never had me. I was forever alone in our friendship, carrying the weight of keeping both of us alive, but now, it looked like our very broken dynamic had the chance to shift and transform into something that resembled a true, equal friendship.

I wasn't quite sure what to do with it, but I could physically *feel* the sincerity in his words.

"I forgave you a long time ago, Judah," I stated honestly, thankful that the mask had come off. "Was I pissed? Yes. Do I still get bitter when I think about it? You bet your ass I do. But all I ever wanted was for you to get the help you needed, and as soon as you made the choice to do that, forgiving you was easy. It's trusting you that will take time to rebuild."

It stung to say, and I caught the wince he tried to hide, but J recovered quickly. "I know. I've only just learned to start trusting myself, so my hope is that as my own trust grows, yours will too."

Stunned by the wisdom in that statement, I blinked at him. "Dr. Blake must be a fucking knockout therapist. What the hell?"

At that, Judah laughed and shook his head. "She's a wordsmith, that's for sure, but she taught me a lot."

"It sounds like it," I replied, refocusing on putting the car in drive, getting ready to take us home. "I take it you liked her?"

"Not at first," he admitted. "But honestly? Looking back on it all, I'm pretty sure she saved my life."

That was the last thing he said as we pulled out of the Cliffside parking lot and headed back toward the Hollywood Hills.

Welcome home, Judah.

CHAPTER 18

JUDAH

FREEDOM WASN'T LIBERATING. Not this time.

No, *this* time...freedom was intimidating.

I was perched on the fine ledge of stability, knowing damn well that any little thing could push me over the edge and right into a breakdown.

The last two times I got out of rehab, I'd already known I would end up high as fuck again before the week was over, so I'd craved that first episode. I'd *wanted* someone to fuck around and kick me off the tight rope of sobriety. I'd been waiting for it.

Now, though, everything was different, and all I wanted to do was lock myself in a room and just keep writing.

As Pharaoh drove, all I could think was that turning my phone on was a risk I wasn't willing to take. Passing houses I used to party in served as horrid little reminders of my previous mistakes, then driving by venues I'd played at triggered cravings I had to choke down, and suddenly, my entire life was blanketed by sickening temptation...

And I was fucking *scared*.

I no longer felt strong enough to be outside the walls of Cliffside, and the closer we got to my house, the more haunted I felt.

The Hollywood Hills was full of fucking ghosts.

They watched me through the car windows as we passed, smiling eerily in my direction like they knew something I didn't, reminding me of all the horrors I'd face coming back into the industry. Their suffocating energy forced me to remember the pressure I was under, the mistakes I made, the times I'd driven drunk on those very same roads trying to escape my own internal hell, not giving a shit about my life or the lives of those I could have taken with one bad accident.

They got so loud, so terrifying, that out of nowhere, panic rose in my chest. "I can't go home," I blurted out.

Silence reigned for only a tick of time before Pharaoh murmured a confused, "What? What do you mean?"

I shook my head back and forth, unable to formulate a full response, only able to repeat, "I can't stay at my house."

The girls in my bed…

Fuck, my lungs were burning.

"Okay, whoa." Pharaoh pressed his foot on the break, slowing the car as he glanced left and right to find somewhere to pull over. "Hold on, J."

He drove a few more feet before throwing on his hazards and parking in front of a random, darkened home. He immediately turned to face me. "What's happening right now?"

Words tumbled from my mouth quicker than I could filter them. "I want to sell the house. I have to. I just… I-I-I c-can't—"

Fuck, I'm so weak.

"You can't go back," he finished for me and placed his hand on my shoulder while I sucked in lungfuls of air. "Hey, breathe. It's okay, man. It's all right. You can stay at my place for now."

All I could do was nod and close my eyes, trying to remember everything that Dr. Blake had said to me, everything she'd taught me.

I didn't know how much time had passed, but I fell deep into my head and tried to remind myself that I could start over, I could press the reset button and re-create my life, that the shit I'd done was over. I never had to repeat the same patterns or make the same mistakes. I wasn't fated to live brokenly for the rest of my life.

Set boundaries. Set up routines. Surround myself with light. Joy. Laughter.

Except all I could feel was this *visceral* fear of failure.

I wasn't strong, I wasn't ready, and I wasn't even close to healed.

How was I going to make it?

How was I—

"Just fight a little longer, my friend,
it's all worth it in the end.
But when you got nobody to turn to,
just hold on and I'll find you.
I'll find you, I'll find you.
Just hold on, and I'll find you…"

A song began to play through the speakers of Pharaoh's car, and the woman's voice was so fucking pure, so beautiful, that it had my eyes opening. The melody, the words, the fact that Pharaoh had chosen the song specifically…it wasn't hard to figure out that all of it was intentional.

The energy within the lyrics alone transported me to a different kind of home. One that lived in my heart, my mind, in all the empty cracks and crevices of my soul that couldn't be filled until she was standing right in front of me again.

And when I turned to look at my best friend, I saw his phone in his hand, saw the messaging app pulled up. Saw her name at the top.

He was texting.

No…

All I could do was blink at him as tears formed in my eyes,

and before I could even say anything, he confirmed my suspicion with a single nod.

He'd told Phoenix.

And the song was from her.

From there, I broke.

CHAPTER 19
Phoenix

I HAD JUST GOTTEN HOME, had only pulled into the driveway a few seconds before the text came through.

Pharaoh: He's out, he's with me, and he's not doing well. Doesn't want to turn his phone on, says he's selling the house because he can't go home. He's trying, P, but he's panicking about something. We're in the car, pulled over on the side of the road, and I don't know what to do because he said he didn't want me to tell you what was going on when I talked to him last week. It's why I haven't reached out. I still don't know why, and I'm sorry I didn't say anything sooner, but... Fuck. If anyone would be able to help right now, it's you.

Instantly, my heart flew into my throat, and I tried not to fucking gag on the pressure.
Judah's out.
He's free.
But he's still broken.
Knowing that Judah wanted me in the dark felt like a swift kick to the soul, but this was the first time I'd heard from Pharaoh in a handful of days, so I knew he really didn't have

many other options. He was going against what Judah wanted because he felt his friend was truly struggling.

I was too pussy to call, too nervous to ask any questions, so instead, I simply sent the first song that came to mind and said nothing else.

Music spoke to Judah, it spoke to both of us, and at one point, his music saved my life.

There was only one record I could think of, one song that was capable of fitting his situation while also providing a sense of hope and love that I so desperately wished I could express to him in person. I'd been listening to it all week after hearing it randomly one day while searching for new music.

"I'll Find You" by Lecrea and Tori Kelly played through the speakers of my own car as I fought tears, picturing Judah listening to it at Pharaoh's request.

After Pharaoh's text, it didn't take me long to figure out what was going on with Judah, and once I did, I could physically *feel* the weight of his pain on my shoulders.

My skyscraper was on his way home and it was almost nighttime, the sun was setting, and demons always came to haunt when the sky turned black. It was no surprise that his fears had shown up and attacked.

Two girls died in his house, in his *bed*.

His phone held contacts to every dealer he'd once used.

Sure, Judah was trying, but he was also terrified.

No matter how strong they tried to be, it had to be fucking petrifying for a recovering addict to leave a place life Cliffside, especially if they genuinely wanted to stay sober. Heading back to their old life, knowing where every tempting mistake lurked, having to relive those triggering memories... I felt for Judah in the realest of ways.

A part of me was pissed at Pharaoh for listening to Judah and keeping me in the dark, but I also knew that Judah's recovery was more important than my feelings right now.

While I didn't understand why Judah felt the need to continually push me away, while I was hurt and feeling alone, I cared more about giving Judah whatever he needed to ensure he walked on steady ground again.

Even if it meant he would walk without me.

After another ten minutes passed with no response from Pharaoh, I played the song one more time and cried, letting myself feel his presence again, now that he was home. Judah was free. He was back and I had no idea what would happen next, but I sobbed through the unknowns. I let out every fear, every worry, and when those tears ran out, I exited my car and prayed that whatever Judah was going through really would be worth it in the end.

※ ❋ ※

THE HOUSE WAS empty when I got home, and for once, I was grateful for it.

Frankie was spending the night with Silas, and the guys had Trixie at their place, so I was left to my own devices. After writing in my journal for about an hour, I took a bath and nursed a glass of wine, attempting to calm my frayed nerves.

Knowing Judah was out of rehab and able to start living again? That connection I used to feel was shining brightly again. There were no more walls between us. He could reach out whenever he wanted to, and if I were desperate and disrespectful, I could reach out to him.

I wouldn't, but the fact that I could was enough to reignite the emotional link I'd tried to bury before his overdose.

I couldn't help but drown in my own thoughts, overthinking how this would all play out, especially knowing Judah wanted basically nothing to do with me. It had gotten so bad at one point that I'd given myself a headache, which in turn pissed me off, completely ruining my plan to relax. Just when I thought I'd be going to bed with no further information, my phone began to vibrate on the narrow edge of the tub.

It was Pharaoh.

Thank god.

My heart slammed against my rib cage as I slid my thumb across the screen to activate the call and lifted it to my ear. "Hey."

Phar's sigh was thick. "Hi."

"You okay?" I murmured into the speaker, feeling my lungs constrict painfully.

"I've never seen him like this," Phar whispered, sounding like he was trying to hide the fact that he was talking to me. "He's terrified, P."

"He doesn't want to fuck it up," I assumed.

"No, this is different," Pharaoh corrected. "In his mind, he *can't* fuck it up."

"Too much pressure," I stated, shaking my head. "He's trying to do it all himself because he doesn't want to look weak."

"That's why he asked me not to call you," Pharaoh stated, reminding me of the painful truth.

It took me longer to respond, but when I did, I asked, "You think?"

"I know, P," Pharaoh confirmed. "He doesn't want you seeing him like this."

Judah's rejection stung in the worst of ways, but I almost admired his choice. He didn't want to lean on me or make it about me. He wanted to prove he could do this all on his own, prove to everyone that he was trying, but I knew better than to expect him to be okay right now. He didn't have to have it all together, he just had to hold onto his will to live. That's all I ever cared about.

I didn't believe that people who struggled were weak. In

fact, I believed the opposite. Those that fought to live were the strongest people I knew, and even in moments they feared their own ability to make it through, weak was the last word that came to mind.

"We're staying at my place," Pharaoh informed me when I failed to reply. "He's in the shower, and I'm gonna order some food so we can talk. Luckily, he has a phone call with his therapist tomorrow, and I'm hoping she'll be able to help him."

Oh, thank god.

"That's good," I stated, feeling slightly better. "He's trying adjust, and it's got to be a shock to the system after three months of steady routines and solitude. I'm not surprised that being back in here is scary for him."

"Me neither," Phar agreed. "I'm just not sure what to do. He wasn't like this the last two times."

"That's a good thing, though," I muttered. "He didn't stay sober back then."

There was a thick pause before Pharaoh said, "I really think he'll do it this time, Phoenix."

Pride swelled in my chest, even as the hope I held for a future with Judah had diminished with his rejection. "Good. That's…really fucking good, Phar."

Tears pricked the corners of my eyes, but I smiled anyway, feeling proud of my skyscraper, proud of the choices he'd made.

And just when I thought our conversation was over, Pharaoh stated, "I have to tell him we slept together."

Fuck.

My stomach hit the floor.

"Now is not the time, Phar."

"Then when?" He sighed into the phone. "The longer I wait to tell him, the worse it will be. If I wait too long, he'll think I didn't believe he was strong enough to handle it and he'll rebel in exchange."

Panic seized my lungs. "Or he'll rebel *because* you told him before he was strong enough to handle it."

"Then what do you suggest I do, Phoenix?"

Pharaoh was getting frustrated, no doubt because of the guilt. It was shitty news to give, and Judah didn't have a good track record when it came to shit like this.

"I don't know," I admitted, genuinely unsure of the right move. "It's going to suck either way, but why do you have to tell him? I can do it too, you know."

Telling Judah I'd fucked his best friend was the last thing I wanted to do, but Pharaoh had just taken on the responsibility and I was just as guilty as he was.

"Absolutely not," Pharaoh replied immediately. "For one, he's avoiding you right now, so if you were to tell him when he eventually pulls his head out of his ass and talks to you, then it would look worse on me for keeping it from him. Two, I don't want it falling back on you. You don't need that."

"We both made a choice, Pharaoh," I said, sighing.

"Yes, we did, because Judah fucked up and we were desperate for connection," Pharaoh pointed out. "I'm just going to get it over with. I'll tell him and he can talk to Dr. Blake if he has to. After that, he can talk to you whenever he wants to, and you can tell him your side of the story."

What a mess.

"I don't... I still don't think it's the right move to tell him right now," I warned again. "Look, I know you feel like shit and so do I, but I think you should wait at least a few days. Let him settle in before you tell him something like this."

"Fucking hell," Pharaoh cursed. "You're probably right."

"I know I am," I replied sadly. "Just relax with him tonight. See if he opens up. Make him feel at home. He doesn't need to feel like an outcast right now. Wait until you're one hundred percent sure it's the right time."

I wanted to be there so badly, it fucking hurt.

My nose tingled with unshed tears, and my head began to cramp again, right at my temples. My tummy felt hollow, my heart ached, but Judah had a right to do this his own way. If he didn't want me a part of it, I had to respect that.

"I doubt I'll ever be that sure, but thanks, little P," Pharaoh muttered. "I'm gonna go. I'll let you know if anything happens."

"Mm-hm," was all I could say as I bit my trembling bottom lip to keep the pain inside.

"Bye, babe."

When the phone went dead, I choked on a loud, gut-wrenching sob, and with one hand covering my mouth and the other holding my heart in my chest, I let it all out.

I cried for Judah, for myself, for Pharaoh, and those girls whose lives had ended far too soon.

I bathed in the sheer agony of every shitty choice Judah made in the past, the way he'd ripped apart our relationship and effectively shredded any moment of happiness into tiny pieces all out of spite. I relived the fistfights, the time he showed up at my door drunk and covered in blood, the way he ruined his career and lost every one of his friends. I grieved the man I used to know, shed tears for the guy I almost lost to a bottle of Percocets.

Because he was truly gone.

And then I continued to cry because the version of Judah that lived on didn't want me, not yet anyway. No matter how much I said I understood, no matter how much respect I had for his journey…I was gutted, pissed, jealous that Pharaoh got to help him and I didn't.

Pharaoh got to meet this new version of my skyscraper. He got to hold his hand and lift him up so he could stand on his own two feet again…

While I was left to wait for a call that might never come.

CHAPTER 20

JUDAH

"I THINK SELLING your house is a great idea," Dr. Blake said through the phone. "You made a lot of memories in that home, but if it's triggering to you now and you have the means to get yourself a new place, then I agree, you should do it."

"Okay." I nodded, continuing to pace the back patio of Pharaoh's small apartment, feeling slightly better about my rash decision to get rid of my home.

"So what else is going on?" Blake asked. "How are you feeling?"

Awful. Chaotic. Like I left rehab far too soon.

That's what I *wanted* to tell her, but it wasn't sure the last part was particularly true. It was only my mind that was a goddamn mess, leading me to fear the worst, telling me I wasn't ready to handle being back in LA.

When in reality, aside from my panic attack, everything else had gone smoothly.

Pharaoh did exactly as he said he would and cleared out my phone after we ate dinner last night and we watched a movie on the couch. He seemed to accept my apology, even though I hadn't even gotten it all out yet, and must have been reading my mood because he didn't push me to talk or even ask any questions. He let me settle in on my own terms, and on the surface, it felt like everything was fine, but on the inside, I was falling apart.

"It actually kind of pisses me off that I'm about to say this," I started, then sighed in annoyance. "But for some reason, you're the only one I feel comfortable talking to right now."

I expected Dr. Blake to at least find that a little bit funny, but instead, she just clicked her tongue. "You were so confident before you left yesterday. What happened?"

"The reality bus followed me home?" I questioned. "I don't know. I just got in the car and immediately started feeling the weight of my old life. It's all still here, Doc. I'm the only one that's different, but because of what I've done and all the shit I have to make up for, there's this weight on my shoulders that makes me feel like I have to *prove* that I'm different. Which adds hella fucking pressure."

"You knew that would happen," Blake pointed out. "We talked about this."

"Of course, but it's one thing to expect something and another to actually experience it."

"Well said," she responded. "But remember, you have to start small. Start with one person or one experience at a time. You said you were going to meet with your band first and foremost, right? You're hanging out with them tonight? Perfect, focus on that. Don't think about what you want to accomplish tomorrow until you feel ready."

"It's not just that, though," I admitted. "It's the fact that even my band comes with memories I'd rather just forget, and instead of experiencing that shit in my nightmares like I did at Cliffside, I'm seeing it all play out in real-time. Everyone is a trigger. Every person, place, and thing reminds me of shit I thought I'd already processed."

"Which is understandable," Blake replied soothingly, "but healing isn't linear, Judah. Just like you had to adjust to life inside Cliffside, it's now time for you to adjust to life back home. You're different now, you're sober for the first time and trying to stick with that. That means every single thing will be handled from a new perspective, and you'll need to figure out step-by-step how you want it all to play out."

Fuck my life.

"Nothing is easy," I said on a groan.

It was *that* little comment that got a laugh out of Blake, which had me rolling my eyes. "Got that right, kid, but it does get easier."

"So this anxiety is normal?" I asked, just to clarify.

"Perfectly," she confirmed. "It's even more encouraging to hear you openly talking about it. Your concern means you care, Judah. The fact that you're trying to avoid things that make you feel bad is on the one hand, healthy, but on the other, not so healthy. It all depends on how you process each feeling. Before rehab, whenever you were uncomfortable, your aim was to run from the feeling by suppressing it. That was your natural instinct, but now you're trying to find healthier ways to deal with the same feeling, and that's the most important part."

Yeah, the cravings were no joke.

Last night, I'd been up until three AM wishing I had a Xanax to take the edge off my anxiety, and it had taken everything in me not to make a phone call. The only thing that kept me from doing that very thing was scrolling through my old text thread between Phoenix and me.

I read it all again—the good and the bad.

Once again, she kept me steady without even trying, without even knowing the power she had over me.

"I just have to take it one day at a time," I reminded myself out loud, not really thinking about Blake.

But still, she said, "Exactly, and you can always call me if you get stuck. Don't go through this alone."

"I won't," I promised, knowing that I would be able to

keep that one. I didn't want to fuck this up, not even a little. "Buuuut, I kind of jumped the gun a little bit. I have the meeting with Pierce and Vale today, and then I already told Pharaoh to reach out to Kavan and Ricco and see if they could come for dinner tomorrow night."

Selfishly, I wanted to rip the Band-Aid off and get all of my apologies over with so I could figure out who I still had on my team and who I'd lost. I was sick of wondering.

"Well, what's done is done," Blake said, brushing off my concern. "The important part is making sure you're not taking on too much. How do you feel?"

"Stressed," I answered immediately.

"Too stressed to handle it?"

"No." I shook my head, even though she couldn't see me. "I think I've figured out my strategy. When I woke up this morning, I decided that my vulnerability is going to be my greatest asset when it comes to getting the truth out. Yesterday, when Pharaoh picked me up, I tried to pretend like I was fine, better than fine. I was great, I was sober! But that was bullshit, and I could tell he was immediately suspicious. My mask backfired as soon as we hit the road. With everyone else? They know me as the guy that used drugs to mask my feelings and help me numb out. I think everyone in my circle deserves to see the real me, I just have to come to terms with the fact that the real me is still struggling right now and that's okay."

There was only a small blip of silence before Dr. Blake responded in a semi-awed, but mostly loving tone, "I'm proud of you, Judah."

Every time she said it, I felt a little better.

The woman was a doctor, someone trained in the field of helping people like me, and if I could make her proud, then I was doing something right.

"Thank you," I whispered, memorizing the warmth in my veins, hoping it would help me get through the next few days.

"You're welcome." I pictured the small smile she always gave me in moments like those. "Now, you know I'm going to ask about Phoenix…"

As usual, the sound of her name dropped a pit in my stomach and ignited a sense of longing in my chest that was so intense, I had to remind myself to breathe.

"She, uh…" I cleared my throat before continuing, "She sent me a song yesterday."

"She did?" Blake sounded surprised.

"Through Pharaoh," I explained. "I guess he texted her when he noticed something was wrong with me. I'm not sure what he said, but while I was lost in my head, he started playing this song and the lyrics kind of pulled me out of panic mode. I saw her name on his phone."

We hadn't spoken about it since.

"How did you feel?" Blake asked for the second time.

I had to swallow down the emotion crawling up my throat. "Not so alone anymore."

"You want to talk to her." It wasn't a question.

"Of course I do," I whispered back.

"But?"

"She deserves better than to see me like this after everything I've put her through."

"I think you might be underestimating her feelings for you, Judah," Blake replied with a sigh.

"Even if I am, I don't want to be a burden to her, or to anyone else for that matter," I stated as clearly as I could. "When I speak to her again, I want to be in a good enough space to support her as well."

"That's a very healthy way of looking at it," Blake affirmed, but I could tell she didn't necessarily agree with how I was going about it. "I just don't believe she would view your recovery as a burden, no matter what stage you're in or how far you think you've come."

"I'm not going to wait long," I told Blake. "I don't think I could even if I wanted to."

"Good. You shouldn't. I think you're doing a lot better than you give yourself credit for, and I have a feeling that once you speak with your friends and begin the journey of mending those relationships, you'll find that you're ready to reach out to her."

"I hope so," I replied, though my response wasn't as confident as hers.

I would be a motherfucking liar if I said I wasn't desperate as all fuck to see Phoenix again, but I knew better. I was still petrified of her reaction, fearing that she wouldn't forgive me, that she wouldn't accept my apology or take me back, and I genuinely wasn't sure what would happen if that were the case. I wasn't willing to risk my sobriety by facing her rejection right away, so securing my friendships outside of her was key. It was my security blanket.

Thanks to the song she'd sent, I knew that at the very least…she still cared.

That was enough for now.

"You know you can call me whenever you want to talk, right?" Dr. Blake questioned before we ended our call. "If I don't answer right away, I'll call you back as soon as I can."

"I know," I confirmed. "Thanks, Doc."

"You're welcome, Judah. Have a good day, I'll talk to you soon."

After hanging up, I let out a sharp breath and sat down on the concrete of Pharaoh's patio before falling flat on my back and closing my eyes to avoid the sunlight.

I fucking liked Dr. Blake, even though she was a giant pain in my ass most of the time. Sill, she'd really come through for me on more than one occasion, and her wisdom was unmatched. I'd started out my journey not trusting anyone, only to find myself trusting her more than I trusted myself.

Blake was a solid rock I could lean on, and I planned to take advantage of her strength as I kept going down this road.

"Hey, you finished?" Pharaoh asked suddenly, scaring the shit out me.

"Fuck, man!" I shouted as I threw myself into a seated position again and squinted in his direction. He appeared to be freshly showered and dressed for the day. "What the hell?"

My best friend smirked down at me. "Were you sleeping?"

"No, you prick," I shot back. "I was just…chillin'."

"Uh-huh," he replied, trying and failing to hide the wide ass smile that bloomed on his face. "So, you're done with your therapist?"

"Yeah," I muttered as I ran two hands through my hair. The strands were too fucking long and starting to tangle between my fingers. "I need a fucking haircut."

"We can go in a little bit," Phar offered. "But first, can I talk to you?"

Fuck.

I hated those words.

"Uh, sure," I replied anyway, watching him let go of a deep exhale as I stood up and dusted off my jeans. Based on the heaviness suddenly blanketing the patio, I knew whatever he was going to say wouldn't make me feel good.

No matter what it is, you can handle it.

Nothing is worse than what you've done to him.

My inner voice attempted to hold me steady, but anxiety pooled low in my stomach, threatening to knock me off balance all over again as he made his way to the small table sitting under the shade. I followed, taking a seat across from him as apprehension bled through my veins.

Quickly, I tried running through topics he could bring up, thinking of all the things he could've wanted to talk about, and none of them were good.

"What's up, Phar?" I asked a few seconds later, feeling impatient as I shifted in my seat.

My best friend cleared his throat and ran a hand down his face, looking nervous as all fuck, which only served to make *me* even more nervous than I already was.

"Look," he started, "I was up all fucking night thinking about this, and there's simply not a right time to tell you so I need to just fucking get it out."

The whole sentence was rushed, and instantly, my face began to heat up.

"Okaaaay," I said, drawing the word out. Still, he just kind of stared at me, clearly overthinking whatever it was he wanted to fucking say, but he was taking way too long. "Dude, you're scaring me. Just fuckin' say it."

He blinked once, clicked his tongue, then blurted out, "Phoenix and I slept together."

One second passed, then two, pretty sure there was a third. Then…

A bullet pierced my heart.

"I'm sorry?" I choked out as all the blood left my face.

My body went cold. My fingers felt numb.

"It was, uh, the day you destroyed her house," he went on to explain. "After our fight in the backyard."

Phoenix and I slept together.

I couldn't seem to formulate a response. Wasn't even sure my brain was working.

Did I hear him right?

"We were…lost, J. We didn't know what to do anymore, didn't know how to cope with what you were doing, how you were acting, and we needed to just shut off the noise for a while."

Phoenix and I slept together.

Like an idiot, I tried to picture it—the two of them together.

I tried to imagine them touching, kissing.

Who made the first move?

Who undressed whom?

"Judah," Pharaoh whispered, trying to regain my attention.

I bet he fucked her good. He probably tried to fuck me right out of her system.

"Judah." My name was louder this time.

Did she like it?

Did she regret it?

"J." A hand touched my forearm.

"Hmm?" I responded this time, meeting his eyes but not really seeing anything.

"Say something," Pharaoh pleaded gently.

I didn't.

I wasn't sure *what* the hell to say. Wasn't even sure what to think.

Phoenix and I slept together.

Was she in love with him?

I mean, I knew he was in love with her. Anyone could tell. I just never thought it would be a problem, never imagined the two of them together, but now...

I felt nothing.

For the first time, without the help of drugs, I felt nothing.

And I couldn't help but think that it had everything to do with getting what I wanted.

Getting something I knew I deserved.

I hurt them, so they hurt me in return.

It was karma, it was consequence, it was *deserved*.

"Okay..." I muttered blankly. "Thanks for telling me."

"Thanks for..." Pharaoh trailed off, sounding confused, but then damn near begged, "Judah, talk to me."

"There's nothing to talk about." I replied evenly, calmly, feeling completely detached.

"Judah, there's a ton to talk about... You don't have any

questions? You have to have questions. I can give you answers."

He wanted to make me feel better, wanted to justify the choice he made to sleep with my girlfriend, but…

"No. I don't have any questions."

Not for him, at least.

As I said, I already knew how he felt about my little bird. I saw it long before I'd fucked everything up, so the more I thought about it, the less and less of a shock his confession was.

Honestly, if I were him and he were dumb enough to let a girl like Phoenix go, I would have fucked her too. What did shock me was the fact that I felt…relieved.

Broken too, of course.

In fact, I kind of wanted to tear my own skin off and burn myself alive, but there was a welcomed relief that came with the news.

"I'm going to head out for a bit," I stated, still sounding like a robot. "Need to get my hair cut. Can I take G-Dog? I promise to get a new car tomorrow."

My old ones were getting sold too. I'd decided that last night.

"Of course," Phar replied in a low, guilty voice. "But, Judah—"

"I'm not mad at you," I interrupted, picking up on how shitty he felt over the whole thing. "I'm not mad at either of you."

How could I be after everything I'd done?

I deserved to live with knowing my girl fucked my best friend. I deserved to live with those images rotting my brain down to mush, haunting me until I couldn't take it anymore. I deserved knowing that Pharaoh took it upon himself to make her feel better, make her feel alive, make her feel something other than the pure fucking agony I'd fed her for months on end. I deserved to taste the guilt, the regret, the godawful jealousy that now seeped through my bone marrow like a disease.

I deserved all of it.

With that, and before my best friend could say another word, I walked back into the house, grabbed the keys, my wallet, and my phone off the counter, and left his apartment.

I had a lot to think about.

CHAPTER 21

PHARAOH

I DIDN'T SEE Judah again until later that night, when he got back from spending hours alone, but I wasn't sure what would happen next. Pierce and Vale had shown up as requested, and I genuinely feared Judah's mental state after telling him about Phoenix and me, but my anxiety came to a crashing halt as I took in his appearance.

Judah strolled into the living room sporting a fresh fade, looking different than I'd ever seen him before. Both sides of his head were now shaved closely to the skin, and while his blond hair remained messy on top, it was styled in a way that made it look like he had a thick, modernized mohawk. The cut actually looked natural and somehow matured his overall appearance compared to the organized chaos of his original look, but it was still a shock at first glance.

"Hey, guys." Judah greeted the room with a humbled sort of confidence I wasn't expecting, given how our conversation had gone earlier. I thought he'd be in a mood, lost in his mind, or worse...high. "Sorry I'm the last to show up. Traffic was fucking awful."

I couldn't see any signs of drug abuse or even alcohol. In fact, Judah seemed more put together now than he had been before I'd told him anything at all.

Pierce and Vale were sitting on the couch across from me, both guys wearing identical, hesitant expressions, like they didn't want to make any sudden movements that might risk setting Judah off.

I, on the other hand, knew better.

The guy sitting down on the chair to my left was no longer the same one we knew before his overdose. This Judah had gained a certain amount of control, a new level of emotional intelligence, even if the underlying panic disorder hadn't gone away.

His newfound strength was a bit unnerving because it seemed to put a wall between the two of us. I was so used to Judah either leaning on me, riling me up, or outright pushing me away with that rebellious, toxic energy, whereas now, it seemed that he simply just…didn't need me. He had taken his growth seriously and wanted to do it, wanted to stand on his own.

I still wasn't sure if he was capable of that or not, and it had me more stressed out than I'd ever tell him.

"What's up, man?" Vale asked Judah in a voice shook a little before he cleared his throat. "You, uh, you look…good."

Judah scoffed a little, but it was sad before he glanced down at his hands. "I don't feel so *good* right now, but thank you. I'm clean, and that's what matters."

My chest squeezed.

I wanted to save him from the intensity of their judgements. Even I could feel the invisible lasers both Pierce and Vale beamed in Judah's direction, searching for any sign of bullshit, and while I knew Judah definitely deserved their distrust, I couldn't squash the protective nature I still carried around.

"Pharaoh said you wanted to talk to us," Pierce stated, sounding more defensive than Vale, obviously wanting to skip the pleasantries and get to the crux of what Judah had brought us all there to talk about.

"I did. Well, I-I do. I just—" Judah stumbled awkwardly over his words before shaking his head. "Fuck it, I'm sorry. This is…awful."

It was. The whole thing was giving me secondhand embarrassment.

The energy in the room was heavy with suspicion, and so much weighed on this moment that it made even *me* feel sick. I knew what Judah wanted to say, so I hoped to God he was able to pull this off. All of us needed it.

"All right, listen," Judah started again after taking a deep breath, then made a point to meet each of our eyes, one by one, before saying, "I'm sorry."

No one moved.

I wasn't even sure anyone was breathing.

But Judah plowed through the silence with a thick dose of truth. "When I started rapping, I was just a fucked-up kid on drugs, trying to find a way to say what I needed to say without directly saying it. It was by fucking chance that Hendrix found our video online and offered Pharaoh and me a deal."

I remembered that day clearly. Judah had started taking his father's pills, and thanks to the effect they had on him, he'd gained more confidence, found his voice. I'd been drumming in the school's band for years, so I already knew the basics and had a passion for it.

"As soon as we agreed to pack up and leave, Hendrix wasted no time introducing us to you guys, and you've known me as this crazy motherfucker with a lot of baggage and a pill problem for nearly eleven years now."

The guys had been a godsend—young like us, ripe and ready to take on the industry. In the beginning, they didn't care about Judah's issues because it wasn't apparent just how much of a problem they'd become as time went on.

But everyone was on drugs in Hollywood, and everyone had a fucking drinking problem. It was how we all survived, so really, Judah fit right in.

Now, after all this time, we had nothing left and it was Judah's fault. It wasn't something that could be easily forgiven or even understood. He'd taken away careers and squashed a decade of hard work.

"I can admit now that I was a mess," Judah confessed as he briefly looked down at his hands before glancing up again. This time, there was that newfound sincerity in his eyes. It shone brightly, and I had no doubt that the guys would notice. You couldn't miss it. "Over the past year, my drug problem, along with my unhealed internal bullshit, came before the good of this band, the good of our career. That was because our career was one of the problems I was facing. My insecurities have been eating me alive, day in and day out, since I signed our first contract, and I've spent all these years hoping drugs would somehow fix them. I know now that wasn't ever possible because those insecurities stemmed from my childhood and the events that took place long before you guys came into the picture, but I was too young, too confused, and then eventually too high to understand how to *actually* fix them."

Pierce glanced at Vale, but Vale was watching Judah with rapt attention, taking in every word.

"I was too naïve to know any better, so I took on the role of TheColt. It was the worst decision I could have made because I didn't even knew who the real me was, much less a stage name that came with an image I could barely control. I got lost in the industry, and as the years went on, that identity became a noose around my neck because I felt like I could never live up to the pedestal I'd been willingly placed on." Judah ran a hand down his face and sniffed. "I was a fraud."

I winced, despite knowing he was telling the truth.

All of the things Judah said, I'd already known for so long, it was almost shocking to hear him say it out loud. I never thought he'd get to this point, this level of self-awareness.

I'd hoped for it, of course, but never expected to be sitting in a room like this, watching him face himself and admit to our friends just how bad it truly was.

"But that brings us to today," Judah continued, "after I destroyed everything we worked for, without thinking about how my decisions and my actions would affect you guys."

Pierce struggled a little to meet his stare, but when he did, I was able to pinpoint the exact moment he'd decided Judah's apology was worth listening to.

"I'm sorry for all of it.," J stated again. "I left you guys in the dust because I was selfish, I was broken, and you didn't deserve it. None of it was your fault or your problem. I wasn't ready to be the face of a band like ours, yet I'd taken the opportunity to follow Hendrix to LA because I wanted to get out of the trailer park we'd grown up in and I wasn't about to turn down the chance to escape. I didn't even hesitate. I threw myself into the thick of it, only to run it straight into the ground after trying to build on shaky ground for so long."

"And now?" Vale asked, cutting off Judah's story, most likely wondering if there was more. If there was a reason Judah wanted to meet so soon after getting out of rehab.

Anticipation grew in my veins, because I'd done my research and found out that neither Pierce nor Vale had begun working with anyone else. They had no real plans to start something new anytime soon, and instead, both of them taken the last three months off to enjoy themselves after all the shit that went down with Judah.

This was the perfect opportunity to pitch Judah's plan, I just hoped the guys would be willing to take another chance on him.

"Now…I have something I'd like to offer you." *Hell, why am I nervous?* "In rehab, I spent a lot of time talking to my therapist about my career, and we worked to figure out what I *actually* wanted to do versus what I thought I *should* do. I ended up realizing that I never actually wanted the label or the contract. I wanted to get out of where I was when Hendrix found me, so I took the opportunity, but I never stayed up at night thinking about going on huge tours and achieving international fame. I never dreamed of owning a house in the Hills or a driving a Maserati around the Boulevard. Sure, they were perks that came with the job and I was high, so I was down as hell, but now? I'm sober, and with my sobriety came the willingness to tap into my own heart and actually *ask* myself what would make me happy. When I did that, I figured out that what I wanted most was to make music with the people I loved and be able to play that music for people that could relate to what we're saying. It was that simple."

Fuck. Even I wasn't prepared for the confidence Judah was gaining as he talked. While he was obviously unsure of what our response would be, it was clear—he didn't care. He wanted us to join him, but he would find what he was looking for either way.

Then he dropped the bomb.

"So…I wrote an album."

There was only silence for a solid three seconds before Pierce bellowed, "You *what?*"

Judah smirked. "I wrote an album," he stated again. "Fifteen tracks."

"Bro…" Vale whispered, bending forward to put his elbows on his knees and his hand over his mouth.

"It's finished, it has a title," Judah informed the room, appearing proud of himself. "And I know we have no label, no manager, and you guys don't trust me, but I had Pharaoh reach out to you right away because I want you two on this with me. In the end, it's up to you, but I'm letting you know up front that we have a very real, very raw set of songs that we can fix up and record. I told a real story here, I'm speaking honest-to-God truths, and I don't give a single fuck about making it on the radio or selling out an arena. We can make this happen independently, go full indie. We can do it on our own terms, build our own team with no bullshit, no rules, and zero expectations aside from our own."

"We'll make less money," I cut in then, wanting to show my support and let Judah know I was in all the way, "but only at first, as we get set up. TheColt fans aren't going anywhere, I can say that with confidence, but we won't have the promotional opportunities the label provided."

"Fuck those opportunities," Vale spat, sounding a little bitter. "They're all fake, prissy bullshit anyway, and they all came with strings. We don't need to show up at another artists' party just to pose for a picture, when the artist himself can't stand us. None of that is real."

"But this album is," Judah promised. "I need your help to fine-tune and polish it. Once we do that, we get to recording. While we polish, we can find an independent agent, someone that can get us in with the streaming services and eventually get us set up with smaller tours."

"Judah, this is…" Pierce started, then stopped after failing to come up with the words.

"Again, I know you guys don't trust me," Judah pointed out. "I seriously don't expect you to because I wouldn't trust me either, but let me prove it to you. There will be no contract, so if a better opportunity comes up, you're welcome to take it. If I fuck up, you're welcome to leave, but I can guarantee you won't want to."

"Listen to this guy," Vale scoffed, but he was grinning, which had my chest warming with excitement.

"I was so dead set on punching you square in the face, I swear to god," Pierce muttered with a smile. "How the fuck did we get *here*?"

Judah ignored the comment but sported a smirk of his own. "We'll start at ten, every day."

"You're serious about this," Pierce stated then, getting down to business. "You really think we can make it on our own?"

With that, Judah swung those blue eyes toward me and held my stare.

In that moment, I knew he forgave me for what happened with Phoenix, even though I had no idea what was truly going on in his mind. Either way, *somehow*, Judah had accepted the position he put Phoenix and me in, and was dealing with the consequences of his actions, in his own way, in order for us to start completely fresh.

There was no petty bullshit, no fighting, no outrage or rebellious setbacks...

I gave him a single nod, letting him know that I was on board, proud, and ready for whatever came next. With my stamp of approval, he turned back to our bandmates.

I watched a small, knowing grin bloom on his face before he answered Pierce's question with confidence. "I know we can."

CHAPTER 22

JUDAH

THE NEXT DAY, I spent way too much time in the shower trying to come up with a solid plan of action for my conversation with Ricco and Kavan.

Talking to Pierce and Vale went better than expected, but at the same time, I wasn't nearly as nervous to speak to them as I was to sit down with the other two. Ric and Kav had become so close to Phoenix and Frankie that they almost felt like guard dogs, ready to rip my throat off at first chance.

I couldn't blame them, of course, and I respected their fierce level of protection over the girls, but it didn't make me feel very confident when it came to laying out a proper apology.

I wanted what I said to sound right, feel right, and contain evidence of all the genuine regret and understanding I harbored. I needed them to know I was serious about not fucking up again, not only because I was ashamed but because my stint in rehab left me with a serious taste of what it would be like to be truly alone, without my friends, and it was fucking terrifying.

"You want me to stay?" Pharaoh asked as he slipped on a pair of black boots.

His offer was tempting but I shook my head. "Nah. As

much as I want you here to hold my hand, I can't fuck around and act like a baby bitch."

Phar scoffed, "Baby bitch? I live here bro, and besides, if I were there for the conversation, it would just look like you had my support."

"Yeah, well, at this point, I don't think anyone doubts that I have your support," I replied, "which, of course, I appreciate more than you know."

After Pierce and Vale left the night before, things were a bit weird between Pharaoh and me, given his confession about sleeping with Phoenix, but I couldn't stand the awkwardness, so we talked. I told him very simply…I understood.

Did I like it? Fuck no. Was I pissed? Hell yeah. Was I aware of the fact that I had no right to be pissed? Absolutely. Was I going to hold the incident over either of their heads? Nope. Because at the end of the day, I'd already obliterated my relationship with Phoenix at that point and she was a free woman. And Pharaoh wasn't required to stay loyal to me when I'd done him just as dirty as I did her. It was a clusterfuck, to say the least, but it was a mess I wasn't willing to derail my progress over.

I *did* ask questions though.

First, I asked if anything had happened between them before that night and he said no, which only made me feel slightly better.

The next question I had was harder to get out because the answer could have gone either way, but I needed to know if Phoenix and he were still together in real-time. Phar had said no, that they were never actually together at all, and his confession felt like a thousand-pound weight had been lifted off my chest, because my biggest fear after learning that they'd slept together in the first place, was that Phoenix and Pharaoh had only forgiven me because they'd fallen in love with one another in the midst of my downfall. I feared they only still cared about me because their newfound relationship made the whole experience worth it.

I feared I'd be left out in the cold.

But because I knew my best friend, I had one last question...

"Do you still love her?"

I expected him to take a while to respond, to have to think about how he wanted to word his response, but almost immediately, he said yes. And all I could do was sit there on the couch with a pit of raging jealousy in my abdomen as Pharaoh admitted that he believed he might always love her, but at the same time—this part was harder for him to get out—he had come to terms with the fact that P's heart would always belong to me.

Rapidly, before I even knew what was happening, that jealous pit churned, unraveled, and rerolled itself into a wad of disbelief.

The statement had me wondering if I could Instacart a shovel so I could bury myself alive.

Because...*what?*

How? *Why?*

I couldn't wrap my fucking head around the idea that Phoenix would give up a guy like Pharaoh, for someone like me, *especially* after everything I'd done. After the way I treated her.

Before I knew it, the deeply rooted self-hatred embedded in my DNA came screaming to the surface once again.

I didn't understand, thought my best friend *had* to be lying.

There's no way.

I didn't fucking *deserve* her heart.

I didn't deserve his loyalty.

I didn't deserve their forgiveness.

I ended up having to call Blake around midnight because what Pharaoh didn't know was that he'd given me more evidence that Phoenix might actually take me back and our entire conversation sent me spiraling into a cyclone of imposter syndrome and survivor's guilt all wrapped in one.

As soon as Dr. Blake answered in a voice full of exhaustion, I flew into a monologue made up of long-winded run-on sentences that didn't stop until I was crying. I felt every ounce of jealousy, couldn't get away from the intensely detailed picture of Phoenix and Pharaoh in bed together, and it had me spinning the fuck out, because how—even after all that—could the two of them seriously want me back in their lives?

It made no sense.

But Blake, being the Angel that she was, talked me down until my tears dried up and my nose was grotesquely stuffy. She explained the power of forgiveness all over again and reminded me that while I didn't believe it yet, Phoenix and Pharaoh knew in their hearts that the man I was last year was not a true reflection of the man I was at my core. They had separated my actions as an addict and my choice to get clean.

Blake told me that in her eyes, it was very clear that all P and Pharaoh wanted was the real me. She believed they slept together because they were both itching for a connection they couldn't find anywhere else, given the intensity of losing someone they both loved equally, just in different ways.

The whole thing was an awful, enlightening experience, and while I only got about five hours of sleep, I was grateful because by the time I fell asleep I was so fucking exhausted I didn't even dream.

Pharaoh's voice interrupted my thoughts, and the timing was almost too perfect. "I wasn't sure what to expect when I picked you up this time around, but it definitely wasn't this, Judah. Your growth is...evident."

...is it?

Slowly, I lifted my head to meet his eyes, and in those darkened black pools, I saw pride.

I swear, I tried to smile, tried to push my lips up and into a grateful curve but it didn't work. Instead, I felt unworthy, unsure, but I hid it and tried to think of what to say.

What I'd chosen as my response wasn't nearly as heartfelt as I wanted it to be, but it was the best I could come up with in the moment. "Let's hope Kavan and Ricco will feel the same."

Phar tilted his head and gave me a small smile, one that was full of understanding as he encouraged, "They will, dude, I promise."

It was true that I'd done a lot of internal work and I did feel like I was on a different mental, emotional, and even spiritual level now that I was sober, but I also wasn't about to rest or celebrate my progress until I had people to celebrate with.

Pierce and Vale's hesitant forgiveness was a great start, but I still felt their apprehension the previous day, so I wasn't throwing a party over our conversation. I'd be lucky if they showed up to our first writing session later this week.

"They'll be here soon, right?" Pharaoh asked once I'd looked away, and his question brought on enough nerves to make me feel like I needed to take a shit.

"Yeah, any minute."

"All right, I'll make myself scarce," Phar replied as he stood from the couch and moved to grab his keys off the island. "Call me when they leave."

I smiled as best as I could but knew it was weak. "Will do."

※

ABOUT FIVE MINUTES LATER, I heard the front door open.

"Bro, why you gotta push me? I'm walking as fast as I fuckin' can."

"Because you're *slow*, dude! Your 'fast' is equivalent to a turtle's."

"Oh, shut up."

The sound of Kavan and Ricco's bickering flitted down the small hallway, through the kitchen, and into the living room, causing me to stand and wipe my hands on my jeans to try and get rid of the disgusting moisture my anxiety so gracefully left behind.

It didn't take long for the two of them to become visible, but it was Ricco that saw me first.

My tall, swagged-out friend stopped dead in his tracks, which caused Kavan to run straight into him.

Of course, he bitched immediately, "Dude, what the fu—"

But then he saw me.

"—uuuck…" he finished.

My chest tightened.

"Fuck" is right.

I decided right there that my reunion with those two would be more emotional than Pierce and Vale, simply because they carried different energy entirely.

Kav and Ricco always wore joy like a cloak, they smelled of family and togetherness. And even from all the way across the room—separated by furniture and light fixtures, plants and general *space*—I could physically feel P's energy embedded in their auras.

Frankie's wasn't far behind.

Once again, it was shockingly evident that those girls really were the link that brought everyone together and I was the only one cast to the side.

So much time had passed, so much damage had been done, so much—

"Judah, hey," Ricco breathed as if in shock, interrupting my revolving thoughts, "you look…"

"Fuckin' *good*," Kav finished for him, sounding eerily identical.

Vale had given me the same compliment, but his recognition felt forced, where Ricco and Kavan's surprise was dipped in…relief.

"Uh," I drew out, scratching my forehead as I once again tried to pull off a genuine smile, "t-thank you."

"No, but like," Ricco shook off the hand Kavan had placed on his shoulder and confidently padded into the living room, walked right up to me, and with zero shame, grabbed my face between his palms. He turned my head from side to side as he enforced, "You look *really* good."

"Yeah, dude," Kavan agreed, stepping up next to his brother in order to join in on the close-up examination of my physical body, "those fuckin' bags you had under your eyes are *gone*. It changes your whole look!"

"Nah, it's the haircut," Ricco pointed out as he let go of my face, only to scan the rest of my body with his keen hazel eyes. "You even gained the weight back."

Scaring me a little, Kavan let out an excited laugh and clapped his hands together, before asking, "So you're sober?"

This is not *going how I thought it would.*

"Y-yeah," I responded, feeling out of sorts from all the extreme attention, "I, uh, I-I am."

"*Actually* sober?" Ricco pushed.

Kavan clicked his tongue and gave his brother a harsh side-eye before clarifying, "He means, are you going to *stay* sober?"

I nodded as confidently as I could. "I mean, t-that's the plan…"

"Have you talked to Keon?" Ricco questioned. "Sage?"

Nausea curled in my gut.

"No," I replied stonily.

Pharaoh and I discussed Keon shortly after I got out

because he wanted to know my plan regarding my sobriety. We both knew that remaining in contact with people that lived the lifestyle I just got out of wasn't going to end well for me so I asked him to remove both Keon and Sage—along with my other dealers—from my contacts as well as all social media.

It wasn't a foolproof plan, they could still reach out to me at any time, but it was better to just cut off my end of the deal in order to avoid any temptation.

Apart of me didn't blame Keon for adding fuel to my fire by providing me with an endless pharmacy because it wasn't his decisions that led me to overdose. I was in control of all my actions back then, but I could still recognize that if Keon were really my friend, he would have noticed—and cared—about my fast descent into dangerous territory.

Those weren't the types of friendships I needed in my life and Ricco and Kavan had a right to wonder about my decisions when it came to friendships.

I stood still as a statue as both guys eyed me for a solid twenty seconds, seeming to weigh the possibility of my answer being fact or fiction, before Ric's voice shattered the silence.

"All right, bet," he grinned and rubbed his hands together, "that's good fuckin' news, my dude."

Kav's casual tone cut in as he explained, "Pharaoh told us you were serious, but I wasn't sure if he was just sayin' that because he didn't want us to rip you a new asshole so soon after getting out. I wouldn't put it past him."

I wouldn't either.

"No, uh, he told the truth," I confirmed unsteadily, "though, I'm not sure what he said exactly, so—"

"—oh, he didn't say anything crazy," Kavan assured me. "I'm just a nosey bastard and wanted to know if you were gonna start poppin' pills again from the jump like you did last time."

I fucking hate this.

"He said that wasn't going to happen," Ricco added, "told us you were actually super serious about your sobriety this time."

"I am," I bit out, now feeling defensive due to the amount of fucking energy they showed up with. It was too much. Too informal and easygoing.

"All right, cool." Ricco's nod was relaxed before he left the room entirely and strolled into the kitchen. As he opened Pharaoh's fridge and pulled out a Red Bull, he asked, "So, how are you, man? How was rehab?"

Like an idiot, I just stood there, blinking, unable to think of a reply because…*what?*

Why were they so fucking chill?

Why weren't they pissed?

What is happening here?

"J, you good?" Kavan questioned from my right.

"I'm confused," I blurted, unwilling to fake it. "Why are you guys acting so…friendly…right now?"

All that could be heard was the fizzing pop of Ricco's Red Bull can being opened. I watched as Kavan's eyes met Ricco's in the other room. They seemed to have a quick, telepathic sort of conversation before Kavan met my gaze again and sighed before admitting, "Well, honestly, we weren't sure *how* to act."

I narrowed my eyes. "What do you mean?"

"This is new territory for us, J. You've never actually been sober before," Ricco responded a bit sheepishly. "We didn't want to put pressure on you by being dicks and holding the past over your head, but we also didn't want you to think we didn't care if you were committed to staying clean or not, because we do. But we just figured that getting to this point wasn't easy, so we decided that if what Pharaoh said was true…we were going to come in with some positivity."

A laugh fell from my mouth, but it was bitter. "I wasn't expecting positivity. You guys deserve to act like dicks."

"Why bother?" Kavan questioned with a raised brow. "Everyone in this group, including you, have been through enough. Sure, you were a fucking monster for a while there—and trust me, if we thought you'd end up turning the sobriety bus around and playing games all over again, we'd be having a different conversation right now—but you seriously do look better. It's clear you're not high as hell, and that's progress in and of itself since it's been two days since you got out."

They're not wrong.

It was progress.

Ricco added with a shrug. "We know this is a process. Us adding pressure out of suspicion isn't going to help you stay sober," Ricco added with a shrug. "We just want to know how you are and what happens next."

Overwhelmed was one way of putting it but stunned was another.

This was a far cry from what I expected to go down between the three of us, and while I was confused even a little suspicious, I wasn't about to argue any further, especially since I could answer those two questions and include my apology while I did it.

As I lowered myself into the same chair I sat in the day before, I coughed to try and alleviate the developing pressure in my chest. All I could think about was how helpful a shot of vodka would be. How if I had taken even just one oxy, I'd be fine, there would be no space in my head for worries.

Within a few ticks of time, my mouth began to dry and panic started to seize my system, so I decided to ask for the next best thing. I addressed Ricco, admitting, "Yeah, uh, I'm gonna need one of those Red Bulls to get through this. Will you toss me one?"

The caffeine wasn't going to help—in fact, it would probably hurt, I knew that—but I needed something other than water or Sprite to get a hold of the cravings. Ricco seemed to understand because the smile he gave me displayed a bit of pity, but he did as I requested with good faith and didn't say anything about it.

Once everyone was settled in the living room and I'd chugged half the can, I steeled myself, briefly closing my eyes, reminding myself that both Kavan and Ricco had already shown more forgiveness than I'd expected, so I was safe for now. As long as I continued to be honest.

As long as I didn't fuck it up.

Vulnerability is key to connection.

"Rehab was hell, if I'm honest," I started once I'd opened my eyes, "but I'm finding that I'd almost rather be back at Cliffside than out here."

Kavan shifted in his chair, angling his body to face me as he listened.

"I'm exhausted, and I'm running myself in circles, wanting to prove to everyone that I'm on the straight and narrow when all I really want to say is I'm fucking sorry and scream. It feels like all my insecurities have intensified now that I have so many reasons to hate myself and it makes everything worse. I feel like shit, I'm drowning in guilt, and it eats me alive every minute of every day. But I almost don't want the pain to go away, because I know it's what I deserve, it's a punishment I think I need to live with, but my therapist insists that living with self-imposed consequences will backfire eventually."

"It will," Kavan confirmed with a dip of his chin.

My sigh was thick. "Deep down I know that, but once the drugs wore off it was like the floodgates opened and I got to experience every shitty thing I did in technicolor, mixed with all the memories of my childhood that I tried to bury. It was torture."

"Can I be honest?" Ricco asked, then.

I nodded and took another sip of my drink.

"We don't even need the apology," he stated simply, and

eyebrows pulled together. "Those words don't mean anything to us anymore, but it's clear that you feel like hell—whereas in the past that wasn't the case. It's not my place, nor do we have any interest in adding to that guilt. And the fact that you were so freaked out by our positivity says enough all on its own, man. You expected us to come in here guns blazing and you were going to take it because you felt it was deserved."

"Addiction is a disgusting fucking disease, J," Kavan spoke in support of his brother. "You're a victim in more ways than one and the only thing that truly pissed us off was the fact that you buried your head in the sand and hurt us, hurt Phoenix, instead of dealing with it. You chose the pussy way out and we couldn't get down with that. Your decisions are your own but when those decisions started to directly affect us and cause real damage to our friends, we had to walk away. But all that doesn't negate the fact that you were a victim from the start. We're able to see both sides."

Blake had been right, my friends really could see my situation from a three-sixty point of view, but I was still left itching with unworthiness. But in the name of growth, I knew I needed to accept their grace because if I didn't I would be shooting myself in the foot.

I was re-building my foundation and it was going better than I thought it would, better than I thought it *should*, but I refused to reject it.

Instead of directly replying to their points though, I switched topics and stated, "When I was in rehab I told my therapist about you guys. And because she was a nosey psychological terrorist that was determined to break down every part of my life, she asked me what I admired, and what I was jealous of when it came to the two of you."

Ric smirked like an asshole. "This'll be good."

Smartass.

"I told her that I admired both of your abilities to live

freely, as if nothing ever bothered you, even though—while I don't know all the details—I know the two of you have first-hand experience with trauma like I do. I told her I was jealous of your ability to keep any lingering effects of that trauma in the family. You never let your past get in the way of your relationships. Any bullshit you have to deal with, you do it together, just the two of you, without tainting your friends or family in the process."

For once, both guys were quiet, so I kept going, "Even before Pharaoh and I were discovered and moved to LA, it wasn't like that for me. I never fully opened up to Pharaoh even though he lived two trailers down and knew ninety percent of my familial bullshit. I was so fucking ashamed that I hid the darkest parts of my life and dealt with it alone. He only found out about my father's accident and my mother's subsequent drug habit after my first stint in rehab, because I told him during a fight. I didn't do it with maturity or vulnerability. And he was pissed because he thought I'd taken my first pill from a dude at school. I was a fucking coward, always have been."

"But that shit is *embarrassing*, Judah," Ric returned in a softer tone than normal, "and you were a goddamn kid when all this started. Admitting to your best friend that your mom was getting high off your father's pain pills, on top of the abuse you already wore all over your skin? You wanted to keep a secret, man, and that's understandable in a lot of ways. You didn't want all that tragedy to be real, and if you said it out loud, it would be. It would be real, and it would *hurt*. You were protecting yourself in the only way you knew how."

"Dude," Kav called out, requesting my attention. When I met his eyes, he said, "Ricco and I only told each other everything and gained this bond because we lived in the same house growing up."

"Wait, what?" My tone was made of pure shock. I'd never learned the real story behind their childhood, never met their families, and never cared to push for information. Now I *wanted* to know more. "Everyone knows you're not actually related but I always considered you guys' brothers. I thought maybe your moms were best friends or something..."

Ricco scoffed bitterly and shifted in his seat before glancing at Kavan and nodding his head, signaling for him to continue.

I watched closely as Kavan ran a hand down his face, which had dread pooling in my stomach, because this was the first time I ever saw the two of them so subdued, so in their heads. They were always extremely put together, full of bubbly personalities and loud ass conversation.

This was different. This was the truth.

Kavan's confession was swift. "We grew up in foster care together."

Oxygen got caught in my windpipe.

...what?

"The woman that raised us also raised four other kids," Ricco further explained. "I was three when the state sent me to that house and Kavan came a few months later."

All I could do was listen as Kavan picked up the story, "Our foster mother still jokes about how even back then we were inseparable, before we could even put together a coherent sentence. We never wanted to connect with the other kids in her house. It was always the two of us against the world."

"You...you guys were never adopted?" My question was hesitant because I didn't want to pry but figured if they didn't want to tell me, they could say so.

But Kavan shook his head as Ric answered sadly, "No. Our foster mother needed the money from the state, and once you adopt a kid officially, you no longer get paid. She only took in six kids because six kids meant enough money to live."

Fuuuuck.

"Her husband was a truck driver. Gone all the time," Kavan went on. "He died when we were eleven."

"Shit, you guys," I breathed, feeling sick.

"Yeah," Ricco said on a sigh. "As you can imagine, there wasn't enough love to go around, but we survived, and it's the reason Kavan and I are so close. We chose to stick together. We're brothers in every sense of the word and we made a family of two as soon as we knew what the word meant. Then dance became our lifeline. It kept us off the streets."

At that, Kavan chuckled a little. "It took us like seven fuckin' years to realize we were any good, though."

Ric smiled in return. "But as soon as we did, we decided to make a career out of it and busted our asses after school to save up enough money to take real classes. As we got closer to graduation, we dropped classes, worked more, and saved to move out and live on our own. Eventually, we moved to LA, and you know the rest, but man…your story isn't ours. It's not worse, it's not better, it's just yours."

I remained silent, trying to digest what I'd just heard, but Kavan wanted to further his brother's point. "Judah, you were handed a shit life. You didn't deserve what happened to you, and I'm not here to ask you to prove shit to me. I just want you happy. *We* want you happy. You brought two women into our lives that give us more love than our foster mother *ever* had to spare. We expected that love to transform you like it did the two of us, but instead, it seemed to destroy you."

"Don't get me wrong, we do love our foster mother, and sure, she's family," Ricco made sure to say, "but because of you and the connection you found with Phoenix, we found our *real* family. We found true peace, true companionship, dude, and we never wanted you to be a fuckin' outcast. We wanted you and P to be in love, to thrive and grow and learn together. It wasn't ever supposed to be like this."

He was getting worked up, and I could feel those goddamn tears lingering in the back of my eyes.

"You were supposed to hold her down, man." Kavan clicked his tongue. "She's got issues, you've got issues, Ric and I have issues, we all know Frankie's a mess. We're misfits, homie! And you shredded us apart because you didn't want to face your shit, and trust me, I understand, but no fuckin' more, okay? No more pushing us away, no more making yourself an outcast because your parents made you think you were meant to be an outcast. Those people fuckin' suck. *Fuck* them. They're not your family."

"We are," Ric demanded in a tone full of determination. "*We're* your fuckin' family and we can't lose you again."

Saltwater slid down my cheeks but I didn't bother hiding the evidence. Instead, I repeated wetly, quietly, "I'm...so sorry."

Overwhelmed, annoyed with myself, hurting over their past and my own, my head fell into my hands and before I knew it, I couldn't stop the breakdown, couldn't pretend to be unaffected by the power of their forgiveness. The sobs only got worse when I felt two pairs of arms wrap around my body, one on either side.

"Never again, man," Ricco whispered. "You're *done* with this bullshit. You're done running. From now on you run to *us* when shit gets hard, you got it? You hear me? I'm not letting you fuck this up again."

"You almost died on us, J," Kavan bit out, sounding like he was holding back tears of his own. "We almost lost you and I...I c-can't again. I fuckin' can't."

Yeah, well, I couldn't speak, could barely breathe, as I realized that while I hurt both of them, it was almost worse because I left them behind. Chose my addiction, chose pills and chaos, instead of celebrating what we'd found. They lost a friend when I set our friendship on fire. They lost *family*. And while I never considered myself worthy of that title, never allowed myself to truly get that close to them, they were willing to bring me into their fold. Had wanted it all along.

"I'm sorry," I repeated, and again, I gave in to the emotion but this time it lasted until it got dark outside and the three of us were sweaty and gross from the close proximity we'd been in for god-only-knew how long.

Pharaoh ended up coming home shortly after we broke apart, looking worried since I hadn't called, but that worry vanished and understanding dawned when he saw our puffy eyes.

"We need food," Pharaoh nodded, almost to himself. "Yeah…I'm gonna order food."

"Good idea," Ricco chuckled throatily.

And for the first time in three months, I felt like maybe, just *maybe*, if shit hit the fan with Phoenix, and by some chance she decided to walk away…I might actually be alright.

I'd been forgiven, been gifted another chance.

I still had a family.

CHAPTER 23
Frankie

"OH, COME ON," I bitched, glancing back and forth between Silas and Kav, "this isn't fair."

"It's totally fair," Silas laughed and dropped his hand on my thigh in an attempt to make me feel better.

"Bullshit! I'll be alone *all* day, and it's my *one* day off this week!"

"Sorry, babes," Ricco threw in, strolling back into the living room holding Trixie after letting her out back to pee, "It's dude's day."

"Plus, you hate golfing," Kavan pointed out, throwing me under the bus.

I slapped on my best pout and crossed my arms over my chest. "Whatever."

It didn't work.

Silas actually stood up with a fucking smirk on his face and made his way to the kitchen.

Phoenix was working all day, and the guys had planned a stupid golfing trip that *apparently*, I wasn't allowed to invite myself to. On any other day, I wouldn't have given a shit, but I was hoping we could go somewhere in the city and do something fun because everyone had been so busy lately, I was feeling neglected. It had been a while since I'd gone to Grand

Central Market or even the fucking pier. I would have settled for anything, honestly, but instead, I'd be forced to fill my day all on my own.

"Call one of your other girlfriends," Ricco suggested and dropped Trix on the couch next to me.

The fluffy thing jumped into my lap and immediately began seeking attention. Uncrossing my arms, I began to smooth my hand down her back as I replied, "Fuck that, I don't feel like playing the rich LA girl role today."

The guys wouldn't understand what I meant, but Phoenix would.

Whenever I had to be around my other female friends, I was forced to strap on my mask and play the part, simply because they were too shallow to see what I saw when it came to the lifestyle we were born into. My relationship with Phoenix was the only thing that kept me grounded, and I often thought about what would have happened to me if she hadn't moved in with my family at such a young age.

"We leave in an hour, boys, so get your shit together," Kav called out, only serving to alienate me even more.

While the guys rummaged through our kitchen searching for snacks to bring along on their little date, I grabbed my lukewarm coffee from the glass table in front of the couch and resumed drinking it while scrolling through my phone. That was until Trixie shoved her snout against my hand, making me drop the damn thing and spill coffee in the process.

"You little bitch," I laughed, both loving and despising the fact that our dog had such a human-like personality. She gave no fucks. If the girl wanted attention, she was going to get it.

When I bent over and grabbed my phone from the carpet, it was vibrating.

"This better be Phoenix calling to tell me she had a cancellation and is coming home to spend the day with me," I grumbled to myself as I flipped the device over to check the screen.

It wasn't Phoenix.

"Holy shit…" I breathed, stared at the name, then screamed, "Guys?!"

"What?" Silas and Ricco called back at the same time.

My heart slammed in my eardrums as I yelled back, "Why is Judah calling me?!"

"Fuck," someone cursed, but I was too busy watching the call go unanswered and turn into a missed call notification on my lock screen to figure out who it was.

Instead, I stood from the couch in a rush, forcing Trixie to jump down, and turned to face the kitchen.

All three guys were staring at me.

"Hello? Why the *fuck* did Judah just call me?"

He still hadn't spoken to Phoenix since getting out of rehab five days ago and the panic I felt instantly had everything to do with the pain I knew my best friend was in over his lack of communication.

Why would Judah call *me* before talking to her?

What the hell is happening?

"He, uh," Ricco started, then stopped to clear his throat. "He told us he was going to call you but asked us not to tell you about it…"

There was smoke coming out of my ears, I was sure of it.

"*Excuse* me?" I narrowed my eyes on the three men in my kitchen as that panic turned into anger faster than they were prepared for. "Someone better explain to me what the *fuck* is happening right now before I go absolutely apeshit on your asses. And quick reminder…dead men can't golf."

"I hate that motherfucker right now," Kavan murmured under his breath as he ran a hand over his forehead. But then he met my blazing stare and explained quickly, "It's not bad, all right? Judah is just doing things his way right now. He's trying to do the right thing by everyone."

Bullshit.

"And somehow the 'right thing by everyone' is talking to everyone *besides* the person he hurt the most?" My rebuttal was laced with suspicion, but I was confused as all fuck. "There's no way I'm answering his call before Phoenix gets a chance to talk to him! That's a fucking betrayal, dude!"

"Franks," Silas stepped forward, but I cut him off.

"—no hold-up, when the hell did *you* talk to Judah?" Despite my incredibly mixed feelings for Silas, it hurt a little that he kept something like this from me.

"Yesterday," he admitted. "We had lunch at Pharaoh's."

"You had lunch at Pharaoh's," I laughed bitterly, and pressed my palm to my forehead. "Great. And would you like to tell me what he said? Why does he want to talk to me?"

"He's apologizing," Kavan explained. "But not only that, Franks, he's making a point to go into detail about what made him who he is. It seems like each person he talks to gets the story they need to hear in order to understand why he acted the way he did toward them."

"Okay sooooo, he's talked to Pharaoh, you guys," I waved a hand. "Who else?"

All three men were silent, staring at me like they wanted to tell me, but couldn't.

"Are you s-serious?" I stuttered. "You're not going to give me anything else? I need a fucking reason to return this phone call because I have *no* evidence that tells me it's a good idea. Instead, I'm thinking you're all acting pretty fucking sketchy right now."

"We don't know what he wants to say to you, Franks," Ricco admitted. "He didn't tell us anything like that, he just told us you were the next person he needed to talk to."

"But he also asked us not to say anything to you because he didn't want Phoenix to find out," Kavan added. "Which I know sounds shitt—"

"—*sounds* shitty?" I cut him off, feeling tears stinging my eyes, even though it had virtually nothing to do with me. This was P's pain I was feeling. The anger was hers too. But I felt everything she did because she was my person, my everything. "No, it *is* shitty! He's supposed to be making things *better* right now, not hurting her all over again! Do you not see what a shitty position this puts me in? Phoenix and I don't keep secrets from each other, and Judah knows that, so he planned it perfectly. Do you not see the manipulation? How are you guys so okay with this?"

"Fuck," Silas cursed, dropping his head before picking it up again and saying, "Babe, please. It's not like that, I swear. Judah is doing what he needs to do, and it is a good thing, I fucking *promise* you, but we genuinely don't know what it is he wants to say to you or why he needs to talk to you before Phoenix."

"If he's trying to talk to you, Frankie," Ricco added, "we can safely assume Phoenix is next."

That statement threw a little water on my fire, making me feel only slightly less pissed.

"He's right," Kavan added. "Pharaoh told him they slept together and he's still coming to talk to you. If he wasn't interested in talking to Phoenix, he would ignore the both of you completely."

He knows they fucked?

"Yeah," Silas added, clearly trying to give me more reasons to calm down. "And honestly, if I were him, I would go to the best friend first too. He has a better chance of getting Phoenix back if her best friend is on board."

Son…of a bitch.
They're right.

"Fuck my life," I muttered, turning around so I could think straight.

Judah was in recovery and the last thing he needed was a pissed-off Frankie Skyes standing between him and the love of his life. Talking to me first *was* a solid idea, even though the secrecy was sketchy as all fuck.

"Get out," I demanded on a whim, not bothering to look at them, "now."

"Franks—"

"OUT!" I shouted, feeling *way* too much at once and needing the space to think.

Suddenly, I was fucking grateful the three of them would be out my hair for the day because I needed to decide what to do and *fast*.

Lucky for me, they didn't argue any further. In fact, they didn't even say goodbye.

And as soon as they were gone, I began to pace, feeling like Phoenix, thinking about the pros and cons of calling Judah back without telling my best friend. Apart of me wanted to bust his ass and call P instead. Get her opinion. But the other part of me knew this was an opportunity to see if Judah was serious about staying sober.

Maybe that was the whole point?

He had to know I was going to be more critical than anyone when it came to his wish to re-enter P's life. The guys were loyal to him *long* before we came into the picture, and while they were pissed at him less than a week ago, it seemed like whatever he said had washed away the resentment.

Judah was either a brilliant bullshitter or he had given them a pretty solid reason to forgive him, and given the man's track record, bullshitting was never one of his strong suits.

"Son of a bitch," I whispered out loud this time as I closed my eyes.

If I called Phoenix and told her, she would tell me to call him back.

I knew she would.

But if I talked to Judah *before* telling her and I didn't like what he had to say, if I even *suspected* that he would hurt her again...would she be angry that I didn't tell her before I returned his call?

I was left to choose between my loyalty to Phoenix and my trust in our self-made family. The guys seemed to think Judah's secrecy had a purpose, a good reason, and they went as far as to do as Judah asked and keep the secret from me, so they must have believed he had good intentions.

I knew without a shadow of a doubt that Ricco and Kavan would *never* let Judah back into our lives if they thought he'd hurt us all over ag—

My phone started to vibrate.

Shit.

Slowly, hesitantly, I looked down only to find Judah's name flashing up at me again.

"Fuck!" I cursed and jumped up and down a little. "God-damnit, Judah, *why?*"

I stared for a few more seconds feeling strung the fuck out, until...

You know what? Screw it.

If I don't like what he has to say right now, I'll call Phoenix immediately.

With very little time to decide, I threw all my trust to the Universe and answered the phone.

✶ ✦ ✶

FEELING like the shittiest friend on planet earth, I sat down across from Judah at the table he'd reserved for us.

Urth café was one of my favorite spots in all of LA so when he told me where to meet him, I just rolled my eyes. If he thought the location of this meeting would give him any brownie points, he was sadly mistaken.

"This better be good," was my only greeting, as I pushed my sunglasses to the top of my head.

Judah didn't even smirk as he replied, "I think it'll be worth your time."

"Yeah? And will it give me a solid excuse to explain why I'm meeting you behind P's back?" I bit out, still pissed.

"Yes." He nodded once, appearing calm and collected, with a new, strange sort of confidence. "I hope so."

Fucking hell. "Fine, then get to it."

As I talked, I studied Judah, and I had to admit, he looked healthy, much better than he had before the overdose. A new haircut, fresh eyes, fresh outfit with matching accessories. He was put together, he'd put on weight.

"I'm sorry," he stated first, which didn't faze me, given how many times he'd said it before. "And not just for the way I treated Phoenix or the physical shit I did to your house, but for barging into your life and causing more chaos than you signed up for."

…that was new.

Getting better.

I tipped my chin, silently encouraging him to keep going.

"When I saw Phoenix on the rooftop of Silas' party that night, it didn't take me long to figure out that she was hurting. It took me only a little longer to realize just how deep that hurt went, and instead of noticing it and thinking of all the ways to help her heal, I saw her as someone who would make me feel less alone."

I knew this already, as did Phoenix, but there was something about hearing it from Judah himself.

I adjusted in my seat as he continued, "When I first started opening up about my relationship with Phoenix in rehab, I told my therapist that I should have walked away. I should have left Phoenix where she was and picked one of the other drowning females in that party to latch onto. But as soon as I said it out loud, I wanted to take it back." Judah huffed a small, sad laugh. "Because it didn't take me longer than two seconds to remember that if I *had* done that, if I would've walked away and left Phoenix up there alone, neither of us would be where we are today."

I was almost annoyed because he was right, and I had said that very thing to Phoenix on more than one occasion.

But rather than agreeing, I remained silent as he went on to say, "While I was in there, after hours and hours of breaking down our relationship, I figured out that Phoenix had already chosen herself by coming back to LA when she did. She left New York behind her and had a plan to see life differently, right?"

Right.

But even I didn't know the extent of her will to live at that point, since I had no idea she almost tried to commit suicide before coming home. Not, at least, until all the shit with Judah went down.

A minuscule part of me was still hurt by that, by the way I'd found out, and I was still confused about why she chose to keep it to herself, but I recognized that Phoenix's life was so much different than mine and the way she handled her parent's death was her choice. I could either accept it or resent it. I chose to accept it and do everything I could to make sure she never ended up in that dark place again.

Judah kept going. "Phoenix had chosen life just before she met me, while I was still coasting, flirting with my addiction as it came in waves, depending on the amount of bullshit I was dealing with on any given day, but had absolutely zero plans to get better when we met. The industry had chewed me up and spit me out, I wasn't writing, wasn't making any real connections, wasn't even confident in my identity as TheColt. I planned to maintain, maintain, maintain. Stay numb, stay high, and live until I couldn't anymore."

Judah met my eyes then, and I could see the truth hidden there. I could see the emotion, the sincerity of his words. "But then Phoenix wandered onto that roof…"

My stomach dropped.

God, he was…actually *talking*. Judah Colt was opening up and spilling his thoughts all over the table and I couldn't do anything but listen and wonder where he was going with this confessional.

"And the sad truth is, if P didn't put up a fight that night, I wouldn't be sober right now." …*is that true?* "It's because of her resistance, her choice to live, that I rebelled and pushed myself to the breaking point. Without having to chase her, without fighting with her, without pushing her away, and then losing her entirely, I never would have seen just how deep my addiction went. I never would have acted out the way I did when she stood up to me, I wouldn't have destroyed your house, or ruined my band. I was an isolated incident for so many years, and while it was good for the people around me because I wasn't causing outright chaos, I still would have ended up overdosing again. Eventually, it would have taken a turn, especially since I wasn't able to write until her. The pressure would have forced me over the edge and I would have done myself in. But… " he paused and took a deep breath, "if I had never met Phoenix and overdosed anyway, I wouldn't have woken up to P's letter."

Slowly, little by little, the ice in my veins began to thaw.

"Phoenix never wanted me to live *for* her, she didn't want to be my reason for living, she wanted to be my partner, and I hated it because I didn't want to live in the first place. And yet, when I tried to kill myself, I didn't get what I wanted. I was forced to live another day, look at the damage I'd done, face the utter chaos that was my life, and yet…without her letter, without her unconditional faith in me, I never would have taken rehab seriously. I wouldn't have had a reason to."

"And you did?" I asked, then, speaking for the first time since he started. "Take it seriously this time?"

For some reason, he smirked at my question. "I wouldn't have had the balls to sit here alone with Frankie Skyes if I hadn't."

Ah. "Touché."

That smile fell as he went on, "I know I did more harm than good where Phoenix was concerned, but without me, the two of you wouldn't have met Ricco and Kav. You wouldn't be dating Silas. You guys wouldn't have formed a family together, and unfortunately, somehow, it was my bullshit that pushed you guys together. Phoenix deserves that. *You* deserve it."

"And you needed to get help," I responded, understanding what he was saying.

Instead of confirming what I said, he tipped his chin in my direction and pointed out, "You're the spiritual one of this group. If anyone is going to understand that fate was behind this, it's you."

"And you believe that?" I asked. "You think all of this was to get both you and Phoenix to a place where both of you could truly be happy?"

"I think it goes even deeper than that," Judah replied. "Kavan and Ricco needed family just as much as the two of you did. Pharaoh and I needed to separate. He needed to feel like he was worthy of being chosen, like he had a place in this world outside of the one I had carved out for him right next to me because I wasn't good for him. I've spent most of my life dragging him down, into my shit, and he doesn't deserve that." *No, he doesn't.* "And I needed to learn how to stand on my own."

Feeling a little overwhelmed, I glanced around us, trying to spot any stray paparazzi, but thankfully, the patio at this location was in the back of the building, completely surrounded by brick and away from the street.

When I met his eyes again, I asked, "So why did you need to talk to me before you talked to Phoenix?"

"Because she needs to be the last person I talk to."

His statement hit me square in the gut. "But why?"

"Because Phoenix wanted me to have a life outside of her. She wanted me to maintain my friendships, enjoy my career. She wanted to be my partner, not my whole reason for living, and now she isn't." He stated simply, then pinned me with his honesty, his truth. "She's my reward."

CHAPTER 24

JUDAH

"JESUS CHRIST," Frankie groaned a minute later as she rubbed her temples. "Phoenix is going to kill me."

"No, she isn't," I replied, feeling better now that I'd spoken to all of the people I needed to. Now that I'd gotten almost everything off my chest. "Because you won't tell her."

"You bastard!" Frankie mock whispered. "I can't *not* fucking tell her that I saw you!"

"You can if you aren't home when *she* gets home tonight," I offered, already having a plan.

That had Frankie pausing.

She narrowed those blue eyes on me and asked, "What do you mean?"

"I'm going to talk to her tonight," I admitted, feeling the butterflies in my stomach take flight and soar into my lungs. "So if you don't want her to know you met with me today, then stay at Silas' and make yourself busy."

"Yeah? And what happens when she tells me you called her?" Frankie threw back. "I refuse to lie to my best friend."

I shook my head. "By the time she calls you, she'll already know about our conversation."

"*You're* gonna tell her?" Frankie raised a suspicious eyebrow.

"Of course I am." The fact that she was still stunned by my foresight was almost insulting until I remembered it was Frankie I was talking to. "I'm going to tell her everything."

"Uh-huh," Frankie nodded. "And what exactly is your plan after that?"

I chuckled a little. "I'm sorry, but I'm going to say the same thing to you that I said to everyone else: let me handle it."

"Judah—"

"I know you hate this," I cut her off by holding a hand up between us. "But this process is horrific enough, Franks. I am baring my fucking soul to everyone around me and each of you have every reason to tell me to fuck right off. And yet, I'm still putting myself out there, even if in the end I have to face rejection. And quite frankly, I don't even know what Phoenix is going to say, if she wants me back, or how she'll react to what I have to tell her, but—"

Frankie put her palm against mine, and said, "My turn to cut you off."

I stared at our connected hands—hers being so much smaller than mine—and swallowed as Frankie said gruffly, "First you told her not to respond to your letter while you were in rehab, and she understood even though it wasn't easy for her. Then you tell Pharaoh not to update her, which of course he eventually did because you needed her help but were too stubborn to ask, *then* you left her waiting for five fucking days. You should be glad neither of us knew you'd been talking to our friends because it would have made it worse."

"That's why I told them not to say anything," I threw in, even though I knew she wasn't done.

"Whatever, fine," Frankie brushed me off. "Still, after spending the last *three months* worrying about how you were doing, if you were okay, she was left to question if you'd even want her when you got out. Judah, at this point, she truly believes that you don't. She thinks you've grown past her and she's trying to accept that. She's trying to respect your recovery, but fucking *trust* me, she's hurting. And if you think for even one second that she doesn't want you back?" Frankie pulled her hand away from mine then and sat back, crossing her arms for emphasis as she stated, "You're delusional."

While Frankie's words warmed a part of me, they didn't completely reassure me, because of all the apologies I'd given out, of all the stories I'd told, and conversations I'd had, the one with Phoenix would be the most difficult.

Sure, I wasn't living for Phoenix Royal anymore, and while, I'd come to the conclusion that if Phoenix didn't take me back, I wouldn't immediately nose dive into a bottle of pills, I also couldn't imagine what a life without her would look like.

She really would be my reward, my gift, at the end of all of this. I wanted her to be my support system, to stand beside me and help rebuild my life, but a part of me still believed I didn't deserve it.

Giving up or walking away out of fear though? That wasn't an option.

But with Phoenix, there were so many things I wanted to say, I didn't know how I was going to break it all down into simple terms. It was one of the reasons I'd waited this long.

I thought about calling her two nights ago—after talking to Kavan and Ricco—because the two of them were just as confident as Frankie was when it came to how Phoenix felt, and while they were still protective over her, they seemed to recognize in me what Pharaoh saw. They believed I would do everything I could to be the man she deserved and that was enough for them.

But I just…couldn't do it.

I wasn't ready.

I told Dr. Blake the same thing when I talked to her the day before and she agreed with my choice to continue making my rounds. She even said the more of a foundation I had built for myself, the more support I had in my corner before speaking to Phoenix, the better off I'd be if something went wrong.

It was the idea of something going wrong that had me nervous as all fuck.

"Judah, come back," Frankie called out softly, touching my hand again, which now laid limp on the table as I zoned out.

"Sorry," I muttered, blinking away my anxious thoughts.

"It's okay," Franks reassured me. "It's almost refreshing to know you and Phoenix still get trapped in your heads sometimes. Too much growth too fast would have me worried."

The mention of Phoenix and I in one sentence had my heart beating faster.

But then Frankie changed the subject. "How have you been handling the paparazzi?"

"I haven't been paying attention," I told her. "Pharaoh deleted all the social media apps on my phone and suggested that I keep the whole thing on do not disturb when I'm not using it to make a phone call or shoot a text. He goes through it at night for me and deletes all the bullshit messages that come through.

"Wow," she breathed, appearing truly shocked. "That's kind of brilliant, but I meant when you leave the house. I haven't seen a ton about you online. Have they been following you?"

I shook my head. "I think I've got them confused because I'm not staying at my house and I haven't even driven my own car since I've been back. I only really left the house once to get a haircut and I went to a barber that works out of his house in the Hills in a gated community so there was no chance of getting caught. Except for now, of course. This is my first outing."

"Damn." It looked like Frankie's head was going to pop off

with all the things I was telling her. "Why aren't you driving your car? Are you staying with Pharaoh?"

I nodded. "I'm selling everything. Starting over."

She whistled, chuckling a little. "You aren't fucking around."

"I can't stand that house," I admitted, feeling those dark, negative feelings lurking beneath the surface of my skin. "I drove drunk in those cars. I could have killed someone."

Else.

I could have killed someone *else*.

The shame of it all was too much to live with. Everything I owned reminded me of the shit I shouldn't have done, the awful choices I made, and once I got to thinking about them, the craving to numb out came back.

It was just easier to get rid of it all and start fresh.

"Hey." Frankie touched my arm this time, and when I met her eyes, I picked up on the empathy swimming in those blue depths. "I forgive you."

Shock slammed into my system, rocking me to my core, but before I could ask Frankie why she just came out and said it, I found her looking at a small family sitting on the opposite side of us.

A mom, father, and a little girl couldn't be older than nine or ten years old.

She spoke almost on autopilot, "Even my parent's—who've never committed the type of crimes you have—couldn't sit me down and explain to me why they treated me the way they did. They are grown-ass adults and they would never admit to being selfish or fucking up. They could never do what you did today, but what you did, what you said, is all someone like me wants. We want the person that hurt us to apologize and mean it." I did my fucking best to mask the emotion flooding my system, but I wasn't sure I was succeeding as she went on, "And not only did you make time to talk to me, specifically, you did it because you love my best friend. And that girl is the only other person that's ever apologized to me."

Fucking hell. I never realized.

Both Phoenix and I had caused Frankie pain, and both of us were left having to prove to her that she didn't deserve how we treated her.

"You never really owed me anything," Frankie continued, "aside from destroying our house and punching my sort-of-boyfriend in the face. But you still wanted my forgiveness because you recognize the importance of family, of my place in P's life, and that deserves to be taken into account. Do I hate you for what you did to her? Yes, absolutely. But was I the first one to recognize the power of your relationship with her in the first place? Yes, I was. And I one hundred percent believe that the Universe is just cheeky enough, just shitty enough, to put all of us through *living hell* to get us where we need to go. And you, Judah Colt, have the ability to change the world with your story if you do this right."

"If I stay committed," I added to her statement.

Because for the first time, I believed her.

I thought of Cassie and Brian, being reminded of the fact that they were fans of mine before they too ended up in rehab. I couldn't stop the tragedies from taking place, but with my music, I could give hope, show kids like me that there was a light at the end of life's dark tunnel.

But what I never understood about that light, was that—like magic—you had to believe it was there in order to see it in the first place.

"I missed your pep talks, Frankie Skyes," I joked, hoping to lighten the mood by giving her a compliment after the boost of confidence she had just gifted me.

My statement earned a chuckle before she warned, "You better get used to them, because if you need a new house and a new car? I'm assuming you're gunning for a new career too. On top of winning over my best friend...phew. The next few months are about to be crazy for you, baby boy. You're gonna need all the Frankie Skyes pep talks you can get."

Unable to help it, I laughed out loud, feeling lighter than I had in quite some time. "I'm sure you're one hundred percent correct. I look forward to the challenge, and with your help, it might not be such a challenge at all."

"That's the spirit," Frankie winked.

CHAPTER 25
Phoenix

"FUCK!" I shouted, then slammed the palm of my hand against the steering wheel of my car after I pulled onto my street and saw *another* crowd of paparazzi, this time blocking my fucking driveway. "What the *hell* is going on?"

There was no way I was getting through, not without subjecting myself to camera flashes and strangers banging on the windows of my car like I experienced trying to leave Death's Door just over an hour ago.

I hadn't checked social media yet, but I didn't need to, given the questions they'd flung in my direction.

"Baby Bird! Is it true that TheColt is out of rehab? Was it really him spotted out to lunch today? Who was the blonde he was with? How long has he been out? Do you know where he's staying?"

To say I was about ready to run them all over was an understatement.

I'd been nauseous ever since.

Even though I had yet to speak to Judah, Pharaoh had told me that J wasn't staying at his old house in the hills on the night I sent him the song, but beyond that, I was clueless regarding Judah's whereabouts or what he'd been doing since he got out Sunday night.

That little fact was part of the reason my life felt like a living hell this past week.

Five fucking days.

Judah had been home for five days and I hadn't heard a goddamn word.

See, this was what I'd been worried about the entire time he was in rehab.

That hope that I held onto? What was the point of it?

I was more hurt, more disappointed, now than I would have been if I had just written Judah off from the beginning and squashed that hope before it had a chance to grow. Even the letter he sent me now resembled a cruel joke.

The only thing keeping me even remotely level-headed was the selfishness I knew I was internally expressing. I knew I was being too hard on Judah, given he'd *just* gotten out and technically, he was doing exactly what I'd wanted him to do the entire time…he was putting himself first.

All along I wanted him to have his own life, his own thing, and then add me to it so I could just simply enjoy it *with* him.

But now that it seemed he'd done as I asked, I was regretting my wish to keep him at such a distance because really… where the fuck was he?

Would I even get closure?

Is this the part where our mutual friends no longer remain mutual and we all go our separate ways?

After days and days of dealing with all *that*, the mention of Judah having lunch with a blonde did me in.

I'd spent the majority of my drive home crying. Listening to a mix of SHY Martin and Julia Michaels, I mourned my relationship, nurtured my jealousy, and did whatever I could do to release the pain for good.

I couldn't think about it anymore.

Enough was enough.

"Okay, but what do I do now?" I asked myself out loud

after I'd pulled over at the end of the street and turned my lights off so the crowd facing my house wouldn't see me sitting in my car.

My makeup was a mess thanks to all the crying I did and when I got sick of my hair sticking to my tears, I threw my hair in a messy bun while driving with my knee. But this bun was *not* the cute version, and the last thing I needed was to have those photographs all over the tabloids tomorrow. Especially if they had caught Judah out with some other girl.

I didn't need the world knowing I was the heartbroken, jealous ex.

Even though it felt like I was.

Attempting to hold back another round of tears, I shot a text to my group chat with Frankie, Ricco, and Kavan, given I had no idea where anyone was right now.

Phoenix: There's a camp of paps outside the house and no one is home. Where are you guys?

As I waited, my nails anxiously tapped against the center console and my leg had begun its bouncing routine.

After a handful of seconds with no response, my anxiety peaked.

This can't be happening.

"Nightlight" by ILLENIUM started playing softly through the speakers, low enough to ensure the stalkers down the road couldn't hear it, but it didn't need to be loud for me to get slapped in the face by the emotion I was wrestling with.

Is TheColt out of rehab?
Yes.
Have you seen him?
No.
Will TheColt and his Baby Bird reunite?
I don't fucking KNOW.

Slowly, one by one, tears fell from my eyes, and when the drop of the song hit, I was a goner, left to sob into my hands to muffle any sounds, feeling pathetic and alone, wondering how the *fuck* I was still in this position.

How was I still so heartbroken?

Why couldn't I catch a break?

Is my karma that bad?

I was getting lost in the negative thought pattern that just *loved* to trap me, so when my phone vibrated, I silently prayed it was Frankie letting me know she was on her way home. She would be able to come up with a plan to evade the paparazzi and get us inside without being photographed. Even if I had to leave my car at the end of the road and hop in her fucking passenger seat with a hoodie over my head, I would do it. I didn't care.

But when I flipped it over to check who it was…the world spun.

My vision blurred thanks to the moisture in my eyes, so I blinked rapidly and swiped the sleeve of my shirt across my face as my heart lurched in my chest and my entire body went ice fucking cold.

No way. No fucking way.

Sure enough, it wasn't Frankie.

Instead, *his* name was there on my lock screen, clear as fucking day.

"Oh my god…" I cried through my fingers, now shaking like a leaf as FaceID tried to unlock the phone. Except it wouldn't work because I was a goddamn disaster, so I typed my four-digit pin as fast as humanly possible to reveal the message…

Judah: Current Location.

"Holy shit," I whispered, realizing that it wasn't a direct message. He'd dropped a pin to his location.

My heart resembled a sledgehammer, beating against my

rib cage and echoing across my body as I clicked on the pin.

A map to Mulholland Scenic Overlook popped up.

He was in the Hills, at one of the many places you could pull over to catch a breathtaking view of Los Angeles. It was just after nine p.m. so the place would technically be closed but—

Another message came through and interrupted my thoughts.

Judah: Meet me?

Just two little words.

Those two words had the power to free thousands of butterflies from a cage I previously welded shut and send them soaring through my body, forcing more tears from my eyes as the double meaning of his question hit me straight in the soul.

I Wanna Know by RL Grime began playing as the letter I wrote Judah flashed in my mind, almost in slow motion.

"... figure out what makes you tick, what triggers you, what makes your heart pound, and what makes it explode.

Take this experience seriously, make it the last time you have to do this, and then come back.

Get the hell out of there, come back, and reintroduce yourself to me."

Time came to a screeching halt as I read his text over and over.

"Meet me?"

He was…he wanted to…

Then it hit me.

I was about to meet the new Judah Colt.

And by the time the drop in *that* song hit, I was pressing send.

Phoenix: I'm on my way.

CHAPTER 26
Phoenix

I DID the best I could to make myself presentable, but it was pretty much impossible to get anything done given how fast I was driving and how uninterested I was in wasting time by stopping to fix my face. I'd seen Judah at his worst. I'd seen him at his lowest. And I'd be a motherfucking liar if I showed up and tried to pretend like the last five days weren't absolute hell for me.

He could deal with the evidence of that heartache.

All I could focus on was getting to that outlook, knowing that he was already there, waiting.

As I sped my way toward the Hills, I mentally ran through the events of the day, of the week, and wondered how much of it was really worth stressing about. Who was the blonde the paparazzi were talking about? Where had Judah been? What was he doing all week?

Truth was, I didn't care about the details anymore. Now that I was *this* close to being in his presence again, all I could think about was physically laying eyes on him—making sure he was okay, seeing for myself that he was alive and breathing—because it hit me all over again that he had almost fucking *died*.

The whole experience felt a little like DeJa'Vu, like a

flashback to when I got the phone call from Pharaoh asking me to come to Paris because he was worried about Judah. Back then I was just as nervous, just as anxious, but the circumstances were so very different. The only similarities between now and then resided in the fact that I had no idea what to expect.

When I landed in Paris, I wasn't sure what I'd find, didn't know how bad Judah's situation was but I knew it wasn't good. Only to find out I wasn't even *close* to prepared for how bad it had gotten. Whereas in the current moment, there was a fresh level of mystery surrounding our reunion, and my gut was *screaming*, reminding me that I was about to come face to face with a whole new version of the man I fell so toxically in love with. This version of Judah would be someone I'd never met, never got to know.

He would be sober, free, completely foreign to me.

And it all happened faster this time around, leaving me with much less time to overthink because rather than having to endure an eleven-hour plane ride, all it took was a quick twenty-minute drive. Before I was truly ready, I was pulling into the empty, darkened parking lot of the Mulholland Outlook.

And there was only one other vehicle parked there.

A motorcycle.

One I'd never seen before.

Breathing proved difficult, and I parked sloppily because no matter what I did, I couldn't curb the trembling of my hands long enough to steer my car in a straight line. Even my chest shook, my whole *body* was alight with nerves and bittersweet anticipation as I scanned the area, trying to find him.

Except, it was too fucking *dark*.

There was only one streetlight—aside from the twinkling lights of the view below—and that was shining a good ten feet away.

I was going to have to get out of the car if I had any hope of finding him.

Fuck, I can't.

My nose tingled as tears burned their way into my vision.

There was so much riding on that moment, and I couldn't help the fear that lingered from all of our past encounters. I didn't know what I would do when I saw him, what I would say, I would—

"Get out of the car, Phoenix!"

My head snapped up. My lungs seized.

Judah.

The sound was muffled thanks to the hunk of metal I was trapped in, but I heard his words clearly enough to know he was close.

But where?

After glancing left and right again, and coming up empty, I gave up and unsteadily opened my door. As soon as my shoes hit the dirt a bomb of nerves went off in my stomach. I tried to get a hold of them, but even my face burned as I shut the door behind me and turned around, feeling exposed.

If I hadn't heard his voice a minute ago, I would believe I was completely alone, standing on trembling feet with only nocturnal insects for company.

Where the hell are you?

I wanted to call out and ask Judah directly, but my vocal cords wouldn't work. They'd been tied shut by trepidation, refusing to work properly.

Somewhere in the outlook, Judah was watching me.

He's so close.

I could feel him, but I couldn't fucking see him.

All that could be heard outside of the wildlife was the sound of my shoes crunching across the dirt as I made my way toward the railing of the outlook, if only to have something to hold on to as I bit my tongue to keep myself from calling out to him. I refused to look like a fool in the middle of this strange game he was playing. I didn't particularly understand what was happening, but somehow, I knew Judah had a plan.

Then, just before I reached my destination, there was movement to my left, near the light, and I jumped, suddenly worried now maybe Judah wasn't there at all, maybe I was about to be killed by a vicious stranger in the Hollywood Hills.

But all of that fear vanished when I slid my gaze toward the sound and…saw him.

Oh…my god.

Like a scene straight out of a movie, my Skyscraper stood under the spotlight. Tall, tatted, damn near *glowing*, the sight of him had my bottom lip dancing with emotional affection.

My hand hit my mouth as I drank him in, noticing instantly that his head was shaved into a smooth fade on each side. The blond hair left on top was still messy but controlled by hair product and cut short enough to stay out of his eyes.

And those eyes?

They were *glued* to me as he walked slowly, casually, in my direction.

His pace was both frustrating and welcome as I held my breath and took in the pink muscle tank he wore—all baggy and ripped—but I damn near choked when I noticed the way his legs now filled out his black skinny jeans. He'd gained weight, put on muscle, which was showcased—along with the wide variety of tattoos inked on his flesh—through the shredded denim, much like his shirt.

An audible gasp left my throat as it all hit me.

Tears welled against my bottom lashes when I found no signs of sleeplessness, no hint of the permanently faded man I'd known before. Judah's body was no longer breaking down from the abuse, but instead, he appeared *healthy*. He was strong, lean, and clean-cut, no longer dehydrated and exhausted.

He looked...*alive*.

And just when I thought my perusal had gone on too long, when I started to feel awkward for not saying anything, *he* began to speak.

"So," he started, talking loudly enough to ensure I could hear him clearly across the excruciating distance between us, "what makes me tick?"

It took me a second to understand the question, but when I did, my whole body lit up with goosebumps.

My letter.

"An overactive mind," he answered simply, but then went on, "I like a challenge, but hate being set up to fail. I'm *always* down for a sarcastic debate or a petty, yet friendly war between friends over something incredibly stupid. And you'll probably find me showing up to a red carpet in a completely out-of-the-box outfit that only *I* would be caught walking in, just to turn heads and start gossip that I *may* end up resenting becauseeee...I get hung up on other people's opinions. I'll need to be reminded that I started the fire in the first place and getting torn apart in the media comes with the territory."

A wet laugh popped out of my mouth, knowing every word of what he just said was true.

"What triggers me?" A low chuckle of his own blanketed the space between us as he called out, "Well *that's* a trick question because *everything* triggers me...turns out I'm bipolar."

My heart squeezed as his shoulders lifted in a small shrug, and to anyone that didn't know him, it would look as if Judah thought his diagnosis was no big deal, but I saw the sadness hidden in the grin on his face.

If anything, J was resigned to the truth, he'd been forced to accept the diagnosis even though he definitely didn't like it, and it left me to battle against a desperate need to hug him, to say something. But I couldn't.

I was rooted in place, trapped by his confessions because I

could only assume he was acting out a plan he seemed to have crafted long before this moment.

I was helpless to see it through, to hear what he had to say exactly how he wanted to say it.

"Now, what makes my heart pound?" he mused, only about six feet away now, but rather than continuing to put one foot in front of the other, he slowed to a halt and turned to look out at the stunning view of LA, while my eyes remained locked on him.

He spoke toward the city lights, "The air in my lungs supplies the beat of my heart, of course, but there's a mixed bag of things that get me worked up enough to feel it beat that hard—hard enough to consider it pounding." He paused, taking his time, before exhaling a breath and telling me, "Fear, insecurity, guilt…my past for sure. The sight of my mother in my dreams or random flashbacks. When I'm backed into a corner by my own self-hatred, or I'm in a situation I can't control, my heartbeat turns into a drum." I could barely breathe as his voice took on a more somber tone. "When I was a kid, I had to listen to that drum so many times, I started interpreting it as anger. That anger turned into a need for either revenge or destruction, whichever was easiest to find in that given moment."

A tumbled lump of empathy sat lodged in my throat as he glanced at me and said, "But then there are also the good things that earn a fast, pounding heartbeat, and those are the things I'm learning to focus on. Like when I'm standing in the wings before a show starts and the intro begins to play. When the fans begin to scream and the nervous energy in my stomach floats into my heart? *That* pounding is the good kind." *God, he's breathtaking.* "But my favorite is probably, the racing of my heart after a good fuck—"

I couldn't help it, I snorted—small and light—but then quickly covered my mouth, remembering the seriousness of the situation. Still, I earned myself a sideways smirk from Judah and the sight of it had *my* heart pounding.

"Knew that would make you laugh," he gloated, then looked back out toward the view and kept going, "But there's also the euphoria I feel when the crowd gets lost in the lyrics of my music. When they shout them back at me, loud enough to fill the whole stadium, to the point where I could throw my mic away and never use it again, but the show would still go on." I watched with rapt attention as his chest rose and fell with another heavy breath. "Those are the things that make my heart pound. All different ways, all different reasons."

I was speechless, completely dumbstruck, and he was silent for so long I thought that might have been it, but I knew there was one more question and had a feeling that maybe he needed more time to think of the answer or collect his thoughts.

So, I waited with barely tempered patience for another minute, until he turned toward me again, resuming his slow pace in my direction. But this time he slipped two hands in the front pockets of his jeans, but his eyes? They *blazed*, wholly focused on me.

Sucked into that blue flame, I swallowed the lump in my throat, and rasped, "What makes that heart explode, Judah?"

A small, tender smile burned across my Skyscraper's lips at my final question, but he didn't reply until the wide gap of space between us was nearly closed, until he was *just* within touching distance.

"Well, that's the easiest question to answer," he told me softly, sweetly, "*you* do, Phoenix Royal. Only you can make my heart explode."

Jesus...Christ.

My soul sang as the rough timber of his confession ignited electric tingles through my veins, as my nose burned, and my vision blurred.

"You asked me if I could find peace hidden in my chaos," he started again, but paused as his throat bobbed with a visible swallow. "You asked if I could get excited about life again if I could find hope for a brighter future. You told me to dream a little at first, then bigger, louder, until I felt strong enough to dream unapologetically. You told me to figure out what I wanted."

The rest of the letter stung the back of my mind, and with it came memories of how hard it was for me to dictate the fucking thing in the first place, how awful it was to speak to Judah through his best friend, knowing that he'd almost died.

"You told me it was time to start a new life and warned me that this was my last chance, that I wouldn't get another one," his voice shook, causing a string of tears to fall rapidly down my cheeks, coating my face in moisture as he spoke.

"I *listened*, Phoenix," he choked out, "I heard every word."

My legs began to shake as I did everything in my power to push away the impending breakdown, but I wanted to touch him, hug him, feel his arms around me so I could be sure he was real, that he was standing right here, that he was alive and well and—

"Fuck, I *hated* you for it at the beginning," Judah admitted gruffly as he stepped closer. "I ripped up your letter, I hated that you were gone, that you were stronger than me—more evolved. I didn't understand how you could head off on some fucking vacation and leave me rotting in all my mistakes by myself, but my God, Phoenix," he shook his head sadly as my heart cracked in two, "it was *terrifying* to realize how deep I'd gone, how lost I'd gotten. The fact that *hate*, and *you*, were even in the same line of thought...?"

I licked my top lip, tasting salt as I sniffed and shuddered against the intensity of the moment.

"It had been like that for a while, though," he continued, looking off to the side, toward the view once again while I was left staring up at him, feeling small beneath his towering height, "I had gotten so used to hating you, *blaming* you, because it was easier than loving you and dealing with the fact that my own choices led to losing you." *Fuck, I can't.* "But it wasn't until rehab that I learned the true depths of the feelings I had for you in the first place. And that was only because I was forced to look at our relationship from beginning to end and track down all my mistakes, all the hidden subconscious projections and toxic patterns I subjected us *both* to."

He sounded so mature, so…smart.

Self-aware and factual. Enlightened.

"But after all that, after all the tears I shed, all the nightmares I had, after all the shame and guilt I felt over the way I treated you and the decisions I made…" His eyes met mine again and this time, that blue gaze glittered.

My control wavered as the remaining space between us disappeared.

The tips of his shoes hit my own in the dirt and suddenly he was so tall, so real, so *right there*, that when he lifted his hands and used both thumbs to wipe away my falling tears, all I could do was close my eyes and hold my breath.

"After staring myself in the face, after greeting the darkness in my soul and digging through all the nasty shit I had screaming in there, I met *you* all over again. I could finally see your kindness, I tasted your strength and used it to build my own. I remembered your blind faith in me, then witnessed, experienced, and *felt* your resilience. It was *your* determination to find happiness that pushed me to want my own, and by the end of it all…I'd fallen more in love with you, Phoenix Royal, than I'd ever been before."

That pent-up sob finally broke free and my body nearly crumbled from the force of it, but he caught me, and whispered, "I'm so sorry, Phoenix."

Fuck his apology, fuck the pain, fuck the past, he was *here*.

With trembling limbs as I completely fell apart, I moved desperately to wind my arms around his waist and mold my body to his as tightly as I could, needing to feel his warmth, hear his heartbeat, if only to ensure he was alive and well.

And I did, *he was.*

I would recognize that beat anywhere, and it had me crying harder as my soaked cheek hit his chest. His own body vibrated with barely controlled tears he pulled me impossibly closer and repeated, "I'm so fucking sorry, baby."

And for the first time, I physically *felt* the truth in his words. I heard the agony, the realizations, the lessons learned, all in the tone of his voice, and it *hurt.*

Thinking of the internal work he'd done by himself, all on his own, had me aching, because I knew exactly what it was like to hate your own reflection and have to break down why. It was fucking lonely. Terrifying, heartbreaking, fucking *earth-shattering.*

His name slipped from my lips in a tortured whisper, and the only response I got was his chin hitting the top of my head, and four wet droplets of saltwater falling into my hair.

And. I. fucking. *bawled.*

I could feel every modicum of his pain, every ounce of his guilt, and it had me ready to commit murder. I wanted to rip his parents apart—limb from *fucking limb*—for bringing my Skyscraper into this world and treating him so cruelly, so ruthlessly, that he grew up and considered his existence worthless. That he felt he had to numb out his childhood by taking enough pills to kill him. My train of thought got so dark I held on tighter, pulled him closer, until my body resembled a fucking straitjacket around his.

Minute by mine, tear by tear, we fell back into one another, and I slowly but surely felt our bond—that blown-out connection—finally waking up. The electricity that had once gone out was being turned back on, and the light between us flickered, gaining strength as the frequency of forgiveness fueled the voltage.

"I'm s-so sorry," he cried softly, as one hand skated up my back and into my hair, while the other came to cradle my cheek, keeping my head against his chest.

Unable to handle the shame and agony written in the syllables of that sentence any longer, I slid one arm from behind his back and gripped his forearm. My fingers squeezed the muscle as I whispered choppily, "I-I forgive you, J."

I wasn't sure he could hear me, wasn't even sure I'd spoken the actual words out loud, but his body heaved with another wave of regret, leaving me with an incredible need to make it better. To get him to understand that I was fucking *done* suffering.

I hated the shame, the guilt, I wanted to assassinate our past with my bare hands, because I just wanted *him*.

I *wanted* this fresh start.

Breaking free of his hold took some maneuvering, but when I managed it, my eyes trailed up, and I was once again tiny and frail as Judah loomed over me. His shoulders blocked my view of anything behind him, and his arms around my body made up a sort of bubble for just the two of us which was perfect given how long it had been since I'd been this close to him.

Meeting that blue stare, I lifted a hand to his face and took in the tiny red lines that now snaked through the whites of his eyes. This time, they were due to the tears, and all I could think of was how beautiful it looked. How different *this* shade of red was compared to the bloody, morose shade the drugs left behind.

My bottom lip trembled, my heart was a wild animal in my ribcage, and I wasn't sure if I could get the sentiment out, but still, as I wiped running tears from his face, I whispered, "T-thank you, Judah."

As if those words caused him physical pain, his eyes clamped shut.

But still, J leaned into my touch as he grated out an almost bitter, "For what?"

"F-for taking the l-leap," I pushed out, even though it was damn near impossible to speak steadily, "for s-starting. For sticking it out. For being willing to try and love yourself as much as I-I love you."

Those eyes stuttered open, and disbelief lingered there, on almost every feature of his face as he checked to see if I was serious.

And when he found what he was looking for, all he managed to say was, "Fucking *hell*, Phoenix," before he broke again, crumbling in front of me, nearly on top of me, sending us both to the dirt, where I held him as he cried.

The force of his sobs, the intensity of his hold on me, it was all evidence leading me to believe he spent the last three months wondering if he could repair all the damage he'd done, struggling to believe I could still find room in my heart to love him after what he'd done to it.

I felt his exhaustion, his worry, and knew he'd spent the last five days trying to be as strong as he possibly could in order to move forward with so many unknowns.

I was witnessing the result. The truth.

Judah clung to me—with both arms around my middle and his head in my lap—while I rode the waves of his emotions right alongside him. My left hand sank into his hair, as my right hand ran its way up and down his spine, letting him know I was there, I was with him, where my tears were silent, and his were not.

And that's where we stayed for another thirty minutes.

Together, in the dirt, we both let go of all the pain, felt our way through every up and down, every failure and success, in the only way we could. We shattered. We remembered. We regretted and re-lived until we couldn't cry anymore, and the agony was no longer a rolling boil, but rather a steaming pot of potential.

Just when my legs started to grow numb, Judah shifted without me having to say a word by putting a hand to the ground and pushing his body into a seated position next to me.

In silence, I wiped my face with my hands while Judah used the bottom of his shirt, as both of us did our best to clean up the evidence of our emotional reunion. And when my skin was dry and chapped, I inwardly cringed, knowing my hair was an absolute disaster. So, I reached up and pulled out the scrunchie, letting the mass of messy brown waves fall around my shoulders before I gingerly began to untangle the knots with my fingers.

A few moments later, Judah's voice shattered the quiet as he admitted, "Rehab sucked."

My heart surged. "Yeah?"

He met my stare. "Yeah."

"…but?" I raised an eyebrow.

I lost those puffy eyes as he glanced back toward the view, causing a lump to form in my tummy.

He was quiet for another minute before he whispered roughly, "But I'm so fucking glad I went."

Fuck, my chest.

"Me too," I whispered.

Adjusting again, Judah planted two feet on the ground and wrapped both arms around his bent legs, before resting his cheek on his knees to look at me. He was quiet, but the blue of his eyes told so many stories as he scanned my face.

I let him stare and stared right back, recommitting his features to memory, until he did finally speak, in a voice that was gruff and exhausted. "This wasn't how imagined our reunion."

I smirked a little. "No? How did you expect it to go?"

He returned my small smile and admitted, "The first part went as planned, but your little 'thank you' fucked the whole thing up."

At that, I laughed outright but the sound was horse. "Damn, I'm sorry. How dare I ruin your plan with two words."

"How dare you is right," he lifted his head and pushed his shoulder into my own. "You had me crying like I was back on Blake's couch."

The thought cracked my heart as I questioned, "Blake?"

"My therapist," he clarified. "I did a lot of...*emoting*. As she called it."

Was *she* the blonde he was with this afternoon?

I still had questions, and the headlines from this afternoon were included, but something told me it wasn't important enough to talk about right now, not after everything that had just gone down. Even with my lingering jealousy, I highly doubted Judah was on a date with some other girl... and besides, the media lied all the time.

Right?

I kicked my shitty thoughts to the curb, hoping I'd have another chance, later on, to dig deeper into what he'd been up to since he got out, and instead stuck to the topic at hand.

"Did you like her? Your therapist?"

Judah scoffed. "Don't tell her I said this...but I loved her. Still do."

Warmth hit my system knowing that he bonded with the woman that helped him through rehab, even if it was hard for him to admit.

"Are you still able to see her now that you're out?"

He nodded. "Have a phone call at nine a.m. tomorrow morning."

"Good," I replied, and released a tired breath, feeling too many things at once.

As we fell back into silence, I let myself get used to Judah's energy again.

The two of us stared through the railing in front of us and out into the sparkling view of Los Angeles. The outlook he'd chosen was one of my favorite spots in the city, and even though I never told him that, it felt like somehow, he knew.

Or maybe we had that little fact in common.

"All right, so I wanted to ask you this in a much different way," Judah stated a few minutes later. "But I don't have it in me anymore—way too fucking tired—and something tells me you won't care."

My lips lifted just slightly.

"I won't," I promised, feeling the same weight of after-breakdown exhaustion, "ask away."

Despite being tired, Judah moved his body in the dirt and shifted so that he was now sitting directly in front of me. Nerves pricked my skin as those butterflies woke up and began to flap their wings in my stomach. Judah folded his legs, so I did the same, bringing us closer until we were still again.

That's when time seemed to slow to a near halt.

Judah watched me, but for the first time, it felt as if he actually *saw* me.

All of me.

He was looking at me the way I deserved to be looked at—like I was beautiful, in all my strength and determination, but also like he cherished me, like he couldn't believe I was real.

The difference in his stare, the gratitude and reverence in his gaze had me wanting to hide and caused a small blush to creep into my sticky cheeks.

"W-what?" I stuttered out.

"You look like a mess," he stated with zero hesitation.

"Hey!" A shocked laugh tumbled free.

"Not in a bad way," he smirked knowingly. "In a fucking good way, little bird."

At the nickname, both of us sobered. Our smiles fell but our breath quickened to the same heated pace.

Silence reigned for a few seconds, but then he quietly, nervously questioned, "Will you go on a date with me, Phoenix Royal?"

Do not cry again.

God, but it was *so* hard.

Back before I received his letter, and even after that, I assumed the first time I saw Judah again, I'd still be pissed, still be bitter. I thought I'd only accept groveling and hardcore proof that he was serious, that he was sober, and I figured I'd make it hurt. Punish him for all the shit he did to me.

But the fact was, I could see the change without Judah even having to speak because that change had reached his soul. It was written in the air between us. I could taste all the work he did on himself, feel it under my skin.

A date would give me a chance to solidify and bring to life what that change looked like in the physical sense. I could get to know him again. I could ask fun questions, hard questions. I could hold his hand and flirt. I could just…be.

There were so many things I wanted to know, *needed* to know, and after spending so much time thinking we might never make it to this point…

"Yes," I nodded once. "I'll go on a date with you, Judah Colt."

"Thank fuck," he exhaled in relief, with a brief closure of his eyes. But then he seemed to shake off the sadness in his limbs, before he leaned forward, and placed his elbows on his knees. The move brought our faces closer together, made it easier for him to meet me eye to eye.

I held my breath as he stated, "We're starting over."

There it is.

His first demand.

"Okay," was all I said, already knowing he wasn't finished.

"We're gonna do it *right* this time."

I nodded. "Yes, we are."

"I'm gonna charm the *fuck* out of you."

"O-oh?" I choked on my shock.

"I'm gonna tell you the *truth*," he promised, "whenever the opportunity presents itself."

"Good *or* bad," I threw out.

He tipped his chin. "Good or bad."

"Okay, what else?"

I like this game.

"I'm gonna ask for your advice and actually take it," he stated simply.

"This should be good," I wiggled my eyebrows.

He issued a warning, "My life is a mess."

Please. "I'm well aware."

"There'll be paparazzi."

I clicked my tongue. "I can handle it."

For the last one, his blue gaze pierced my chest. "You'll have my back and for once…I'll have *yours*."

My pulse skyrocketed as I whispered, "That sounds like a deal I can agree to."

"Good," he nodded with finality and then surprised the shit out of me by standing and holding out a hand.

Confused, I grabbed it, and he pulled me up.

Standing in front of him, I wasn't sure what he was up to, but the last thing I expected was for him to start walking backward… *away* from me.

There was a fucking grin on his face as he stated, "I'll see you tomorrow. Pharaoh will drive you to the shop and I'll pick you up at 8."

Stunned, I called out, "That's *it?*"

His smile was blinding as he called back, "For now!"

"What?!" I yelled, watching as he mounted his fucking bike.

He can't be serious.

"Goodnight, Baby Bird," was the last thing he said before that engine roared to life, his blond hair disappeared under a helmet, and dirt was blown toward me as he peeled out of the parking lot and into the empty street.

"Son of a bitch," I muttered as I ran to my car and locked myself inside just in case some predator was lurking in the trees. "What the hell just happened?"

※ ❋ ※

"OH MY GOD, I am *so* sorry," Frankie called out as soon as I stepped through the door. "Judah made me keep quiet, and even told the boys not to respond to your text earlier. I was at Silas' house, and he took my phone because I wanted to tell you *so* bad, but I also knew it would ruin everything and Judah wanted to handle it and he had a whole plan and—"

"—it's *fine*, Frankie," I insisted, cutting her off with a smile on my face. "Though I do need you to clarify pretty much everything you just said, but first, help me shut these fucking curtains before those paparazzi start filming us through the goddamn window."

Her blue eyes widened. "Right, okay."

We parted quickly as Frankie ran into her office while I tackled the dining room windows.

By the time I got home, I didn't care that the paparazzi were still out front, because at that point, if they wanted to spread a story, they could. I was back in contact with Judah, and I didn't give a fuck about anything else.

"You look like you were crying," Frankie called out, unwilling to wait before interrogating me. "Did that bastard hurt you again? Because I swear to fucking God, Phoenix…"

Rolling my eyes, I shouted back, "No, Frankie, he didn't hurt me."

"Good," she responded just as I shut the last curtain. "I was about to take back every nice thing I said to him."

Excuse me?

I padded into her office, wondering what the hell she was talking about. "You said nice things to him?"

"Sure did," she muttered, "unfortunately."

Wait a whole ass second...

Putting two and two together, I leaned against the doorframe, and concluded, "So *you're* the mystery blonde."

"Ugh," she sighed dramatically. "I knew we shouldn't have left at the same time, but Judah said he didn't care because it was a part of his plan.'"

"*What* plan?" I narrowed my eyes as she stalked past me, heading down the hall.

"The plan to get you back, stupid."

"Okay, name-calling? Really?" I chuckled in surprise. "You're in a fucking *mood* tonight."

"You know I hate being out of control!" Her rebuttal was loud. "That fucker was *allll* business, though. He refused to tell us his plan and asked us to keep all this shit a secret. BRO, he wouldn't let me tell you *anything*, so of course, I had to live with being a shitty friend and it made me—"

"Crazy?" I finished for her, biting down on a laugh as I sat at one of the chairs at the island.

"Yeah, *crazy!*" She agreed, pointing at me as she opened the cabinet where we stored our liquor. "Judah Colt makes me crazy."

Laughing openly now, I suggested, "Why don't you just start from the beginning and tell me what happened?"

"Okay, yeah," she nodded quickly, still all worked up, "that's a good idea. Just let me make this shot reeeeal quick..."

She focused intently on the two shot glasses on the island

in front of her, pouring tequila into both of them before sliding one to me and downing the other before I even had a chance to pick up my own.

"Ahh," she sighed, "that's better. Alright, so basically? This brand-sp new, totally sober version of Judah Colt is no joke."

Tipping my glass back, I swallowed the contents then requested, "Explain," as the liquor burned its way down my throat.

"So apparently, all week, Judah's been talking to everyone in our group," she started, "Pharaoh was first of course, but then on Monday, he met with his band. I have no idea how it went because none of us have seen Pierce or Vale since it happened, but Pharaoh told us tonight that 'things are happening' which is cryptic as all fuck but fine, whatever. So, *then* I guess on Tuesday he met with Ric and Kav, and of course, I was *pissed* because like…why wouldn't they tell us, right? Well then I found out he met with Silas on Wednesday, and I got even *more* pissed because COME ON."

Even though I'd spent the week alone, wondering how he was doing, feeling completely alone, and more than a little heartbroken, pride swelled in my chest.

Judah wanted to speak to his friends, his family first.

It meant he was taking what I said seriously, and while it sucked, I told him I didn't want our relationship, his *life*, to be all about me, and before rehab, before his overdose, he wouldn't have given a fuck about what his friends thought of him. He would have run everyone over and barged back into my life without a care in the world, demanding that I take him back.

What Judah had done this week was a bigger deal than Frankie realized.

"And then, here I am this morning, begging the guys to let me go on a fucking *golfing* trip with them." My eyes went wide. "Yeah, I know, I was *that* desperate. But anywho, they wouldn't let me go because it was a 'dude's day.' So, like twenty minutes later I get a call from Judah, and low and behold, all three guys already knew it was coming. So, naturally, I kicked them out, had a complete meltdown, then answered Judah's *second* call due to peer pressure, and ended up at Urth Café with him this afternoon, where I inevitably accepted Judah's very heartfelt, very convincing, and very annoying apology because he fucking *charmed* me into it."

Her story was so long-winded, I busted out laughing, unable to help myself given what I already knew about Judah's ability to apologize now that I'd experienced one myself.

"Yeah, you're laughing, but I was *not*," she bitched. "Especially when he told me on the way out of the cafe that he *wanted* the paparazzi to get a glimpse of us. After we'd been photographed, he told me to go to Silas' house—spoiler alert, there was no golfing trip—and to let him know when you texted us because *somehow*, he knew you would reach out to me if there were paparazzi camped outside the house and I wasn't home. I told him I wouldn't be a part of his shitty plan, so Silas stole my goddamn phone and let Judah know when you texted our group chat."

"Which is why instead of getting a response from you guys, I got a text from him," I put it all together. "Son of a bitch."

The smile on my face was massive as I realized that he really did plan the whole thing.

"Wait, what?" Frankie asked. "Seriously?"

"Dude, he texted me not even a minute after I texted you," I chuckled, shaking my head. "It was instant. He dropped a pin to his location and asked me to meet him."

"All we knew was that you agreed to meet him! Judah refused to tell us how or where it would go down," Franks explained, but then squealed, "Oh my god, tell me everything!"

So, I did.

And that was how I spent the rest of my night—reliving my reunion with Judah, telling Frankie about the tears, the truths, the breakdowns, and finally, the moment I'd been waiting for since Pharaoh's phone call on that plane.

The moment we pressed that reset button.

CHAPTER 27

JUDAH

"WELL, it's safe to say the paparazzi have found you," Pharaoh announced, stalking through the front door of his apartment with a sour-looking pout on his face. "They're everywhere bro."

"Yeah, I know," I cringed, feeling like shit for subjecting Pharaoh to the media chaos. "They want updates on my situation with Brandon."

"It's not just that and you know it," Pharaoh bitched as he flopped onto the couch and closed his eyes. "Between you being freshly out of rehab, Phoenix, the mystery blonde, our career going up in flames, *and* the Brandon bullshit? Forget about it. They're not going away anytime soon."

He was right, of course, but I didn't know what to do about it because it was always Hendrix that cleaned up my messes with the tabloids. "Fuck, we need a PR manager."

"Correction," Pharaoh started, sounding bored and tired, "*you* need a PR manager."

Standing from the chair, I anxiously made my way into the kitchen. "Okay, sure, *for now*. But what happens when we announce this new album? We're going to need someone to help set up interviews and shit."

"You need to do an interview now," Pharaoh suggested. "Or at the very least, release a statement."

That did *not* sound like something I wanted to do.

"I don't even know *how* to release a statement," I groaned, opening the fridge in search of something to drink. My throat was drying up more and more by the minute. "Who takes care of that shit?"

"PR Managers," Pharaoh mumbled.

I clicked my tongue, tacking on an eye roll for dramatics. "I meant where would a PR Manager send the statement?"

"Not a single fuckin' clue, dude, but we need to figure it out, so they go the fuck away."

Sighing, I shut the fridge and leaned against it as I pinched the bridge of my nose and thought through the massive list of shit, I needed to take care of in the next few weeks.

I had absolutely zero clue what I was going to do but still, I said, "I'll handle it."

The last thing Pharaoh needed after all this was to clean up more of my mess. I was already living with him, driving his car, and now the paparazzi were stalking his apartment complex. It wasn't ideal for anyone involved but he was right, one statement could solve the issue.

"You know I'll help you," Pharaoh let loose a sigh of his own as he sat up to meet my eyes. "I'm just in a mood."

"What's goin' on?" I asked, jumping on the opportunity to talk about him for once.

"I don't know, man, I slept like shit and then I got to thinking about this class I'm teaching down in Northridge, and with the winter session ending, I wanted to do something bigger in the spring...I just don't know how to tell Carmine that I want to branch out."

He was speaking fucking gibberish. "What are you talking about? What classes?"

"Fuck, sorry," he shook his head, "I forgot you weren't really…uh, paying attention at the end of last year."

There was that guilt again, followed closely by the shame demon.

It only got worse when he explained, "Phoenix and I teach classes to kids from low-income families under a program that a woman named Carmine launched last year in Northridge. P ran a drawing class, focused on the art of tattooing, while I taught percussion to a group of fifteen kids."

I pictured it, thinking of the two of them giving back to our community, showing off their individual passions, and the vision in my head made my chest swell and ache all at once.

I'd missed it.

Seeing Phoenix interact with kids, watching Pharaoh light up as he ran through the basics of what he did for a living…

Forgive yourself and be present in the moment. Do not drag past mistakes into a present situation when you can strive to fix it instead.

My inner voice was beginning to resemble Dr. Blake, but it was right. I had an opportunity to integrate myself back into their lives and I could do it genuinely this time, I could show them I cared, that I *wanted* to be a part of it.

The first time I tried to speak, nothing came out, so I cleared my throat quickly and tried again, "T-that's awesome, dude. But what's the problem?"

"Carmine," he answered, "I don't know how she would react if I told her I wanted to expand the program, turn it into a 30-40 student class and move it to a bigger venue."

My eyes widened. "That's a lot of kids, Phar. How would you handle them all yourself?"

"I wouldn't," he responded, getting up from the couch and beginning to pace. "I want to make a program of my own and invite a few new drummers I've met over the last few months to teach. They play for smaller bands, mostly indie, and I think not only could they use the exposure, but they're also talented enough to teach a new generation of drummers. But not the kind that can afford fancy classes. These kids can barely afford lunch at school."

He would need a whole lot of practice drums and a serious plan if he wanted to pull this off. "What if you still taught for Carmine and held the big class once a month?"

His black eyes hit mine. "Is that enough time to learn anything significant?"

Shit. "Probably not. Buuuuut, you could gift the kids their own practice drum and start a virtual YouTube series, maybe? They could learn from home."

"How would they watch, Judah? They don't have devices, probably don't even have internet."

Fuck, he's right.

"Thirty kids, thirty phones…" I did the math in my head. "Alright I have an idea but it's insane."

An excited grin spread across Phar's face as he clapped his hands together and said, "Hit me."

"What if we searched the internet and bought old phones off people," I started, thinking on my feet. "These kids don't have access to the internet or Wi-Fi unless they're in public, right? So that would be where we gather our *lovely* group of friends and host an uploading/downloading party."

"I'm listening…" Pharaoh dragged out, staring at me intently.

I could see the gears working in his head.

"We would have to ask the parents for permission for this plan, but what if we filmed your videos and skipped YouTube all together? We could get every kid set up with a phone and just manually upload the videos to each device. It would be a bitch to do with that many kids, but hell, they'd have a month's worth of classes in one place and they could watch over and over if they wanted to. Even pass it on to a friend."

"Fuck, that's brilliant!" Phar nearly shouted, but then deflated pretty quick, "It's going to be pricey though. Even if we find super old iPhones being sold for two or three hundred apiece. That shit will add up when we get to the twenty or thirtieth one."

"I'll take care of it," I promised, wanting to be of use. "It's a damn good idea and thanks to my reckless behavior, our music has gained some serious traction over the last few months. I can afford it."

"You have to buy a new house," Pharaoh countered.

"Yeah, and it'll be smaller than the one I currently own, plus we did upgrades, so it's worth more than what I bought it for," I pointed out, and when he looked at me like I'd just told him aliens visited me in my sleep, I pushed, "Seriously, it's fine. You just need to get me the brand of practice drum you want the kids to use, and I'll order them. I'd imagine it'll take some time for those to come in, though."

"Well, that's fine, given the fact that I have to film a whole fucking *series*," Pharaoh smirked before his face fell serious. "But, Judah, you seriously don't have to do this."

"Yeah…I do," I confessed, feeling the weight of my childhood creeping in. "You and I both know what it's like to wonder where our next meal is coming from, we both know what it feels like to live in a family that doesn't have enough money to keep the electricity on, much less pay for an extracurricular class." Phar glanced down at his hands as the same kind of memories began to assault him too. "If we had been given an opportunity like this, it could have changed everything for us."

A small, bitter sound left his mouth. "Damn right."

"So, I *do* have to," I stated softly. "I've gotta do what I can to give these kids some kind of hope because the shit I just went through? I wouldn't wish it on anyone."

The lack of inspiration, the belief that I'd never find a way out, and then avoiding the problem altogether was what led to my downfall, but if we could give these kids some hope from the jump and start them off young? We could prevent a problem from developing in the first place. Give them something to dream about and let them know they had support in the process.

Yeah, this needed to happen.

"Thank you," Pharaoh whispered, meeting my stare again, this time showing me just how grateful he was. "But not just for wanting to help. For caring enough to listen in the first place."

The fact that he had to thank me for such a small thing told me just how shitty of a friend I'd been for all these years, and again, I was left feeling like a giant pile of useless garbage.

It took me a minute to get out of the dark corner of my head, the one where I stored my giant pile of self-hatred, but I crawled out of there when I reminded myself that it wasn't about me.

This whole situation wasn't about me.

I was making up for lost time, and every person in my life needed to know just how much I really did care about the things they loved. I didn't know how to before, still didn't really know in the current moment, but I was walking blindly and hoping my soul would help me out.

"You shouldn't have to thank me for my support," I muttered quietly. "But I understand why you did, and all I'll say is, don't thank me again. Instead, hold me to a higher standard and expect that from now on, I'll be giving a shit. I'll be a better friend."

Clearly at a loss for words, Pharaoh just watched me for a few seconds, but then nodded as a small smirk began to grow across his face once again.

"What's that look for?" I asked, feeling suspicious and a bit bashful.

"I'm thinking Cliffside might work some sort of voodoo magic on its patients," he chuckled. "You're…just not the same."

"Is that a *bad* thing?" I laughed.

"Not even a little," he shrugged, smiling widely now. "It's just fucking shocking."

"Yeah, well, no one is more shocked than me," I threw out before heading toward the room I was sleeping in. But before I locked myself in, I called out, "Did you make sure to give Phoenix her helmet this morning when you dropped her at the shop?"

"Ha. Yeah, dude, she's all set," he yelled back.

"Perfect."

I grinned to myself.

It was going to be a damn good night.

CHAPTER 28
Phoenix

"THESE MOTHERFUCKERS ARE *RELENTLESS*," Kenji complained from the window of Death's Door, as he stared out at the crowd of paparazzi outside. "I don't know how you handle this shit."

"I don't," I muttered, focused on finishing up a design for my first appointment on Monday. "Just pretend they're not there."

"Bullshit!" he shouted, scaring me into looking up from my iPad, eyes wide. The man looked unhinged. "Can I go say something? Please?"

"No, Kenji, you can't," I warned, "because then there will be a story about you defending me, and they'll follow you home and stalk you until you tell them what I'm hiding. They'll think you're my secret boyfriend and it'll turn into a whole mess. Right now, they don't care about you, they want me, so just…I don't know, come chill."

"Easy for *you* to say," he mumbled under his breath.

"Dude, the shop has never been more popular," I pointed out. "You're winning here."

"At the expense of our fucking privacy? I can barely focus!"

"Because you're feeding the attention!" I shot back. "Aren't you done for the day? Just go home!"

It was seven-thirty, the shop was nearly closed, and he had no reason to be there. We'd both just completed three back-to-back clients, and he even planned to come in on his day off tomorrow to do a full-sized thigh piece because the client was willing to pay over a thousand dollars more than what he would have charged, just to have it as soon as possible.

"I'm not leaving you alone," Kenji replied, sighing out a harsh exhale. "No way."

"Judah will be here soon," I reminded him. "It's fine, Kenj. I'm good."

"Absolutely not." His tone resembled finality. "What if he doesn't show up? You have no fucking car, Phoenix. I'm not leaving you with the horde of crazies outside."

I rolled my eyes. "That's sweet and all, but Judah wouldn't just leave me here."

Even when Judah was high as fuck, if I called, he'd answer. I never had to worry about him forgetting about me. That was the very *last* thing that would happen.

"I'm still not leaving," he insisted. "I'll wait with you and we can all leave together."

"Fine," I caved. "But please hush for a little bit, I'm so close to being done with this."

I was off tomorrow and the last thing I wanted to do was spend time on my iPad, working. I'd done so much fucking drawing lately I was developing a permanent hand cramp.

I deserved a break.

Kenji listened, turning up the music in the shop before he started stress cleaning. I loved working for the man, and that love only grew over the last few months. We'd become partners—more than just owner and employee. The two of us thought about bringing someone else onto the team, but that idea only lasted five minutes, after we discussed all the things that could go wrong.

Our workload was crazy, our schedules were booked months in advance, but we liked it that way, and the thought of having to train someone to keep up with our pace, or even risk their design and quality not matching our own? Nah, it wasn't worth it.

Twenty minutes later, my phone pinged, letting me know a text had come through, and without even looking at who it was, anticipation grew in my tummy.

"That better be him," Kenji stated from across the room, sounding salty as hell.

Luckily for me, it was.

Judah: Put your helmet on before you leave the shop. I'm going to pull up, you run out and hop right on. We'll drive through the crowd.

A wide-ass smile bloomed on my face.

Phoenix: Aye aye, captain.
Judah: Two minutes, little bird.

"Get your stuff and bounce, Kenj," I instructed, still grinning. "Judah will be here in two and he's basically gonna do a fucking drive-by."

Despite his initial annoyance, Kenji smirked, "Of course he is."

My whole body was alight with a mixture of excitement and serious nerves as I said, "It's a good thing I won't be at the shop tomorrow because if these guys are wondering about the status of Judah and I's relationship, they're about to get a juicy little tidbit."

It felt like alligators were swimming in my belly, knowing

that the paps most definitely get photos of Judah and me on his bike, but that was an extreme benefit of wearing helmets.

They wouldn't be able to see either of our faces.

Small miracles and all that.

"Good point, they'll probably leave as soon as they figure out you're not working," Kenji agreed.

"I doubt they'll even show up," I shrugged as I shut down my iPad. "They'll probably follow me home tonight and camp out there instead."

Kenji's face puckered up as if he'd just eaten half a lemon. "You need to move into a gated community if that's the shit you're gonna deal with."

"That's not a bad idea," I mused. "But eventually Judah and I will become old news. Especially if he speaks to a media outlet at some point and just gets it over with."

"Is he going to do that?" Kenji asked.

"I have no idea, honestly."

It's not like we'd gotten a chance to talk about anything the night before, given how emotional our reunion was. I hoped to talk about those things tonight, as well as catch up on what he's been doing after learning from Frankie that he'd begun to mend his relationships with our friends.

Suddenly, the crowd outside started making more noise, moving quickly down the street with their cameras up.

"Shit, he's here," I rushed out, and tossed the strap of my bag over my shoulder. Running behind the counter, I grabbed the brand new shiny black helmet and pulled it down over my head. I made sure the visor was in place, just in time to hear Judah's bike roaring toward the shop.

Fuck, here goes nothing.

"Bye, you little minx!" Kenji called as I secured my messenger bag against my hip, opened the door, and high-tailed it toward Judah, where he straddled his idling motorcycle in the middle of the street and stared in my direction.

I couldn't see his face, couldn't tell if he was smiling or frowning but I could feel the intensity of his gaze, even without the evidence.

Somehow, I was able to quickly, gracefully, throw my leg over the back of J's bike, arrange my bag behind me, and wrap two arms around his waist in record time.

Before I knew it, J was revving the engine, warning the screaming paparazzi around us to get out of the way or get run over.

Some cut it incredibly close, trying to get as many shots as possible, not caring that their flashes were nearly blinding us. But Judah couldn't be distracted. He gassed the engine and flew forward, straight through the swarm of paps, and down the road, speeding us away from the prying eyes.

It wasn't until we hit Pacific Coast Highway that I relaxed, settling into the feeling of Judah's body in front of me. The fact that he was here, that I was wrapped around him, had me smiling behind the mask of my helmet. I felt like screaming, shouting to the sky that miracles were real, even though nothing major had really happened yet.

We talked—him more than me—and we cried.

That was it.

And yet the whole exchange had been transformative, was proof that change had occurred. It was evidence of deep, inner soul work that would allow us to build on a more solid foundation, and I felt foolish for even thinking that those feelings we shared before everything fell apart, were fake or false.

Our relationship was littered with immaturity and toxicity, but at the base of it all, it was real. We just didn't know what to do with it or how to nurture our connection properly. And if I were honest, I wasn't positive that we knew how to do that even now, but it was safe to say that we both definitely knew what *not* to do, and that was a good enough start.

Judah drove for an hour, heading deep into malibu and

even past the coastal town, bringing us to an in-between place where houses were few and far between and the beach was empty. The sky was dark when he pulled over, appearing navy blue, as he parked the bike in an empty lot that reminded me a little of the place we'd celebrated Frankie's birthday. But this time, there were stairs we could use to get down to the sand, instead of dangerously navigating massive rocks to get the job done.

When the engine cut off and we both pulled off our helmets, all we were left with was the crashing symphony of the ocean down below and the rare passing of cars. Anxiety and excitement felt one in the same as my fingers worked to smooth out my hair and regulate my breathing.

Neither of us spoke, but the silence was loud.

I could feel Judah's energy sinking into mine once again, but this time there was a sense of calm integration like he was getting used to being in my presence again and it was a feeling I understood well. I'd been doing the same.

When my hair was as good as it was going to get, I took a deep breath and got off the bike, using J's shoulder to help steady my body as I adjusted to the feeling of solid ground after an hour of enduring the bike's vibrations.

He silently held my elbow and watched me until I was good to stand on my own.

I was too nervous, too heated to watch him dismount, and instead turned. My boots crunched along the gravel as I walked to the railing overlooking the beach, and I focused on the sound of *his* boots as he hung our helmets and locked up the bike.

Every inch of my body was aware of him as neither of us spoke, and it remained that way until he called out, "You're beautiful, you know that?"

Butterflies danced, as I glanced over my shoulder to look at him.

He was leaning against the bike, arms crossed over his chest, as he stared at me, and in the darkened night, those blue eyes looked like stars. True admiration lingered in his gaze and the sensation of his affection ran all the way to my toes.

I tipped my chin. "So are you."

Our eyes locked and an energetic battle began as the two of us tried not to smile. Eventually, he stood up straight and headed toward me, showcasing that natural-born swag as he walked.

The leather jacket he wore had my thighs clenching and drool pooling in my mouth but I swallowed down my arousal, knowing this date was about a whole lot more than physical attraction.

"I wanted to do a whole *thing* tonight," Judah confessed when he was in front me, when his body was within touching distance. "I was planning the candlelit dinner and even bought roses, but with the paparazzi stalking me in the city I just—"

"—are we really candlelit dinner kind of people?" I asked, cutting him off.

Already able to tell that he felt bad about not being able to do what a man would normally do when trying to win back a girl he'd fucked over, I wanted to wash that guilt away. I genuinely didn't care what he did.

All I gave a shit about was what he said, who he was, how he treated himself, and in exchange, how he treated me going forward. The rest was nonsense.

"I don't know," Judah answered as he stepped forward, "are we?"

I shook my head, realizing we really *didn't* know what kind of people, what kind of couple we were. We never got that far, never did things normally.

"We went so fast in the beginning," I stated, then reached forward to brush some dust off the t-shirt peeking out under his jacket. "We never really got to the true get-to-know-you part."

"If I recall correctly—" he wrapped his fingers around my hand before I could remove it from his chest, "—we absolutely *did* get to that part. We played twenty questions on a beach just like this."

"Ha," I let out a small laugh, remembering that night. "Okay, sure, but it did *not* go well."

I'd made false promises that night. Promises that came back to bite me. *Hard.*

"No, it didn't," he agreed, but there was a smirk on his lips, and I decided right there and then that Judah's eyes were the prettiest at night. They truly did resemble stars, and that specific shade of blue had become a beacon, a symbol, my favorite color. "What do you say we try again?"

My stomach flipped, my cheeks heated, especially as he laced his fingers through mine and began to walk, pulling me toward the stairs.

"You want to play twenty questions…?" I clarified nervously, not loving the odds of that going well given our track record.

"Yup," he called back, sounding determined.

"Are we going to do it the *right* way this time?"

"You betcha," he answered, but then paused suddenly on the steps, causing me to stumble. Luckily, he still had my hand and managed to turn at the last second, so catching me was easy. Now standing eye to eye, he held my waist as he murmured, "I've got a long list of questions, but I'm sure yours is even longer."

The palms of my hands burned against his chest as I said, "you're probably right."

"Good," he grinned, brushing a piece of hair off my face before tucking it behind my ear. Then, after making sure I was steady on the stair, he pulled back and lifted both hands between us, and rushed out, "Rock paper scissors for who goes first. Ready? Go!"

I blinked once, twice, then caught up, launching into the first round with determination to win.

"Ha!" I called when my scissors beat his paper.

"Again."

His hand covered my fist in the second round. "Fuck! Wait, are we playin' two out of three?"

"Four," he corrected.

"What if it's a tie?"

His shoulders lifted on a quick shrug, "We ask a question at the same time."

A laugh bubbled up my throat, "That makes no sense."

"True," he nodded, appearing hella focused, as we started the third round.

He chose scissors while I picked paper right at the last second.

Judah gloated, with a sexy as fuck grin, "Guess that means I won."

"Damnnit," I bitched, and pushed him backward. "Fine, go."

His laugh warmed my chest. "Don't be a sore loser, it's just one question."

Still salty, I muttered, "You know I hate losing."

Judah hit the sand first, and when he did, he spun to face me, rocking a smile that could have killed me if his energy wasn't so alive. "I sure do."

"If this were football, you'd get a penalty for rubbing in your touchdown," I sassed. "Just ask your question, mister."

He lifted his arm in my direction. "Hand first."

My heartbeat picked up its pace.

As I laced my fingers through his, I prayed this attitude of his wasn't due to drugs or a false start. I found my fear lurking in the background, behind all my excitement, and I hoped it stayed there—far, far away—as we began to walk.

I scanned the area, pulling in mindful breaths as I kept

myself in check, trying to stay grounded given the uneasiness of my current situation with Judah. He was acting fine—better than fine, really—but I wasn't able to just forget everything that happened. Forget that he was capable of going full monster on me at any moment.

I forced myself to brace for impact, just in case.

"Okay, so," he drew out, squeezing my fingers gently, "I'll start easy. What *is* your idea of a perfect date?"

The answer was easy. "I don't have one. And not because I'm super chill and don't care about romance or anything, but really just because…I've never actually been on a date."

"Wait, what?" Judah gaped down at me and stopped our forward motion in the sand. "What do you mean?"

"Before you, I never even had a boyfriend." *I can't believe I never told him this.* "I fucked around in high school, and in college I just turned that up a notch. I was never interested in dating or falling in love given the whole situation with my parents."

That particular memory always zapped me into a different mood. Bringing out bitterness and fear, tainted with a sadness I could never fully express or get rid of.

"I should have known that," J mused quietly. "Neither of us have really done this before."

"No," I stated. "We haven't."

Staring up at him under the cover of night, I wondered what would happen when we got to the *really* difficult questions. I feared pushing him too far, saying too much, or not saying enough and triggering those heated, toxic, arguments we used to have.

"I guess that just means we can figure it out together," Judah supplied, sounding more confident than I was. "We can plan dates together from now on, until we get the hang of it. Or we can surprise each other, and if one of us doesn't like it, we can make a pact to tell the truth."

"A pact?" I smirked, even though that worry was still creeping through my veins.

He lifted the hand that wasn't holding mine, and made a fist, leaving only one finger standing up.

"Pinky promise me," he requested, "that we'll always be honest about what we like and dislike."

Unable to resist, I held up my own pinky, adding, "And we won't get butthurt or take it personally if we don't like what the other has to say."

"Deal," he whispered as our pinkies wrapped around one another. "Seal it."

I knew what he meant, but time slowed as I realized we hadn't kissed yet. Hadn't kissed in months.

But when I lifted my head to put my lips to my fist and he mirrored the motion, leaning down so that our eyes tangled as we sealed our new deal. The air around us grew thick with unspoken tension and chills danced down my spine.

Why does this all feel so…strange?

I pulled back quickly and cleared my throat before unlinking my finger from his. My shoe sank into the sand as I began to walk again, pulling him after me.

We had so much fucking history. It felt like there was a giant addiction-sized elephant in our energetic bubble and I wasn't sure what to make of it. Again, I thought I'd be punishing him for the things he'd done, I thought he'd be groveling on bended knees to get me back but instead, it felt like I really was on a first date with a brand new person.

Where was *my* Judah?

I only saw a glimpse of him here and there. The rest was someone else entirely.

"My turn," I stated, trying not to think about all the what-ifs and focus on the moment. "Now that you're out of rehab, sober, and free to do what you want…what will you do next? What do you picture for yourself in the future?"

"That's two questions," he pointed out. "You've gotta pick one, baby bird."

"Fine." I rolled my eyes. "The second one."

More than anything, I wanted to know where his head was at, and that question was sure to give me a solid idea, but for some reason, it caused him to pause. I felt the shift immediately, causing me to look back at him.

Gone was the flirty Judah, and in his place was the recovering addict I'd met last night. His eyebrows were pulled together just enough to let me know he was contemplating something, while he chewed on his bottom lip. The light in his eyes had gone out, replaced by a darkened sort of worry.

Wanting to remain steady and supportive, I slowed my pace and gave him room to think.

We'd walked another twenty or thirty feet further down the beach before he spoke quietly, "Truth?"

I blinked, remembering our first conversation on the rooftop of Silas' house, and once again, deadly creatures swam in the pit of my stomach.

Still, I glanced up at him and whispered, "Always."

"I'm trying not to think too far ahead," Judah admitted in a voice laced with exhaustion. "I get anxiety when I think beyond things I know for sure, and find it hard to travel into territory I haven't discovered yet. For example, I have a meeting with my lawyer this week about Brandon's case against me, and I know what I need to say and how I want it to go. But if I try to think about what happens after that, when *my* lawyer talks to *his*, I find myself imagining up all the ways it could go wrong and then I tumble into expecting the worst, which turns into a seriously bad case of panic. My brain can't handle too much at once right now, or maybe ever. So, I guess I don't know how to answer your question."

The mention of Brandon had secondhand anxiety slithering

through my veins, so I couldn't even imagine how *Judah* was handling it.

"It'll get better," I promised, "I can't exactly tell you *when* —because I still deal with the same thing—but it does get better." Judah had actually presented me with the perfect opportunity to see if he could actually handle me giving him advice, so I went on to say, "If you think about it, you're literally reprogramming your brain right now, trying to break old patterns and find healthier ways to deal with your anxiety. It doesn't happen overnight; it takes consistency in order to see results."

Judah laughed, which was a damn surprise, but it ended on a sigh before he said, "You and Blake would get along swimmingly. She said almost the same thing to me when we talked this morning."

"Oh, yeah, how did that go?" I asked, curious to see what he'd tell me now that we had an open-door policy when it came to honesty.

"It went as it always does," Judah admitted. "We talked about the last couple of days, but we mostly talked about you."

My tummy dipped, wondering what his therapist thought of me. "And?"

"And I'm pretty sure the woman wanted to throw me a party. Virgin Pina Coladas included," he scoffed in a lovingly annoyed tone.

I chuckled a little. "Why's that?"

"Because I've spent the last three months telling her how you'd never take me back and I'd end up alone and angry at the world forever." His tone was monosyllabic. "She always knew that wasn't true. Said you'd be able to see the change in me."

"I can," I said right away, but then paused when a shocked expression crossed his face. "I mean, I can feel it..." I didn't want to give him a free pass after the shit he'd done, but I also couldn't deny what was glaringly obvious to me. "You—your energy is just different."

"In a good way?" He asked, sounding nervous.

"Yeah," I shrugged. "I don't know, J, the more I spend time with you, the more I feel like you've changed so much that I really might not know you at all."

At that, he sucked his teeth and nodded, looking away from me.

"What?" I asked, now nervous myself.

Did I say something wrong?

He shook his head.

"Judah, look at me," I requested, and when he gave me his eyes, I saw resentment, a little bit of anger, but I wasn't sure why it was there. "What's happening here?"

"It's the drugs," he spat out. "You're right. You *don't* know me. I don't even know me, yet. I'm doing the best I fucking can but when you say that, I get all fucked in the head because I'm terrified that you'll hate who I really am compared to who you fell for."

Whoa.

"I feared the same thing," I admitted softly, stepping forward. "I feared you'd grow past me, wouldn't love me after the drugs were out of your system. I *knew* everything would be different, J. I knew you wouldn't be the same guy, and I knew the drugs made you who you were before, but that doesn't mean I'm not willing to get to know you again."

"You shouldn't have to," he laughed bitterly. "I'm not worth the investment."

"Why don't you let me decide that?" I asked, realizing that my Judah was most definitely still in there, he was just too scared to come out. Judah was posturing, trying to appear confident when he was a mess of worries inside. That insecurity was still there, the guilt wouldn't go away for who knew how long, but there was room for me. There was still space for me to come in and prove that he was worthy of being loved for the man he was outside of his vices, especially if he loved *me* properly this time.

We really could grow together; he just didn't believe it because he'd never tried before.

When he didn't answer I said, "Pause for a second and don't think about the immediate future. Think about ten or fifteen years down the line when all of this is behind us, you're settled and happy…what do you want to do? What dreams do you have on your bucket list?"

He chuckled sadly and admitted, "Babe, I barely have a bucket list."

Feeling some type of way about how much damage Judah's addiction did on his ability to dream, I said, "Alright, then make some shit up on the spot. Off the top of your head, what do you want?"

"You," he stated simply, glancing down at me with a fiery stare, "but I also want to travel."

My soul surged at the first part, getting caught in my throat, making it harder to ask, "Travel where?"

"Europe at first," he mused, then starting to walk again. "I want to backpack, I think, because even though I've been there multiple times, I never truly explored. I would stay for a whole summer and actually *live* there; see the culture and learn how they spend their day to day lives as non-tourists." His face had taken on a dreamy sort of expression. "I'd like to see Barcelona, too but man, I'd love to go to Egypt."

Moisture pooled in my eyes, but I blinked it away, focusing instead on the conversation at hand. "What about Peru?"

"Absolutely," he nodded down at me. "Even Israel, we could explore the dead sea."

I'd succeeded in getting him out of the negative hole in his head and guided him onto a new pathway of thought, and all of a sudden we were dreaming together, creating a list of places we wanted to go. Before I knew it there were over thirty destinations on our travel list.

I laughed through his horrible attempt at an Australian accent and he made fun of me for wanting to go to Costa Rica to hold monkeys in the wild.

"You're going to get your face eaten off," he chuckled. "Wild monkeys are mean as fuck."

"If you're nice to them, they'll be nice to you," I waved him off, smiling to myself.

"Sure, if you don't make any sudden movements," he laughed. "Where's the fun in that?"

"You're ruining this for me," I let go of his hand and stepped away.

He grabbed my arm and pulled me back, "Fine we can go see monkeys."

"Thank you. Adding it to the list," I gloated as I typed "Costa Rica" into my phone. "Alright we've spent enough time on this, it's your turn."

There was a few blank seconds of time before I felt his mood shift once again, falling into that darker territory where his fears lived, and while I wasn't exactly looking forward to his question, I knew we had shit we needed to get out in the open.

Judah took his time though, and just when I thought he would never ask the question, he whispered, "Do you love Pharaoh?"

Fuck.

I'd forgotten that Pharaoh told Judah what happened between us. He told me about it the day after, explained that he wasn't sure how Judah felt because he didn't freak out, he just got lost in his head then left. I told Pharaoh that he needed to sit Judah down and talk about it when he saw him again but I never found out what happened after that phone call.

Judah's question for me wasn't accusatory in any way,

instead, it felt like he was genuinely asking me how I felt, with an underlying tone of wondering what I wanted.

My breath left my body in a deep exhale, before I answered honestly, "Yes. I do. But not in the way you think."

"But you slept with him," he stated quietly.

"I did," I nodded once, tussling with worry over Judah's reaction.

"Will you tell me why?" The question came out so gentle it made him sound like a little boy that just wanted to understand why life was so fucking unfair.

"Because I was upset," I told him. "I was pissed at you, sick of feeling alone, done with crying, but more worried than anything. I just…needed to shut off the noise for a while."

"But you had feelings for him," he assumed. "I know you, and I know you wouldn't have slept with my best friend out of revenge."

He was right. "My feelings for Pharaoh were growing at the time, yes. We'd spent so much time together at that point and had formed a pretty deep friendship. But I think both of us knew we could escape for a while, and we jumped on the opportunity. I was shaken up, he wanted to make it better—make *something* better—since he couldn't fix you, and it was a survival instinct between two people that lost the person they loved the most. We wanted the connection we couldn't have with you, but found it with each other."

That might have been too much information but I had to tell him the truth. Sugarcoating facts wouldn't help him at that point, Judah needed to know what we went through as a result of his own choices. My sleeping with Pharaoh was a result of Judah's actions. There was no way around it.

Judah was shockingly calm and quiet, until he asked, "Do you resent me for pushing you that far?"

"Truthfully, no," I told him. "Because at that point, I didn't want anything to be about you. I was more grateful that Pharaoh was there, willing to escape with me."

"And if I had never gone to rehab?" he went on to ask, "if I'd never overdosed? Do you think you would be with him?"

My stomach was in knots.

"No, I don't," I told him honestly. "Would we have tried? Probably. But I think in the end of it, Pharaoh and I being together would have made it worse for you—sober or not—and neither of us would have been willing to do that."

"You would have given up a chance at love, just to keep me from crawling into a hole I would have ended up in anyway?" He sounded surprised, but it was tame. Tempered and mature.

I had to stop walking. He paused too.

When I lifted my head to scan his face, there were questions written all over his features, and I couldn't help it, I reached up, standing on my tippy toes, to smooth the creased line between his eyebrows.

"Judah, at that point, I had already lost my one great love," I admitted. "It wouldn't have been hard to walk away from Pharaoh, because I'd already experienced the hardest and worst sacrifice. I had to give up *you*. If I would have ended up with Pharaoh—or anyone else for that matter—I'm sure I could have found happiness, but you still would have been my biggest regret, even though it wasn't my actions that split us apart."

My love for Judah was permanent, written in stone, and I was convinced we had a soul contract both of us agreed to sign long before we were born into this world.

"I'm sorry, Phoenix," Judah whispered again.

He's...sorry?

The old Judah would have lost his shit, gone completely bananas, and yet this Judah wasn't freaking out, wasn't overreacting. In fact, in my opinion, his response was an *under*reaction, which had me skeptical.

I had to know. "Are you mad at me? At Pharaoh?"

"No," he shook his head and reached out to run the outside of his index finger over my cheekbone. "Am I jealous? Yes. Does it make me want to burn the city to ashes? You have *no* idea. But can I fucking blame you? No." His hand fell away and regret coated his stare. "Phoenix, I fucked…Jesus, I made you—"

"Judah," I called out, stopping him with a hand on his arm before he tried to go through the memory of Layla and what he did on the rooftop. "We experienced it already. You learned from it. You digested it right?"

"Yes," he choked out. "But Phoenix, I did it out of revenge because I genuinely thought it would turn you into a monster, just like me. I thought you'd retaliate and I wouldn't be playing the game alone anymore. How did I read you so wrong?"

"Are you actually asking me? Or are you backsliding into doubt because you're feeling guilty?" I questioned gently, knowing he already talked through this in rehab. He had to if Dr. Blake knew about me. "You don't feel like you deserve my forgiveness."

"I don't," he stepped back, running two hands through his hair. I watched as his eyes glazed over, as he fell face-first into that negative spiral he was so familiar with. "I don't deserve you, *period.*"

"I disagree," was my only response because I wanted to let him have his moment.

I didn't cut it short because he needed to feel his way through this. He needed to process my willingness to accept who he was *now* over the man he was when he was addicted.

"Is it seriously enough that I recognize how shitty I was and apologize for it, though?" He laughed bitterly. "Sure I cried, sure I told my therapist every disgusting detail and got down to the bottom of why I did what I did, but how is that enough to earn forgiveness from you?"

"It isn't," I agreed. "Because it's not just about the forgiveness, it's about the work you put in after. It's about ensuring that you never make those decisions again. It's about trusting that you won't."

"Yeah, and how can you trust me after all that?"

"Because I never lost faith in you," I replied, getting emotional. "Even when you were acting like a total fucking psychopath, I saw the light inside that soul of yours and all I ever wanted was for you to see it too. But I didn't want you to just simply *see* it. I wanted you to *wear* it, own it, and you're on your way there, Judah. You're wearing that light in your soul like a necklace right now, and *that* is the version of you that I trust. It doesn't matter what else you've done, because you've done the *one thing* that guarantees a beautiful outcome…as long as you never lose faith."

I stepped forward then, as he stared at me like he couldn't figure out where I'd come from. Like I was a beautiful alien.

I placed my hand in the center of his chest. "As long as you keep wearing this light, as long as you nurture it and help it grow brighter, we won't ever face those problems again."

"Because addiction isn't my identity," he stated, sounding like he was reminding himself.

"And neither are your mistakes."

"But I hurt you so bad," he reminded me in a whisper, dropping his forehead to mine in defeat.

"I hurt you too," I stated, needing him to see that it wasn't one-sided. "I broke a promise I made by walking away from you and it hurt. I hurt you. Which only fueled your addiction, darkened your actions, because anger and revenge were all you knew at the time. But now, after all the work you've done, you know better. And so do I."

Though the whole conversation wasn't fun, it still felt like the stepping stone we needed.

Our past needed to be flushed out, felt, and forgiven before we could move forward.

"I won't fail you again," he promised shakily, like he was trying his best to stay strong. "You didn't want to be my reason for living, and you're not. I'm putting my life back together for *myself*, in the way *I* want it to look, and I told myself if you didn't want me when I got out, then I'd take that as my consequence and find a way to live with it. But even if you would have rejected me, you have to know that you would still have been my inspiration. I never had a role model, no one ever taught me how to be a man or how to hold my own. I had to learn through trial and error, but you? *You* became my light, and I know I chased it for the wrong reasons before, but you can bet…I won't make that mistake again."

My Skyscraper.

"*That,* right there," I started, then grabbed both of his hands in my own, "is strength, Judah Colt. You recognize where you went wrong and are now promising that you won't repeat the same pattern. So, now, all you have to do to deserve me—to deserve love in general—is to stick to that promise and accept that *I* have enough faith in you to know that you'll do it, that you mean what you say. It's my choice to make, don't make it more complicated than that."

"Complicated is just about all I know," he muttered, smirking sadly, "but I'll try."

"Good," I nodded, stepping back before asking, "Now is it my turn?"

"Mhm," he responded, and resumed our walk.

"Alright, tell me about your week this week," I suggested, following after him. "where the hell have you been?"

I already knew the answer, thanks to Frankie's crazy explanation last night, but I wanted to hear it from him. And I was glad I asked because he talked for a good thirty minutes, telling me about his plan to speak to everyone else first, knowing that it was healthier for him to start up a foundation outside of his relationship with me.

I listened as he went through each conversation he had—including the one with Frankie—and asked questions where I felt it was appropriate. There were a few times where I had to remind him that forgiveness didn't mean we all forgot what happened or that we weren't still upset. Our forgiveness spoke more about our belief in the fact that Judah was more than just an addict and his choices didn't define him. We held onto hope and he came back proving that hope was warranted.

Now it was about him walking the steps forward.

He told me he bought a new bike and planned to get a new car within the next week, explaining that he hated the thought of his Maserati and what he'd done while driving it. I asked how it was staying with Pharaoh and he said it wasn't home but he was grateful for the opportunity to sleep there while he figured out his next steps.

He asked me about tattooing and how everything was with Kenji and the shop, so I gave him a lengthy update on the last few months and told him how in a way, our disastrous relationship had accelerated my career. People wanted to know me, wanted work done by me, just for the bragging opportunity. It was odd and uncomfortable for me at first but I'd gotten used to it and learned to look at the positives.

By the time we finished firing off questions back and forth, an hour and a half had gone by.

"My turn?" I asked as we stopped near a big ass rock and sat down on it.

"Sure is," Judah replied, turning his head to scan my face.

But when his gaze hit my lips, it lingered for just a second too long.

Whoa.

I looked at his. Pink, familiar, *mine*.

Fuck.

"Favorite food?" I blurted, ripping my eyes away.

"Uh, mac and cheese..." he replied with a confused tone. "You knew that already, though. Try again.

"I don't have to try again," my rebuttal was quick. "A question is a question."

"Your question was bullshit," he laughed, and his next statement was a taunt, "Your turn, again, little bird."

Fuck, he's onto me.

The stupid bastard knew I was scared to ask what I suddenly wanted to ask.

It was just that after everything he confessed, after talking about Pharaoh and getting through that conversation without an explosive fight or a toxic storm of words, then spending so much time hearing about all the intense, emotional, apologies he'd given out? I found myself wanting to be closer to him. I hated the last little bit of oddly shaped space between us.

Ricco and Kavan had forgiven him, Silas and he were on the mend, even Frankie had reluctantly agreed to let him past her protective gates around me, and yet...

We were still so far away compared to what I was used to. There, on the beach, he felt like another man, yet wholly similar to the Judah I knew and I couldn't stand that awkward resistance.

The emotional guards I had put up on purpose were quickly slipping inch by inch sinking into the sand beneath my feet—leaving me vulnerable and exposed.

Bittersweet affection crawled up my spine as I weighed my options.

I looked at him then, only to find him watching me too.

I could ask another question about his time in rehab or coax him into telling me more about his next steps, but all I wanted to do was jump into the deep end and remind myself of our chemistry, investigate whether or not we still had at least *that*.

"You're taking too long," Judah sing-songed, jumping down from the rock to stand in front of me.

"Please," I spat. "I gave you all the time you needed earlier."

"I'm a recovering addict," he shrugged. "That's your job."

A scoff was my only response.

"Ask the question," Judah pushed.

"No," I stated instantly. "You don't deserve it."

He quirked an unaffected eyebrow, "I don't deserve a *question?*"

Shit. I'm making this worse.

"I don't know yet," I replied anyway. "That's what I'm thinking about."

"You're making absolutely zero sense."

I know.

I paused again, chewing on my bottom lip as those butterflies flew relentlessly in my stomach.

"Phoenix," Judah called. "Ask the—"

"—fine, will you kiss me?"

Time stood still.

When I met his stare, those blue eyes flashed, blazing with new heat as he stepped forward, and grated out, "You're right, I don't deserve it."

"And yet?"

I held my breath.

He stepped between my dangling legs. "Yet, that isn't a very appropriate question for a game like this, little bird."

I know.

"I don't care," I whispered, "answer it anyway."

"Why?"

He was so close, hovering over me as those blue eyes held me captive.

"Because I need to know if we've still got it."

Determination went off like a bomb. "Oh, we've still got it."

He answered the question.

With two rough hands cupping my face, he bent forward and fused his lips to mine.

Hard.

He wasted no time reminding me exactly what it felt like to be kissed by Judah Colt.

But then, as his tongue hit mine, that determination to prove our chemistry fizzled out, and the experience turned into something entirely different.

Softly, his lips moved against my own, and the pressure, the gentleness of the way he did it sparked a nostalgic longing in my chest. A whimper fell from my mouth and into his as he parted his lips again, inviting me to taste him in an explorative sense.

And even *that* was different.

Where he once tasted of pain and cigarettes, this flavor was brand new, reminding me of the first peek of sunshine after a hurricane, or a rainbow during a storm.

The temperature rose as he pressed forward, bending me backward just enough to have me wrapping my arms around his neck to anchor myself to him. His palm hit the rock next to my hip as his mouth caressed my own.

Pillowy, wet, profound. His kiss spoke of a thousand apologies.

"Phoenix," he whispered my name against my lips, and it sounded like a plea, a confession. A question?

I kicked it up a notch, pulling his bottom lip in between my teeth to remind him that I wasn't fragile, I was able to forgive him and move forward. My responding kiss said that I never resented the lust-fueled passion he held in his veins for me; I *craved* the fire that drew my moth to his flame.

And it worked, because with a growl, he lifted my body, encouraging me to wrap my legs around his back as he walked us around the other side of the rock, toward the taller ones.

"I missed you," I whispered between kisses, feeling the crushing weight of our separation, admitting to myself that it didn't matter what shitty fucking choices he made in the past. I didn't care.

Not when I got *this* guy in return.

The Judah that pushed me up against a rock, kissed me like he knew what he had. Like he wouldn't ever risk breaking the precious diamond he'd found on a rooftop at a party, ever again.

We were meeting all over again, getting lost in the feel of each other's affection as our lips moved quicker, speeding up to a pace that would lead to shedding clothes if one of us didn't pump the breaks.

He sucked my bottom lip into his mouth and let it go slowly, before saying, "I'm not fucking you on a beach."

The chuckle I gifted him was husky, "Why not?"

"For one, it's cold," he pointed out, swooping in for another wet kiss. "Mmm, and second, sand is a fucking *no go* when my pants are this tight and we have to ride the bike home."

"Fair enough," I agreed, grinning as I leaned forward to press my lips to his again, not caring if all we did was make out. I wasn't done with him yet. He felt too good, and I knew the days, weeks, months to come would include more tough conversations and challenges. I was taking the good moments where I could get them.

"Okay," he stated heavily, a few minutes later as he struggled to catch his breath. "*You* need to ask a better question before I say fuck the cold, the sand, *and* the bike."

Even as I, too, struggled to breathe, the air between us was darkened with lust but light with love, and I wanted to bottle up the feeling and sell it for millions.

"Fine," I agreed, feeling high without the drugs. "We never got to finish talking about what your plan is with your house. *Or* what you're gonna do about Brandon and your career? And before you bitch, I know it's more than one question, but we reached twenty a while ago so spare me the nonsense."

"Is my little bird feeling left out?" he taunted, leaning forward to smile against my cheek before placing a kiss in the same spot.

"Don't make me beg," I warned.

"All right, all right" he gave in, pulling back to look at me. "Let's walk back though, because we still have to drive home eventually."

He dropped me to the ground, grabbed my hand, then explained, "I know Pharaoh told you I'm selling the house. My plan is to get it up on the market in the next couple of weeks, then start packing. So aside from the lawyer shit and Brandon's case, I need to find a new house and figure out what car I want to buy."

"Can I help you?" I asked, feeling eager to be a part of helping him set up after spending so much time fearing I wouldn't be able to.

"I was hoping you'd offer," he admitted sheepishly. "I don't want to push you into anything, though. I know we need to have our own things going on."

"Me helping you get your life set up and you refusing to live for anyone *but* me, are two very different things, J," I pointed out. "I don't want to be your entire reason for existence, but I *do* want to be intimately involved in the life you set up for yourself. I want to hear about and be a part of what you do in your day-to-day experience, as well as support you wherever I can. And as long as you do the same for me, we'll be golden. It's just about balance."

"I know," he said with a sigh, "But I struggle, still. I don't want to fuck this up, I don't want to lose you because I expected things of you that I shouldn't have. And given my track record, I think I'm entitled to that. I don't trust myself when it comes to you and me."

I hated that he felt that way, but it was also to be expected with Judah. Every emotion—no matter what it was—Judah felt with such intensity that it would be difficult for him to get past the guilt and shame. I had to be patient and meet him where he was at.

"Trust will grow with time," I assured him. "That includes everyone, not just you and me. You have a lot to make up for, a lot of wrongs to right, but you'll figure out exactly how to do that as you go along, and if you'll let me, I can help with the loose ends. You were right earlier when you said you needed to take it one day at a time. One moment at a time, even. For right now, all your relationships have been given a new start. Focus on building upon that foundation and the rest will settle as more time goes on."

Judah was trying, that much was obvious, but I wasn't blind to his apprehension. He still doubted himself, doubted our trust, and really, I didn't mind it. It was healthy for him after all the shit he'd put us through. I didn't like to physically walk through that web of doubt—mainly because I always wanted to erase his pain—but I knew it was a necessary part of the recovery process.

We walked in silence back to the stairs and climbed them slower than we'd descended, and by the time we got to the top, Judah's energy was low enough to worry me.

He was lost in his head again, probably running through the list of shit he had to make up for, spinning in circles trying to figure out how he was going to make it all better. It put an odd sense of pressure on my shoulders and separated us once again. He was gone, no longer my Judah, but was instead...unreachable.

I'd learned so much about him tonight, but I had hours, days, lifetimes, worth of questions left to ask. I didn't want him to shut me out, didn't want him to push me away, and needed him to understand that as long as he was sober, as long as he stayed loyal and present with me, I was there. I was down. I was...his.

There was no one else for me, and Judah feared I'd walk at any moment, that I'd wake up and realize that I deserved better but he was a fucking idiot because if that were going to happen, it would have happened when I fucked his best friend.

Anger surged for reasons I couldn't figure out until I realized my own abandonment issues came to show their ugly heads. I held back as best I could and watched as Judah climbed the steps in front of me. I took a deep breath, reminding myself that this was only night one. It was only our first date, and now that I'd gotten to spend more time with him, ask more questions, gain more insight into his thought process, there wasn't a chance in hell that I was going anywhere.

He just needed to know that, believe it.

When we hit the top, he went straight for his bike and dug the keys from his front pocket. He straddled it without saying a word to me, but when he went to slip his helmet over his head, I grabbed it from his hand.

"P," Judah sighed my nickname.

I hung the helmet back on the handlebar and threw my leg over the bike in front of Judah, facing him, so I landed right in his lap, where he couldn't avoid my presence.

He closed his eyes and rubbed them with two fingers. "What are you doing?"

"Not giving you the space you think you deserve," I muttered quietly.

"Phoenix—"

"—No," I cut him off. "I'm not allowing you to get lost right in front of me anymore. We did this already. I saw this movie and I didn't like it. I won't allow you to fall into a river of self-pity when I can help ease your mind."

"Oh?" He laughed with a bitter bite and opened his eyes to blink at me. "How will you do that?"

He thought I couldn't read him, didn't understand that I knew what he was thinking even when he was throwing dishes around my kitchen and breaking end tables in search of pills.

"You've taken on a lot by coming back here with a list of people to apologize to and immediately heading off on that apology campaign. It's great, what you did, but now you're wondering if you can live up to the standard you set for yourself," I stated confidently, empathetically. "You're trying to stay clean, fighting cravings, moving, restructuring your life, and you don't even have a job anymore. Your entire life is up in the air, and you don't handle stress well. It's too much, Judah."

"What was I supposed to do?" he shot back with eyes full of frustration and emotion he couldn't keep hidden. "I didn't want to be alone!"

Oh, Judah.

"The fact that you can admit that so quickly and honestly right now tells me everything I need to know, J! You can accept that you *aren't* alone anymore, start to trust it. I'm right here. I'm sitting *right* in front of you, hand out, palm open, ready for you to just take it." I held out my hand. "I spent months wondering if you would come back to me. I had no idea if you were going to tank your floating ship as soon as you got out or if you'd take your healing seriously. I didn't know if you'd push me to the side and run off to someone else or if you'd even like me now that you're sober. But the last thing I expected was for you to come back like this. You spent the entire night being open with me, you didn't hide a thing, and you kept a promise you made to me last night. How can I trust you more than you trust me right now?"

That question threw him for a loop, I could see it on his face. His eyes bounced between mine, appearing bewildered, confused, until all that spilled into defeat once again.

"I'm sorry," he stated as he slipped his hand over mine. "You're right, I just—"

"—don't want to get your hopes up," I finished for him.

He nodded. "I live in the land of 'what if I'm not enough and it all falls apart' and I stay there because it's what I know best, but that's when the cravings hit and the anger comes back, and at that point? Getting out is damn near impossible."

"I know," I affirmed, lacing our fingers together. "But from now on, when you're around me, don't go to that place unless I give you a reason to. Unless I tell you that you've done something to make me question you, don't question yourself. I can promise to be open with you. I can't speak for everyone else, but when you're with me, I'll give it to you straight, J."

Awe crept into his eyes, and I felt my own start to water from the intensity.

"How are you so brilliant at this?" Judah asked, scanning my features as if he were trying to crack a code. "How do you know exactly what to say?"

I smiled sadly, "I know you, Judah. Probably better than I know myself."

"I want to do that for you," he whispered brokenly. "I want to hold you up like you hold me up, and I'm so scared I won't be able to do it."

"You will," I reassured him. "All it takes is paying attention and genuine care. You're a little behind, but I'm an open book. If you talk to me, I'll talk to you."

"And then we'll have each other," Judah confirmed.

"We'll have each other," I agreed with a nod.

"I need your help," he finally admitted.
"Just tell me the problem and we'll figure out it."
"I still don't think I deserve you."
"Maybe you don't, but you will soon."

And then I kissed him because I could. Because I wanted to. Because for once, I got the truth out of Judah without gaslighting or screaming or bullshit all up in the way.

I got to talk, he got to respond, and we came to a healthy conclusion for the first time in our relationship. It was a start, a *good* start. One that fueled my hope, reopened my heart, and reminded me that no matter what, miracles did exist.

Growth was hard, sometimes it threatened to kill you, but it was achievable even in the worst cases, like Judah. So I celebrated his choices, rewarded him for his honesty, all with the touch of my hands and the taste of my tongue.

And if his reaction was anything to believe, it was enough for him.

Judah wrapped both arms around my body, lifting me so that we were pressed together on the bike, and for the next however many minutes, we lost ourselves in each other's kiss. It was cold and late, and the waves roared in the background, but for once, we were at peace.

That feeling wouldn't last forever, it was only the beginning, but for that moment, it was everything we could have asked for...

And more.

PART THREE

CHAPTER 29

JUDAH

"J, CHECK YOUR DAMN PHONE," Frankie called out from her office down the hall. "Did you get my email?"

My phone?

I was too busy watching Phoenix draw up a tattoo design on her iPad, even though I was supposed to be looking at houses for sale in Los Angeles. Cringing with guilt, I twisted on the couch to search for the stupid device but couldn't find it anywhere.

Somehow, over the last three days, their dog Trixie had become quite obsessed with me, and was currently curled up in my lap, reminding me that the phone was probably under the dog.

"Shit," I cursed, picking up the ball of fluff and holding her out to Phoenix, who wasn't even paying attention. "P, baby, take Trix."

"Huh?" she muttered, then noticed the four paws dangling right in front of her face. "Oh, sorry, what's happening?"

"Frankie's yelling at me," was all I said as I snatched up my phone and unlocked it quickly, before the ice queen came at me with a pitchfork. "I think she sent me another listing, but I was watching you and now she's getting impatient."

Phoenix chuckled as Kavan abandoned Ricco in the

kitchen—leaving him to continue cooking—and made a beeline for Trixie. He clicked his tongue, "Give her to me, you stingy brats. She needs more attention than you're willing to give her."

"You're making dinner, bro," I muttered, scrolling through my emails, "how much attention are *you* gonna give her?"

"I can throw a ball and mix red peppers at the same time," Kavan stated with a whole lot of sass, "don't start with me, Colt."

"I got em!" I shouted back to Frankie, ignoring Kav. "I also got an email from Julia saying my statement will go out tomorrow."

"What? Really?" Phoenix perked up next to me. "Thank god."

"About damn time." Frankie responded, but her voice was closer now. P and I turned to see that she'd actually left her office to come and have a conversation. "I didn't think it would take her a full twenty-four hours to get ahold of someone."

"Eh," Phoenix shrugged. "We sent it to her on a Sunday, so she probably didn't do shit until yesterday."

"True," Frankie agreed. "Alright, what do you think of the one I sent you?"

Once Frankie had slept on my apology, she came around much quicker than I thought she would and actually jumped down my throat yesterday, talking about my search for a new house. She had taken it upon herself and gone full real estate agent, saying she wanted to help me look around. I wasn't sure about it at first, but Phoenix gave me one of those looks. One that told me I'd better take the offer or risk Frankie's wrath, so I did.

Surprisingly—even though she had absolutely *zero* experience—the little blonde seemed to be good at just about everything.

"Phew," I whistled, my eyes widening as I took in the home she sent me online.

"Let me see!" Phoenix leaned in, damn near climbing on my lap to get a closer look at the property Frankie found.

It was a Spanish style home, sort of like the girls' place, but it was double the size, and seated below a mountain in Thousand Oaks. The home wasn't in the Hollywood Hills, but rather all the way out in Ventura County. I'd decided yesterday that getting away from the heart of LA would be better for me in the long run.

"Four bedrooms," Phoenix pointed out as she read the screen, "Five bathrooms. Yeah, that's good. Damn! Look at the kitchen!"

"Your domestic ass is drooling all over my phone, little bird." I tapped the back of her head. "I can't even see."

"Sorry, sorry," she murmured, leaning away just enough for me to look *with* her.

Frankie sounded like a true agent as she explained to us, "It's an older build, which isn't a problem given how well it's been taken care of, but I figured the price was solid. It's less than your budget, but that's what happens when you take that chunk of change and move it out of Hollywood. You get more for your money."

"J?" Phoenix looked up at me and those brown eyes searched my face as she sat back a little, taking one of my hands with her. "What do you think?"

I lifted the phone higher and brought it closer to my face so I could scroll through the pictures one more time. I went through each one as Phoenix played with my fingers and waited.

By the time I got to the last one, a smile bloomed on my face.

I met Frankie's expectant stare and said, "I think I wanna see it in person."

"Yay!" Franks squealed, obviously proud of herself since I'd turned down the other five listings she sent me in the last twenty-four hours. "I'll call the listing agent tomorrow!"

"Perfect," I nodded, but then made sure to say, "Thank you, Frankie. I really appreciate your help."

"Please," she waved me off, "with everything else you've got going on, I wasn't going to let you scramble alone."

Aka, she needed to be busy, and she was getting bored, so taking on a new project was exactly what she needed.

Still, I left my smile where it was.

And she wasn't kidding.

I spent most of the morning yesterday talking to my lawyer, figuring out how we were going to get Brandon to either drop the case or make it as easy as possible to settle on a deal. Luckily for me, shit like this was pretty normal in Hollywood and a payoff would most likely work.

The last thing I wanted was to pay Brandon to go away, but I also didn't want to make my reputation in the media worse by getting photographed walking in and out of a courthouse. On top of that I still needed to go car shopping this week.

If Frankie was able to find me a home within the budget I'd given her, then the money I'd make off the sale of my current house would easily pay Brandon, get me a new car, with enough left over to get Pharaoh exactly what he needed for his virtual percussion class.

I wasn't broke, not by any means, but for the first time since I got discovered, I had to watch what I was spending.

It was sad, but music sales skyrocketed while I was in rehab, along with YouTube viewers, but it worked to my advantage because my royalty checks were big enough to help me rebuild the rest of my foundation and provided a solid cushion while the band and I spent the next couple of months recording the new album.

Phoenix still had no idea that I was back in the studio, or

that I'd written an album at all, but I wanted to keep it that way, given how personal it was, how heavily she was involved without even knowing it. The album itself would tell a story, and she was a major part of that story. Surprising her with my hard work was one of my goals, but I feared the day she questioned me about what I was doing every night.

"Dinner is almost done, losers," Ricco called out. "Frankie, where's Silas?"

"How am I supposed to know?" Franks scrunched her nose. "I'm not his keeper."

"No, but you are his girlfriend," Kavan threw back, completely oblivious.

Trying to hide my grin, I opened my messaging app and told the room, "I'll text him."

"We'll set the table," Phoenix added, gaining my attention as she got up from the couch. She too was holding back a smile as she leaned down to plant those pillowy lips against mine, but before she could pull away, I grabbed her chin between my fingers. "You're not getting out of this, missy. I know you're busy, but I want that new ink. *Soon.*"

That smile grew to full capacity as her eyes met my lips. "I hear you, Skyscraper."

"Good." I gave her one last peck before she turned to walk away, leaving me to find out where Silas was.

Apparently, our first family dinner couldn't commence until the big guy was present.

As I waited for a reply, I got up to help Ricco and Kav arrange all the food they made on the island in a buffet style, so everyone could fill their plates before sitting down at the dining room table.

"Damn, this looks good guys," I complimented, taking in the scent of tomato sauce and freshly baked bread.

"Stuffed shells, my dude," Kavan clapped me on the back. "Over Christmas—when the girls were gone—Ricco and I had nothing to do so we went home, and our mom forced us to learn this recipe when I told her the girls' cooked most of the time."

"They cook like *half* the time," Ricco corrected. "We cook too."

"Uh, yeah, okay," Frankie called out sarcastically. "If P and I don't cook, we order out. You only cook for Holidays."

"Cooking is a fuck ton of work," Kavan rallied. "Don't be sassy."

The sound of the front door opening threw Trixie into a tailspin, giving her best attempt at an intimidating bark until she ran around the corner, just as Silas called out, "I'm here, I'm here."

I walked around the island, and peered down the hallway, watching the exchange.

"What happened?" Phoenix questioned immediately, scanning Silas from head to toe. "What took you so long?"

"I picked up a stray dog," Silas informed her with a grin and a wink.

"Oh, fuck off," Pharaoh's voice hit our ears, making P's assessing eyes soften beautifully as she took in my best friend.

"I thought you had to work!" She accused, now grinning from ear to ear.

"I did, but the session ended early, so I told Silas to pick me up since he was right around the corner from the studio," Phar explained and reached for her.

Phoenix fell into his arms and hugged him tightly, and I didn't miss the way Pharaoh's whole body relaxed as she held him.

It was situations like these that made my seemingly neverending shame hit its highest peak.

As I stood by the island, I watched Phoenix extract her body from Pharaoh's and ask him about his day, while Frankie greeted Silas with a small kiss. Ricco and Kavan shouted profanities and cracked jokes with everyone—jokes that I didn't understand, because while they all spent the last year getting to know each other, I was too busy digging myself a deeper hole.

I'd missed so much, and it...hurt.

So much so that the cravings hit me in just the right spot, telling me that the liquor cabinet was right behind me, within reaching distance. If I was too pussy to be so obvious about it, I could just fake a sickness, sneak out, and find someone—anyone—that would link me up with a prescription that wasn't mine.

The room caved in, and I squeezed my eyes shut, counted to ten, and breathed deeply through my nose as images of Phoenix and Pharaoh fucking began to whip through my mind's eye.

It had me clutching the counter, squeezing until my fingers went numb.

I couldn't do this, I couldn't watch them all together like this and survive feeling like the odd man out, especially knowing it was my own motherfucking fault. I did this, I alienated myself, I pushed them all together and—

"Hey." P's voice hit my ears, but it was whispered and very close. "Breathe, J."

I opened my eyes, wanting to cover up my weak moment, not knowing who was around, but found only Phoenix and she was standing close enough to block my breakdown from the other's view.

No one had seen.

Understanding fell over her features as her tiny hand covered my whitened knuckles. "Want to go have a cig before we eat?"

All I could do was nod, grateful that she was able to read me, that she was paying attention and was able to find me in time, before the others could notice what was happening.

I started smoking again just yesterday, on my way over to Phoenix's house, in a desperate attempt to try and rid myself of the nerves that taunted me. I wasn't sure what it would be like to spend time around everyone again, and I knew that Ricco and Kav would be at the girls' house when I came over.

Phoenix smelled smoke on me immediately and asked about it—not in judgement, but more in curiosity, figuring something might have gone wrong—I was honest with her about what happened on the ride over and explained that I stopped at a gas station after hiding my identity as best I could. She understood, even reminded me of her offer to sponsor me. She said her offer still stood and she planned to stay sober, right along with me.

I, however, hated that idea, and told her that I'd think about it, but even if I said yes, she would only have to stay sober if I was around. Otherwise, she could do whatever she wanted.

I didn't want to take away her ability to let loose every once in a while, not after everything she'd gone through. She agreed and told me to let her know.

I planned to speak with Blake about it and get her thoughts, but it looked like after tonight's ordeal, I'd have quite a bit to talk about during our appointment tomorrow morning.

"All right, talk to me," Phoenix requested as I sat down in one of the chairs on her back patio. "You fell into your head pretty fast back there."

Patting my lap twice, I waited until she sat down to explain, "It just feels like shit, watching you all interact, knowing that I could have been a part of it if I hadn't been so out of control." As she lit two cigarettes in her mouth like a pro, I kept going. "And I know it's no one's fault but my own, it just fucking blows to experience it firsthand, you know? Because then, I'm left wanting to run away and numb out."

"Because you don't like feeling like you missed out, or like you can't catch up," Phoenix concluded as she handed me one of the two cigs. "You'd rather not feel anything at all."

"Exactly," I replied, before taking a drag and letting the nicotine char my lungs. "I just…hate that I'm like this."

Distracting myself, I slipped my hand under P's hair and held onto the back of her neck, reminding myself that while she had other relationships, other friendships, she was outside on the patio with me because she cared. Because she understood. Because she—like Blake—believed there was nothing wrong with struggling, it was all about speaking up and asking for help.

"You're adjusting, J," Phoenix reminded me. "This group was only formed in the last year, and while that *is* a significant amount of time, in the grand scheme of things…it really isn't."

Then she got up, which had me frowning until I realized she was just turning around so that she could straddle me, rather than facing the opposite direction. When she was settled, and because I needed physical proof that she was real, I ran my fingers over her forehead and down her temple, as she spoke again.

"We have so many years ahead of us, Judah. Plenty of time to make new memories and more inside jokes, ones that you'll be a part of now that you're home where you belong. This transition phase is only a season."

Only a season.

She was right and with the realization, some of that jealousy, that anxiety left my system, leaving me feeling more in control, though the cravings would take time to get rid of.

I watched my little bird as she hit her cigarette and blew the smoke over her shoulder, exposing that neck again, leaving me no choice but to loosely wrap my hand around it.

I'm an addict after all.

"You make it sound so simple when you say it like that," I

stated gruffly as my thumb moved back and forth under her jaw. "You put it in terms I have no choice but learn to accept."

Her smile was beautiful, even though it was small and full of empathy. "It's just about shifting your perspective into a positive one. I had to learn how to do it quite a bit when I lost you."

"I'm sorry," I repeated again, for probably the thousandth time since we'd reconnected.

"I'm not," she whispered, sounding almost ashamed as she ashed her cigarette over the side of the chair.

"What do you mean?" I questioned before pulling in another hit.

"I don't know." She shrugged and began to play with the silver chain around my neck. "It just feels like even without all of the chaos, I would have just spent all this time trying to keep my head above water. My mental state was fucking garbage when I first moved here. I was faking it for Frankie's sake but between the memories of my parents and my own fears, I don't know that I would have pulled myself out of it. It was you and everything that happened between us that pulled me out of my shell and showed me just how strong I was."

"I could have done it in a better way, baby," I stated sadly, hating that she thought my hurting her was a good thing, all because it showed her true colors. "I don't want to believe that I needed to do the damage I did, just to get you where you are right now. I'd like to think that you would have gotten there even if I'd done right by you."

"Who knows," she lifted those small shoulders, "I just think it all happened the way it was supposed to."

Moving my hand to the back of her neck, I pulled her forward, close enough to brush my nose against hers before landing a kiss on her lips.

"I agree with you there," I said against her mouth, "but I'm not sure I'm exactly a fan of fate's choices when it came to our life plan."

At that, she let out a tinkling laugh. "The universe can be a real jackass sometimes."

"Ha," I chuckled. "You can say that again."

A thought hit me, and I had to ask, had to know where she was at. "Do you still think about your parents? You used to believe your love killed."

She let out a small, bitter laugh and glanced down, now playing with the hem of my t-shirt as she admitted, "I still believe that."

"Phoenix," I clicked my tongue, using an index finger under her chin to raise her head.

"How can I not?" she asked me, seriously. "You fell for me and almost died, J. It's not a coincidence in my eyes—nothing is—but I have learned to accept it. Frankie asked me once if I'd be willing to spend the rest of my life with you, knowing that you're an addict and after thinking about it I said, yes. It only makes sense. You could relapse, sure, but I could also snap at any moment. We're both fucked in one way or another, and if you're willing to take a chance on me, then I am too."

"I don't believe you'll snap," I replied forcefully, feeling like shit knowing that another one of my choices solidified her stubborn mindset.

"And I don't believe you'll relapse," she threw back in a tone similar to mine.

While I doubted her opinion and she doubted mine, deep down, both of us hoped the other was right. It was a twisted fucking system, but it was ours.

"Well, aren't *we* the world's greatest couple," I muttered sarcastically, tacking on a small smile at the end.

"Ha," she laughed a little, "the best."

"I guess it is what it is, though, huh? We'll never really know how our future will shake out," I stated almost to myself.

"I know it'll take work, and we both have to remain committed and honest, but yeah. The shit our parents left us to deal with won't change, so you're right, it is what it is. We just have to take it one day at a time."

We sat in silence after that, letting our worries float away with the smoke, and I continued to remind myself that when it came to Phoenix and the rest of my friends, I had to deal with being the odd man out for a little while, but I still had *this*. I still had her. And only the two of us understood what it was like to be us. We bonded over our damage and now planned to help each other through it. This was what Phoenix wanted all along, but I couldn't see the benefit, or even the point when I was high. Now, though, I'd never felt so…safe.

I wasn't alone, I hadn't been since that June night on the rooftop last year, but I was too faded to see it before now. The Universe had given me my person, my partner, and I had tried to ruin her because I didn't know any other way of doing things.

I wouldn't make that mistake again.

After a few final hits of our cigarettes and another kiss, we ended our impromptu smoking session.

Gracefully, Phoenix climbed off my lap, then held out her hand, and said, "Come on, Skyscraper. Let's go make some memories."

CHAPTER 30
Phoenix

OVER THE NEXT MONTH, life seemed to pass in a blur.

Frankie was able to get Judah, Pharaoh, and I in to see the house in Thousand Oaks a few days after she found it and Judah decided to make an offer on the spot, which was accepted the following day. Frankie decided to keep working with Judah and the two of them got to planning right away, spending the last three weeks packing up Judah's old house, to get ready for the closing date.

Meanwhile, I was drowning in work, having very little free time, since I was still finishing up the winter season of drawing classes with the kids as well as spending my night's designing tattoos in order to stay ahead of my schedule.

Luckily—or unfortunately, depending on how I looked at it—Judah seemed to be just as busy. He frequently came for dinner, especially when he knew Ricco and Kav would be there, but he never stayed the night and he always left by eleven p.m. A part of me was grateful that we didn't have to be glued to each other to feel like we were making this work, but another part of me wondered if we were making it work at all.

Judah and I still hadn't spent a night together.

It had been a whole *month.*

We hadn't even really made out since that first time on the

beach, and I was…worried to say the least.

"I just don't get it," Frankie mused after watching Judah turn down another one of my invitations to just stay here instead of Pharaoh's guest room. "He doesn't even have a good excuse."

"He doesn't need an excuse, Franks," I groaned, flopping backward onto the couch. "He told me he isn't ready."

"Ready for *what?*" She huffed. "You two have fucked plenty of times and your chemistry used to light up the goddamn room. Where did it go?"

The drugs.

All I could fucking think was that the drugs had everything to do with his attraction toward me in the beginning. It was the only thing that made sense, given it was the only thing missing between now and then.

"Maybe he thinks he'll have performance issues," Frankie pondered when I didn't respond.

And she was right, that was another thing that could be linked to the drugs. Some of the shit he was taking back then would have made it far easier to blast me in bed like he used to. Maybe something was wrong? I had no idea, but it wasn't even about the sex. It was about intimacy, period. I was too busy for proper dates, but even when we were alone together, we simply talked on the patio, or I'd go watch a movie or binge Netflix for a few hours with him and Pharaoh.

"I don't even care about that, though," I groaned. "I just want him to touch me more than the basic shit we're doing now."

With zero class, Frankie snorted, "You sound like you're in high school and you haven't lost your virginity yet."

"I know!" I shouted. "And we all know that is *totally* not the case. Judah Colt used to have no fucking issue shoving his dick down my throat."

"Woo, graphic," Frankie fanned her face like an asshole,

"tell me more, you little slut."

"Don't start," I tried not to laugh. "You know I'm a boss in bed."

"Facts," Frankie agreed immediately, "maybe you just need to remind him of that."

"No, I need to *talk* to him," I corrected her, and I'd known it for a little while now, but I was hoping the issue would resolve itself on its own. "For some reason the thought of seducing him feels gross. Judah is in his head about something, I just don't know what it is."

"Hmm," was all Frankie said before we got lost in thought for a little while.

I wanted to be held, wanted to sleep next to him again, but literally every time the opportunity came up, he had a reason not to. I was trying not to feel rejected but fuck, it was hard.

Then Frankie perked up and asked, "What about when you do his tattoo? You're still drawing it right?"

"It's done, actually," I admitted, feeling the sting of nerves in my tummy. "I just haven't told him."

"What the hell? Why not?"

"Because everything feels weird right now, and the design I drew is personal as hell. I don't want to do it when we're like this."

Judah had been pressing me to get this design done for him since we reconnected, saying he was pissed he fucked up his opportunity in Paris, but I still took my time. I wanted it to be special, I wanted to show him how proud I was of him, but also give him something that would be a symbol or a token to remind him how far he'd come.

Except, somehow it felt like the fire between us was gone. The animalistic passion I'd once thrived off of was nowhere to be found and I seriously didn't know what to do about it. The love we felt was still there, our connection was still intense on an emotional level, but without the flames, it wasn't the same.

On the rare occasion I pictured my relationship with Judah when he was sober, I imagined us to be unified on all fronts, sure, but I actually expected the heat to be turned up a notch, given that we'd proven nothing could truly tear us apart.

That love/hate, thing we had going on was toxic, but it was once apart of us, and in the bedroom, we displayed the same energy. He never held back, and I never backed down. Now, it felt like he was walking on eggshells around me, terrified to lose the fragile thing we had going.

"I think maybe this has a lot to do with his healing process," I told Frankie. "Think about it. The last person I fucked was Pharaoh, and the last person *he* fucked was most likely Sarah or Rachele. I don't know if that's true, per say, but I would definitely assume they all slept together. He's admitted to having survivors' guilt, and this could be a symptom of that."

"Fuck," Frankie muttered sadly, "I didn't even think of that."

Feeling a new kind of pressure, and more fear than I'd like to, I admitted, "This shit is so complicated."

"Yeah, it is," she agreed, "but you're Phoenix Royal, and you've dealt with worse. So, before you go into a downward spiral, remember that you are on your way to getting everything you wanted. You already have the dream career, you built a family here in LA, and you fell in love. It was a goddamn fucking train wreck for a while there, but when you held onto hope…it paid off. The girl you were in New York is long dead, you buried her, and you've blossomed into a fucking *goddess*. You and Judah are going to figure it out, you're just taking baby steps to get there."

She was right.

"Ughhhhhh," I groaned, then sighed, then sat up on the couch and stretched out my aching muscles. "Fucking hell, I'm beat."

"You need to get some sleep, and stop stressing," Frankie suggested. "But before you go to bed, help me."

I met her blue eyes, feeling only slightly jealous of the fact that she was still drop dead fucking gorgeous—even with a messy bun and baggy clothes—and asked, "Sure, what's up?"

All she said was, "Silas."

"Oh lord." I rolled my eyes. "What now?"

"He's starting to get suspicious," Frankie informed me. "He feels me pulling away, and last week he pointed out that even though the media thinks were in a relationship—thanks to all the times we've attended events together—we've never actually discussed being in a committed relationship. He said he noticed every time he brings up commitment, I get all weird."

That didn't surprise me.

"Can't you just explain to him where you're at?" I wondered. "If he's down for you, he'll understand that you're not seeing anyone else, labels just freak you out and you're working on figuring out why, but you're still not ready for anything too serious."

"We're glorified fuck buddies and he wants to actually date me," Frankie explained, "That's the problem. I spend a few nights there a week, he comes here sometimes, but we don't actually leave his house unless, again, there's an event. We've never gone on a true date since the first one he took me on."

"And you don't want to date becaaaause…?"

Her features set into a hard line, lips pursed and serious, as she stated, "dating leads to engagement, engagement leads to marriage, and that's a whole ass motherfucking *no* for me."

Yikes.

"You're going to have to tell him that, Franks," I warned, despite knowing how scary it was to think that far into the future. "That, right there, is pretty straight forward. If he doesn't want to continue after knowing that you're not ready to head in that direction, then there's your answer. But if he does accept it and says he doesn't care, then believe him. You just have to tell him the truth."

My girl let out a sharp groan, making me cringe a little.

She sat up straighter and tucked her legs under her body, shaking her head as she said, "He's going to fucking hate me."

"No, he isn't," I disagreed, "you're impossible to hate."

"He'll be disappointed and that'll be worse."

"But you'll be able to breathe easier knowing that the conversation is done," I offered. "You're always the one preaching to me about the universe setting things up on purpose, and you totally believe in fate and all that, so if he's supposed to stick around, he will. And if he doesn't then you know he's not your person."

"Ugh," she sighed again. "Alright, you're right. Go to bed now. I'm just gonna sit here and think myself into a tailspin."

A laugh slipped out before I could stop it.

"No ma'am." I shook my head, standing from the couch before moving in front of her. I held out my hand. "It's time to wash your face, brush your teeth, and get all cozy in your designer bed sheets. *Then* we think ourselves into a tailspin."

I got a mirrored laugh from her in return, but hers was loud and bright.

"We are so fucked up," my best friend muttered as she let me pull her up.

"Bet your ass," I replied, lacing our fingers together as we made our way into our shared bathroom. And because my best friend was a genius, she connected her phone to the sound system and hit shuffle on our shared winter playlist.

From there, we danced to FLETCHER's voice, singing the lyrics of "Healing" at the top of our lungs as we completed our nighttime skincare routines.

It was exactly what we both needed.

CHAPTER 31

JUDAH

"ALRIGHT ONE MORE TIME, dude, you got this," Phar's voice floated through the speakers of the sound booth as he pressed the button that allowed me to hear him. "Give me all you've got, yeah?"

All I could do was nod as I slipped back into the role I once resented. Instead of harboring the shame and guilt that came when I thought of TheColt, I held onto the power the name gave me, the legacy I could leave behind as I squared my shoulders and stared at the studio mic in front of me.

"She Held Me Under" was finally almost finished—we only had one more layer to go, but I wanted to take it from the top and lay the whole track down again.

Perfectionist tendencies were making themselves known, and it had everything to do with this being the first song I'd complete after getting out of rehab. First song I'd ever made sober.

Being in the studio again was jarring at first, reminding me of the hours and hours I used to spend getting high in order to find the confidence to do what I was doing right now, and while I missed the synthetic ease that the drugs provided, I didn't miss the internal breakdowns and seemingly endless battles with self-doubt that occurred once the high wore off.

Here, now, I was finally in the fucking *zone*.

Clear headed. Excited.

This time as I slipped my headphones over my ears and fell victim to the grumbling, throaty bass of our new track, I was telling a new story—keeping even the messiest parts—written into a fictious metaphor from my previous point of view.

The one I knew best.

She held me under like a twist of fate
Tiny circles, squares, or any shape
Out of sight out of mind,
Ran swiftly out of time.
all I could think was how she walked away
then my air ran out, my mental sight came out to play

In that darkened tunnel all over again
I screamed and screamed
A shattered man.

Black lights, long nights, fist fights in a haze
Wrong, right, real, fake, it was all a mistake
Yet in the blink of an eye, I was a monster of rage
Chaotic epiphanies in a mind full of doubt
Getting better was useless, it's all broken now

No faith left to gift,
no fucks left to give
A cacophony of madness,
Submitting to sin

It's alright now though, look where I am
Sterile rooms of dissapointment
At least I'm alive

Except that wasn't true, though
It was no wish of mine
I wanted her to take it all
My life, my lies
To end up six feet under,
the only real dream I had
But that didn't happen, left ruthlessly living instead,

No faith left to gift,
no fucks left to give
A cacophony of madness,
submitting to sin

But in the end who cared?
Not the one that held me under
Not the one that claimed my fate
She was long gone now in a city of snakes
It's okay, though, it's alright,
remember you're alive!
Second chance is all that matters
Fine third, that's a lie.

Choose wisely little demon,
Forgive all your little lies
Ancient nightmares come to haunt
Submit or face time.

"Fuck yeah, Colt!" Vale shouted through the speaker, when I opened my eyes.

I saw him standing there, right behind the sound board with a wide ass smile on his face and his hands shoved in his hair, looking as if he couldn't believe what he'd just witnessed. Pierce was standing on the couch, clapping loudly even though I could barely hear it. But even with the wall of glass between them and me, their excitement slithered over my body like a new skin.

I couldn't really respond, wasn't sure what to say.

The creative power in my veins made it harder to come back down to Earth. I'd gotten lost somewhere—back in time—as I retold the story I'd written and felt my way through the lyrics. The memories that inspired them in the first place came back with a vengeance, but rather than feeling anything even remotely negative, I felt *fueled*, high in the realest of ways. My endorphins skyrocketed, allowing me to feel true, real, natural pride.

Enthusiasm. Exhilaration.

What in the hell did I just do?

Suddenly, Pharaoh busted through the door of the studio we were renting and barreled toward me with full intention to tackle. Luckily, I was steady enough to keep us from crashing into the line of guitars to my right as his body hit mine with a hard thump.

"I'm so fuckin' proud of you, man," he boomed into my shoulder, clapping me hard on the back. "That was the best version you've laid down yet, and I am just…"

All I could do was sputter out a startled laugh, just as at a loss for words as he was.

"It's only the beginning," he whispered, "this is only the fucking beginning."

He was right.

We'd only just started recording a few days ago, after spending the last three weeks getting all the lyrics I'd written lined up with the production we had in mind. The four of us didn't want to waste the money on renting a studio if we were just going to spend hours at a time reworking the lyrical frame, but once we knew the fifteen songs I had written were ready to go, we decided to hit the ground running.

"Bro, you good?" Pharaoh stepped back and shook me a little, meeting my eyes. "You look like you saw a ghost."

I was totally fine, actually. Hell, I was better than fine. I was just...

"I feel amazing," I whispered, looking down at my hands as if they'd done something without my permission. "I feel like I finally did something worthy of being famous for."

"Jude, come on, you know the shit we did before was just as good," Pharaoh offered, but when I met his eyes again, he relented. "Alright, fine, it wasn't *this*. But it was still good."

Shaking off the past I waved a hand at him. "I know, I know, whatever. It doesn't even matter because whatever the fuck we just did was pure magic."

The smile that bloomed on his face had my chest lighting up like a firework. Not once in the decades I'd known him, had I ever seen him look that happy. Not even after a solid show or the first time one of our songs hit the radio.

There was even happiness in his voice as he agreed with me, saying, "It sure as fuck was, brother."

The crackle of the speaker system met our ears right before Vale's voice filtered through. "Come on, you two. Let's listen to that shit back and see what we need to do about production."

It was still early, only three in the afternoon, so we had plenty of time to wrap this up before we were scheduled to be done at eight, but I found myself getting antsy to get working on the next song.

This feeling was addictive.

The good kind, though. The kind Dr. Blake was talking about.

Self-confidence, humble pride.

It was all very new, but extremely welcome.

THE REST of the afternoon was spent guzzling pizza and junk food while the guys and I watched Vale work magic on the sound board. We listened to the damn track so many times it had my ears ringing, but I was more than happy to be sick of it because it meant we'd done something right.

Around six thirty, there was a knock on the door of the studio, sending a pit to my stomach and that too-familiar defensive anger boiling to the surface as I spat out, "We still have an hour and a half!"

Pharaoh put a hand on my shoulder and squeezed as he stood from his seat, saying, "Calm down, Tasmanian devil, I know who it is."

What?

"Who is it?" I called after him, not trusting his idea of a surprise.

But when he opened the door, the room tilted as I immediately got to my feet.

There's no fucking way.

"H-Holly?"

# CHAPTER 32

PHARAOH

I STARED down at the little blonde as she winked at me, then ducked under my arm and entered the studio with her usual confidence.

"Hello, boys," she greeted with a quirky wave.

Pierce was struck silent, while Vale's energy went from extreme focus to extreme delight as he ran to embrace our tiny ex-assistant.

She was already being swung in the air as he asked, "What the fuck are *you* doin' here, Holls?"

"Put me the hell down and I'll tell you," she replied with a wheezy laugh, clearly struggling to breathe as our bassist and producer squeezed the shit out of her.

Vale listened and set Holly back on her feet, then stepped back as Judah made his way forward, appearing pale and a little scared.

He almost looked sick to his stomach.

"Holly…" he breathed out her name, but then stopped, seeming unsure of what he wanted to say.

Luckily for him, Holly took care of the talking part all on her own.

"We don't have a ton of time, so I need to make this

quick," Holly announced to the room as she set her messenger bag down on chair and pulled out a notebook, along with a pen and her water bottle. "Pharaoh called me about a week ago and told me everything. Including Judah's apology train, the fact that he wrote an album in rehab, and that *you* three have agreed to give his bitchass another chance." She smiled a semi-malicious grin. "I hear you're going full indie."

"Facts," Pierce smirked, nodding at her. "But what brings *you* to the misfit party?"

It was clear to me that Holly's easy-going mood did very little to soothe Judah's anxiety, and when she shrugged again and said, "I want in on it."

He seemed to like *that* even less.

"What?!" Pierce and Vale shouted at the same time, both sounding stoked as hell, while Judah seemed to get more fidgety.

"Pharaoh gave me the rundown," she explained. "He asked if I would be willing to come back and I said I'd think about it. After twenty-four hours, I made my decision, and now here I am."

Judah shook his head in disbelief before saying, "Hold on, Holly—"

She held a hand up to cut him off.

"Don't," she stated a bit forcefully. "Am I pissed at you? Sure. I lost my job, after all. But do I care what you have to say? Not particularly. Mainly because I didn't know you like the three of them did, so in a way you were just a shitty boss. But lucky for you, my father was an addict so I know how this goes and I know what true sobriety looks like. You're working, according to your best friend, you're taking it seriously, and that works for me. But also…" she pinned him with her blue stare, spewing *don't fuck with me* vibes, all over the studio. "I *will* know if anything is suspicious with you. I'll be paying more attention than I did last time, and just like I told my father ten years ago, I'll tell you the same thing: you won't backslide. Not on my watch. But if you decide to be stupid and throw away your life again when I'm *not* around? That's your choice. I suggest you choose wisely."

They stared at one another, eyes locked and loaded with unspoken words, but all she got in return was a subtle nod from Judah. It was the first time someone didn't want to hear what he had to say and her unflinching attitude was bound to throw him for a loop. I studied him, watching out for…well, anything.

He was angry, but it didn't seem to be directed toward her. It was internal, purely personal, which was almost worse.

Holly didn't seem to notice—or maybe she just didn't care—because she flew right into the next thing.

"I have more news," she told us all.

"Let's hear it," Pierce replied enthusiastically with a clap of his hands, while Vale sat down on one of the two couches in the studio.

We all followed suit, finding places to sit while Holly pulled her phone, as well as her iPad out of her bag. The girl was stacked, totally prepared, and all I could hope was that Judah would understand that while Holly wasn't exactly warm toward him, she didn't need to be in order for her to do her job.

Not everyone was going to forgive him from the jump. This was a part of being a recovering addict.

"Pharaoh knows all of this already," Holly started once she was ready, and as soon as she said it, everyone in the room turned to look at me. I leaned forward as anticipation bled through my veins. I did know what she was about to say, and I was fucking *stoked*. "But basically, after everything went down, Hendrix obviously told me the band dissolved and I had no job. Lowkey, I was prepared for that. I had a feeling something shitty was about to go down, so I had my resume ready to go."

I glanced at Judah, trying to gage his reaction, but found him listening intently, even though his eyes were a bit unfocused. I held my breath as she continued, "It took about two weeks, but then I started interning part time for a guy named Rex Johnson, and I know, he sounds kinda douchey but don't judge the boss by his name. This guy is legit. He used to be a band manager, but when his last band broke up, he decided to start training other managers or even assistants. He's been in the business long enough to breed people like me into people like him. Which worked for me because I didn't want to be an assistant forever, you all knew that," she paused and eyed the four of us.

It was true.

Holly was paying her dues in the industry when she started working as TheColt's assistant. I didn't know what she actually wanted to do, but when I found out she wanted to become a manager, I knew I made the right choice when I called her.

Holly continued, "But what Pharaoh *doesn't* know, is that I actually went to Rex and told him I was thinking about working with you guys, on top of training with him. I said I knew I'd be busy but I didn't care, because this was my dream. Well, low and behold, he has worked with *many* struggling artists before, and a few of them have gone the indie route and done it successfully."

She involved Rex?

Holy fuck.

"I told him you guys were working on an album and that you wanted to put it together pretty fast in order to get it out as soon as possible…" Holy *shit*. "Aaaaaand, he offered to make my training more hands on and help me actually manage you guys, legitimately. All I need is the album and he'll show me how to do the rest."

Four seconds of pure silence followed her statement until the room erupted.

"NO FUCKING WAY!" Vale shouted.

"You're a *lying* little pipsqueak," Pierce accused in a mocking tone as he ran forward with a massive smile on his face and snatched her up off the couch and into his arms. "You *better* not be lying to me."

"I'm deadass, I swear," Holly laughed, grinning from ear to ear. "You better get to work, boys. We've got an album to release."

"Jesus Christ," I muttered, rubbing my forehead as I processed the fact that we wouldn't have to struggle our way through getting this album out. When I approached Holly, I was just hoping she'd be willing to assist us again, do the shit she used to do. But actually *managing* us? That wasn't even in the realm of possibility as far as I knew.

Floating in a state of shock, my eyes found Judah, who was still sitting on the couch, staring at his hands.

I sighed, then, knowing he was thinking of four hundred reasons he wasn't ready, or he didn't deserve it, but I also knew there was nothing I could do for him right now.

That was the thing about Pierce and Vale's forgiveness. They were willing to work with him, they were excited about what he'd produced, but it was obvious to anyone paying attention that they didn't really care about Judah himself.

He was struggling, everyone could see it, but Judah had done too much damage to those relationships for them to want to pause the celebration to help him process.

"Hey," I kicked his boot with my own. "Wanna go have a cig?"

When he looked up at me, his eyes were haunted, unsure, but he surprised me when he said, "No, I'm okay."

I tilted my head in confusion. "You sure?"

"Uh, y-yeah," he nodded choppily, then cleared his throat, "it's just a lot to take in."

"But it's good, right?" I pushed, trying to get a read on his mental state.

It took him a few seconds to respond, but when he did, his voice was full of watery gratitude, "It's…amazing, Phar."

Relief flooded my system. "Fuck yeah it is, buddy."

"Th-thank you, for reaching out to her." His voice was low enough that the other's couldn't hear, but it still held a sense of awe and disbelief.

"I had a dream about her," I admitted. "Not sure why, but when I woke up, I just made the call."

"Huh," Judah murmured absentmindedly.

"So now what?" Vale called out, loud enough for both Judah and I to glance his way. "What happens next?"

Holly spoke from Pierce's arms, "Well, first, I'll sit in on your session tomorrow and you guys can tell me where you're at with the production. We'll have to go from there, but just as a reminder—I am *hella* knew with the whole managing thing —I've only been working with Rex since January so I'm definitely not Hendrix. Still, my plan is to keep you all updated with what I'm learning as I go, but pretty much everything will be run through Rex first, aside from normal assistant shit that I already know."

Judah shook his head beside her, and said in a low, but reassuring voice, "We have basically zero idea what we're doing either—we're all newbies—we'll just have to figure it out as we go."

She watched him for a moment, almost studying his expression, before replying with a small smile and a dip of her chin, "Yeah, we'll figure it out."

Well, that went decently…I think.

"Fuck, I am *too* excited," Pierce muttered under his breath and slapped Vale on the knee.

Holly let out a small chuckle as she organized her materials in her lap. "Then let's get our shit together, shall we?"

And that's what we did.

Together, we made a list of things Holly could do without Rex's help, then we complied a set of questions for her to ask him at their next meeting. We just needed to figure out what we needed to do in order to prepare for an album release. That was new territory for us, but Holly promised she'd come back with answers as soon as she could.

We talked for another hour, and finished right at eight, when our studio time ran out.

After everyone left and it was just Judah and I walking across the parking lot to our vehicles, I said to my best friend, "You need to call Phoenix."

For a second, panic flashed in his eyes. "Why?"

"Because you've been working every day since you got home and I know you haven't spent a single night with her." Judah deflated, blowing out a gust of air as I kept going, "Dude, she doesn't know you're in the studio. If she did, I wouldn't be saying shit. But she doesn't, and I know her, she's probably starting to question what you're doing. She may even think you're avoiding her."

Yeah, I didn't feel great about telling Judah to spend the night with a girl I was still in love with, but I did it more for Phoenix than I did Judah.

She didn't know he was working his ass off, but I'd watched him turn down her offer to stay the night one to many times for me to feel good about him lying to her.

Not that he was *lying*, per say, but it was still a secret and Phoenix wasn't dumb. I was willing to bet any amount of money that she was, at the very least, confused about his lack of time and attention. But on the other end, his absence could make her suspicious and that was the last thing I wanted for either of them. Judah wasn't worthy of distrust at that point, he just wasn't used to being in a healthy relationship and taking care of his career at the same time.

He wanted to prove to her that he could live his life outside of her, make himself proud, and still cherish the fuck out of her. I understood it, I really did, but he still needed to find a way to spend real, actual, *intimate*, time with her, not only because she deserved it, but because he did too.

And quite frankly, I needed time alone for a night.

"You're right," Judah replied. "I just want to finish this album so I can give her more of my time. Keeping this a secret isn't really doing me any favors."

"You could always tell her," I suggested. "You know she'd freak out."

"I know, but there's something about the idea of showing her the finished product…" he trailed off then shook his head. "I just have to tell her I have a secret and it's a good one. I can explain to her that I'm not avoiding her, I'm just working on some things."

"She's fucking smart dude," I warned. "She'll figure you out if you're not careful."

His groan was loud. "I know. But you're right. I should probably go there tonight."

"Is there any other reason you've been avoiding it?" I questioned, wondering why the fuck he'd wait a whole month to have her in his arms all night. I wouldn't be able to resist.

"I don't know, honestly," he admitted as we reached G-Dog. "I'm in my head about it, that's for sure, but now I'm using work as an escape instead of drugs. It's healthier in one way, but not so much in another."

His new level of honesty was still shocking to me, but I ran with it and said, "Just talk to her, J. Lay it all on the line so you aren't under so much fucking stress. If you want to keep the album a secret, fine, do that, but at least figure out how to ease her fears and your own in the meantime."

He nodded in understanding but then narrowed his eyes on me and leaned up against the tire on the back of my Wagon. As he got comfortable he asked, "You good, dude?"

Was I good?

Uhhhh, that's a hard question to answer.

Generally, yes, everything was fine. Everyone was getting along, it looked like our career was standing on two feet again, and yet…

"Yeah, I'm fine." I gave him a half smile. "Just concerned about the snare in the third verse. Gonna go home and practice until I figure out what's missing."

J's eyes bounced between mine in suspicion. "You sure that's it?"

Get out of my head.

"Yeah, man, I'm good."

"Uh huh," Judah mumbled, nodding his head slowly. "I don't believe you, but I'll ask again tomorrow."

Great.

"Whatever, dude," I faked a laugh, "go get your girl."

"I'm on it," he replied slowly, still watching me as he pushed away from the SUV, "but call if you need anything, yeah?"

"Of course," was my only reply before I made quick, yet casual work of getting into my car.

Knowing Judah would keep an eye on me as he got settled on his bike, I pretended to organize my shit in the front seat and fucked around on my phone for a minute, but as soon as the engine roared to life and he left the parking lot, I stopped and sighed. The back of my head hit the headrest behind me and the truth settled on my shoulders,

I wasn't fine.

My mind was full of thoughts I used to never have room to think about.

Memories. Daydreams. Flashbacks every time I closed my eyes.

Now that Judah was sober and hyper focused on doing the right thing, he was no longer the center of my life. There was no reason for me to focus on him anymore, and because of that, my own issues were creeping back up and making themselves known.

I'd done so much complaining, so much bitching about how I spent years in Judah's shadow, but I'd forgotten that his struggles covered up my own. Judah's life had become a distraction from my own string of shitty choices and while I hated his constant disasters a month ago, I found myself...fucked without them now.

If I learned anything from Judah's journey, it's that the mind worked in powerful, mysterious, *infuriating* ways.

And mine was spiraling.

Ghosts from my past had come back to remind me that while Judah's actions were darker and much more obvious than mine, I was just as selfish as he was. For the last week my dreams had taken me back eleven years and reminded me that I, too, had chosen my own wants and needs over someone else's, all while knowing full well that I'd be breaking a heart in exchange.

A heart that didn't deserve it.

One that was pure and scared and in danger like the rest of us.

Except I didn't have a drug addiction to use as an excuse to be that shitty to someone I loved. All I had was a plane ticket, a massive chunk of money I'd done essentially *nothing* to earn, and a chance to live a brand-new life far away from that hellhole.

And I took the opportunity without a second thought.

I packed what little shit I had and got on that plane without even saying goodbye.

...I left a flower in a minefield.

The realization hit me hard a few nights ago and I had absolutely zero idea what to do going forward. All I knew was that I needed time alone, I needed Judah to spend time with Phoenix so that I could think in my own space—silently, under the cover of night and in the midst of all my shadows.

Even if I was suddenly terrified of the dark.

CHAPTER 33

JUDAH

I STOPPED at a gas station on the way to P's, filled up my tank, then decided I'd better call her before just showing up and barging in on a girls' night or something.

After two rings, her sweet, unintentionally sensual voice caressed my ears with a simple, "Skyscraper."

A grin spread across my face. "There she is."

"What's up?" I could hear the mirrored smile in her tone, giving me the confidence I needed to turn things up a notch.

"Well," I drawled, "I've had a very long day, I'm in desperate need of a shower, and I'm itching for some ink…"

Phoenix let out a small laugh, "I was wondering when you'd start hounding me for that again."

"Which part?" I flirted, taking a risk. "The shower or the ink?"

I wasn't expecting the heavy pause but was rewarded by one breathy word. "Both."

Anddddddd my dick was hard.

"I'm on my way."

Hanging up without bothering to hear her response, I started my engine, knowing that I was finally going to take the step I'd been too cautious to take over the last few weeks.

Phoenix had no idea, but I was struggling more than I let on.

It was awful watching my friends smoke and drink like they didn't have a care in the world, while I was stuck with cigarettes and soda to get myself through whatever group hang out I was attending. That shit ate at me on the daily, and the only thing keeping me from throwing all my progress in the trash were the hundreds of little goals I'd set for myself on a daily basis.

Dr. Blake suggested setting up a routine, making sure I had something important to focus on throughout the day.

Everything I did was strategic and I stayed busy, surrounded by the people I loved the most. Even though it was hard sometimes, I'd specifically told every one of my friends that I didn't want them to stop their lives for me. Phoenix included. If she wanted to smoke a blunt before dinner, she could. I didn't give a shit. But she was the only one that remained sober when I was around. It pissed me off at first because I thought she didn't believe in me, like I needed to be babied or watched over, but she was Phoenix and she knew immediately that I'd gotten lost in my head. We talked about it, she explained that it had nothing to do with her belief in me, but rather her celebrating me. She wanted to support me and told me to fuck off when I said it wasn't necessary.

I left it alone after that, and actually found that I was able to see more clearly than I'd been able to while I was on drugs. Before my overdose, a conversation like that would have ended in ruin, but this time around I was able to see the truth and believe it rather than get lost in my own subconscious fears.

All in all, I took pride in sticking to my sobriety, if only because it was the only promise I ever kept.

I was prescribed Lithium to treat my Bi-Polar disorder, Lexapro for my anxiety, and a drug I couldn't pronounce that helped reduce the cravings I still fought from the opioid abuse. The medication cocktail wasn't fool proof, I wouldn't say that it worked one hundred percent of the time, but I was doing my best and I was fucking proud of myself. Knowing that everyone in my life—all of the people that had chosen to forgive me—got to see me winning against my addiction on a daily basis? That was fuel for me.

And tonight, I'd hit a big goal that I set for myself weeks ago.

Given the nature of my relationship with Phoenix and all the shit I did wrong, the last thing I wanted was to jump right back into a full-blown relationship and fall into the co-dependent trap that I'd set for us in the beginning. I was still capable of it, I still wanted to be wrapped up in her at all times because she was an addiction in and of herself. I didn't want to fuck up the most important thing in my life, so I created boundaries. Not for Phoenix, but for myself. Instead of losing myself in her, I made it a goal of mine to set up my career first.

I'd told myself that once I laid down the first track on my new album, I'd allow myself to dive into the deep end with Phoenix. I'd give her everything I had left and figure out how to balance both once the time came.

Blake warned me about forming attachments and how if I wasn't very careful, I could fall into more of those addictive tendencies that could eventually cause more problems between Phoenix and I. It was a hard pill to swallow, but I knew she was right. While I wanted Phoenix to be at my beck and call constantly, I didn't need her to be. She had her own life, her own career, and we both deserved to achieve independent success.

However, I was still me, so I knew if I were going to be truly independent, I needed to lay the foundation of my career first, before blowing the roof off my obsession with Phoenix Royal.

And because she was intuitive and brilliant, Phoenix knew not to push me. I could see the disappointment written all over her face when I continued to shut her down night after night, but even without knowing that I was heading straight to a writing session with the guys, she let me go without a fight.

She trusted me.

And I recognized how in some cases, it would be shitty of me to not include her in what I was doing, but Dr. Blake reminded me over and over that my recovery journey was about *me*, and I needed to do whatever I thought was necessary to find a way to stay sober.

This was it.

If I'd done it the opposite way, I wouldn't have given a shit about the album, I would have spent every fucking day wrapped up in that girl, and nothing else would have mattered.

Was I still formulating my life around Phoenix Royal? Yeah, a little bit. But a zebra can't change its stripes.

I am who I am.

Phoenix Royal was written in the marrow of my bones. It was crucial to set everything else up before I slid inside that girl again, but tonight…

It was going down.

I'm coming for you, baby bird.

We have a long night ahead of us.

CHAPTER 34
Phoenix

"YOU MIGHT WANT to leave the house," I warned Frankie as I walked into the kitchen, trying to ignore the swarm of honeybees trying to make a colony in my stomach.

My best friend scrunched her nose and stared at me from the island where she sat with her laptop open in front of her. "Why?"

"Uh—" I let out a small, flustered laugh, and put a hand to my forehead, "—because Judah just called, and he's...on his way..."

Her features fell into confusion. "...okay? He's here all the time."

"Yeah, well," I started to explain, moving to the fridge to grab a Truly so I could chug it before he arrived, "he's coming to *shower* and get his tattoo."

"Oooo," Frankie wiggled her eyebrows like an asshole. "Shower? That man has barely been in the bathroom other than to take a piss and leave."

The top of my can popped as I opened it. "Yeah, that's what I'm getting at."

"Oh my god, you're finally getting laid!" Franks squealed, causing me to cringe against the high-pitched sound. "Damn *right* I'm getting out of here. You two are gonna need the whole house to yourselves."

The thought had me nervous as fuck.

Which was ridiculous because it was Judah we were talking about, but I still felt so detached from him that the thought of being intimate with him again gave me anxious butterflies.

"Fuck my life," I muttered before lifting the drink to my mouth and downing it in one go. As the carbonation burned my lungs, I resented the fact that I couldn't have another—given I'd be inking Judah's skin permanently and the last thing I wanted was to fuck it up because I was a pussy and needed alcohol to even face him.

"What the hell is happening to you?" Frankie laughed as I let out an un-ladylike belch.

"I don't know!" I yelled back, sounding like a lunatic. "I'm freaking out."

The bitch tried to cover her smirk as she closed her laptop and stood from the island, but I still saw it.

"Clearly," she nodded and stepped toward me. "How about you just calm down, and tell your bestie what's wrong."

"No," I blurted, scowling at her. "You're laughing at me right now and I'm not loving it."

"I'm laughing because it's Judah dude!" She let her smile show fully now that she was in front of me. She grabbed my shoulders. "You're about to get what you've wanted for *weeks*. Don't fuck around and get all bashful and weird. Take the bull by its horns and lock his ass down."

Take the…

I busted out laughing, feeling the lightness spread to my toes as I bent forward to get it all out.

Frankie was right.

It didn't erase my nerves, but she did her job and loosened my internal panic.

"I needed that," I pushed out through my chuckles and wiped my eyes. "I *really* needed that."

She laughed with me, but it wasn't nearly as boisterous. Still, she said, "I know you did. But seriously, calm your tits, pretty girl. You've got this."

With that, she smacked my ass and made her way into her room, leaving me in the kitchen alone.

As the laughter faded, anxiety came back, but I didn't have much time to think about how many things could go wrong, because as I was recycling the Truly can, I heard our front door open.

Shit.

Fucking *shit.*

"Honey, I'm homeeeee," Judah called out, sending volts of electrical awareness through my body.

I cleared my throat as quietly as I could, then let him know, "I'm in here!"

His boots beat down on the wood of our hallway as he headed in my direction, while my heart echoed the loud sound, syncing with his movements already. But then he rounded the corner and sauntered into the kitchen…

I swear to all fuck, I lost my breath.

My Skyscraper looked like he'd spent hours pulling on his hair, and it was now messy and sweaty atop his head, making my mouth water as my gaze flitted south, taking in those bright blue eyes as they blazed in my direction. His lip was quirked north, telling me without words that he had plans for the night. Plans for me, for us, but I wasn't in on the secret.

Biting my lip and ignoring his stare, I took in his outfit to buy myself some time.

He wore a black T-Shirt, showcasing a neon pink skeleton couple on the front, with dark grey skinny jeans and his pink Doc Martin's. I fixated on the thick silver bracelets circling his wrists, thinking about how uniquely sexy he was.

My breathing was already erratic, but as I forced myself to meet his eyes once again, my sight got caught on the silver chain around his neck, made to look like barbed wire.

A whispered, "Fucking hell," slipped out before I could stop it.

His tone was teasing, full of taunts, as he slowly questioned, "What's wrong, baby bird?"

My stare locked with his. "You're hot and you know it."

At that, he let out a dark laugh, but before he could respond, Frankie blew into the room.

"Hi Judah, bye Judah," she called out. "Phoenix, text me in the morning and don't you *dare* forget or I'll cut your fucking nipples off."

"Whoa, watch it!" Judah called back, scowling at my best friend as she ran down the hallway.

"Love you!" Was the last thing she said before the front door shut and I was officially alone with Judah Colt.

Instantly, as if the Universe knew just how to fuck with me, the temperature of the room skyrocketed, sending my heart flying toward uncertain excitement.

"Soooo," Judah started, drawing out the word slowly, "care to share with the class why you're so…worked up?"

Ohhhhh, fuck off.

He knew the answer to that question.

The tension in the room was palpable, for Christ sake. No one would be able to miss it, much less the two of us. And the heat was only turned up a notch as Judah began to walk toward me again. Unconsciously, I stepped backward and into the counter, where both of my hands clutched the marble to hold myself steady.

"I, uh—" *get it together, Phoenix,* "—I'm just…"

"You're just…" He stopped in front of me, leaning down just a little in order to whisper, "Just *what*, Phoenix?"

With him standing that close, all I could do was crane my

neck to look at him, lifting my chin in order to meet those blue eyes. His energy was fucking loud, and finally, terrifyingly, it was entirely focused on me. I could physically feel his thoughts, picture his ideas, and taste his desire to touch me, but he was holding back because he still loved to make my head spin.

This was the side of Judah that had yet to make an appearance since his overdose. This was the spark I missed, the passion he held deep within even just the tone of his fucking voice. It set me on edge, had me spiraling through all the possibilities while at the same time keeping grounded—completely rooted in the here and now.

His intensity had me whispering back, "I just…missed you."

His pupils blew wide, my heart lit on fire.

"*You* missed *me?*" That gaze darkened further as he asked his question, but I couldn't answer, not when his hand grazed my waist before sliding up my side, over my chest and around my throat. The pressure was featherlight, yet it was enough to steal my breath as he demanded, "Shower. *Now.*"

I bit my lip and sucked in a breath through my nose before letting go of the counter and lifting a hand to his chest.

"Yes, sir," I replied, pushing him backwards and toward my room, letting him know I was more than down.

The silence was charged as I led the way through the house and into my bedroom and it had me feeling like I was walking through a thunder cloud. At any moment the storm would start and once it did? There was no telling what kind of damage would be done.

As we entered, I turned off the main lights and flipped on my purple LEDs, giving the place a more relaxed feel in an attempt to calm the raging hormones in my veins. Right next to my bed was the massive massage table I used whenever I tattooed someone at home, and Judah noticed immediately.

"Oh good, she's all set up."

I had no idea why, but whenever he talked about me like I wasn't there—as if he were thinking out loud—it did something to my insides. I was already starving for his affection but I'd be a sloppy mess in no time if he kept it up.

That's when it hit me.

Holy fuck, I'm going to see him naked again.

I cleared my throat, fearing I'd choke on my next words, but before I even had a chance to say anything Judah's hand was wrapped around my throat again, but this time, from behind. He pulled back, forcing my body to hit his as he rumbled, "I can feel your thoughts from here, little bird."

I tried to breathe normally. "Yeah? Then what am I thinking?"

His fingers hit my temple as he swiped a chunk of hair from the side of my face, giving him room to lean down and whisper in my ear, "You're already wet and you don't know what to do about it."

My eyes fluttered shut as I inhaled his scent.

Judah Colt was once again *everywhere*—too much and not nearly enough.

When I said nothing, he pushed, "Am I wrong?"

This was it.

This was the moment I'd been waiting for ever since we reconnected, the moment I thought might *not* happen given his previously avoidant behavior.

Anticipation lit up my bloodstream. "Why don't you find out for yourself?"

That hand around my throat tightened just enough to cause a small moan to slip from my mouth, but it was gone before I knew what was happening.

"Lift your arms," Judah instructed in a voice like gravel, as his fingers appeared at the bottom of my t-shirt. I listened, extending my arms in the air so that he could pull the fabric over my head. "Good girl. Now turn around."

Knowing he was in charge had me shaking, wondering if maybe I really would get everything I wanted. Was it possible that the darkly sexual and passionately dominant version of my Skyscraper hadn't died that day?

I fucking hoped so, because it seemed like Judah was back in control, giving me a chance to surrender to the intensity of our connection and live in the bliss. I needed that, wanted it more than I could even express, so I did as he said and faced him.

But rather than waiting for further direction, I reached for the hem of his shirt, and began to lift it, silently requesting he take it off. Given his height, he didn't bother making me struggle, but instead pulled the garment off by grabbing the back and tugging it over his head, leaving him bare chested in front of me for the first time in too long.

My hand immediately landed on the tattoo depicting broken glass, as I surveyed all of the others showcasing his pain, his nightmares, and the ways he tried to tell the truth before he really even knew how.

But he didn't let me look for long. His index finger gently connected with my chin, where he applied just enough pressure so I'd lift my head to meet his eyes. My heart galloped at the emotion simmering in his stare, depicting a whole world of things he wanted to say.

Instead of launching into a monologue, though, he quietly, sincerely, said, "I'm sorry it's taken me so long to be here with you like this." His thumb brushed my bottom lip. "I promise my absence will make sense sooner rather than later."

Not knowing what was occupying Judah's time and attention had the potential to make my fears spin into significantly negative patterns, but I always came back to my friendship with Pharaoh. I trusted him, I knew that if he had even *one* inkling of doubt, or thought *anything* was suspicious when it came to Judah, he'd tell me. And he hadn't.

In fact, the two of them seemed closer than I'd ever seen them before, and it made me happy because now, it seemed more balanced, less stressful. They were back to being brothers, and I knew both Judah and Pharaoh needed that

I had no factual reason to doubt Judah, and even if I did…I somehow just knew he was telling the truth.

Even though it hurt to be left in the dark, I nodded in reply and stated, "I trust you."

I didn't realize the magnitude of what I'd said, but Judah sure did.

The sexually charged energy vanished as his eyes fluttered shut and a look of pure torment crossed his features. I grabbed his waist as he shook his head and pinched the bridge of his nose, obviously trying to clear the intrusive thoughts plaguing his psyche.

"Hey, don't do that," I soothed, knowing there was a very real possibility that Judah could vanish into his head. "Talk to me, J."

With a thick exhale, he leaned forward to press his forehead against mine. It took him a minute, but eventually he whispered, "I don't deserve your trust yet, Phoenix."

"No, you don't," I agreed, knowing he was right. "But I can't change how I feel, and you shouldn't try to change it either. Unless my trust is misplaced."

"It isn't," he insisted, "I swear. I just…I know I'm keeping shit from you and—"

Swallowing down a lump of past pain, I asked, "Is whatever you're doing helping you?"

"Fuck," he whispered painfully, sounding like he was struggling to withhold information. "Yeah, it's helping, but the more you ask, the more I want to tell you. It's supposed to be a surprise. It all is."

It all is?

There's more than one thing?

He genuinely seemed bothered by my questions, and I recognized the odd paradox we were in. I couldn't get suspicious every time he tried to surprise me for the rest of our lives, just because he had a past. This was where he got the chance to earn my trust again, but I was giving it more freely than I thought I would after everything we'd been through.

I couldn't help it. More so than ever before, I felt like I could read him. I thought maybe that was why he was avoiding spending time alone with me, but at the end of the day it didn't matter. I trusted myself, and my gut knew that Judah wasn't doing anything shady, he was building a life for himself outside of me.

I had space to work, time to spend with Frankie, and Judah had Pharaoh and whatever it was he was doing all the time. He was growing, he was still sober, so his system seemed to be working, and it was obvious that he wasn't trying to hurt me by keeping me in the dark about this hidden part of his life. Still, though, there was a lingering sadness I would have to work to ignore until he finally revealed his secrets.

"It's alright," I promised him, tacking on a small smile. "If whatever you're doing is making you happy then I'm fine with the major case of FOMO I have right now."

He chuckled sadly, still looking pained, "If I told you even a hint right now, it would give away too many details and your brilliant ass would piece it all together before I even had a chance to reveal the rest."

Yeah, he wasn't being shady, he was just doing what he thought was best and that worked for me. Even though I hated it.

"You've got that right," I chuckled a little. "It's probably for the best that you keep the details to yourself."

"All you need to know," Judah started, as he brought back

the heat by wrapping two hands around my waist and pulling me against his chest, "is that your boy is about to make you very, *very* proud."

My chest nearly exploded with all the emotions that took flight in my ribcage, and just when I thought it couldn't get any worse, Judah lowered his head to my temple, and whispered thickly, "Oh, and I missed you, too."

My sanity nearly cracked as love, lust, and total adoration shot me straight in the heart, blaring bright and nearly blinding me with the need to tell Judah how I felt about him already, without any of the shit he was doing behind the scenes. There was so much I needed to express but I just couldn't seem to put my thoughts into words. It was too much, too intense, too real between us. It felt like words weren't enough.

So instead, I told him with a kiss.

Tilting my head, I lifted my lips to his and wound my hands around his neck, settling into the feeling in my heart and the pride that simmered there, as I memorized the barely tempered pressure of his kiss.

As his lips parted, it felt like he was breathing those unspoken words right back at me—telling me he felt the same, agreeing that the physical distance between us had taken a toll, but still reminding me that it didn't wipe out the emotion.

His tongue spoke the language of love as it danced with mine.

"Fuck," he groaned against my lips as those hands squeezed my waist, holding me against him with a solid grip, "I *really* fucking missed you."

My answering moan fell into his mouth as our bodies melted into one another and our kisses became more intense, more purposeful. I'd forgotten how smooth his bottom lip was, how easy it was to suck it into my mouth and bite down. I hadn't forgotten how he reacted whenever I caught him by surprise, though.

The answering growl and sudden bruising pressure of his hands was more than expected. It was highly anticipated. So much so that I jumped—knowing he'd catch me—straight into his arms. Immediately, I abandoned his lips, intending to give some attention to his sharpened jawline, but before I could, his teeth met my collar bone.

"Ahhh, shit," I hissed as my head fell back, body arched in his arms. "Fucking hell, J."

His tongue smoothed over the mark, but then trailed up my neck, leaving a wet path of liquid lava on my skin as he went. My pussy pulsed against his stomach as he took his time tasting me, reacquainting himself with the flavor of my perfume since we hadn't even made it to the shower yet.

"You have the softest skin," he purred as those perfect pink lips left a trail of kisses along my jawline. "I can't mark it here, but I know a little something about a pressure point that tends to make you go—"

"—Ah, Judah!" I cried out as his teeth bit into the spot on my neck that never failed to leave me limp, completely at his mercy.

"There it is," he smiled against my neck, licking the spot for good measure. "I think it's time for a shower, because I want this," he snapped the clasp of my bra against my spine, "off."

"Ow!" I chuckled, smacking his chest, as I tried to calm my body down.

And to think, this was just the start of our night. It was only nine p.m.

I am so fucking screwed.

CHAPTER 35

JUDAH

I FELT LIKE A FUCKING ASSHOLE, leaving Phoenix to have to wonder what the hell I was doing while I distanced myself from her, but I had to keep reminding myself that in the end, it would all be worth it. All she ever wanted me to do was write my music from the heart and give my fans the true version of myself because even though I was messy, chaotic, and unable to see the light ninety percent of the time…my listeners could relate.

Phoenix was right when she gave me that pep talk last year. I had the opportunity to be a pillar in my industry, showing my fans that while my head was dark, my will was stronger. My fortitude was more powerful than my nightmares.

This album would be me baring my fucking soul to anyone that listened and my goal was to show P that I could handle the criticism this time around. I was trying to come to terms with who I was and get prepared for people to hate the music I put out.

There was nothing wrong with my truth, there was nothing wrong with me expressing that truth, and it was about damn time I figured that out. Would it be fucking difficult? Hell yeah, but that was the point. Phoenix would be there, ready to support me, just like she wanted to be.

It was an odd gift—not one that could be bought with money—but it was a gift none-the-less.

"Do you know what you're doing?" Phoenix asked as I sat her on the bathroom counter and started gathering what we needed for our shower.

"Uh, yes, I know how to turn your shower on," I stated with sarcasm dripping from my tone, "It hasn't been *that* long."

"Okay, well," she shrugged, showcasing that bratty smirk, "I'm just checking."

"Mhm," I nodded, holding in a smile as I turned on the faucet and adjusted the heat to near-boiling, fully aware of how hot Phoenix liked her water. "So, you ever gonna show me what you designed for me?"

I really wanted that tattoo.

"No," she responded confidently.

With the water now set, I turned to look at her, finding those honey eyes dilated as she stared at me. Liquid lust shot through my veins, making me flex my fingers, closing them into a fist in order to keep from touching her, or better yet, fucking her right there on the counter.

I was trying to elongate the night, make it special. Take it slow.

"No?" I bit out, stalking forward. "Why not?"

"Because," she breathed, eyes fluttering as I stepped into her space, "you're just gonna have to trust me."

"Hmmm," I hummed, running my nose along the top of her head. "I suppose I can't complain about that."

She was trusting me after all the shit I'd done. The girl could ink a fully detailed penis on my body and I wouldn't even blame her.

"You better go get the towels, handsome," Phoenix reminded me. "Wouldn't want the water to get cold."

My answering laugh was gruff and throaty, thick with

restraint I was quickly losing control over because the way she said it made it sound like a warning, proving she was in the same position as I was. Both of us were finding it hard not to give into what our bodies were screaming for.

Quickly, I did as she instructed, grabbing two massive, designer towels—thank fuck for Frankie's spoiled ass—and sat them on the counter next to Phoenix. She remained unmoving, choosing to watch me rather than continue to undress, but the show was over now, and I was done waiting.

Reaching forward, I used my index finger to pull the center of her bra away from her skin as I demanded, "Off."

Without responding, she listened, reaching back to unclasp the strap, but when she was finished, I lost all sense of self as she let the garment fall to the floor at my feet, gifting me with a stunning view of her naked chest.

Faint tan lines still lingered, showing me the exact shape of her bikini, but her skin was still naturally golden, causing my mouth to dry up as my breathing intensified.

My little bird was a fucking masterpiece.

As I studied her, she jumped down from the counter and closed the distance between us, sauntering my way and going straight for the button on my jeans.

"Hey now." I caught her wrist, stopping her from going further because I wasn't done looking yet, I wanted to take it slow, but when she looked up at me, there was a new kind of confession lingering in her stare. It was hard, hurt, and unbalanced.

"The last time you and I were in this room together, you were bloody, shit faced, and couldn't do a damn thing for yourself," Phoenix reminded me, causing my heart to move into a guilty kind of beat. Her voice was suddenly cold and distant as she explained, "I need to do this. Erase the memory. Or at the very least, replace it with a new one."

She immediately looked back down and pulled her wrist

from my grip but I grabbed it back again, feeling like an absolute fucking asshole as I choked out, "Wait a second, P."

She paused, as those lustful flames between us entirely vanished and heartbreak took their place. I noticed her shoulders beginning to shake as her eyes remained downcast, causing that shameful anger in my chest to rise, making me wish I could smash my fist into the mirror in front of me just to get rid of the nearly three-sixty view of the moment I was experiencing.

But instead, I pulled her body into mine and smoothed my hand down her back, trying to shut out the fact that I couldn't even remember what she was talking about. It had to have been linked to the morning I woke up in her living room and found my backpack missing from my car, given I hadn't been invited over for a long time before that.

If I'd shown up faded...I couldn't even imagine what she had to do to get me cleaned up.

"I'm so sorry," I whispered into her hair, knowing those three words would never be enough.

"Y-you could b-barely walk," she responded shakily against my chest. "I kept trying to hide my tears but I don't know why I bothered. You wouldn't have cared. You were fucking *gone*."

Jesus Christ.

My stomach was a hardened knot as I bit down on my bottom lip to try and hold back the emotion threatening to suffocate me.

I didn't know what to say, I didn't know how to tell her she didn't deserve it while knowing at one point, I thought she did. I knew she was crying, I knew she was remembering a moment she would much rather forget, but it was all made worse when her hand on my chest curled into a fist, leaving deep scratches behind as she sobbed, "I thought you were going to die."

Me too.
I wanted to die.

"But I didn't, baby," I responded quietly, pulling her closer as she fell apart. "I'm still here."

"You didn't even care," she cried softly, loosening her grip on my flesh. I wanted her to keep it there. I wanted her to mark me, make me suffer, because the pain was distracting, fueling, branding me with reminders to never do something like that to her ever again.

She needed an explanation.

I thought tonight would be healing for the two of us, but *everything* was a trigger. Every move I made was a reminder because I'd done so much damage, I'd touched every surface of her life and tainted it with my issues. If I were going to come back and try and make it right, I had to make it *all* right. I had to answer to every crime and deal with every consequence of my actions and—not for the first time—I was thankful for Blake and all the shit she made me walk through because I knew how to handle this, I just hated that I had to in the first place.

"The more drugs I took, the less pain I felt," I explained, "you know this, but you don't know how deep it went, Phoenix. I'm terrified of *everything*. Every*one*. Adults are sketchy, friends are shady, my fans are liars, and then you showed up and I thought you'd agree with me. I thought I had the girl you were in New York and never recognized that girl was dead. You killed her by saving your own life. You were stronger than me, braver than me. It made me hate you, made me want to break you, to get revenge but also to see if there was anything else I could do to convince you to be with me, to meet me in the dark."

The sounds coming from her mouth had me struggling to stand. She broke as I confessed, but I needed her to understand the fucking insanity that was my mind. She needed to know it wasn't her fault, but also understand that she didn't have to choose me. She could walk, she had every right to hate me, to leave me in the dust, and maybe it was my martyr talking but I almost wanted that. I deserved it.

"When you refused to drown, when you left me, it did nothing but push me further over the edge, but *none* of that was your fault, Phoenix. And I'm ashamed to admit that I don't remember the night you're reliving right now, but I can tell you this..." my hands ran down the back of her head, trying to ease her heart ache. "I cared. I cared more than you even knew what to do with. Drugs were my love language. The more I took, the more feeling I was trying to bury. And if I showed up here like that, it was because even when I was fucked, you were home, Phoenix Royal. In any state—good, bad, suicidal—you're home. Every decision I made came back to you, even if it hurt you in the process." Her body went limp as she sobbed, but I caught her, holding her to my body as I insisted, "It's fucked up, but it's the truth. All I knew was toxic. I was convinced I'd be forever broken. I'm a goddamn mess, P, and you don't deserve it."

Knowing what I needed to do, I stepped away from her and ran my forearm under my nose to try and clean myself up, but then got right to work.

I quickly removed my pants, socks, and shoes, not giving a shit about the jewelry I wore, then moved to Phoenix, who leaned against the counter with her head down. That brown hair fell over her shoulders and covered her face from view, but her body still trembled. She was locked in a memory, feeling everything all over again and I knew what that was like.

Dr. Blake would try and talk me through it every time I experienced a flash back, but getting out of the memory took time, care, and attention. It took releasing those memories through emotion, and even though I felt sick to my stomach and the cuts from P's nails had blood spilling down my chest—all of my focus was on her.

My entire body was lit with guilt, desperate to make her feel better, remind her that I was there, I was trying to change, that I was sorry. So once I was naked, I bent to my knees in front of her, grabbed the waistline of her leggings—making sure to grab her underwear at the same time—and began to pull them down her legs. Her cries intensified as my own trailed silently from my eyes to my jawline, falling to the floor in small splashes.

I sniffed then instructed softly, "Lift your leg, baby," as I tapped her right calf.

Phoenix listened and knew what to do when I got to the other leg, helping me remove the tight fabric from her body until she was as naked as I was, standing in front of me but still trapped in her own head.

"I just c-can't…" she whispered brokenly, voice shaking, "I-I d-didn't expect…"

"It's okay," I tried to reassure her, but that selfish, disgusting part of me wanted her to just stop. Stop feeling, stop remembering, stop hurting because of me. I wanted to turn it all off, rewind time, and shower at Pharaoh's fucking house to get away from it all.

And yet, even still, I tried to picture what she witnessed that night, and while it only served to make me feel worse, I held on to it because it was another piece to my fucked up puzzle. Another weapon in my armory to use against myself whenever I thought about slipping up or giving in to a craving that could kill me.

I'd driven drunk that night, after fighting Brandon and hitting Silas. I remembered the road twisting oddly in front of me, making it feel like I was in an alternate universe as time bent and other cars disappeared. Everything was muted and grey, but I remember soaring, feeling the most alive I'd ever felt.

Except it was all fake.

And look what I did to her that night without even knowing.

Wanting to kill myself all over again, I battled with those demons, as they taunted, screamed, and echoed back all the reasons I didn't deserve to be here with Phoenix, to keep her, or even take care of her.

But I shut them down by doing just that. By remembering I could prove myself to myself, and to her in turn, that I was worthy of another chance.

I stood, leaning over her small body to grab a thick hair tie from the counter next to the sink and as gently as I could, I gathered her hair out of her face, tying it up in a messy, less-than-perfect knot on the top of her head.

As I did it, she lifted her chin to meet my stare and what I saw broke me that much further.

"Fucking hell, Phoenix," I breathed out, cracked and full of remorse. The bold evidence of her pain served as an invisible blade to my heart.

Her normally bright stare was now red and puffy, caked in melted makeup and the sight had me wishing she'd just put a bullet between my eyes and get it over with already.

And yet…

"I've got you," I promised her, "'K? I know I fucked up, I know I—"

"I mourned you," she cut me off in a voice that was thick and distant. "I thought you'd never come back, never be the guy I knew you were deep down, and I mourned you."

My eyes shut against her words, her truth.

"You left me here to clean you up, Judah," she whispered. "Me. Your girl. You left me with your ghost and asked me to hold you up as you stumbled through my house, drunk as hell, covered in blood, and then acted like it was no big deal. You felt no shame that night, and that was the hardest pill to swallow."

There were rusty nails in my throat, I was sure of it. "And then I made it worse."

"No, *then* I found your drugs," she bit out, staring down at her hands, not giving a shit that she was naked, not even trying to hide, and I didn't miss the symbolism within the moment.

Pure vulnerability wrapped in nightmares.

"I just wanted to find you clothes for the morning," she admitted. "I didn't intend on being *that* girl and search through your shit, but when all I found was that fucking backpack…"

Her tears started up again, but this time they were less loud, less obvious, and more internal as she fell back into her memories, leaving me to chew on the fact that I'd truly shown her what I was like at my worst.

I swallowed my self-hatred and stepped toward her—showing her that despite how shitty I'd been, I could handle her pain, I could handle the truth—and pulled her into my arms.

I expected her to push me away or tell me to get the hell out, but she didn't. She made my hatred worse and clung to me, instead.

Phoenix wrapped both arms around my neck—all too aware that I'd never let her suffer with my height—leading me to reach down and slide an arm under her knees before lifting her in a cradled position.

Her sobs hadn't come back, but I wanted to get her through this in an intimate way, proving to her that I wasn't going anywhere, and when the time came for her to ask questions or get mad and start yelling, I'd handle that too. She deserved it. I didn't just put her through hell, I went there personally, and she followed because she loved me.

I took advantage of that trust and I'd be damned if I did it again.

After checking the water temperature with an outstretched hand, I confirmed it was good but instead of keeping the showerhead running, I pushed the metal tab and ran the water for a bath, no longer interested in anything but holding her close.

She said nothing as water filled the tub, but her silence told me everything.

Because I couldn't help it, because I hated that I could physically *feel* her pain, I whispered once more, "I'm sorry, little bird."

"I know," she muttered against my skin, and as much as I despised it, I appreciated that she never told me it was okay.

Because it wasn't.

CHAPTER 36
Phoenix

BY THE TIME Judah and I settled in the bathtub, I felt like an open nerve.

Half of me was pissed for ruining what should have been a fiery reunion, the other half knew I needed this. I'd been so fucking strong, so forgiving, so understanding, and yet I was still angry. I was still hurting, still confused, still feeling all of the filthy shit I'd felt back when Judah was lost to me.

I didn't expect my reaction, though, and I wasn't even really sure what triggered it in the first place, but when I went to take off his pants and he denied me, my brain just broke, cracking open the heartache box I thought I'd nailed shut.

I hadn't.

But what I *had* done was open a line of communication between Judah and me that I had been too scared to touch before, fearing that I'd piss him off and he'd react like he used to. I didn't want to rock the boat or break the fragile foundation we'd begun to build again, but I was wrong for thinking that would be his response.

It wasn't.

It was the damn opposite.

Instead of throwing shit or raising his voice, he stayed silent behind me in the water and washed my body, my hair, leaving only my face for me to clean, simply because he couldn't reach it. And I was glad I sat facing away from him because the entire time his hands seared my skin, I cried. I cried for the old me—the girl that had fallen in love with a monster and gotten torn apart as a result. I cried because I slept with Pharaoh, leading him on, making him believe that we had a future when in reality my heart had always belonged to the very monster that led me to him in the first place. I cried because I'd been forced into denial, forced to shut my feelings for Judah down and shove them deep enough where it was easier to forget them than it was to find them.

But then, when Judah was finished and I was clean, those tears no longer fell from my eyes, and I felt like for once, I'd told Judah a truth and got the response I deserved.

Except now, my mind was open, my vulnerability had been turned up as loud as it could go, and I wasn't done talking, wasn't finished going back in time to get answers or simply get it all out.

Waiting, I let him wash himself, knowing that if I tried to do it he'd shut me down, and when he was done, I leaned back against his chest, felt his slippery skin against mine, and grabbed his hands when he placed his arms over my shoulders.

Our breathing synced for only a few moments, before I stated, "I thought maybe you didn't want to have sex with me because the last girls you slept with were Rachele and Sarah."

His answering sigh was deep and full of remorse. "I, uh… don't remember those three days, either."

Fuck.

I closed my eyes.

"But you have survivor's guilt?" I asked after a few deep breaths.

"On a major scale," he admitted softly. "I didn't sleep for weeks in rehab, fighting nightmares that kept popping up, reminding me of our bender. Most of the time, you and Frankie took the place of Sarah and Rachele, which, of course, made it all worse."

"Jesus, Judah," I muttered, not even wanting to think about what it would be like to endure those kinds of nightmares.

"Dr. Blake recently prescribed me a new anxiety medication because of it," he stated, twisting a piece of my hair around his finger. "I, uh, I'm not really doing as well as I make it seem."

"Then stop pretending," I replied in a blunt tone, no longer caring about being gentle. "I'm not here for you only when you're happy, Judah. You weren't supposed to get out of rehab and hide all the negative shit from me as a way of proving that you're committed to living sober. That's not the point."

That lingering resentment was showing but I couldn't help it. Knowing he was struggling and I was only just now finding out about it had me pissed off all over again.

"Deep down I know that," Judah stated, "but I'm new to this, P. I'm so fucking used to keeping every emotion hidden until I can't anymore. Then it explodes out of me in ways that cause serious damage. It's how I've spent my entire adult life living. It's not healthy, I know that, but after rehab, I had a handle on the dark shit because I faced every nook and cranny of my fucking *soul* while I was in there. So when I got out, I naively expected my life to be easier. But the more I get settled, the more everything reminds me of the mistakes I made, and I'm too determined to fix it all to worry about opening up to you about it. I don't want you to perceive me as weak."

"Weak?" I couldn't help it, I laughed. "Judah Colt, you are the fucking opposite of weak. You overdosed, nearly died, and I genuinely thought that you were going to come back and get fucked up all over again because it was easier than doing what you're doing right now. Even keeping *this* shit from me makes you strong in my eyes, because you're still hiding this pain and

I had no idea. You're trying to do it all alone and you actually had me fooled, but that's the thing. I'm sick of being fooled by you."

I wasn't giving it to him easily, but he was getting it nonetheless. I was done being shoved in the corner, only to see the sides of him he wanted me to see.

"Fuck." Judah's forehead hit my hair as he exhaled deeply. "I'm screwing this all up."

I released a similar breath, feeling exhausted after the breakdown I'd just had, but still, I replied, "No you're not, you're just falling back into old patterns. Which, I guess is to be expected, but Judah, to me…hiding emotions is the same as hiding drugs. It's still a wall between us, it still keeps me alienated, and leaves you alone. The last thing you need is for one night, it all becomes too much, and you wind up too terrified to tell me how bad your headspace has gotten and how long you've hidden it from me, so you take a fucking pill to escape it altogether." The thought terrified me more than *anything*, which fueled my reaction in a way I hadn't expected. "Don't ruin your progress for the sake of your pride."

Judah remained quiet, but his arms tightened around my chest, pulling me closer into the cocoon of his body, and again…it surprised me. Not only because he hadn't freaked out after my less than graceful chastisement, but because he was still willingly supplying the simple, yet completely transformative affection that kept me grounded.

It had taken an entire argument, a whole ass screaming match for Judah to hear me in the beginning. He pushed any criticism away, and any modicum of help was shut down before I could even complete a full sentence until I had him so worn out that he had virtually no other choice but to listen to me.

But now…

"I've spent the last month trying to learn how to live

sober," Judah explained, "and I still struggle with what that's supposed to look like because truth be fucking told...the triggers that made me want to escape in the first place haven't gone anywhere and *that's* what I'm terrified of being exposed. I don't want anyone to see me as more of a risk than they already do."

I could see where he was coming from when he put it like that. Ricco and Kavan had accepted him back—as had Silas and his band—but we all knew they were still keeping a sharp, thin, protective distance between Judah and themselves. Frankie was probably the only one that didn't feel that way.

"I'm not blind," Judah rumbled, sounding both sad and resigned to his fate, "I know that most people won't ever fully trust me again. I'm an addict. I always will be. And it's up to me to fight that part of myself, so given my track record, most of you guys probably think I'm going to derail this train sooner rather than later but—"

"I don't," I cut him off, knowing he was right, but needing to make sure he understood my side of things. "I don't even let myself think about you relapsing."

There was a long pause, then, "...why?"

"Because I could snap at any moment."

It was a reminder more than anything—a fear *I* still carried around like a tiny designer backpack. It didn't look like anything dangerous could be hidden in there, but it was big enough to hold a gun.

"Phoenix, please." It sounded like he rolled his eyes. "You aren't going to snap. You are not your father."

"And neither are you," I concluded, not believing him for a single second, but wanting to prove a point. "Both of us could lose our fucking minds at any moment if we decided to stop fighting to stay positive, to keep living despite the demons that chase us, but you keep conveniently forgetting that I need you just as much as you need me." Given that I was out of tears, my emotional balance was off, supplying me anger instead of sadness. "You keep leaving me alone, Judah, and that's not your fucking job. That's not what we're supposed to be. We're supposed to keep each other fighting, J, and I'm sick of either being kicked around for wanting to live, or being left to wonder what's going on because you're too afraid to tell me that you struggle."

I was on a roll and couldn't seem to stop talking. "You and I are not the kind of couple that gets to live a normal life. We can't exorcise our demons and get rid of them once and for all. They haunt us, they threaten us damn near constantly, and I don't want to do it alone. I don't want to fight alone. When will you see that I am willingly, knowingly, offering to hold your hand through every nightmare, every panic attack, every insecure tantrum, because all I ever wanted was for us to fight with *those* things and not each other?"

His answer was quick.

"I never learned how to trust. I never instinctually learned what it was, how to give it, or how to earn it. I didn't even realize Pharaoh was the first person I trusted until I was in rehab and Blake pointed it out. My parents fucking *hated* me, Phoenix. From basically birth. And I got used to being hated. I thought I would always be hated. I lived skeptical of every single ounce of adoration because no one told me that was in the cards for me. No one told me I deserved it."

But I did.

"Until you," he confirmed. "You knocked me off my goddamn feet, but I already had a plan. Double fucked and always faded. Here for a good time, not a long time. And like I've said so many fucking times, I thought you were on that boat with me. I thought we were going to do that together. Survival was never the end goal for me until it was the only choice I had."

Knowing Judah was so deep in his own damnation by the

time I met him always made me feel physically ill. Add on the fact that his parents were such fucking monsters? I was softening, becoming empathetic to his life and the lack of tools he was given to live it to the fullest.

"So, I'll be honest, Phoenix, I heard you when you talked about wanting to be there for me, wanting us to be in this together, but before rehab, before I connected the dots, I had absolutely no fucking idea what any of it actually meant." Recognizing what he was saying as truth, I swallowed my anger and continued to listen. "You were so much more emotionally evolved than I was—thanks to your parents showing you love and affection—where I was taught affection by the industry and the women I'd fucked around with. I'd given affection to Pharaoh instinctually because I trusted him subconsciously, but the brutal way I treated everyone else? The fighting? The hard fucking? It all came from what I learned in my own house. It was natural, normal, and I'm just now trying to open myself up to the possibility of learning a new way of existing."

My heartbeat was wild in my chest as I thought of how different Judah and I were, how much he had to learn, how much he already *had* learned.

"My choice not to tell you about my struggle had everything to do with the shame I felt over dragging you into my darkness in the first place. I didn't think you'd want more of the same, Phoenix," he confessed. But he said my name like it was precious, like he knew he fucked up and was just trying to navigate the choppy waters of trying to fix it. "And I know we agreed to talk openly and honestly, but even then, I wasn't dealing with the shit that's started coming up lately. The longer I'm out of rehab, the worse it's getting because, yes…I'm doing it alone. And if you take anything from this conversation, know that it was never about me not *wanting* you to hold my hand—in fact, that is all I ever want in this lifetime. If I'm going to live, it's going to be holding your hand. I just…didn't think it was still possible that you'd want me and all my broken pieces too."

Miraculously, the tears were back.

I wanted to be pissed at him, and a solid twenty percent of me still was, but when he broke it down and explained it to me the way he did—involving his parents, giving me a link back to the beginning, telling me how it all started—I couldn't blame him. Even when he was a total disaster, when he spent every day fucking *every single thing* up, I found it hard to blame him because that addiction was a disease, yes, but it was also a symptom of a much bigger, much scarier, diagnosis. Fear of abandonment was a monster. It was a fast breeder and got off on reproducing demons of all shapes and sizes.

Judah was starting all over, starting completely fucking fresh, but with no one on his side. Everyone else was waiting for the moment he slipped up, they were waiting for him to show even a glimpse of those previous colors, so he hid *every* color just in case it might remind someone of his past and how he used to be.

Which was what led me to intertwine our fingers as I whispered, "Broken, whole, shattered, even non-existent…I want you without conditions, Judah. This hand is mine to hold."

It was a different promise, yet entirely similar to the original one I'd made to him.

You said you wouldn't leave, even if we fought.

Fighting with him wasn't necessarily an issue for me because couples fight all the time, but the issue I lived with constantly was fighting about shit unnecessarily due to secrets, lies, and manipulation of truths he thought I couldn't handle. I was always kept six feet away from the truth. That didn't work for me anymore.

Judah's long fingers squeezed mine as he said, "I hear you, little bird. No more distance."

I hoped he meant it because I was dead serious.
Any more distance and we'd be done.

* ❄ *

LEANING AWAY from Judah's skin, I dipped the tip of my needle in the black ink, and asked, "How you holdin' up?"

"Fine," Judah replied, "wondering what the hell this tattoo is gonna look like."

"It's supposed to be a surprise," I smiled, feeling much better after our bath.

We ended up staying in the water for another thirty minutes, where Judah told me more about what rehab was like for him. He let me in on some of the conversations he had with Dr. Blake during the last six weeks of his stay—where things got more and more intense when it came to his growth—but what really got me was the fact that he admitted he was struggling with not having a place of his own.

Living with Pharaoh was fun and all because they were best friends, but Judah explained that he'd gotten used to his routine in rehab, and being out of it made him realize how much better he did when he was working with a routine. He said he was ready to live alone again so he could truly figure out what he needed to feel more secure.

I asked him why he'd been so distant and he said he set himself a goal he wanted to achieve before he made his way back to me completely. He explained that he was genuinely afraid of losing himself in me all over again and forcing me to put up a boundary that might derail his progress, so he gave himself something to fall back on. A project to complete, apparently. I had a general idea of what he could be spending his time on but I refused to press him for answers, knowing he wanted to do it all on his own and surprise me with the result.

He did, however, say that he wouldn't be so distant going forward because whatever goal he'd made for himself had been completed. It made me feel a little bit like the second option but I was taking the small wins because what else was I supposed to do?

Judah then admitted that sleeping next to me might help with the nightmares he still dealt with—even if they didn't go away—because at least when he woke up, he wouldn't be alone as he tried to calm down.

Luckily for him, I craved that.

There was a part of me that desperately needed to help him, to take care of him, and that was my abandonment issues peeking out at me, but I wasn't questioning that either because *fuck my life*…if it meant that I was going to feel better, feel included, and my relationship would remain stable and happy? I didn't care if it was borderline toxic.

"I know it's supposed to be a surprise but did you have to put it in the *one* spot I won't be able to see basically ever?" Judah grumbled, pissed that I'd chosen the back of his neck to ink my design.

"It fits the aesthetic, and it's not supposed to be seen every day, it's supposed to be worn as a badge of pride," I explained, knowing it wouldn't make sense until he saw it.

"Whatever, you're just lucky I previously agreed to let you have full control because otherwise, we'd be changing it."

I smirked, getting back to work, "Oh, hush. Just trust me."

"You know I can't sit in silence, so talk to me," he requested, making my smirk bloom into a smile. "What's on your mind, lil' lady?"

A lot.

"Everything," I answered honestly.

"As in?"

"I don't know," I sighed, making sure to shade the small tip of the tattoo perfectly to accentuate the linework. "I just…want us to go back to normal, I guess. And I know that's not really possible, but it seems like everything is still so goddamn complicated and I'm tired of it."

"It is complicated," Judah agreed, "but not *everything* has to be."

My stomach dipped a little, picking up on the subtle hint in his tone. "Explain…"

He scoffed. "What's the one thing we haven't done yet?"

Heat blew through my cheeks. "Sex."

"Correct, and tell me, little bird," his voice resembled a sensual purr, "have your sexual tastes changed?"

Oh, fuck…

"No," was all I managed to say, trying to hold back the slight tremor in my hands, fearing I'd fuck up the design. But this conversation was one of my biggest fears. Sex was the one thing about our relationship I hoped didn't have to be reinvented.

His next question came out deliberately slow, "So…you still like it rough?"

I cleared my throat, starting to sweat, "Judah, I'm trying to work here."

"I'll take that as a yes," he concluded. "My hand around your pretty little throat…you still into it?"

"J…" I warned.

"Another yes. That's good." *Oh, holy hell, someone help me.* "And all that anger you still hold inside, all that resentment you pretend you don't feel toward me…you want to take it out on me, don't you?"

There it was. That toxic passion I was hoping wouldn't disappear with his vices.

"You're lucky I'm almost finished," I grated out, wanting to throw my tattoo machine across the room and forget the whole thing.

His chuckle was dark. "Ah, yes, another correct assumption. And once again, lucky for you…there are some things about me that will never change."

I clenched my toes. "That you're a savage in bed?"

"That," he responded, "but also the fact that you turn me into a monster."

My god.

But he was right.

Fucking Judah always felt like an out-of-body experience, one where both of us fell victim to the intensity of our connection and fed from it until we couldn't anymore. It was fast, brutal, and neither one of us liked to hold back.

I feared that we'd lose that—that we already did—given Judah had barely even touched me since that first night on the beach. But now that I was finishing the last of his tattoo, that anticipation had returned full force.

I remained quiet, not wanting to respond until my job was complete, unsure of my ability to handle the sexual tension in the room being spoken out loud.

Focusing hard for a few more seconds, I laid the last line of the final word and pulled back to admire the completed piece. Checking each part—the windows, the door, the tip, the bird flying overhead, and each individual letter—my grin spread, and glee burst through my chest.

It was perfect.

After covering the fresh tattoo in Aquaphor, I snapped off my gloves, and announced proudly, "I'm done."

Judah flipped over faster than expected, flying toward me with wicked intent as he gripped my face and growled out, "Good, come here."

His lips hit mine in a rush of movement, sending me stumbling backward, only to be caught by his arm around my waist. I responded immediately, lifting to my tippy toes and sliding my hands in his hair, pulling tightly, just to be sure I set the tone.

"Don't you—ah, fuck," I moaned as he moved his mouth to my neck and bit down on that spot that drove me wild. "Don't y-you wanna see your tattoo?"

His tongue licked a line up the shell of my ear before he whispered, "Later."

Good enough for me.

I turned my head, finding his bottom lip with my teeth and sucking it into my mouth, giving myself full permission to let loose.

"That's it," he ground out as I jumped to wrap my legs around his waist, "hold on."

He started walking, leaving my room entirely.

Confused, I asked between kisses, "Where are we going?"

"We're going to be thirsty," was all he replied.

Licking my way down his jaw, I said against his skin, "And you feel the need to prepare now?"

His shoulders lifted on a shrug. "I want to fuck you on the counter."

There go my insides.

"Kitchen sex first?" I questioned throatily, smiling because I knew he had a plan.

As we passed through the living room he explained, "I haven't had sex in four months, Phoenix, we both know I'm not going to last long, especially being inside *you,* so the first round will happen here." My ass hit the island. "Who knows where the next round will take place. All I know for sure is that it's about to be a *long* fuckin' night."

I smirked, fully prepared. "Give me all you've got, Skyscraper."

Those blue eyes went up in flames as his hand flew to my throat.

I gasped, not at the pressure, but out of surprise, as he forced me to look up—right into the eye of the storm. "I'll give you all I've got, little bird, but you better give it back twice as hard. And make it hurt."

He wanted to be punished, wanted to know how much damage he'd done and how pissed I was about it.

"But first," he taunted as his gaze slid to my lips, "I have to make sure you still taste the same."

My breath got caught in my windpipe and Judah abandoned his hold on my throat and went straight for the hem on my baggy shirt, lifting it over my head before yanking my boy shorts off in one smooth motion.

Oh shit.

He fell into a squatting position, bringing him eye level with my already soaked pussy, giving him a perfect idea of just how crazy he drove me with that little sex talk we'd just had.

I had no time to prepare before there were two fingers buried in my cunt, and a thumb on my clit. Judah got straight to work.

"H-holy fuck!" I cried out, immediately reaching for the edge of the island, holding on for dear life as Judah expertly manipulated the walls of my pussy like he'd memorized every area and knew exactly how to send me straight to the stars.

And hell, maybe he had, once upon a time, but for someone who frequently forgot moments others could never erase, Judah certainly had this one thing down pat.

"Still so tight," he murmured, as if unfazed. "So pink and raw, waiting to be pounded."

Oh, I needed to be pounded, alright.

I wanted to skip the foreplay—didn't give a fuck about this part—so I tried to tell him as much, starting with, "Judah, can we just—"

"Ah, ah, little bird," he cut me off. "I said I wouldn't last long, which means you get all the special treatment first."

I didn't want special treatment, I wanted to be fucked, but

when his fingers disappeared, only to be replaced by his tongue, I lost all my fight.

"Fuuuuck," I hissed out, as the wet heat of his mouth tortured my clit.

My eyes rolled back, and my grip on the granite was so tight that I feared my nails might break off. Judah's tongue danced against my pussy as he reacquainted himself with the flavor of my essence and did a thorough job of marking his territory.

He gripped underneath my knees with both hands and lifted, bringing my feet to rest on the edge of the island.

And then he spread me wide.

Holy fucking hell.

Those long fingers joined his mouth this time—first two, then three—as if preparing me for what his dick planned to do. I was as grateful as I was annoyed, knowing that the nine-inch monster he was keeping from me was about to do some serious damage, especially since he planned to go all night.

"You're dripping, baby," he pointed out, holding up a hand to prove just how right he was. My juices coated his fingers in a clear sheen before he lifted them to his mouth and licked away the evidence, "and you taste exactly as I remembered."

Goddamnit, he's so hot.

"You gonna fuck me yet?" I panted, feeling lightheaded, and ready to explode.

"Depends," he smirked, sliding his now clean fingers up and down my folds, teasing my clit and making me jump with every pass, "how close are you?"

"Close enough to want to rip your balls off right now," I snarled, glaring at him as I lay nearly immobile on the island. "*Do* something before I do it for you."

His eyebrows rose. "Now that's an idea…mutual masturbation?"

The moan that slipped from my mouth was involuntary as

my pussy throbbed at the thought of seeing him stroking his dick in front of me.

"Judah, please..." I begged, fingers itching to touch myself. I squeezed the granite harder, feeling a nail snap, just as I feared. "Ow, fuck. Do something!"

Slowly, Judah stood up and flashed me a knowing smirk as he dropped his joggers to the floor, leaving him completely naked, standing two feet from the island rocking a hard-on that was nearly the size of my forearm.

"I don't know," he singsonged, looking down at his erection then back up at me, "I'm thinking maybe we *should* just get ourselves off."

Oh, come on. "You wouldn't dare."

He barked out a pitch-black laugh. "I wouldn't?"

With rapt attention, I watched as he gripped the base of his cock with his left hand and held it tight, squeezing as he dragged his fist up the length and hissed, eyes closing with pleasure.

I am going to die.

But you know what? Fine.

He wanted to play? Let's play.

Sitting up, I let one of my legs dangle from the island, while my eyes remained glued to where he held his erection, and slid my hand to my pussy, biting back a groan as my index finger laid that first hint of pleasure.

As if Judah somehow knew what I'd done, his eyes flew open, blazing with blue-tinted lust as he found me in my new position.

When we locked eyes, I turned it up a notch, and instructed with a smile, "Jerk off for me, baby boy."

The groan that fell from his mouth had me tripping over myself as I picked up speed just enough to chase the spark he'd lit inside of me. It wasn't hard, given the fact that he looked like a beautifully sculpted statue come to life, standing in front of me surrendered to pleasure as he watched me play with myself.

I slid a finger down my folds before burying it inside myself, just enough to get the whole thing wet, and pulled it out again, loving the feel of his eyes on me as I lifted it to my mouth and mimicked his move from earlier, sucking the juices clean off.

Flames exploded between us as he pumped his dick faster, hips rocking with the motion of his hand, almost as if he was imagining himself thrusting into me. But just when I thought I couldn't get more turned on, he paused.

"Fuck. Me," I whispered as Judah swiped the pad of his thumb over the swollen head of his erection and collected the pre-cum.

My fingers slowed on my clit as he stepped toward me and demanded, "Open."

My pussy throbbed against my hand, nipples stinging as I opened my mouth for him. With perfected finesse, Judah pressed his pre-cum to my tongue and dragged his finger away slowly. I swear, my eyes rolled so far back in my head I could see my brain as his flavor exploded on my taste buds. The sounds of Judah stroking his dick picked up speed as he stood between my legs, but this time the head of his cock sat only a few inches from my entrance, making me groan in aggravation.

Okay, so this is way hotter than I expected it to be but I'm going to fucking implode.

In sync, the two of us moved faster, driving ourselves further toward the breaking point.

"You're so fucking hot," he growled out, lost in frantic desire, floating in this suspended place of mutual bliss right along with me. "You ready?"

I was more than ready, but Judah wasn't one to finish without me, so at just the right time, he reached forward and gripped my left nipple between two brutal fingers and twisted just hard enough to set me off like a bomb.

"Shit, Judah!" I cried out, trying to hold myself on the counter as my body convulsed, hitting climax faster than I prepared for.

"Fuuuuck," he grated low and slow as cum exploded from the tip of his cock and hit my arm which was still crossed over my stomach. His essence slid down to my hand, which was still working to finish me off, making the whole experience feel more than intimate. "Jesus Christ."

"I…can't…" I panted, trying to breathe through the shaking of my limbs.

As reality came back and my body relaxed into Jell-O, I dropped my other leg so I was sitting normally on the island. Judah let go of his still-hard erection with a sigh and stepped forward, placing both of his arms on either side of me.

He leaned down—breathing just as hard, if not harder—and pressed his forehead against mine.

I couldn't help the small smile that bloomed on my face as I dragged the back of my arm down his chest, covering him in his own cum as I stated, "I could kill you right now."

He laughed, softly, yet still full of arousal. "You'll thank me when I fuck you senseless without having to stop every 30 seconds to keep from cumming."

I rolled my eyes, but lifted my head and lined up my lips with his. "I'm tempted to say you can't jerk off anymore unless I'm there to see it."

"Oh, trust me," he chuckled against my lips, "you're not the only one."

"That was hot," I whispered, moving closer.

"Scorching."

His lips met mine and this kiss was slow at first as his mouth caressed mine with gentle movements and light tasting, until it wasn't anymore, and we were ravenous again. My hands met the sides of his face, wanting to hold him right where he was as my tongue fought with his, as we tried to energetically prove who loved who more, who wanted who the most. It didn't matter—the battle wouldn't be won or lost—because we were one and the same and every feeling was so deeply intertwined it was hard to see which ones belonged to which person.

"Where next?" I breathed against his lips.

"Couch," he replied, swiping me from the counter and into his arms, where I resumed my attack on his mouth, memorizing his taste, his flavor, branding him in hopes that this time, *I* would become the vice he was addicted to.

Judah didn't sit down when his shins hit the cushions, instead he stood still and devoured my mouth with one hand wrapped around my back, and the other buried deep in my hair. His tongue traced my teeth, so I bit down on it lightly just before sucking gently enough to pull a moan from his throat.

"I missed you," he murmured softly, "so much it hurts even right now."

"Show me how much it hurts," was my only reply before he straight up dropped me onto the couch and remained exactly where he was.

"Can do," he promised, "turn around, get on all fours, and hold the back of the couch."

My pussy flooded instantly, knowing that he wasn't going to hold back this time.

"Yes, daddy," I smirked, loving that *this* version of Judah hadn't died with the last.

He was still my own personal devil—in all his deliciously toxic ways—but it seemed he planned to save it all for the bedroom. And for a moment, I felt foolish for even thinking this part of our relationship was capable of fizzling out. How could I? That kind of passion lived at the very core of our connection, seated right next to the love we held for each other.

Lust was there, but it was a tool or a switch we flipped, rather than a driving force.

It was everything I wanted and more.

When I was in position, Judah gripped my hips and pulled back, so I was lined up with the head of his still solid dick, but before he made any moves to enter me, I felt his lips pressed against my back.

"You got some new tattoos," he mused, kissing the moth Kenji had designed for me, right in the center of my back.

"Mmm," was all I could muster up, feeling the burn of need in between my legs.

"I plan to explore each one in detail," he warned me, before licking the right wing of the moth.

But he didn't stop there, his tongue traced it's way up my spine, around the back of my neck, and over the side of my throat where his teeth left little love bites. A moan slipped from my mouth in response as his left hand dropped on top of mine and squeezed.

"So pretty," he whispered, gripping my jaw with the opposite hand to turn my face toward his, where those lips met mine in another searing kiss.

I whimpered, feeling desperate as my hips moved back and against his erection. It felt like a steel rod in between my ass cheeks, reminding me just how lucky I was to have found a man so well endowed.

"J, please," I begged in a whisper.

His fingers released my jaw as he smirked against my lips. "Anything for you."

And then I got what I wanted.

"Holy f—" my breath vanished as his dick slammed home, hitting my cervix with a hard thrust, before his hand disappeared from my own and reappeared on my hip, joining his other one on their mission to nearly kill me.

A satisfied chuckle left his throat as he drove his cock into my channel with more fever than he ever had before, rattling my teeth in the process.

My hold on the back of the couch had my hands aching, but I didn't give a single flying fuck, not when I was finally full of him again, finally surrounded by everything that was Judah Colt.

Something happened when we fucked, when we surrendered to the feel of each other. It was magic—dangerous, destructive magic. His fingers gripped my skin hard enough to bruise, hard enough to leave reddened crescent moon indents in my skin, but that sharp pressure only served to make the walls of my pussy clench harder around him.

"Mother of all fuck," he ground out, not bothering to stop, but rather speeding up. He plowed into me, using his grip to pull my hips back so that my ass hit his groin hard enough to make an embarrassing amount of noise. "God, that *sound*."

I went momentarily blind as stars danced in my vision and my insides screamed, but I was quickly struck with clear sight once again as his palm came down on my right ass cheek with a hard smack.

"Ahhhh!" I cried out, not bothering to filter the octave as my head fell back.

Seeing an opportunity, Judah reached forward and grabbed a fist full of my hair, winding it around his wrist, and yanked me into a kneeling position on the couch.

His mouth hit my ear and those harsh breaths had my pussy pulsing, especially as he snarled out, "Let me hear you, little bird." Except, just as a moan slipped from my mouth, his hand gripped my throat, cutting off nearly all oxygen. "Oops. Just kidding."

I ground my teeth together as he pounded into me, hitting

my g-spot with damn near perfect precision, but where his dick couldn't hit one hundred percent, his other hand slipped between my legs and sealed the deal.

Judah's fingers slid between my folds and went to fucking *town*, causing me to grip his wrist and dig my nails in, given I couldn't make any real noise. I could barely even breathe until he released my throat, and when he did...

I screamed.

My whole body shattered, falling into the depths of euphoria, surrounded by a galaxy of flames as my climax hit its peak.

"FUCK!" Judah cried out then bit down on my shoulder as he broke apart behind me, crossing over his own finish line and bringing us both to the brink of insanity. "Son of a bitch."

"My God," I breathed out as my entire body shook with the aftershock. I had no idea how much time passed, but eventually, the two of us collapsed onto the cushions of my couch, sweaty and spent, as we tried to catch our breath.

After a solid amount of time, Judah muttered against my shoulder, "It's a damn good thing you two cover your couches in blankets because these *definitely* need to be washed."

At that, I laughed—hard and loud—feeling like a thousand pounds had been lifted off my chest. Judah joined me, sounding carefree, and satiated behind me, but it was the hand the wrapped around my waist and pulled me closer that truly sealed the deal of my happiness in that moment.

For the first time since we met, I actually felt close to him.

There were no more secrets—aside from the surprise he was working on—and I could live with that. I could breathe again knowing that every dark and dirty fact was already out in the open and we could grow our relationship knowing there were no more skeletons in our individual closets.

"Uh, you got that right," I laughed. "Frankie would have

killed me if I told her we needed to hire someone to come steam clean the couch before she could sit on it."

"I think she would have taken it out on me instead of you," Judah chuckled. "You can do no wrong in her eyes."

I smiled. "That's true."

Judah's lips hit my temple. "You feel better?"

"Sure do," I gloated like a brat. "Needed that."

"Yeah?" he questioned. "You needed this big ass bite mark on your shoulder?"

His tongue ran over the already forming bruise.

I shivered, then shrugged, "Eh, it's a battle wound."

His answering laugh vibrated against my back. "You're something else."

"I left marks too," I pointed out, glancing down at his arm and tugging on it until he let go of me. When his hand was in front of my face, I pointed at his wrist. "That's pretty gnarly."

His next laugh was louder and much more boisterous as he said, "Oh my god, I can't wait until Dr. Blake sees this. She's gonna freak and ask if I started cutting or some shit."

"Judah!" I chastised, feeling momentarily bad.

"It's fine, little bird," he assured me with a chuckle. "I'll just tell her you're an absolute freak in bed. She'll get it."

I slapped his arm. "Don't you dare."

"Fine, I'll tell her I cut myself."

"Judah!"

"Oh, hush," he chuckled, pulling me closer again. "Calm your lil' titties down."

"My tits aren't little," I pouted.

"Eh, they're not huge."

"Okay!" I untangled myself from his arms. "You are skating on *thin* ice right now."

He just laid back on the couch, looking comfortable as ever and as naked as the day he was born. "I'm hyped up, baby! Also, we're into the whole honesty thing now."

Sitting up now, I crossed my legs and grabbed my tits. "Yeah, well, you don't have to be *that* honest."

Smiling wide, he pulled my hands away and replaced them with his own. "Hey, I never said I didn't love them. I just said the lil' girls weren't huge."

I sneered, "Just stop talking."

"Ha," he scoffed. "Should I do this instead?"

His thumbs grazed my nipples.

"No, stop it," I pushed his hands away.

He put them right back, "Come on, I'll make you feel better."

"No!" I tried to hide my smile as I shoved him away again, but this time, I used my legs too, kicking him straight off the couch.

Unable to help it, I busted out laughing as his whole body disappeared over the edge.

"You bitch!" he yelled as he popped back up, showing no signs of anger, but instead radiated a new, playful energy that I wanted to physically bathe in.

He came for me with clear intentions.

"Don't you dare," I squealed, hopping up from my position, but failing to get very far because I felt like a newborn fawn, all shaky and unstable.

"Oh, I dare, little bird," he growled. "You asked for it."

His fingers hit my sides and the tickle attack began.

In fact, it lasted far too long because he was somehow less affected by our last fuck session and was able to snatch me back every time I tried to get away.

I resorted to grabbing throw pillows from the couch and slamming them against his body in an attempt to get him to stop, but even that didn't work. The trick was simply enduring the awful sensation of tickling until I could get him close enough to wrap my legs around his waist and pull him down on top of me.

When I had him where I wanted him, I kissed those swollen pink lips and poured every elated, inflated, and infatuated feeling I had into it.

"Mmm." Judah sobered fast. His body melted into mine, pressing us further into the couch as he held himself up with an elbow next to my head.

When my lips parted, his tongue fell against my own and caressed me into newfound emotion.

The distinct vibration of love flooded my chest, causing me to cradle his face in my hands, feeling so fucking grateful that he'd found the strength to make the right choice. To live, and to do it fully. He found the courage, fortitude, and self-worth to do the hardest part and now we were both reaping the rewards in a way I previously didn't want to hope for—fearing that it would never be possible.

And yet it was. He was here, he was sober, and I felt like *finally*, I had what I truly deserved.

"I love you, Phoenix Royal," was whispered against my lips, sparking a light in my chest and tears in my eyes.

"I love you more, Judah Colt."

His smile was sweet. "Don't start that argument."

"It's not an argument. It's a fact."

"It's bullshit, but okay." He kissed my nose, then shocked me by moving to stand. Once he was upright, he held out a hand. "What's a *fact* is that I still haven't seen this tattoo. So, get your little ass up, and show me."

Oh fuck, I'd nearly forgotten.

I put my palm in his, took a deep breath to hide my nerves. *Here we go.*

CHAPTER 37

JUDAH

I COULDN'T SEEM to stop touching her.

Holding her hand wasn't enough, so when I pulled her off the couch, I pressed one more kiss to her lips before turning around and saying, "Hop on my back."

Her sensual laugh hit me straight in the soul. "I can walk, J."

"Don't ruin my ego, little bird, at least pretended I broke you in half so you're cripple for the next ten hours," I mused, flexing my hands at my sides impatiently.

"Okay, drama queen," she responded, but gave in, jumping onto my back and securing her legs above my hips and her arms around my neck.

I grabbed one of each and walked us to her room, where all of her tattoo shit was still left out.

"Okay now put me down," she patted my chest. "I have to get the hand mirror."

Groaning, I set her down and complained, "Why did you have to put this thing on the back of my fucking neck? I can't even see it properly!"

She didn't bother looking at me but instead went searching for the stupid mirror, as she replied, "Where the hell did you want me to put it, J? You're covered basically everywhere."

"Um, my calf?" I looked down, finding quite a few places the tattoo could have gone.

Phoenix snatched the black hand mirror from her messenger bag and stood back up to look at me while shaking her head, "Your leg hair would have hidden the detail."

I rolled my eyes. "You're kidding."

She blinked. "I'm not."

"I don't believe you," I crossed my arms like an asshole, "Prove it."

She smirked and it was full of sass. "Gladly."

My dick woke back up, fueled by the fact that she was very much still naked and totally unashamed of her body as she sauntered to the bathroom, despite my comments about her tits.

Which I wouldn't take back.

She was a solid C. Not too big, not too small.

Definitely not huge, but perfect for me.

Following her, I winced at the sharp light of the bathroom but was too excited to complain, wanting to know exactly what she'd drawn for me.

"Alright, handsome, hop up on the counter and scoot all the way back so your spine touches the mirror," Phoenix instructed confidently.

"My bare ass on your bathroom counter?" I questioned with a grin.

She rolled her eyes, "I'll bleach it, just go."

I didn't actually give a shit, so I did as she said, feeling grateful for the cool marble against my skin, given I was still at risk of overheating from the events of the night.

Once I was in position, Phoenix shocked the shit out of me by climbing on the counter and straddling my legs, stopping at my knees, where she settled with the mirror in her lap and a smile on her face.

"Yeah, uh," I cleared my throat as my erection became glaringly obvious, "you better stay right where you are before I forget all about this damn thing and force you to ride me right here, right now."

That smile stayed firmly in place as she replied, "Focus, baby."

"Mhm," I nodded and swallowed. "I'll try."

But as soon as she lifted the mirror and angled it in a way where I could clearly see the new ink etched on the back of my neck, all other thoughts vanished.

With zero finesse, I reached forward and pulled the mirror toward me, leaning in to get a closer look, but P's hand hit my shoulder, as she whispered, "I'll bring it closer, just stay there with your spine straight."

I listened but didn't let go of her wrist as I stared at the design, unable to say a word as my chest tightened around my heart.

Tears pooled in my eyes as I scanned the whole thing from top to bottom over and over in what could only be described as pure amazement.

"P…" I whispered softly, but Phoenix remained quiet, knowing I needed time to process.

She'd drawn a building.

A skyscraper.

A very realistic and extremely detailed skyscraper that was only a few inches tall and sat directly in the center of my neck, just below my hairline. It looked like a pencil had sketched the image with hundreds of individual lines that shaped the many floors and windows. The whole thing was tiered at the top and ended in a long point.

But that wasn't what got me, it wasn't even the words written on each side of the building, forming a circle around the entire design.

"Dream a little, then dream bigger. You're finally free."

It was the little bird perched peacefully on top of the

building—right at the tip—appearing comfortable, as if it belonged there.

"Phoenix..." was all I could say as emotion clogged my throat.

"When I first met you, you were so much taller than I expected you to be." Her laugh was distant, as if she were lost in a memory. "I mean, anyone can google your height, right? Sure. But anyone over six feet tall is hard to picture until you meet them in person. So that night on the rooftop, when I called you a skyscraper, that's all it meant, you know? You were massive compared to me, and it fit. But as time went on, and when everything went down, I found myself praying that my Skyscraper never fell. I prayed nothing would tear you down, and then when you overdosed, you'd taken yourself out all on your own and it was singlehandedly the worst moment of my life because I'd put my faith in you never falling."

Tears fell quickly as I listened and stared.

"But then, when I found out you were still alive, I hoped that my Skyscraper hadn't actually fallen. I hoped it was just hidden in smoke—lost in the remains of your natural disaster—and that in the end, when the storm passed, there would be a miracle, and you'd still be standing tall." Her voice had gotten thicker as she spoke, "But that's the thing about faith. It's a verb. It's an action. Faith is a choice. It's something you build, grow, and learn to trust. And once you learn to trust your own faith in yourself, it becomes a gift, something you anchor and lean on. But not everybody has that gift, not everyone is strong enough to build their faith. But it turns out...you are."

I met her eyes then, nearly blinded by the love, the passion, the brilliant truth shining bright.

"I struggled with my own faith," she admitted. "I didn't want to hope for anything because I didn't want to be let down again. But you did the work—you looked faith in the face after never believing before—and you got to know her. You found that faith in yourself and came back, just like I asked you to in that letter. You dreamed, you cried, you suffered, but you did it. And now, you're here—my Skyscraper—still standing tall, even after the storm."

Stunned, grateful, and completely in awe of the woman in front of me, I pulled the mirror from her hand and grabbed her waist, pulling her toward me.

With my eyes on hers, I stated, "And you, my tiny little bird, said you wouldn't leave, even if we fought." At my words, she closed her eyes, and I wiped away the tear that fell. "You never broke that promise. Even after every fight, every storm, every chaotic and completely avoidable disaster I caused, you're still here. It was *your* faith in *me*, that ensured this skyscraper stayed standing."

I hadn't thought about faith in the way she described it but P was right. I had *none* before I went into rehab, but while I was there, I'd learned all about it. Learned to grow it, trust it, until I used it as my driving force on my way out and back into the real world.

But without P's influence, without her strength, I wouldn't have made it in the first place, and maybe that was the whole point.

I said as much, realizing, "Maybe *that's* what makes us twin flames…"

Her eyes fluttered open, revealing confused brown orbs. "What do you mean?"

"I asked Dr. Blake about the idea of twin flames when I was in rehab," I admitted for the first time. P's eyebrows rose but I kept going, "She basically explained that the idea of twin flames is a very spiritual way of looking at relationships. According to certain beliefs, twin souls are the highest, most evolved level of soul mates, but as we already knew, most don't make it in long-term relationships. And she said that was because twins literally have the exact same soul but it's split between two individual people with two individual mindsets and beliefs. Both partners—both halves of the soul—have to *want* to work through the karma and generational trauma in order to make it because otherwise, they will trigger each other. They mirror one another in every way, making them almost *too* alike. She said that in the eyes of spirituality, one twin will want to move forward and the other will have to choose whether or not they want to follow. If one partner chooses to stay where they are, the relationship won't move forward and the soul will remain split, but if they choose to surrender to growth...nothing will keep the two halves apart."

I sat up a little straighter, thinking hard about our journey and how we got where we are. "Blake said that it's a runner, chaser dynamic that usually makes or breaks the relationship but almost always leads to a separation. During that separation, one half of the soul will grow, change, evolve, and become who they're supposed to be, but that growth will create jealousy and toxic tendencies in the other half, triggering old wounds to appear and that's where the choice comes in." I ran a hand over my forehead as I processed out loud. "I fought this for so long, but I chased and chased and chased you until you didn't answer my call. I'd gone too far and you cut me off. In my eyes, our relationship was completely over, even though that wasn't the truth."

"You had to heal," Phoenix whispered, catching on. "You still had a choice, but I was no longer in the picture. You had to choose to grow for *yourself*, for your half of the soul, and not for me, or even *because* of me."

"And yet, without your growth, I never would have been in such a multilayered position," I added. "I've overdosed before and went right back on drugs. But it was *you* and my connection to you, that motivated me to figure out what the fuck happened that made me who I am, and in turn, I learned how to navigate it. I could finally see you clearly—see *myself* clearly—and get rid of the toxic triggers in my way."

"Holy shit," Phoenix breathed out. "It's...true. But even when Frankie brought it up to me last year, I never actually thought it could be possible but—"

"Faith, Phoenix," I cut in, throwing the word back at her. "Spirituality isn't a tangible thing we can touch, it's a belief we feel in our soul and align our lives with. It's something we have *faith* in. And if I have learned anything since I met you, it's that I can't not *feel* you. Even when you cut me off, even when your end of the connection went dead, you were there. You chose yourself by getting on that plane and ignoring my call. You leaving left me with no choice but to choose once and for all. And I chose wrong."

"But the universe didn't approve of your choice," she reminded me. "You got another shot to pick again."

"Yeah," I agreed with a small smile, "and it was your letter that did me in."

Phoenix shook her head, seeming overwhelmed by what we'd discovered, but still, she said, "If you think about it, we really are mirrors. Both of our parents set us up to fail, both of us have had to crawl out from under their actions and how they affected us, and yet, both of us can't completely escape it."

"And yet—" I smiled a little bigger, "—together, we can get each other through this life. Even with the unknowns, with the fears, demons, and nightmares."

Suddenly, Phoenix smacked my chest.

"Ow!" I protested.

"I fucking told you! That's what I've wanted from the beginning! But when I said it, Judah, I meant it. I need it. Something in me has always known that taking care of you—being with you, supporting you—was what I needed in order to feel whole. I anchor you, you anchor me. We'd be one and the same."

At that, she sucked in a breath. "Oh my god...we—we're twin flames."

That small smile bloomed into a real one, a big one, because *fuck my life*, I didn't care if it was crazy. I didn't give a shit if no one else believed it, if it was wild, esoteric, and completely out of this world. It was the truth.

Our truth.

"Yeah," I agreed, leaning forward to capture her lips with my own, before concluding, "and we're solid fucking gold."

CHAPTER 38
Phoenix

MY MIND WAS STILL SPINNING, floating, whirling over the conversation we just had, but I knew it was going to take days —possibly weeks—for the realization to settle into my system, and I wasn't done with my surprise yet.

"Alright, I have one more thing for you," I stated after I'd kissed the shit out of him. "But you can't look yet. Stay here."

Climbing off his legs, I landed on the floor and headed into my room.

Because he's a stubborn little prick, he followed.

"What did you do?" Judah asked confidently, sounding like our last conversation really lit him up inside.

Judah wasn't like me in the way that I overthought every little thing.

For him, the realization or discovery of twin flames and the fact that we matched up with the stories told about split souls, was a pillar, a beacon of strength and pride. It gave him something to believe in. Where I didn't want to be disappointed if we were ever proved wrong. I feared getting attached and then heartbroken, but that was my thing to deal with.

And it all stemmed from my lack of faith.

I could barely believe that a higher power truly wanted to

gift me something as beautiful as finding the other half of my soul, but the connection was also too powerful to deny.

Fear of abandonment had me chained to my doubts, but I refused to let it hold me back

Shaking my head in an attempt to shut off the negative thoughts, I replied, "Just a little something. Get in bed and I'll grab it when I'm done."

J whistled softly, replying, "Hmm, yes ma'am."

Smirking to myself, I cleaned up my tattoo supplies and packed everything away, then headed into my closet and grabbed the large frame I had made last week.

"Close your eyes," I instructed before I left the closet. "And don't fucking cheat."

"You're bossy tonight," J called back.

"Just do it."

"It's done, princess, my eyes are closed."

I peeked my head around the corner to make sure he was telling the truth and found out he was, so I moved back into the room and made sure the picture was facing my body as I sat down on the bed next to him.

"Okay, so, I knew you'd bitch about the placement of that damn tattoo," I informed him, which earned me a smirk, "so I got you something for your new house."

I flipped the frame around, held it in front of him, and said, "You can open your eyes now."

He removed his hands from his face, blinked twice, and then went still as stone as he saw his tattoo—blown up and on display—framed in front of him.

"Phoenix fucking Royal," Judah whispered, sounding shocked, but giddy all at once as he studied the picture. Gently, he ran a hand over the glass, touching the bird etched at the top of the building, but then he looked at me.

Those blue eyes were full of so many emotions it made my chest ache as my heart skipped a beat. He gazed at me, eyes bouncing back and forth between my own, until out of nowhere he asked, "Will you be my sponsor?"

Time stopped.

He wants…

"Y-you want me to be your—?"

"Sponsor, yes," Judah gave me a small, humble nod. "Blake and I have been talking about it and she thinks it's a good idea since I generally don't trust people and I have zero interest in finding a stranger to help me, but I wasn't sure when to ask or how to—"

"Yes," I cut him off, feeling weightless and completely weighed down all at once. "Yes, I'll be your sponsor."

I didn't even know what it fully meant or what my job would be but I didn't give a shit what I had to do or change or be—I would do it. I would be it.

Supporting him in that way was something I'd wanted from the start of our relationship, even if I had no idea, he had an issue as brutal as addiction. I still wanted to hold him up, support him, talk to him, lean on him, and I wanted him to do the same for me.

"Y-you're serious?" he questioned shakily. "I mean, we'll have to meet with Blake and she can tell you more about it and we'd have meetings to attend and you'll see me in a very vulnerable state if something gets brought up that triggers me. I just…"

He was nervous, embarrassed, about his recovery journey but that was the shit I couldn't stand. "I want to do it, J. I want to be there for you. I'll do anything to make sure you stay happy and healthy, even if it means watching you fall apart and helping you pick up the pieces. There are no secrets or shame in this relationship. Not anymore."

He simply watched me for a full minute before he snatched the frame, set it on the floor, and reached for me. "Get over here, girl."

I went willingly, falling into his arms as he rolled on top of me, landing us in the middle of my bed.

He brushed his nose against mine in an Eskimo kiss, and whispered, "I love you. You know that?"

Heart fluttering, I responded, "I could stand to hear it a few more times."

"Fuck, woman," was all he said before he kissed me stupid. That mouth of his worked magic against my own as our tongues met once again. He pulled back only long enough to say, "Thank you, baby bird."

I responded by sinking one hand in his hair, as the other traveled down his chest and toward his rapidly hardening erection. I knew he had another round in him, but this time, I wanted it to be softer, more intimate, less frantic.

When my fingers wrapped around his shaft, his entire body shuddered, and his lips left mine.

"Three in one night?" he asked with a devilish grin.

"Up for the challenge?" I threw back.

"Not a challenge—" he shook his head, now appearing completely serious, "—a goddamn gift."

Lord have mercy, I am so screwed.

This version of Judah Colt was the one I only hesitantly hoped for but desperately craved. He was wild, rough, and deeply affectionate, but there was still that small part of him that would forever be cracked and bruised. That part of him matched mine. It was what made us who we were—it would bind us together and tie us into an inseparable knot—and for the first time, I felt like I could actually surrender to it.

So I did.

I worked his dick into a hardened rock, making sure to drive him wild enough to skip the foreplay and dive right in.

"Shhhhit," I sucked in a breath as he slid his length inside of me—slowly this time—devouring every aching inch of my channel until he was fully buried inside of me. "So fucking good."

"Mmmm," Judah groaned his response, holding himself above me, moving only when I pulled his mouth to mine.

That round lasted the longest of all three, but that was because we took our time. Our bodies, our connection, seemed to light the room around us, as we focused solely on feeling. Each other, our hearts, our soul. The world around us fell away as Judah made love to me for the first time since we met, bringing us to a level we'd never been on before—one that we wouldn't be able to erase or forget.

And when we both reached the edge, he buried his head in my neck as I held him to my chest, and we rode that wave together, ensuring that nothing and no one would ever come between us again.

CHAPTER 39

JUDAH

WAKING up the next morning was a bit surreal. It was the first time I'd slept completely through the night in the last four months, and I wasn't going to say it was simply because Phoenix was there, but rather it was a mixture of that and the fact that both she and I had put in some serious physical work in the hours before we fell asleep.

Phoenix was still passed out—breathing softly with her head resting peacefully on my chest and an arm slung across my stomach—and I was completely content to stay there. I focused on the pattern of her breathing while thinking through all the things that happened the night before.

I could feel the aching sting of my new tattoo on the back of my neck, but the slight pain was welcomed. It was a beautiful reminder of all the shit I'd been through and the fact that without Phoenix, without her influence in my life—whether up close or from a distance—I wouldn't be where I was.

I spent so many nights in rehab wondering, hoping, praying to a God I didn't believe in, that Phoenix would somehow forgive me for all that I had done to her, as well as the people in our lives. I desperately prayed that I'd find hope again.

It was a slow process, and while that hope still felt out of reach sometimes, it was tangible now. I'd tasted it, seen the results.

And now the only thing in between us was my album and the magnitude of that accomplishment. Once she found out about it, once that little surprise was out in the open, there wouldn't be a single thing standing in the way of our future together.

For once I was actually imagining that future, visualizing what my life might look like two years from now. Three, five, ten...

What would it be like to watch Phoenix grow as an artist, to live together permanently, to vacation or work together? I had so many ideas, I'd thought of multiple different options regarding how my girl and I could collaborate on future projects. Opening her own shop, or even traveling on tour with me and guest tattooing in shops located in whatever city I was performing in.

We could do this—her and I—and I knew she believed in that dream too, even though she'd have to battle with her skepticism.

"You're thinking awfully hard right now," P's groggy, sleepy voice hit my ears, making me smile as I stared at the ceiling.

"Nothing else to do when the queen is asleep," I pointed out, "I certainly wasn't about to wake her."

P's chuckle was small, but it still packed a punch. "You're ridiculous."

"Yeah, well, we knew that already."

Slowly, Phoenix sat up and began to stretch, causing me to glance down at her, watching as she winced through multiple movements.

I couldn't hide the pride in my voice as I asked, "You sore?"

Her eyes hit mine with a glare, "How about *you* try and move right now?"

Taking her challenge, I started to sit up, only to meet heavy resistance and the sting of protesting muscles.

"Mhm," Phoenix sassed when I cringed, "Exactly. Check your ego."

I laughed through a grunt, noticing that even my shoulders ached. "I'm a little scared to stand up."

"*You're* scared?" Phoenix questioned. "I'm pretty sure my vagina went to war with a bat last night."

That did me in. I let out a loud laugh causing her to join me as the two of us struggled to get into a comfortable sitting position.

As we calmed, I pointed out, "It's because we just woke up. We'll just have to drink a lot of water and hope for the best."

She rolled her eyes and grumbled, "I'm not used to you being so optimistic. It's kind of annoying right now."

I chuckled. "Yeah, because you haven't had any coffee yet."

"Fuck," she sighed, "And Frankie isn't even here so I'm gonna have to get up and make it myself."

"Not so fast, darling," I purred, reaching over to grip the back of her neck and gain her full attention, "that's what *I'm* here for."

Shock bloomed in her stare. "Do you know how hard it was to get you out of bed before? Since when are you so willing to make my morning caffeine?"

I smirked, "Since I got used to waking up at six a.m. to fucking meditate?"

"Ah," she attempted to nod, but my grip was blocking the movement, "right."

Pulling her toward me, I embraced the lightness in my

chest, the ease at which I was able to talk about my time in rehab, and hoped that it remained this easy as time went on.

When her lips were only a few centimeters from mine, I requested, "Kiss me."

"Gladly," she whispered, before closing the gap and pressing that sweet mouth to mine.

Flashes from the night before had my morning wood pulsing under the sheets, only made worse as the distinct scent of sex hit my senses. My hands on her skin itched to continue their exploration and make good on my promise to study every new tattoo she'd acquired during our time apart, but I held myself back, knowing we had all the time in the world.

Just not today.

She pulled back first, seemingly having the same thought as I did, as she asked, "What time is it? I don't even know where my phone is."

In order to keep myself from diving in for more, I began the tedious task of getting off the bed. Wincing, I replied, "I think it's in the living room. I'll grab it."

My phone, however, was on the nightstand next to me since I spent a small amount of time scrolling through it as Phoenix did my tattoo the night before. I picked it up, feeling grateful that Pharaoh had managed to turn off all notifications from my social media accounts, so I wasn't bombarded with notifications first thing in the morning. He even muted my email so I only had to see the madness when I was fully prepared for it.

"It's just past noon," I told Phoenix before opening the handful of texts I received from Pharaoh.

Pharaoh: Yo, I think the last of the phones we bought will be done arriving today. I'm waiting on two more, but they're expected to be delivered by two p.m. today.

Pharaoh: Let's get the crew together. Phoenix is off today, correct?

Pharaoh: Frankie said she and Silas are available. They'll be on their way to the girl's house in a few. She texted Kav and Ricco.

"Son of a bitch," I groaned and dropped the phone back on the nightstand.

My ass hit the edge of the bed again.

"What's wrong?" P asked, coming up behind me and draping her body around mine.

When her head peeked over my shoulder and her arms tightened around my center, I turned to kiss her temple, then explained, "You know how Pharaoh wanted to teach a virtual drum class to the low-income kids you guys work with?"

"Hate calling them that, but yes," she nodded against my skin, "he told me last week when he came to visit me at the shop."

I ignored the prick of jealousy that threatened to taint my mood, knowing that Pharaoh and Phoenix had a very close, very real friendship that I basically forced them into by isolating them in misery due to my actions. I had to remind myself often that it was actually a blessing, having my girlfriend and my best friend be so close, but it was hard because I was the alien sometimes when the three of us hung out.

Anyone around them could see their connection and feel the trust and security they felt around one another. It was a hard pill to swallow, but I'd swallowed bigger so I made sure to never let my feelings affect my relationship with either of them.

"Okay, well," I responded, "the phones are in, and we finished filming the series of classes a few days ago. Pharaoh has been working on editing ever since and I guess he's ready.

So, he called Frankie and told her, and of course, she called in the calvary. Everyone is on their way here."

"Ugh," P groaned—loud and dramatic—before flopping back onto the pillows, "son of a bitch."

Took the words right out of my mouth.

"Exactly," I agreed, "but our boy needs our help, so why don't you get that sexy lil' booty in the shower while I start the coffee. I'll join you once it's brewing."

"I suppose," she sighed, "but can you grab my phone first? And I'm gonna need food if we're going to be spending the day dealing with technology."

At that, I grinned as I stood up once again and looked down at her. "Actually, I have a request."

She quirked a brown eyebrow, "A request, huh?"

That sultry voice had me scanning her very naked and slightly bruised body, which only made my dick harder than it already was.

I had to clear my throat before I replied, "Yup, and it gets you out of messing with technology for at *least* an hour."

She sat up on her elbows. "I'm listening…"

"French toast," I stated simply, giving my best attempt at puppy dog eyes. "Pleeeease."

A tinkling laugh fell from her lips as her head fell back in disbelief. "You want my French toast?"

"Yes. Badly," I nodded. "The restaurant, diner, cafeteria situation in rehab served this French toast, and these two kids I met in there fucking *loved* it, but I still thought yours was better, so I never ordered it. But now I want it."

"I have about thirty questions regarding that statement," P told me, looking a bit shocked, "so as long as you're prepared to spend our time in the shower telling me all about this restaurant, diner, cafeteria situation, along with the friends you made, then fine, yes. I'd be happy to."

"Fucking deal," I grinned. "I'll get your phone and my

credit card. You can order all the shit you need through Instacart. I'm sure everyone will want to eat, so you'll need to order a good amount of food."

"Ooooo," she flirted, "Daddy's giving me access to his credit card?"

I winked. "Do your worst, baby bird."

With that, our day began. One that was sure to be a long, exhausting, yet completely fulfilling experience.

CHAPTER 40
Phoenix

FROM THE KITCHEN I stared into the living room, noticing how little space was left, as every single one of our friends took up nearly every inch of the room. There were bodies spread out on the couch, both chairs, the floor. It should have felt cramped, but everyone looked comfortable, even Silas—who was by far the biggest of the group—seemed content as he threw a tiny purple tennis ball for Trixie. The little ball of fluff ran happily down the hallway and back into the living room, over and over, anxiously anticipating his next throw.

We all spent the day as planned—helping Pharaoh set up his virtual class on a wide range of different types of phones. Some were older models of Androids and iPhones, some new and barely used, but the whole exchange warmed my heart as I thought about the kids opening up their new devices to find a series of videos from the one and only Pharaoh Roman, teaching them a form of art that could take them places if they wanted to pursue a career in his field. And even if they didn't, this experience would provide a form of escape from their individual circumstances.

It was magic in the making and I was lucky as all fuck to be surrounded by so many selfless people.

It was late in the evening as I cleaned up all the take-out

boxes and wiped down my counters, but I kept one eye on Judah as he laughed with Ricco and Kavan over a conversation I hadn't been following.

It was a beautiful sight to see—even more beautiful knowing that it would only get better from here. As the days, weeks, months went on, more trust would grow, the bonds would tighten and anchor us together as a group.

"Boo!" A finger tapped my shoulder, causing me to damn near jump out of my skin as my hand flew to my mouth.

I turned to see Pharaoh, grinning down at me like an asshole.

"You prick," I breathed out, feeling my heart rage against my chest. "What the hell?"

He chuckled softly. "You were lost in thought."

"Yeah, I know!" I laughed and fanned my face.

His brown eyes still glittered as he placed an arm over my shoulder and requested, "Come have a smoke with me?"

Shaking my head, I gave him a small eye roll but then nodded in agreement.

As we abandoned the kitchen and walked toward the patio, I made eye contact with Judah and feared his reaction, knowing that he had a jealous streak in him, but his face only dropped for a short amount of time before he steeled his features and threw me a wink before going back to his conversation with Ric and Kav.

"Huh," I mused once we got outside. "That was easier than expected."

Pharaoh laughed as he pulled out a chair for me at the table. "He's on his best behavior."

"Yeah, well, even Judah's best is usually a dick when it comes to me being alone with other guys," I reminded him.

"He lost that privilege," Pharaoh replied as I sat down. "Don't worry, it still drives him crazy."

I didn't want to admit that I took a little pride in that, but I did. Eventually, my resentment toward Judah would fade, but there were lingering moments where I wanted him to feel what I felt, since he spent all that time numbing out while we suffered.

"So what's up, buttercup?" I asked Phar as he took out his pack of cigarettes and removed two. I took the one he handed me. "Are you excited to get these phones to the kids?"

"I am," he nodded, then placed the filter between his lips and lit up. After releasing the smoke, he slid the lighter to me and continued, saying, "I'm nervous about the parent's freaking out, and wondering if I should send some sort of email or permission slip home with them next week before I give them out. I don't want to step on any toes or anything."

I thought about that as I lit my own cigarette. "Yeah, you might want to ask Carmine what she would do. She'll have ideas. Hell, she'll probably want to help."

"She took it a lot better than I thought she would," Pharaoh informed me. "She said that my involvement like this would actually shed light on the program and spread the word. She's been wanting to grow the program and provide other classes, so she hopes that more people will volunteer to teach during the summer term once this spreads across the community."

"I don't doubt that," I replied. "It's a great opportunity for everyone involved, honestly."

"Yup," he popped the "P" then met my stare as he took another hit and talked through the exhale, "but that's not why I pulled you out here."

"Oh?" I quirked an eyebrow.

"I just wanted to check in," Phar shrugged, sounding casual, "make sure everything is good."

"I think everything is good," I stated. "I mean, I'm still in the dark about what Judah has been doing for the last month, but I know that if he was up to something sketchy, you'd tell me."

Pharaoh nodded, appearing genuine. "I know where he's been. I've been with him."

"You have, have you?" I grinned then, more curious than ever, but more relieved than anything.

"Mhm," Pharaoh murmured with a smile that told me he was indeed holding in a secret. "You can trust him. He's up to something, but it's nothing bad."

"And you're involved?" I asked, wanting to clarify one more time as ideas started forming in my head.

"Okay, hold your horses," Pharaoh laughed, catching on immediately. "Please don't go all Phoenix Royal and try to figure this out. Because you will, and then you'll ruin the surprise."

I chuckled. "It's a little too late now. The gears are already turning, but I won't think too hard, I suppose."

He shook his head as if he should have known better than to say anything. "Let him keep this secret, babe. I promise you won't regret it. I just wanted to make sure you knew you were safe."

Instantly, my heart warmed, knowing Pharaoh worried for me. He wanted to ease my anxiety over the situation, and I was struck once again, by how incredible the man was.

"Thank you," I replied genuinely. "I was a bit anxious about it."

"A bit?" he joked.

"Stop." I laughed.

Pharaoh chuckled too but then went quiet for a minute. The swift change in his energy had me asking, "What's going on? You good?"

His sigh was thick. "I'm, uh…I'm okay."

A brick dropped into my stomach, causing me to sit forward. "You're *okay?* What's wrong?"

Pharaoh's entire demeanor changed, folding in on itself as his struggle became evident. It wasn't until now that I noticed the hint of bags under his eyes, the lack of color in his face.

Fucking hell, what did I miss?

"Truthfully, I've spent so long focusing on keeping Judah's head above water, then making sure *you* were okay, that now… I just don't have anything else to focus on besides myself," Phar admitted, sounding like he was discussing an inevitable war. "It's been a whole ass decade since I've been free enough to think about my own life, my own past, and now it's like everything I've ignored is raging to the surface."

Just yesterday I felt gratitude for the lack of skeletons in our closets, but it seemed now that Pharaoh's were making an appearance. There was still so much I didn't know about Pharaoh and it had me wondering *what* in his past was coming back to haunt him.

I didn't get a chance to ask him though, because he continued, saying, "I knew this was coming. When I was living alone and Judah was in rehab, I started having dreams, but they weren't bad, necessarily, they were just…real. Vivid. But during the day, I was still stressing about Judah and wondering what would happen when he got out, so now that he's back in one piece and actually seems to be doing fine all on his own, it's left me with nothing else to worry about."

"So, what are you worrying about now?" I asked, wanting more information, more context.

"The way I left the trailer park," he admitted, not giving me much to work with.

"You mean when Hendrix discovered the two of you?"

He nodded.

"What about the way you left home has you so spun out?" I asked, recognizing how he wasn't willingly giving up the information until I posed the question. Pharaoh was falling back into the habit of curling in on himself, keeping his demons under lock and key, but I knew that if he called me out here, there was a reason, and it went beyond just checking in on me.

I took my job seriously as his friend, knowing I was one of the only people he'd come to trust aside from Judah, and I knew that if Pharaoh's nightmares had to do with his past, he wouldn't want to drag Judah into it.

That was a recipe for disaster, even though it could potentially help both of them in the end.

"It's a lot, P," Pharaoh admitted as I dragged on my cigarette. "A lot of shit went down with my family, my…ex. And I just, I don't know, I'm questioning everything. I'm wondering what I left behind."

I blew out smoke.

His *ex?*

Who the fuck?

"There's a lot to unpack there, Phar," I warned. "I don't want to overstep and pry into your life, but—"

"If anyone can pry, Phoenix," he interrupted to clarify, "it's you."

I thought about that for a second while glancing toward the glass doors to check on everyone else. They were fine, still laughing and scrolling through phones.

"Alright, that's fair," I stated and turned back to meet his eyes again. But for another handful of seconds, I stared into those black orbs, hoping to find any hint of the demons Pharaoh carried on his back, but even then he seemed to guard them, hold them back, as if they'd bite me if I got too close. Still, I swallowed, and suggested, "let's go to lunch tomorrow."

After a thick sigh, he nodded as if he knew it was something he had to do.

And he did, because if he didn't talk to me, who would he talk to?

"I'd, uh…" he paused, trailing off as he ran a hand over his 5'oclock shadow. "I need that."

Oh, Pharaoh.

"Then it's a date," I nodded, feeling a little sick, hating that he was in so much pain, but prepared to help him in any way I could.

"Thanks, little P," he whispered, finishing the last hit of his cigarette before stamping it out in the ashtray between us. I followed suit before he cleared his throat and asked, "Ready to head back in?"

His energy had taken a hit, but I knew that by the time we got inside, Pharaoh would have his mask back on, firmly in place.

"Yeah, Phar, I'm ready."

This group had more issues than we had underwear, but I was making it my fucking mission to get us all to a place where we could beat our demons into the dirt and find our permanent version of happiness.

One way or another.

* * *

AFTER EVERYONE but Judah and Frankie left, I spread out on the couch, lying flat on my back, as Judah packed up the small number of things he brought with him the night before.

Trixie hopped up onto my stomach and walked up my chest before sitting down so that her nose touched my chin. She had zero issues with shoving her snout into my face, looking for attention, even though she'd just been showered in cuddles and pets and kisses from the six other people we had in this house all day.

"You're incorrigible, you know that?" I asked the little blonde ball of fluff. "You're an attention whore."

"She's a princess," Frankie pointed out from the other end of the couch, "what do you expect?"

I chuckled, giving the dog what she wanted, as Judah came back into the room, and ambled toward the back of the couch.

"Tired, little bird?" he questioned in a sarcastic, all-knowing tone.

"Don't pretend like you're not," I replied, not bothering to meet his eyes as I kept my attention focused on Trixie.

That was, until his hand came down on mine, moving it aside so he could pick the dog off my chest and cuddle her himself.

"Hey," I protested. "She's mine!"

"She likes me more," he gloated as Trix the Traitor licked his face. Her little tail ran wild, making me pout.

"Whatever," I rolled my eyes before closing them completely.

Judah's laugh was a satisfied one as he stated, "I'm going to run back to Pharaoh's and grab some shit, then I'm coming back. We both have to work tomorrow so I'll just leave from here when you do."

"Gonna tell us what you're doing?" Frankie asked.

Judah's response was quick.

"No."

"Fine, just tell *me* then," Frankie corrected.

"No," Judah repeated.

"Why not?"

"Because you'll tell me," I mumbled, answering for Judah.

"Ugh," Frankie grumbled. "I hate being left out."

"You know what you're not left out of?" Judah asked, addressing my best friend. "Helping me design the inside of my new house."

That got Frankie's attention *and* mine.

I peeked open an eye just as Frankie yelled, "What?!"

"I'm renovating," Judah grinned down at her. "Pretty much the whole place."

"Which means…" Frankie pushed.

"Which means…" Judah stalled, "I'll need someone to help me decide how to design the inside, furnish the place, and ultimately, decorate."

"Oh *fuck* yeah!" Frankie squealed. "I'm so down!"

"Good, because we start next week," he winked, leaving her to jump up from the couch and grab her laptop saying she was going to pull up the listing again and get a list going.

"I'll send you my hourly rates," she called out right before she slammed the door to her room.

I barked out a laugh as Judah said, "I'm sure they'll be astronomical."

I smirked up at my Skyscraper and said, "You're a cheeky bastard, you know that?"

"What did I do?" he feigned innocence.

"Dragging my best friend into all of your projects to earn her trust and build a friendship," I laughed. "Well done."

He shrugged casually, "All in a day's work."

I shook my head, feeling warmth spread through my body at the prospect of how good our life really could be.

"Get down here and kiss me," I demanded, ready for him to do whatever he had to do, then get back here so I could show him just how proud I was.

He obliged, bending forward to plant his lips on mine, ensuring to make my head spin as his tongue danced against my own in a quick, searing promise.

"I'll be back," he whispered into my mouth, and then set Trixie back on my chest.

"I'll be waiting," was my only reply as he stalked off and out the front door.

# PART FOUR

CHAPTER 41
Phoenix

THE NEXT MONTH and a half were full of long days, and even longer nights, as I worked at the shop and had weekly meetings with Judah and Dr. Blake to discuss the sponsorship and what my role would be. I found that I absolutely loved his therapist and as Judah said, she loved me. We were able to talk through the dynamics of our current relationship versus the old one, and she gave us more advice on how to assimilate our wants and needs individually, into a healthy, functioning relationship together.

It was terrifying at first—being so open with a stranger—but once I saw how Judah interacted with her, I was able to calm down.

On top of that, I was booked damn near solid at the shop, while Judah and Frankie spent the hours after I got home going through design ideas and ordering furniture online. Décor too.

The two of them had quickly become a pair of sorts, because Frankie being Frankie, dove right into the project and made sure she spent a sufficient amount of time with Judah so she could get his approval on her ideas, as well as work the renovations into both of their schedules. She'd told me during one of our girl's nights that while she actually did send her hourly pay rates, he blew right past her numbers and paid her an obscene amount of money to get the job done. She said she protested and refused to accept it but he wouldn't back down.

I knew he was doing it to show her he valued her opinions and trusted her vision, but there was a level of remorse there as well. He was paying her back for the damage he'd done to not only me but our house as well. He was doing what he could.

I was grateful for it, and I knew Frankie was too, but I was also completely fine with the amount of time they spent together because it left me time to support Pharaoh. Who very much needed it.

After our conversation on the patio, where he admitted that he was struggling, I found out just how badly, the next day. I always knew that Pharoah had an old soul—one that was full of knowledge and peace—making him a solid partner and friend, but with that came a horde of memories, locked tight in the back of his mind until it exploded from old age.

I was now the only one that knew what truly happened to Pharaoh before he left that trailer park eleven years ago, and while Judah assumed he had the whole story, I knew the truth. Pharaoh spared him a lot of the details, mainly out of embarrassment and fear, but also because his memories were a weapon against his focus. Against his drive and determination.

It was a story I hated thinking about, much like Judah's past, but I found myself going back through the details often, and my advice was always the same.

Pharaoh needed to go back and face his past head-on, just like Judah, but in this case, Pharoah had actual people he could talk to. Family he could call.

It was daunting and packed full of problems he wasn't ready to face, and I knew how hard that was so I gave him space when he needed it, but also made sure I was free whenever he needed to vent as well.

Pharaoh was a work in progress, as was Judah's house, and between those two things, work, Judah's secret project, and finding time to spend one on one with Frankie…my schedule was packed.

"Are you ready?" Frankie huffed impatiently, stalking into my room like I was holding up a runway event. "We have to leave in like ten minutes, dude."

I glanced down at my shoes, and up at her, "You can see I'm legit *one* step from finished. Calm down, malibu barbie."

"Don't sass me right now," Frankie growled. "I am *stressed*."

I couldn't hide my smile, "You're not stressed, babe, you're nervous."

"Ugh!" She threw her hands out dramatically as she spun around and headed into her room, talking as she went, "Of course I'm fucking nervous! What if someone says something shitty about what we've done? Is Judah going to fall off the rails?"

Knowing full well this had nothing to do with Judah, I slipped on my booties and followed my best friend.

"Is *Judah* going to fall off the rails? Or are you?" I questioned, not bothering to wait for her answer. "Babe, it's all going to be fine. I promise."

Frankie sat down on her bed, wearing a striking pink suit, fitted perfectly to her curves, with a white silk camisole underneath the blazer, and silver jewelry accents.

"I just want him to be happy," Frankie muttered. "And I want it to be perfect."

The thought had my heart swelling, "Franks, he's been with you the entire time you guys have worked on this together. He will love it, he is happy, and it is perfect. You're just nervous about everyone else seeing it, which is normal."

Her blue eyes hit mine, then, showcasing true doubt, which had me wondering what all this was about. Frankie had been fine lately. In fact, her life had turned out a lot better than she thought it would, given how much Judah was paying her to help him, and the fact that she didn't have to take on as many of Julia's events as a result.

She was coming into her own, and on top of that, Silas had told her he didn't give a shit about her not knowing what she wanted. He said he was a grown-ass man and whenever he decided he didn't like their arrangement, he'd let her know, but for now, he was happy to keep it the way it was.

Frankie frequently worked herself into a tizzy way more often than she needed to. She stressed herself out before anything bad even happened. But lately, it had gotten worse. She seemed to always anticipate the worst, which was so unlike her it had me wondering what the hell happened.

"I know, I know," she replied with a sigh, breaking me out of my thoughts. "I just want this to go well, you know? It's Judah's housewarming party, my job is done, and I…"

Oh my god.

"You don't know what you're gonna do next," I concluded for her, now seeing the problem.

"I don't want to go back to just being an influencer, Phoenix," she admitted. "I'm using my brain, my skills, and talents I didn't even know I had, and I'm fucking loving it, but it's almost over. What am I supposed to do now?"

"You start a portfolio," I told her. "You have the before and after shots of Judah's place so you can post those, and once you do, you'll be able to start marketing your talents. You could even start a business if you wanted to."

"I know, it's just fucking scary," Frankie explained. "What if everyone gets to the house today and says the place looks like shit? What if they hate it and I find out I'm garbage at this. That means even though I love it, I won't be able to do anything with it."

"I'm sorry, but I really don't think that's going to happen, Frankie." I moved to sit next to her on the bed and wrapped an arm around her shoulders. "I know you, and I know your tastes. I know your drive and how brilliant you are at making anything and everything look beautiful. Mix that with Judah's stubbornness and his own specific tastes, I know that if he was happy with the end result, everyone will be mind blown by what the two of you have created."

It was true.

Judah always had unique, yet exquisite taste, but now that he was sober and focused, he was flourishing. He seemed to be refining his preferences when it came to luxury and I had zero doubt in Frankie's ability to bring that to life. I believed fully that Judah's new home was stunning.

"I hope you're fucking right," Frankie spat softly. "Otherwise I'm going to have a mental breakdown."

Chuckling a little, I slid in my worry, and asked, "Franks, what is going on? You seem to be more sensitive than normal lately. And it's not a bad thing, but usually I'm the one having mental breakdowns. *I'm* the sensitive one in this friendship."

"Well, that comes with the territory. You're a cancer," she pointed out elegantly. "But my Sagittarius ass is aching for adventure, but I'm scared I'm going to fail because I want it so badly I can barely see straight."

Her parents never believed in her, never supported her in the way she needed. No one had told Frankie she was good at something aside from spending money and looking good, so it was no fucking wonder she was worried about whether or not she truly had what it took.

"Listen to me," I started, gripping her chin and turning her head to face me, "you are Frankie motherfucking Skyes, and you are *more* than just a pretty face with rich tastes. You are intelligent and innovative, you're not afraid to take risks, and that's what makes you so fucking good at what you do. If you wanted to be like everyone else, you could be, but you're branching out and doing your own thing, putting your own spin on fashion, interior design, event planning, and hell, you could do whatever you damn well pleased. *That* is what this city needs, what this world needs. More of Frankie Skyes. So quit doubting yourself before I have to take more drastic measures and do some real damage."

Her laugh was a little wet, but she kept her eyes as dry as possible to ensure her makeup stayed in place as she replied, "Shit, I am a mess."

"Nah," I disagreed. "You're transforming. Fear comes with the territory. You just have to learn how to put a muzzle on that bitch."

My best friend shook her head and pressed her forehead to mine. "I love you."

"I love *you*," I replied, then patted her lap. "Alright, enough of this, we need to leave before Judah has a similar breakdown and the whole night is ruined."

That got her up and moving, and within five minutes, the two of us were in her Porsche and on the road, speeding toward Thousand Oaks, California.

CHAPTER 42

JUDAH

"SO, what are we doing for P's birthday?" Ricco asked me as we stood in the driveway of my new place, waiting for Frankie because she was the only one with a key.

Somehow, I'd gotten roped into *that* arrangement.

When she originally told me the plan, I said no right away, but she laid on the puppy dog eyes, and it was over from there. The annoying little blonde wanted the whole family to see the inside of my new house at the same time, and *apparently*, that included me.

Frankie let me help her with the majority of changes and I picked out the décor items inside the house, but the actual execution was all managed by her. I still hadn't seen what the workers had done over the last six weeks, but I was anxious to find out.

Frankie had come over earlier in the day to let in the caterers, who were now hard at work in my new kitchen, making dinner for the seven of us.

"I'm working on finalizing some details," I told both Ric and Kav, "I'll let you know the plan next week."

"You're gonna go all out, aren't you?" Kavan smirked, bouncing back and forth on his feet like he was prepping for a UFC fight.

I rolled my eyes at his antics, but replied, "Does she deserve any less?"

"Fuck no," Ricco answered. "I can't wait to see what you come up with."

Just then, we heard the distinct, clear sounds of "Switch" by 6LACK coming from a car stereo, but because Frankie knew what the fuck was up when it came to music, she had the Remixed version on blast as she sped around the corner and drove up the small hill leading to my driveway.

"My girl," Kavan laughed, clapping his hands as he rocked his hips to the beat.

As the white Porsche stopped to the left of us, I spotted my little bird in the passenger seat, mouthing the lyrics with a saucy, swagged-out smile on her face as the two girls rode the waves of the still-blaring track together.

Meanwhile, Ricco and Kav had their own dance party going on next to me, taking full advantage of the impromptu moment. Knowing this was a memory I wouldn't want to forget, I pulled out my phone and started recording. This was the first time we christened my new driveway with the power of music.

"Yaaaaaaaaaaas, king!" Frankie yelled out the window as Ricco hit a solo freestyle when the second drop hit.

Kavan went next, just as Pharaoh pulled in behind Frankie, followed by Silas, and it wasn't long before both of them joined the small party with wide smiles and bobbing heads.

"Hold on hold on hold on," Frankie called out as the song was about to end. "This next one is for Judah."

Oh shit.

My stomach dropped as everyone looked my way. Phoenix —who was seemingly aware of what was coming next—got out of the car sporting an all-knowing grin, as she rounded the front bumper and made her way to open Frankie's door.

The blonde stepped out, leaving the car running, just as the haunting, religious sound of my current favorite song filtered out of the car and toward me. Phoenix leaned against the now-closed door and crossed her arms over her chest, but met my eyes and winked, telling me without words to do my worst.

A wicked smirk bloomed on my face.

Everyone knew I had recently become obsessed with NF—an up-and-coming rap artist—because I found myself relating, almost too closely, to his darkly honest and sometimes sinister lyrics.

But *this* song? "The Search?"

It was my fucking *favorite*.

And when he started to rap…so did I.

As Frankie held up her phone to record, one by one, Silas, Pharaoh, Ricco, and Kav, moved closer, forming a small circle around me, lining up with the two girls as I covered NF's lyrics with my own flare, feeling every word from the tip of my head to the soles of my feet. The energy in the group began to buzz, lighting me up with that passion I always felt when I played this type of music, but when my favorite part of this particular song was about to start, Phoenix pushed off the car and walked toward me in the middle of the circle, wearing confidence like goddamn perfume.

And right on time, right on cadence, with as much passion as I had, she spat each lyric word for word, right along with me.

"Yeah, the sales can rise
Doesn't mean much though when your health declines
See, we've all got somethin' that we trapped inside
That we try to suffocate, you know, hopin' it dies
Try to hold it underwater but it always survives
Then it comes up out of nowhere like an evil surprise
Then it hovers over you to tell you millions of lies
You don't relate to that? Must not be as crazy as I am

*The point I'm makin' is the mind is a powerful place
And what you feed it can affect you in a powerful way
It's pretty cool, right? Yeah, but it's not always safe
Just hang with me, this'll only take a moment, okay?
Just think about it for a second, if you look at your face
Every day when you get up and think you'll never be great
You'll never be great, not because you're not, but the hate
Will always find a way to cut you up and murder your faith
(woo!)"*

Everyone *exploded.*

Kav and Ricco jumped on each other, while Silas jumped on me, leaving Pharaoh to scramble for Frankie's phone before she dropped it, as she grabbed Phoenix around the waist and spun her around. Laughter took over the whole group as we surrendered to the new energy surrounding us all.

"What a fuckin' way to set the tone, man!" Silas yelled as he gripped the back of my neck in a brotherly vice. "You're a motherfuckin' *monster.* I can't wait to see what you put out next."

Silas was just as in the dark as everyone else about what I was working on, and little did they know, I had taken some serious notes from NF.

He was an artist in this industry that I felt I could actually look up to. He worked for every single thing he earned, and it hadn't been easy for him, but unlike me...he did it sober. He made a name for himself without the bullshit I pulled, and I admired that as much as I envied his wiser choices. I thought about it often. Used his journey as a compass for mine.

"Where the hell did you learn to rap like that, little P?" Pharaoh asked, coming up behind her to grab her in a choke-hold-style hug. He smacked a kiss to the top of her head. "We need to get you in the studio."

My girl laughed, trying to shove him off as she explained,

"No, thank you, my rapping skills are for car rides, and occasional driveway hangs only."

"Okay, but why?" Kavan pushed, smiling from ear to ear. "Because like...you were on point, girl! That takes some serious swag."

"*I* couldn't do it," Frankie said with a laugh, holding up two hands. "My rapping skills do not exist anywhere."

"Whatever," Phoenix rolled her eyes. "I memorized that one in particular because I knew Judah loved it and figured at some point it would come in handy."

"What the hell?" Ricco threw out. "That wasn't planned?"

"Nope," Frankie popped the "P", appearing proud of herself. "Phoenix and I were just bumpin' on our way in and I figured Judah needed a little moment before we showed off the new house."

I did need that moment.

We all did.

"Well, fuck," Silas laughed. "This group is…"

"Dope as hell?" Pharaoh joked, finishing the statement for him, but he too appeared to be a little stunned.

"Duh," Frankie muttered before turning around to shut off her car and grab her bag from the backseat. When she had what she needed, the little blonde addressed us all, "Alright, enough is enough, let's get inside before the caterer's think we're gonna eat dinner outside."

"I mean we coul—" Frankie slapped Kavan in the stomach before he could even finish the sentence, effectively shutting him up.

As everyone moved toward the front door, I caught Phoenix by the waist, stopping her movement only to spin her around to face me. When those brown eyes hit mine, I grinned and said low and deep, "Hello, Baby Bird."

She didn't miss a beat as she smirked, and greeted, "Skyscraper, so nice to see you."

"Ha," I barked, "*nice* to see me? Girl, you better try—"

Her lips crashed into mine, cutting off my protest and giving me exactly what I was about to demand. She stole my breath with the power of her kiss and every single time it felt like she was repeatedly sealing my fate to hers. It never failed to remind me that losing her would have been the biggest mistake of my existence, even if I had succeeded in ending it. I would have burned in hell with that regret without even knowing what I would have missed out on.

"I love you," she whispered as we broke apart.

"Mmm," I groaned against her lips and wrapped her tighter in my arms. "I love you more."

"Don't start," she warned.

"Hello!!!" Frankie yelled in our direction. "You shit heads have all night to suck each other's faces, let's go!"

Phoenix let out an adorable laugh as she stepped out of my arms, but she remained facing me, allowing the perfect opportunity to scan her form. It was only then I realized she was wearing one of my shirts, which she artfully turned into a dress —much like she did last year—only this time, she appeared to have more time because anyone else would have thought she bought her outfit straight off the rack.

"Holy fuck," I breathed, grabbing hold of her hand and lifting it, "turn around for me."

My little bird did as I requested and shocked me stupid as I stared at the knotted design down her back.

Phoenix wore one of my pink silk button-down shirts but somehow—in order to make it fit her—she sliced a line down the back of it, stopping about a foot from the bottom hem so that when she wore it, her ass was still covered. But the top half was cut in such a way that the knots made the once large shirt, fit like a tiny as fuck body con dress.

"You like?" Phoenix asked, sounding both sassy and sweet as she kicked a white boot up behind her showing off those tan legs. Desire blew through my body as I took in her corded calf muscles from all the yoga she'd been doing.

"Do I *like?*" I repeated, dumbfounded, sweating, and ready to call this entire fucking thing off. We didn't need dinner. I needed her naked, now. "I'm fucking drooling, Phoenix."

"Good," she sassed, "that was the goal."

With a wink over her shoulder, she headed into the house, leaving me with a perfect view of her ass. Not bothering to hide my groan, I followed her up the small walkway and toward the front door, where everyone was still gathered.

"So nice of you two to join us," Frankie rolled her eyes when I finally reached her side.

Clicking my tongue, I adjusted my pants to hide my raging hard-on, and said, "Just open the door, you brat."

"*I'm* a brat?" she threw back.

"Is *now* the time to argue?" I countered.

"I hate you."

"You're a fucking liar. Just open the damn door."

After muttering something under her breath low enough so that I couldn't hear, she stuck her key in the handle and did as I told her to, revealing a brightly lit, open foyer with marbled floors and a skylight directly above, built into the high ceiling.

"Phew," Phoenix whistled, "this is gorgeous!"

"*This* is just the beginning," Frankie corrected, glancing around the space with pride shining in her blue eyes as our group filtered in and began to explore.

CHAPTER 43
Phoenix

HOLY. *Shit.*

For some reason, I was expecting Judah's new place to be smaller than his home in the Hills, even with the pictures I'd seen online, but I couldn't have been more wrong.

The house was *massive.*

When I stepped through the foyer, I headed straight for a sunken living room, surrounded by two small steps, that brought you down a foot, and onto a plush, white carpet. The space was perfect for mingling and had all the bells and whistles—a seventy-inch television mounted above a gas fireplace, two long white linen couches, a glass coffee table, with big, beautiful houseplants spread out on various shelves and surfaces—but because the first floor was an open floor plan, the back wall was made of sliding glass doors that opened up to an outdoor living room.

I could see glimpses of a sparkling blue swimming pool, and three sets of lounge chairs, but I knew there was more around the corner because the whole bottom floor seemed to be baking in the evening sun.

We walked on what Frankie described as woven bamboo flooring, matching the white-on-white design of the home, accented by rich, dark wood furnishings. The main room opened up into a bright kitchen, where a chef was hard at work, surrounded by a handful of caterers, preparing our dinner. I had to stop and admire the beautiful cabinets, and stone flooring, which made the granite countertop stand out beautifully, but when Judah linked his fingers with mine and pulled me along, I told myself I'd have plenty of time to become familiar with the space once today was over.

Together, we passed through a butler's pantry loaded with a wet bar and under-counter refrigerator, that led us straight into the dining room.

I stopped and sucked in a breath as I took in the two-tiered chandelier hanging above the intricately set table, which cast tiny rainbows throughout the space thanks to the light pouring in from the sliding glass doors.

These were open as well, giving us a perfect view of the fountain in the backyard.

"Jeeeeesus," Kavan whispered, staring at the running water like I was. "*That* thing is dope."

"Frankie insisted on keeping it. It came with the house," Judah informed us, rolling his eyes when he looked down at me.

I bit my lip to hold in a smile as I took in the beautiful stone masterpiece, placed perfectly in the grassy area of the backyard.

"This is stunning, you guys," I offered, making sure to lock eyes with Frankie so she understood how proud I was of her and all the work she'd done.

"Come see the outdoor kitchen," she winked at Pharaoh, who appeared stunned by the place.

Low and behold, there really was an entire outdoor living space, with a fridge, a massive grill, pizza oven, smoker, along with a sink and a huge glass dining table.

"Okay, I am never gonna leave," Ricco announced as he fell onto the huge outdoor sofa, and grabbed one of the black throw pillows to place behind his head. "*And* the place is private so I can get my tan on, totally naked."

"Um, excuse me?" Judah called out next to me. "You can kiss my white ass if you think you're tanning naked in my back yard."

"Please," Ricco waved him off, "I'll make sure you're not home."

"Oh?" Judah laughed, incredulously. "How the fuck you gonna get in?"

"With the spare key you'll hide in one of those fancy flowerpots out front," Kavan threw in, sitting down on Ricco's legs, joining his friend on their mission to make themselves home in Judah's new place. "You know you can't leave us hanging."

"You two are not taking over my house like you did P and Frankie's," Judah stated, shaking his head. "No way."

"Sure," Kavan nodded, pretending to agree, "we'll go with that."

I couldn't help it, I laughed, knowing damn well that the two brothers would be barging in on Judah's place, five out of seven days a week, especially if I was here just as often.

"I'm the one that re-designed this place," Frankie added. "I could always make you a key myself."

"You fuckin' traitor!" Judah accused, glaring at Frankie.

She shrugged casually, "Gets them out of my hair."

"Oh my god," I chuckled, placing my hand over my mouth.

"Okay, I'm going to make a mean rack of ribs with this thing," Pharaoh muttered from his place in front of the smoker. "Are you kidding?"

"What about them pizza options thoughhhh!" I squealed, letting go of Judah's hand to run and jump on Pharaoh's back, feeling way too excited for all the possibilities.

From there, the night went on without a hitch, and after exploring the entire second floor, where Frankie had set up three guest bedrooms, a study that Judah planned to renovate into a studio this upcoming summer, and a loft overlooking the second family room on the first floor, we all sat down at the dining room and talked as the caterer's brought in our meal.

Once a massive fried turkey and all the various sides were placed in front of us, Silas did his usual thing and clinked the side of his glass with a butter knife to gain everyone's attention.

Under the table, I reached for Judah's hand, knowing that whatever Silas was about to say, would be emotional for him, and in turn, for me.

"I won't make this long," Silas told us all, causing Frankie to snicker, "but I had to take a quick second and say, first of all, congrats to Frankie for doing such an incredible job redesigning the inside of this place, making it the perfect space for not only Judah, but for the rest of us crazy hooligan's as well."

"Got that right!" Kavan whopped with two hands around his mouth, causing a round of chuckles and Judah to shake his head.

"But with that being said," Silas continued, "we have to address the elephant in the room."

Judah squeezed my hand, so I ran my thumb across the tops of his knuckles, letting him know I was with him, no matter what.

"Judah Colt," Silas turned to meet J's eyes, searing him with an expression I'd never seen him use before. "I always believed in you. From the moment I met your crazy ass, I knew there was some deep, real, raw fuckin' talent under the drug habit and stupid decisions, but I wasn't sure what the hell you were gonna do after the events of this last year. Turns out, you took your life by the balls and refused to give up, and for that, I'm fuckin' proud. More than that, I'm fuckin' excited, brother. I'm excited to see where you go from here, how you bulldoze your way back into the music industry and tell your truth, how you rebrand yourself into a new, genuine, and completely authentic version of TheColt. And all I ask is that you hold on to the monster within you, the one that fueled you to keep going when you were at your weakest point, because to some, it wears a halo, but to people like me? We see the horns. And those horns are earned, brother. You went to hell, you tasted that torture, then you crawled your way out and lived to tell the story. So do it. Tell the fuckin' story."

Chills raced down my spine as Silas finished and a round of hoots sounded off in the room. Yet my hand tightened around J's as heat blew through my body, remembering how well acquainted I was with that version of Judah. I knew all about the horns *and* the monster within him. I recognized that my own monster only made an appearance when he was present. She loved that hellion just as much as I loved the buttery sweet version of my Skyscraper.

"Alright, that's it," Silas laughed, shaking out his shoulders and holding up his glass toward the center of the table. "A toast to Judah and his future, which I am grateful to be a part of. Proud of you, man."

All at once, we leaned forward to clink our glasses in honor of my guy, who seemed overwhelmed by what Silas had said, but I also picked up on the subtle buzzing energy surrounding him as that leg started to bounce under the table.

Silas had a point and it had me wondering when I'd hear another song from TheColt. I wondered what it would sound like, what his music would feel like, now that the filter was gone and Judah was free of his vices.

Who would TheColt be now?

I couldn't fucking wait to find out.

* ❦ *

"PEACE AT LAST," Judah sighed, once he shut the door behind our friends later that night.

It was nearing eleven p.m. and after a long, sober evening full of eating, laughing, Judah opening housewarming gifts, the guys exploring upstairs, and placing claim on the guest rooms, Ricco and Kavan finally announced they had to leave to pick up Trixie from her sitter. Pharaoh, Silas, and Frankie followed swiftly behind them, wishing us a good night, and leaving Judah and me alone.

"Peace is right," I responded, turning to stare up at him with a smile, feeling warm and happy after the success of the night. "Hi, baby boy."

Judah ran a finger from my temple to my lips, as affection burned bright in his blue eyes, "Hi, sweet girl."

Butterflies danced in my tummy but I ignored them as I stated, "There better be a good reason why you told me not to pack a bag for tonight, and it better not be because you expect me to wear *your* clothes all day tomorrow."

Frankie had chosen to do the housewarming party on a night where I wouldn't have to worry about driving to the shop the next morning, so I planned to spend the entire next day getting to know Judah's new place and making myself at home.

"Why don't I show you?" Judah winked as he grabbed my hand and laced our fingers together before pulling me toward the hardwood stairs leading to the second floor.

"Ooooo, do I finally get to see what's behind the big white double doors?" I teased.

Judah refused to show anyone his room, saying it wasn't for them, it was for him.

And me.

I was a puddle of fucking goo at that point, but I liked to think I hid it well.

"You knew you were going to see it, don't pretend like you're shocked," Judah sassed back.

"Yeah, but you make it sound so mysterious," I flirted. "Are we going to enter another world when you open the door? Is Narnia behind it?"

"I'm not even going to dignify that with a response."

"Such big words you use, oh mysterious one."

A laugh bubbled up his throat, "Jesus Christ."

I cut the bullshit as we finished our walk, taking in the gorgeous pieces of art Frankie picked out for the walls, depicting various displays of both rage and happiness, all in muted black and grey coloring.

Judah didn't bother stopping when we reached the door but instead just turned the knob and pushed it open, signaling for me to go first.

I, however, paused two feet into the room.

"Holy...shit," I whispered as my eyes scanned the wide-open, massive space in front of me.

The first thing I saw was Judah's bed—elevated against the farthest wall on a platform you had to climb two stairs to get to. In front of the pitch-black painted wall sat his bed. The thing was huge, with a silver snakeskin headboard, and two glass nightstands on either side—both of which sported fresh snake plants, underneath two mounted light sconces. Except, rather than a normal shade surrounding the lightbulb, his was covered in clear glass shaped like a skull.

Pink LED lights were hidden along the edges of the platform, along with the outline of the bed, which was dressed in a thick black comforter.

There were six pillows on the bed, all dressed in different shades of pink silk, matching the bed skirt hanging from the edges.

"This shit is so sick, I can hardly breathe," I bit out, trying to catch my breath as my heart beat with excitement.

"I designed this room," Judah admitted. "Frankie wanted it to match the rest of the house. I told her to kindly fuck off."

A distracted laugh tumbled from my mouth as I took in the rest of the room.

Floor-to-ceiling windows lined one side, providing a delicious view of the Ventura county mountains, along with the pool down below, while on the other side I was met with a myriad of things to look at. The other walls were painted stark white, but when I turned, I came face to face with three doors. One was blank, while the other two sported pink neon LED signs—one saying "Baby Bird" while the other said "Skyscraper"

"What in the fuck is *this*?" I whispered, walking toward the one with my nickname.

"Open it and find out," Judah encouraged, sounding nervous, yet excited at the same time.

As anxious anticipation curled in my stomach, I reached for the handle and opened the door, finding a black-painted room, full of...

"My clothes," I gasped.

"Mhm," Judah replied, following me into the brightly lit, yet darkened room, "I had the movers pack up your side of the closet in my old place, then went shopping to fill the rest of the space. This closet is obviously a helluva lot bigger but—"

"Shoes?" I cut him off, walking to the far wall, which was full of all different kinds of footwear. "Fucking *bags?* Judah!" I spun around and glared at him, feeling undeserving of the sheer amount of money floating in the room around me. "You've got to be kidding."

He smirked, sliding two hands in his pocket as he met my stare with no remorse. "Not even a little."

"But—but, it's too fucking much!"

"Says who?" he laughed.

"ME!" I yelled.

"Well," he shrugged as if my tone didn't bother him at all. "Too late."

"Uh, no it isn't," I shook my head and reached over to grab a Prada tag hanging from one of the many dresses, "They're still tagged. You can return them."

"I could…" he rocked forward a little, "but I won't."

Narrowing my eyes on him, I growled, "I'm gonna kill you."

"You could try," he shrugged again, still smirking down at me.

Knowing I wasn't going to win, I turned around and muttered, "Stubborn fucking bastard."

Judah's chuckle followed me as I took in the rest of the space, passing by a floor-to-ceiling mirror, a pink velvet chair, and a fuck ton of accessories that I knew cost him out the ass to purchase.

Despite how much I hated him for spending that much money on me, gratitude filled my veins, my heart, my very soul as I glanced at the things he picked out.

Judah knew me.

He knew my style, my favorite colors, designers, brands.

I stopped in the middle of the room, knowing he was right behind me, and turned to face him once again. Glancing up to meet his eyes, I saw that love again. It shone so brightly, I couldn't help the tears that formed on my bottom lashes as I whispered, "Thank you, Judah."

"You told me to dream, then dream bigger," he started and lifted a hand to cradle my cheek, "so when I was designing my room, that's exactly what I did. I want this place to be yours too, even though we haven't discussed you moving in, and I'm in no rush to have that conversation. But I'm finding that when I dream big, I go all the way."

A watery laugh slipped free from my lips.

"You living with me is inevitable," he continued. "Being

spoiled by me, comes with the territory. But this time? I promise not to fuck it up."

How could I be mad at him when he put it like that?

"Kiss me, Skyscraper."

His smile damn near killed me. "Gladly, Baby Bird."

From there, I got lost in the waves of gratitude and newfound peace that our connection seemed to float in. My worries began to fade, my fears were far away, and I was happy. I was inspired. I was excited.

I was exactly where I wanted to be.

CHAPTER 44
Phoenix

"SOOOOO," Kenji drew out the word, wiggling his eyebrows as he asked, "what are you doing for your birthday tomorrow?"

The fact that it was already the end of June had my brain short-circuiting.

"I have no idea," I answered honestly. "Everyone is keeping it a secret."

Kenji nodded knowingly and concluded, "So, Judah is planning something."

"Probably?" I replied with a question. "I'm really not sure what the hell is happening because even Frankie has been super chill about it. Normally she's all up in my shit, taunting the hell out of me when she knows something I don't, but she's kept her cool."

I hadn't pushed to find out though, especially since I was used to secrets by now. For months, while I was working at the shop, Judah was off doing something I still hadn't figured out —though I had my ideas—and after speaking with Pharaoh, I decided to just let him be. Which was difficult at times because I wanted to hear about Judah's day and he would have to tell me a very watered-down version of the truth to keep the lid on whatever he didn't want me to know about yet, but I was getting through it.

"If Frankie is keeping her cool, she doesn't know shit," Kenji stated as he finished shading the last part of my new tattoo. "There is no way that girl is capable of being cool about a surprise."

I had to laugh, knowing he was right.

"Well, I guess we'll find out tomorrow," I sighed, closing my eyes to try and block out the last few minutes of pain.

Last week, Kenji had shown me a drawing of a bat, whose wings were made of flowers and vines, and asked me what I thought. I told him it was fucking dope—because it was—so he asked me if I'd get it myself. My answer was "in a heartbeat" but the last thing I was expecting him to say was "Good, because it's your birthday present. I booked you for the 29th."

But there I was, getting the beautiful bat inked on my left calf, in a spot I'd been trying to fill for a while. I'd been in the chair for about four hours, which wasn't bad, considering my last tattoo—a giant, feminine-looking dragon crawling up and over my hip—took nearly ten hours to complete. I'd gotten the fierce lil' baby last month, during a break in both my schedule and Kenji's and I was still obsessed with her.

Judah was a big fan and had spent just as many hours telling me just how much he loved it.

She was sexy, that was for sure.

"Okaaaay," Kenji sing-songed, "I'm done. And *damn*, does it look good."

I hopped off the chair way too fast and nearly fell, thanks to my center of gravity being off, but as soon as the dizzy spell passed, I ran toward the mirror at the back of the shop and turned around, looking down at my new piece.

"Ahhhh!" I squealed. "She's beautiful, Kenj!"

I couldn't help but give my tattoos personalities and pronouns—especially if they were some form of living creature like the bat and my dragon.

"Couldn't agree more," he beamed, coming up to the

mirror as well. "I don't know what it is about you, but you're probably my favorite person to tattoo. I always nail it."

I scoffed. "You nail every tattoo, dude. It's not just mine."

"Yeah, well, agree to disagree."

My boss was a perfectionist to say the least.

I stared at my new ink for another full minute before I heard my phone ring back at my station where it was plugged into a charger.

"Shit," I muttered as I ran over to grab it.

When I did, I was greeted by my favorite picture of Judah, lost in thought while sitting on the beach. The photo was from one of our most recent date nights—which we tried to do at least once a week.

That particular night, we took J's bike up to Santa Barbara and spent the night in this adorable Airbnb right on the water. It was a beautiful surprise Judah had planned, and it turned out that it didn't matter what we did on our dates—mini golf, going to a movie, riding ATVs in the mountains of Venture County—as long as I was with him, it was perfect.

"Hellllo?" I answered, smiling to myself.

"You best be on your way to my place," was all he said but he sounded a bit wound up.

"And if I'm not yet?"

"I'm going to beat you home," he replied.

Starting to pack up my bag, I asked, "And if you beat me home?"

"I'll already be in bed."

It was nine p.m.

"And if you're already in bed?"

"I'll be naked and ready for you to ride me."

Fuck me.

"I'm leaving in five."

"That's my girl," Judah purred. "Hurry up."

When the line went dead, I took a minute to catch my breath.

Judah had been insatiable lately, but that was fine by me because I might have been worse than he was. There was just so much time to make up for, and I finally felt like I could take full advantage of the fact that he was mine. He didn't feel like a celebrity anymore, he didn't feel like TheColt or just the guy that saved my life. He was just Judah, my Skyscraper, the guy that nearly died due to a series of mental health issues and addiction problems that stemmed from a series of unfortunate events taking place in his childhood.

He was someone I could relate to, that I could protect, and I found myself looking forward to the moment he decided to step back into the spotlight, because this time, I felt more than equipped to handle it. My role in his life had become solidified over the last two months, we'd learned how to pull each other back to earth after a nightmare rocked our world.

I'd been there for quite a few of Judah's panic attacks in the middle of the night. Ones that were triggered by dreams of dead girls and Hell itself, and because Judah had been going through it, it seemed my own nightmares needed to be given attention, since they came back harder than ever before.

Still, neither of us cared. We got through it. We openly discussed that maybe it was a purge of sorts. Thinking that our pasts were getting to know one another, in a twisted, fucked up sort of way, and we hoped that eventually, there would be nothing left to learn and we'd be able to sleep peacefully. But it was those nightmares, those memories, that brought out the monster in both of us.

Inside we were angry and bitter. We were on a first-name basis with resentment and fear, and when we fucked, we let it out. We surrendered, felt, and screamed our way through the pain—together. It was as magical as it was brutal, which I never thought could go hand in hand, and yet they interlaced their fingers easily, as if meant to be.

On top of that, it wasn't easy on Judah when he was surrounded by alcohol or even weed. And I, as his sponsor, had learned what to do and what not to do based on trial and error. The first few times Judah had become angry and pushed me away, reminding me of our previous relationship, but I held strong, taking notes from Dr. Blake and remembering what she taught me about reactive responses.

Judah was a work in progress, but I was finally a part of the process and even though I, too, had to remain sober, it was worth it. *He* was worth it.

"Okay, I'm out of here," I said to Kenji, who was cleaning up his station. "Thank you, as always, for this masterpiece."

"Any fuckin' time," Kenji replied, jogging over to hug me. "Happy Birthday, baby girl."

I squeezed him back. "Thanks, Kenj."

Once I was out of the shop and in my car, I moved as quickly as possible, trying to get on the road knowing that I had at least another hour before I would make it to Judah's house. As soon as the Bluetooth connected to my phone, I hit shuffle on my new summer playlist and laughed—loud and unfiltered—as "Comeback" by JoJo and Tory Lanez began to play.

Fuck my life, man. Too perfect.

I had that bitch on repeat the whole way home.

CHAPTER 45

JUDAH

WHEN I HEARD the beeping of the alarm system, signaling a key had been used to open the front door, I smirked, knowing it was finally time to let out some fucking steam.

I'd had a rough day in the studio because—and not for the first time—I was overcome with a nearly insurmountable number of insecurities thinking about tomorrow and all the things I had planned. Pharaoh tried to help, Pierce and Vale had no fucking idea what was wrong with me, and Holly had been too busy making last-minute arrangements to even notice what was going on.

All I knew was I had cold feet.

I wanted to tell Holly to cancel the whole thing because the album sucked, it was too loud, too brash, too honest, and too fucking bold to come out the gate with. I couldn't step back into the industry like that. Who did I think I was?

Except, Pharaoh wouldn't let me pull the plug, telling me I was in a downward spiral because I was nervous. Sure, yeah, of course I was fucking nervous, but it felt like more than that.

It felt like I couldn't fucking do it.

It felt like a bad motherfucking idea.

All I wanted to do now was tell Phoenix what was happening, but I couldn't because it would ruin my goddamn surprise. So, instead, I planned to fuck her until we both bled.

I heard the pounding of her boots against the floor, meaning she was close, so I stayed still, in my position right next to the closed door of my bedroom, and waited for her to open it.

My dick was already hard, my hands were shaking, and my breathing had become erratic in the last thirty seconds, as I anticipated the release of emotions that was sure to follow as soon as—

The door opened.

I pounced.

My hand was around her throat in half a second, dragging her toward me as I kicked the door shut once again. Her back was against the wood and my lips were on hers not even a moment later.

I heard her bag hit the ground, felt her hands snake under my shirt and all the way up my chest, before those nails tore lines down my skin, drawing a groan from deep within my stomach. I swear, my tongue hit the back of her fucking throat with the way I was devouring her, and she kept pace, biting down on my flesh to assert her dominance, even as my fingers squeezed tighter, causing her to growl under the pressure on her windpipe.

And while I had planned to make tonight all about her—hoping to fuck her through the midnight hour and be the first to tell her happy birthday—it seemed that she was well aware of just how much I needed to be tortured.

Phoenix tore her head from my grasp and sucked in a breath, breathing hard as she stared up at me. Those brown eyes burned with unspoken desire as she dropped to her knees and went straight for the button on my jeans. She wasted no time freeing my dick from its denim entrapment and gripped the rock hard base in a fierce hold.

"Fuckkkk," I hissed, eyes dropping closed for only a moment before I zoned in on the way she teased the head of my cock with the tip of her tongue. She smirked maliciously and showed her pearly white teeth as she bit down on the piercing at the head of my dick and pulled. "Jesus C-christ, P."

Her fingers tightened around my shaft, squeezing tightly, removing all the oxygen from my lungs as blood rushed to the tip, where she continued to tug on the metal, causing my legs to shake and my heart to nearly stop.

But then she let go and pumped me slowly, as she stated, "Someone had quite the day."

My answer was a low, deep growl as her mouth closed over the head of my dick, but all I could feel was the light pressure of her teeth torturing the flesh as she took her time sliding her hand back down to the base.

"Phoenix," I bit out with warning written all over my tone.

"Hmmmmm?" She responded with my dick still in her mouth, causing a long vibration to zing down my length.

Fucking hell. "I'm gonna need you to fucking do something."

She pulled back with a wicked smirk. "Or?"

My eyes were hard, hooded, and dead serious as they met hers. "Or I'll snap and shove my fuckin' dick down your throat without permission."

That smirk formed into a full-blown taunting grin. "Since when do you need permission?"

This girl.

With two hands, I held the back of her head and responded, "Open up, little bird."

She did.

And down went my cock.

I slammed my hips forward and fucked her face until she choked, gagging on my length, while I raged against the demons in my mind. Her mouth felt like liquid silk as saliva pooled around my shaft and dripped down her chin, and I didn't even have to wonder if I was going too hard, giving too much, because she encouraged my savage motions by grabbing my balls in her fist, rolling them together to send a blinding sensation up my spine.

"Son of a *BITCH*," I snarled out, gripping a fist full of her hair to ensure a tighter hold, as I pushed harder, pumped faster, knowing she could handle it, that she wanted it, even as her face turned red and those brown eyes leaked saltwater from the force.

It wasn't until I was seconds from exploding that I abruptly stopped, pulling out of her mouth with a quick motion, causing a wet sound to follow, one that had my engorged cock pulsing.

Phoenix wiped her eyes, breathing heavily as she remained on her knees, watching me as I stood over her. She was still smiling, but it was dark, downright dangerous. Especially as she said, "You should probably go sit on the bed and wait for me."

"Oh, I should, should I?" I crooned, kicking my jeans all the way off before lowering myself in front of her, sitting with my legs sprawled out on the carpet, hands casually braced behind me. "I don't think I need to go that far to get what I want. Not when I can get it right here."

Phoenix sucked her white teeth and nodded as if to agree, but then stood and walked closer, stepping on either side of my legs, until her skirt-covered pussy was at eye level.

I felt her tiny hand sink into my hair, where she gripped a handful and tilted my head back so I could meet her blazing stare. With her free hand, she began to drag up her leather skirt, revealing a lacy pink thong, delicate enough to tear apart with my canines.

In a husky, lust-fueled voice, she demanded, "Eat it first."

My girl is a goddamn dream.

"With pleasure," I agreed, flashing her a vile grin as my dick pulsed, bouncing against my abs.

P's foot hit my chest, kicking me into a lying down position, so she could lower her knees to the ground and plant that pussy above my face.

Wasting no time, I gripped her thong in my hands and snapped both sides, before dragging the fabric out from between her legs, creating friction against her clit, causing a long moan to fall from her mouth.

I had to resist grabbing my erection just to get some goddamn relief, but I craved the sting of need, the ache of desperation. And I had very little time to think about the pain in my balls, because Phoenix wasn't looking for a sensual licking. No, she wanted to ride my face, as I did hers, and that's exactly what happened. As soon as my tongue hit her cunt, her hips lowered and breathing became damn near impossible.

That hand hit my hair again but this time she yanked my head up, further in between her legs, and she began her relentless attempt to use my face as a tool to get herself off.

And I had zero complaints.

I sucked, fucked, and devoured the delicious folds of her pussy as she chased that climax.

Her cries were loud, unhinged, as my fingers dug into the flesh of her thighs, using them for leverage as I pulled her clit between my teeth and held still, flicking my tongue against the swollen bud, letting Phoenix ride her way out of my hold, causing a scream to break free of her throat.

Her juices dripped into my mouth, coated my chin, my nose, my cheeks, as she did what she had to do, and I supported her the whole way through. But because I knew her body better than even she did, I felt that distinct pulse against my tongue, the throbbing of her clit, and knew she was mere fucking seconds from exploding, which I wasn't going to allow.

When we came, we came together.

With more force than she expected, I lifted her body as well as my own, until we were back in a seated position, and before she had time to bitch at me for cutting her orgasm off right at the brink, I placed the tip of my dick at her entrance and slid right in.

The two of us groaned, completely in sync, as a vibrating, hot sensation blew through my body and damn near set it on fire.

"Fuuuuuuuck," Phoenix hissed—seemingly lost to her own needs—and got right to work.

My little bird fucked me with expert precision, jumping up and down on my dick like it was the end of the world and our last chance to fuck. The sight of her lost in desire, drowning in sensation, had me reaching forward and pulling closer. I latched on to her mouth and let her taste herself, kissing her until neither of us could breathe, as those hips rocked over my cock and the slight change of position added a new kind of friction, bringing the finish line that much closer.

"Fucking goddess," I breathed into her mouth, not even sure that she heard me as she cried out my name. I licked a line down her jaw, holding the back of her neck in a vice-like grip as I made my way to that pressure point, knowing I wasn't going to last more than a few more seconds and she still needed that final push.

When my teeth clamped down on that perfectly sensitive spot, she went off like a bomb, bringing me down in her shrapnel. I came in a whirlwind of sound, lost sight of the room around me, and fell dick first into the kind of heaven only Phoenix's body could provide.

The cosmos swirled behind my closed eyes as I shot my seed inside of her, as my hands roamed her body, snaking up her back and over her shoulders, pulling her even closer—as close as fucking possible—as she shook with her own release.

"Oh my god," she cried a bit desperately as my sweaty forehead met her neck and my arms squeezed her body to mine. In response, P's hands drifted into my hair and held me there, returning my affection as we let go of the darkness and fell back into our usual selves.

"Wow," Phoenix whispered breathlessly against the top of my head.

"Mhm," was all I could say as my chest rose and fell rapidly.

The two of us remained silent for a few minutes after that, until both of us were firmly planted back on Earth.

That's when the investigation started.

Because my girl was too smart for her own good, Phoenix pulled back and held my face between her hands, and searched my eyes, trying to find answers to why I was so feral.

"What happened?" She asked seriously, carrying a hint of demand in her tone.

I ignored the question and sighed, turning my head to kiss the palm of her hand, before patting her ass, signaling that she get up. She didn't force me to answer, but instead did as I non-verbally asked, and then followed me into the master bathroom, where I started the shower while she peed.

When she was done, Phoenix remained patient as I walked around the large space, but it wasn't until my back was turned away from her as I took a piss of my own, that I admitted, "I'm an insecure piece of shit, and got bit by the anxiety bug."

She isn't going to like my phrasing, but at least it's the truth.

"First of all," Phoenix started, "don't talk about yourself like that, please. Second, what were you feeling insecure about?"

When I turned around, she was leaning against the counter on her side of the bathroom.

Yes, there were two.

Frankie suggested a his and hers style bathroom and I agreed instantly because I liked the intimacy of it all.

I leaned against the counter on my side while trying to come up with a way of telling her what happened without giving any of the surprise details away. After the last two months, I'd gotten used to telling Phoenix all the embarrassing shit about my thought process, so it wasn't hard to admit I'd hit another wall today, it was just hard to explain which wall I hit, given she couldn't actually know all the details until after tomorrow.

"I'm doing something for your birthday," I told her, knowing that wouldn't be much of a surprise, "and I guess I just found myself bumping heads with the perfectionist in me. I got cold feet, then spiraled into a case of 'I'm not good enough', and then landed in 'I can't do this', until Pharaoh had to step in. Which, of course, only made me more anxious because I hate when people see me like that. It was just fucking awful."

That was a very tame version of what happened to me that afternoon, but I couldn't tell her the rest until her birthday was over and the cat was out of the bag.

"You're killing me, you know that?" she asked, eyeing me in the mirror as she turned around to wash her hands, even though we were about to get into the shower. "I can't even properly help you right now because I don't know what you believe you're not good enough for."

I smirked and crossed my arms, "You're brilliant. Think on your feet, baby bird."

She scoffed and rolled her eyes, but then stalked toward me and grabbed my hand on her way into the shower, pulling me along behind her. When we were both inside the massive space, standing underneath the one-and-a-half-foot wide rain-style showerhead, she wrapped her arms around my waist and pressed her naked body against mine in a hug.

The water beat down on us from above and created a wall of sorts around us, making me feel safe, surrounded, and comfortable enough to close my eyes. I held her tight, letting the stress of my day evaporate, and drank in the overwhelming power of her love for me.

Phoenix didn't even need words to get her point across. I could read it all in her energy. She was letting me know that, of course, I was good enough—I could do anything I wanted and fuck what anyone else had to say.

But it wasn't until I was in her presence like this that I could remember it, that I could *feel* it.

She had music in her breath, affirmations in her eyes, and peace in her soul, even though she didn't believe it.

She didn't have to, because I did.

Just like she believed in me in a way I didn't think I would ever be able to.

"I love you," she called out over the sound of the water.

I tightened my arm around her shoulders and sank my hand into her wet hair, holding the back of her head against my chest as I responded, "I love you more."

From there, we took our time washing each other's bodies, not speaking, but instead just savoring the moment, and each other all at once. And when we got out, we dried off, brushed our teeth at our individual sinks, then headed straight to bed, where we lied naked under the covers with our legs intertwined and her head on my chest.

"You're good enough, Judah," Phoenix whispered as I stared at the ceiling. "Whatever happened today, whatever you have planned for tomorrow, I know it will be a success. It'll turn out exactly as you wanted it to or even better if you let yourself believe it."

She had no idea how much I hoped that was true because there was so much riding on this one day. I couldn't imagine what would happen if I fucked it up.

"I'm nervous," I admitted, speaking to the ceiling. "And I know you don't really know what I could be so nervous about, but you're the only one who will understand just what nerves do to me."

"One bad thought leads to ten others," She concluded.

"Exactly," I agreed. "And they won't go away. Even now. I just keep thinking about all the ways it could go wrong and I'm really fucking regretting not involving you in this."

"Why don't you just tell me?" She asked with a sigh.

"Because I can't, P," I gently pushed. "I have to do this without you, just to prove to myself that I can. I don't want to lean on you for every single little thing and tomorrow is going to be a glimpse into my future and I need to face it alone."

There was a thick pause before she said, "All right, fine, but listen, you have time. You have time to get it right. It's not one and done, Judah. You don't need to put so much pressure on yourself to get it right the first time, or even the second or third. You're still getting comfortable in this new mindset and the last thing you need is to push yourself back toward your vices because you just want to escape. Nothing you're doing is worth that."

She was right. And I was close to that point.

There were multiple times in the studio that afternoon where I thought about sneaking out back and finding a way to contact Keon or Sage—whom I still hadn't spoken a word to since I got out of rehab. But we knew how to be sneaky; I knew how to get what I wanted without anyone else finding out, but I bit down on the craving, reminding myself that I hadn't gotten this far just to throw it all away.

I had to do this sober. I had to do it for *myself*.

"I know," was all I said before Phoenix pushed up onto her elbow and kissed me, marking my lips with her flavor, minty and sweet.

I cupped her cheek and deepened the kiss, sliding my

tongue against hers, earning myself a pretty moan. Rolling on top of her, I had no intention to fuck her to sleep, but that's what happened as midnight came and went.

Phoenix Royal was officially one-quarter of a decade old.

"Happy Birthday, Baby Bird."

CHAPTER 46
Phoenix

WHEN I WOKE up the next morning, sleep held me tightly in its grip, more so than usual, making opening my eyes difficult as fuck. I planned to wrap myself around Judah and convince him to stay in bed all day but when I rolled over to reach for him…he wasn't there.

My eyes flew open, then fell immediately into a narrowed state, wondering who the fuck he thought he was, leaving me alone in bed on my birthday? I was just about to throw off the covers and go in search of him when I kicked a piece of paper into the air with my sloppy movements.

Shit.

I reached for it, but it slid off the far end of the bed and onto the platform, causing me to grumble under my breath as I lifted my heavy ass body and crawled toward the edge of the bed to try and grab it.

Our little fuck session last night had my legs screaming in the aftermath, telling me I hadn't done nearly enough working out in the last few months to keep up with our latest style of lovemaking.

Hanging over the side of the bed, I snatched the neon pink paper and groaned loudly as I pulled myself back into a sitting position.

"Wow, that was much more difficult than it should have been," I murmured to myself as I opened the letter, only to find Judah's handwriting, scrawled in sharpie.

Come and find me.
But put some fuckin' clothes on first.
-J
Ps: happy birthday, little bird.

This dude.
I smiled to myself, despite my exhaustion.
He better have coffee.

My plan was definitely *not* to put clothes on, but he probably knew that which was why he'd made a point to remind me to. After quickly brushing my teeth and throwing on a random all pink sweatsuit from my obscenely full closet, I bent forward, gathered all my hair, and threw it up into a messy knot on the top of my head, not wanting to waste any more time.

I was feeling a bit grumpy since my original plans to go back to sleep were instantly squashed, but when I opened the door to find pink rose petals lining the entire hallway in front of me, all of that disappeared into thin air.

"Oh my god," I whispered, glancing around at the vases full of pink and black dyed roses that covered various surfaces around the second floor. I touched one, feeling the silky black petal between my fingers and grinned, knowing Judah must have either hired someone to set these up while we slept, or got up early enough to do it all himself.

When I hit the stairs leading to the first floor, tears pricked my eyes and warmth spread through my entire body.

Dangling from the high ceiling we're hundreds of tiny, intricately crafted origami birds made out of different shades of pink and black paper.

As if on cue, "More of You" by JP Saxe began to play as soon as I started to descend the stairs, making those emotions spill into a trail of water down my cheeks as the opening lyrics hit my ears. I bit my lip to stop the trembling as my chest threatened to crack under the pressure of my gratitude. Yet, it wasn't over.

Downstairs, the place had been turned into a balloon filled paradise, as every surface seemed to float in shiny pink metallic balloons of all shapes and sizes. Those same flowers were littered everywhere, along with bowls of both sour gummy bears, pink and black M&M's and skittles.

My laugh was wet as I continued trying to find him.

When I hit the kitchen and still found no evidence of human life, I heard the distinct sound of doggie paws headed my way.

I sucked in a breath.

Trixie.

My little girl came barreling into the room, and I bent quickly, snatching her up when she jumped into my arms excitedly, immediately licking the tears off my face and making me laugh harder at her enthusiasm.

"Hey sweet girl, what are you doing here?" I asked the dog before kissing her face, and running my hand along her back, only to find another note tied to her collar. I clicked my tongue. "That cheeky bastard."

Out back.
PS – ur hot. Love the hair.

What the hell?

Where the fuck was he?

I'd been watching the windows the entire time I walked, looking for any evidence of people outside, but came up blank.

Confused as hell, I set Trixie down and said, "Come on, girl, outside."

The little dog knew exactly what that meant, but rather than running toward the doors directly in front of us, she ran all the way down the hall, past the living room, past the family room, and into the small reading room, that came with the house. Judah was going to turn it into an office, but it remained unfurnished for some reason.

Feeling a bit anxious to figure out Judah's endgame, I followed Trixie toward the door and opened it. She ran forward, sprinting into the backward, as I stepped out onto the patio and into the area where the fire pit sat, only to be scared stupid by a whole ass crowd of people screaming, "Happy Birthday!"

I jumped and let out a squeal as confetti bombs exploded in my direction.

As tiny pieces of multicolored paper rained down on me, I heard laughing but was too stunned to join them as I glanced around and saw a whole crew of strangers, obviously hired, coming around the corner of the house, holding bouquets of balloons.

"She can't even think straight!" Someone called out with a loud chuckle, signaling me to glance to my right, finding my entire group of friends walking toward me with bright smiles on their faces.

"There she is," Ricco winked, making everyone laugh harder as I took in each of them.

Kavan, Silas, Frankie, Pharaoh, and Ricco all surrounded me carrying boxes of sidecar donuts and grinning like fools.

That was when I did laugh, because even Kenji was there, smiling from ear to fucking ear, and all I could think about was how we were *never* going to be able to eat nearly eight dozen donuts, between the group of us.

"My girl is twenty five!!!" Frankie screamed and shoved

her box into Silas' arms before barreling forward to attack me with one of her bear hugs, crushing my lungs in the process. "Happy birthday, baby!"

"Let me in, let me in," Kavan yelled, rushing forward to wrap his body around both of ours. "Ricco, get in here!"

Both Frankie and I laughed, remembering the group hug at the airport back in January when everything was still up in the air and felt daunting and grim. Now, though, the past seemed to be behind us as everyone else dropped their boxes in the grass and came forward to join in.

Frankie and I were crushed in the middle of our pile of bodies, and loved every second.

It wasn't until someone cleared their throat that the group disbanded, leaving me alone in the center of the circle. It was Judah that stepped forward, then, wearing an identical sweatsuit to mine, except his was black.

As he made his way toward me, he stated, "The only reason they got away with hugging you first, was because I had to run up and change as quickly as possible so we could match."

My smile was wide as he stopped in front of me.

My mind whirled, trying to catch up to the chaos around me as I grabbed the strings of his hoodie and pulled him down so that we were nose to nose, "Were you spying on me, Skyscraper?"

"Haven't you learned yet?" His lips brushed my own. "My eyes are always on you, Baby Bird."

With those words and a kiss to top it off, the small crowd cheered, and once again set off those goddamn confetti bombs, which only made me feel bad for the cleaning crew that would have to sweep the little motherfuckers up later on.

But my guilt quickly vanished as Judah pulled back and said, "Alright, so this year, your birthday is going to be a little bit different, but I promise that by the end of the night, you'll understand why."

"A little?" Ricco chuckled under his breath.

"Shhh." Silas smacked his arm.

"Okaaaay," I drew out, pointing to all our friends. "It's looking pretty similar to last year, just in a different house and with a helluva lot more donuts."

"I told you everyone getting a dozen was going overboard," Pharaoh muttered loud enough for us to hear.

Judah threw a *shut up* look in his best friend's direction, before bringing those baby blues back to me, where he explained, "I felt guilty for not being able to spend the afternoon with you today, so I went a little crazy, but it's fine. Again, you'll understand later."

"We can hand out donuts to random people," Frankie offered.

"That's creepy," Kavan shut her down.

"Unless they're homeless," Ricco threw in. "Ohhhh, we should give some donuts to the homeless people!"

"Will you guys shut up?" Judah called out, trying not to laugh.

I, however, openly snickered at the ridiculousness.

"I'm pretty sure if all of us give a box of donuts to one homeless person, those bitches will spread through the community pretty fast," Silas decided to tack on, no doubt to piss off Judah. "I'm just sayin'"

Frankie tapped his abs. "Good idea."

"Do we think that one homeless person will actually share though?" Pharaoh asked, continuing the charade.

"OH MY GOD," Judah called out. "Can we fucking not right now?"

"I mean," I shrugged, "as long as I get to keep a box, I think this idea is pretty solid, though Pharaoh has a point. Whoever you pick, you have to make sure there are a few more people watching the exchange, so they know to ask for a donut. This way no one hordes them."

"Won't that cause a fight, though?" Frankie asked. "I'm just imagining—"

"Okay, I'm done," Judah grabbed my wrist and dragged me further out in the grass and away from the group, while I busted out laughing, unable to help but tease him, knowing he wanted this whole thing to be perfect. When we stopped by the fountain, he looked down at me with an incredulous smile. "You're an asshole, you know that?"

I grinned widely, "I know, but you're so cute when you're frustrated."

"I agree," Kavan stated from behind us, which only made Judah's eyes roll into the back of his head as he noticed everyone just simply followed us.

My cheeks hurt from smiling, but once everyone was together again, I said, "All right, we're done. Go ahead, J, what did you want to say?"

Judah's eyes scanned over all of us, making sure we were serious about letting him talk. Ricco held up two hands and Kavan mimed a zipper closing over his mouth, while Silas pulled Frankie in front of him and draped his arms over her shoulders.

Pharaoh, however, was a wildcard with a devious smirk.

Judah pointed a finger in his direction, "You keep your mouth shut."

"Damn, you guys are adorable," Kenji stated with a brilliant white smile, joining the conversation as he sipped on what looked like champagne. "Why haven't I been hanging out with this group more often?"

"Because you haven't been invited before now," Judah ground out. "For fuck's sake, Phoenix, look at me."

Biting my lip to hold back a smile, I did as he asked, and lifted my chin to meet his eyes.

By now, he was done trying to be cute about it, and just simply said, "The guys and I have some things to do, so I've paid Kenji here, to drive you and Frankie to a day spa, where you'll be spend the afternoon getting whatever services you like. Then Kenji will bring you back here, where I've hired a beauty team to come to the house and get you and Frankie ready. Your next ride will arrive to pick both of you up at seven-thirty sharp."

My eyes widened, "And where are we going?"

Obviously more relaxed since his speech was done, he wagged his eyebrows and stated, "That's for me to know and you to find out. Now let's go eat some of these damn donuts—that I now can't stand—because we only have about thirty minutes until you have to leave for your appointment."

"Woo!" Kavan shouted and began obnoxiously clapping his hands. "Good talk team!"

I shook my head and eyed Frankie, who threw a wink in my direction from the comfort of Silas' arms before Judah threw a hand over my shoulder and leaned down to whisper in my ear. "Happy Birthday, sweet girl."

Every time he said the nickname, it had my pussy throbbing. There was always a hint of sarcasm within the two words, letting me know that while he did think I was sweet, he knew there was a side of me that was anything but.

"Thank you," I smirked back, basking in the double meaning.

I had a feeling I was in for a *very* interesting day.

※ ❃ ※

"YO, my skin is smoother than a baby's ass cheek," Frankie sighed as we slid in the back of Kenji's car after spending five hours getting collagen facials, aromatherapy massages, and algae body polishes. "That herbal sauna should have been on my list to add onto J's house. I need one of those in my life on the *daily*."

Kenji laughed from the front seat, calling back, "I got lost on the altitude pool deck. That shit was award-winning."

Judah paid for Kenji to get whatever he wanted as well, as long as he left Frankie and me alone to spend the afternoon together.

"I'm excited to get all glammed up," Frankie did a little shimmy in her seat.

"Do you know where we're going?" I asked my best friend, trying to sound nonchalant, but feeling anything but.

Before we left for the spa, Judah's energy had shifted and those nerves from the day before were on full display. I doubted anyone noticed, but I saw them immediately. He was worried about something, but it went deeper than I expected. It was personal to him.

After spending two months learning about his triggers and hearing stories about his past, I was able to quickly pick up on the difference between anxiety that came from general things, and anxiety that was linked to his healing journey.

This was the latter.

He was in serious thinking mode, getting lost in his head, and I didn't get a chance to ask him what was up before he and Pharaoh ushered us out the door. The only thing that had me feeling calm enough to enjoy my day, was the fact that Judah wasn't alone. His best friend was with him, and while Judah didn't have the easiest time opening up to even Pharaoh, I knew that Phar wouldn't let him spiral into a tizzy he couldn't get out of.

Still, in the back of my mind, I worried.

"I actually don't," Frankie sighed, which caused me to study her closer, looking for lies. "Judah was *supposed* to tell me, but then I got too excited, and he got freaked out, thinking that I would blow his fucking cover, so he didn't tell me shit."

Frankie was an awful liar and given her obvious frustration, I knew she was telling me the truth.

"Well fuck," I exhaled heavily, now at a loss when it came to trying to figure out what had Judah feeling so worked up. "I guess we'll just wait and see."

Frankie, oblivious to my concern, mused, "I hope this beauty team brings a good array of dresses because I am *not* trying to look average tonight."

"Wait," I held up a hand, "they better not be bringing dresses! Do you have any fucking idea how many designer outfits I have untouched with the fucking tags still on, in my closet at his house? We don't need more!"

At my outrage, both Frankie and Kenji busted out laughing, like my statement was ridiculous.

"Oh honey," Kenji sighed like he pitied me. "You haven't been paying attention to how Hollywood works."

"Fuck off," I grumbled, rolling my eyes as Frankie continued to chuckle next to me.

I knew how it worked, I just hoped Judah wouldn't play into the stupidity of shit like that. Why would we buy two more brand new outfits when I had a whole closet full?

Hell, it was ridiculous.

"He wants to spoil you, babe," Frankie's voice was gentle as she bumped her shoulder against mine. "Just let him."

Yeah, whatever.

I just knew how much he had to pay last month to get Brandon to drop the case against him, so without knowing how much Judah was actually worth, I worried he was spending too much on me. Especially since he wasn't releasing new music or even acting as a social figure in the industry at the moment.

But Frankie was right, and what the hell did I know?

I wasn't about to act ungrateful when the man clearly went

all out, with a whole lot of care and thought behind each action.

"I need some music," I called out to Kenji. "Hook me up to the Bluetooth."

"You got it, dude."

As soon as everything was set and I hit shuffle, Frankie and I perked up, grinning at each other as "Love Me Land" by Zara Larsson filtered through the speakers.

Yeah, this was exactly what I needed.

Me, my best friend, and night full of unlimited possibilities.

Happy Birthday to me.

CHAPTER 47

JUDAH

"OKAY, YOU NEED TO *CALM* DOWN," Holly warned, putting two hands on my shoulders as I hung my head.

"I am freaking the fuck out," I admitted, as if it weren't completely obvious.

"Yes, I know, but Judah listen to me," she pushed, pulling my chin up to meet her stare. "This album is your best yet, I fucking *promise*, and I can tell you right now, everyone is going to think the same. But at the end of the day, they don't even fucking matter, right? That's what we've been talking about for months now. This industry can kiss your ass."

I was sitting in the dressing room of the small venue we'd rented out, while the crew we hired to set up the stage.

While I appreciated Holly's words, she was the very last person I wanted to talk to, so I counted to three and pushed my fears aside. Then switched the subject. "Did you give the letter to the limo driver?"

"Yup," Holly nodded, seeming relieved to be talking about something she could control. "And the guys are already on their way back to your place. I made sure Silas had everything you requested for their drive back here."

I blew out a breath. "Alright good. And the tickets?"

"All gone," Holly grinned wickedly. "The venue will be at capacity. That Julia woman is no joke."

Yeah, no shit.

I should have known when I had Holly reach out to Frankie's PR manager to see if she'd get invitations out to influencers about tonight's event, that she'd be able to get the job done, but for some reason, I doubted anyone would want to come.

The tickets were free, given the guests would act as a form of equally free marketing. They were required to post to their social media accounts in order to spread the word about what I announced tonight, but that little fact was exactly what had me losing control.

So much could happen.

Hate. Criticism. Belittling my words.

It was daunting, downright terrifying, to think about my most honest stories being ripped apart by the media, but I started this, and I knew I had to see it through.

"Dude," Vale called out from the open doorway, smiling from ear to ear with Pierce in tow, looking just as excited. "You fuckin' ready?!"

I swallowed the ball of anxiety in my throat and nearly lied to his face before Holly cut in, saying, "No, he's not fucking ready. He needs a pep talk. So, get it done while I make sure everything is solid out there. Rex should be here soon."

Oh, fantastic. Rex was coming too.

I groaned and dropped my head in my hands.

"Ohhhhh, no you don't," Pierce stated, coming over to pull my head up by my hair. "You listen to me, ya little asshole. You did *not* put us through months of hiding and tell us to lie to basically everyone, just to pussy out now. Hell, we weren't even allowed around Phoenix because you didn't want to spoil the fucking surprise! Bro! This is our fucking time! *Your* time!"

"Who gives a mother fuck what anyone has to say tonight?" Vale added, sounding genuine, "This album is a fucking banger, bro, and I've watched you ring your heart dry, all over the floor of that studio for too long now, to let fear stop you."

"We've been down this road before and it wasn't any fun," Pierce admitted. "The guy we've come to know over the last few months is not the guy we knew last year, and the world deserves to know him too. It's time to rip the fucking band-aid off and tell this story. We've got money to make, bitches to fuck, and a whole lot of celebrating to do."

Vale nodded his head toward Pierce and added, "And honestly? We can't wait to see that girl of yours because it's been way too fuckin' long."

They didn't get it.

Neither of them could understand that while their words were meaningful in their own way, they did very fucking little to ease any of my fears. The battle was with my own mind and could only be won by sheer willpower and truths I couldn't quite figure out.

In order to get them out of the room, I stood up and stated, "Whatever, just keep your hands to yourselves."

"At least it got him standing up," Pierce murmured in Vale's direction while grinning at me like a dick.

I snarled out. "I'll get it together. Just give me a minute."

After each of them patted me on the back and left the room, I sat down on the couch and took a few deep breaths, picturing Phoenix, wondering if she'd gotten my letter yet.

Unsure of the time, I grabbed my phone, only to find an unread text message from my little bird waiting for me.

My hands shook as I opened the message.

Phoenix: I love you, Judah Colt.

Fuck.

Tears pricked my eyes as my demons screamed, refusing to be put down by three little words. But I was stronger because of them. I saw the meaning, felt the truth, and knew that even if tonight ended in ruin, I would still have her.

I couldn't type fast enough as I wrote out my reply.

Judah: I love you more, Phoenix Royal.

"Dude, you good?" I heard Pharaoh's voice before I saw him.

I remained staring at my phone screen as I replied, "No, I'm not."

"But?" He pushed.

"But I'm gonna do it anyway."

"There's the Judah I know."

P's little reminder had me standing from the couch with new, yet fragile, confidence in my veins. It was enough to keep me steady, but not enough to think completely positive.

Tonight, I'd be re-introducing myself to a world I couldn't stand, and despite knowing that the feeling was probably mutual, I swallowed my fear, because I had shit to say, and this world was gonna listen.

TheColt was back and it was showtime.

CHAPTER 48
Phoenix

"MISS ROYAL, THIS IS FOR YOU."

The limo driver—an older gentleman with white hair and a knowing smile—handed me a neon pink envelope, matching the notes Judah had left me earlier this morning.

"Thank you," I nodded, returning his smile as I took the letter from his hand. My stomach was a mess of nerves as I stepped away from the fancy black limousine and began to open the envelope.

"From J?" Frankie asked, coming to stand beside me as everyone else, minus Pharaoh and Judah, climbed into the limo.

"Mhm," I muttered, distractedly.

Pulling out a piece of black cardstock, I read the words written in silver sharpie.

"Baby Bird,
Last year, you made me promise to ask you if I ever wanted you to come to one of my shows, instead of just manipulating you into attending. I thought it was funny, you absolutely did not."

I laughed at that, remembering how pissed I was about the whole thing.

"And while I know this isn't much better, I hope you can forgive me, given the circumstances.
At first glance, this may seem like I've made tonight about me rather than your birthday, but it will make sense in time, and I have a feeling you will appreciate why I did what I did, and why I chose today to make it happen.
After tonight, there are no more secrets.
But in exchange for my secrets being out, I have to issue a small warning.
There will be paparazzi. There will be headlines. There will be…noise.
We've lived the last few months in virtual silence, hiding away from the world as I worked up the strength to make my presence known again in the industry, but that time is coming to a close.
What I can promise you is…this time will be different.
This time, I'll lean on you when it gets hard.
This time, your voice will be heard, your advice will be taken, and your time will be respected.
I'm doing this my way now, no longer following my demon's lead.
Tonight, you'll meet TheColt once again.
Remember, he loves you as much as I do.
See you soon,
J
PS – smoke the fucking blunt. It's your goddamn birthday."

"What the hell?" I whispered, trying to blink away the tears in my eyes in order to make sure I read his letter properly. "No. No way."

"What does it say?!" Frankie questioned impatiently.

I threw it at her, "Read it out loud."

As she did, I paced the driveway, listening to the words carefully, making sure I understood what he was saying.

You'll meet TheColt once again.

"Holy fuck," Frankie breathed, then repeated louder, "holy *fuck*, Phoenix!"

"I know!" I yelled back, letting this new information settle into my system, and as I did, a watery smile formed on my lips.

Little by little, I pieced together the clues, his insecurities yesterday, the nervous anxiety from the morning, the secret project, and the fact that he was okay with keeping this hidden because he knew that I wouldn't be able to bitch about the end result…

"He's been writing," I concluded, then met my best friend's shocked stare. "He's been *writing* Frankie."

She nodded vigorously, "Enough to hold an event of some sort, apparently."

"Ladies, I'm sorry to interrupt," the limo driver cut into our freak-out session, "but we have to leave if we're going to make it on time."

Shit.

"Right, right, okay," I nodded in his direction and grabbed Frankie's hand, pulling her toward the open door. "Let's go."

As soon as we stepped inside the limo, Kavan, Ricco, and Silas all turned in our direction, each of them wearing shit-eating grins.

"Oh my god, you knew!" Frankie yelled out. "You fuckers *knew* and didn't say anything?!"

"Please," Kavan laughed, reaching over to grab a bottle of champagne that floated in ice, "and risk pissing off Judah? No way. We weren't going to ruin the surprise and be the reason he fell off the deep end again."

Well, when he put it that way…

"Jesus Christ," I muttered, rubbing my temples as I prepared myself for what was to come.

Judah's warning wasn't to be taken lightly. If he really was coming back with new music, the paparazzi would be no joke. We'd be swarmed by media outlets trying to gain information on TheColt's next steps, and because I was so close to him, they'd consider me just as good of a source as he was to find that information.

However, I found myself significantly less stressed than I would have been last year.

It could have been because I spent so many months being chased by paps while he was in rehab, or because I was closer to Judah now than I ever had been before, but the idea of being under the public eye again didn't grind my gears like it used to. For some reason...I felt like I could handle it.

Like *we* could handle it.

As long as we did it together.

"Phewwww," Silas clapped his hands as he stared into a wooden box on his lap. "That boy stocked us *up*, y'all. Motherfucker came *through* with the high-quality bud."

Remembering the final statement in his letter, I smiled.

Judah supplied blunts for the limo ride.

"He also sent a playlist," Ricco informed us. "It's downloaded to my phone."

Son of a bitch.

He went all out.

I had absolutely no idea how Judah was able to piece his career back together, but I knew I was about to find out, and that little fact had anticipation and pride filling my lungs with new air.

This was what I wanted.

This was what I pictured, what I was hesitant to pray for, fearing I'd never get it.

Judah had done the damn thing, all on his own, and I was on the ride of my life.

"WOOOO," Kavan shouted, fanning his face as "Motley

Crew" by Post Malone began to play through the boosted speaker system of the limo. "YEEEEAH BOY."

"Pass me a blunt!" Frankie called to Silas, who handed her a perfectly rolled piece.

As she lit it, I relaxed, nodding my head to the music, feeling the adrenaline of TheColt leaking into bloodstream. If I knew anything about this new version of Judah, it was that he wasn't coming to play.

And that had me more excited than anything.

※

THE HIGH WAS thick after so much time not smoking but I was grateful for the haze of weed as we exited the limo into a sea of paparazzi. Silas' bodyguards met us at the door of the limo and kept the crowd back, allowing us to move swiftly through the crowd and into the back entrance of the venue. We weren't completely out of view from the people still entering the building from the front, but it was better than fighting fans *and* paparazzi at the same time.

After hitting traffic on the highway, we arrived later than expected, so I wasn't sure we'd have time to see Judah before whatever was about to happen, happened. When I went to ask Kavan if he knew where J's dressing room was, he didn't have time to answer before Holly stopped our group's forward motion.

"Oh my god," I breathed heavily as nostalgia hit my chest.

"Ahhhh!!" Frankie squealed, rushing forward to wrap Judah's former assistant in a hug.

Holly seemed prepared for it, catching Frankie with barely even a stumble, laughing as she did it.

Once the shock wore off a second later, I ran forward, joining the two girls in a group hug, feeling a surge of gratitude, knowing that Holly had chosen to give Judah another chance.

There was no doubt in my mind that without her, he wouldn't have kept his cool while preparing for all of this. It was making more and more sense how he was able to keep this part of his life a secret.

"Dude!" I yelled as I stepped back. "What the hell is happening?"

Holly smiled. "Okay, while I am so happy to see you all, and I would love to answer your questions, we have *very* little time to get you to your seats so we're gonna have to wait until after."

I was disappointed, but at the same time, too excited to care.

"Do your thing, lil' lady," Kavan called out. "What's the move?"

"You guys have a gated off section right in the front, but Phoenix," Holly's blue eyes met my gaze, "I'm going to come grab you after the second song, okay? He's only doing a few songs, but the last is the most important."

Nervous butterflies took flight in my stomach as I replied, "Sure, sounds good."

"All right, follow me," she stated with an all-business attitude as she walked us through a door that led to the main floor of the building.

The venue looked to be an old fire hall that had been remodeled into a place that could hold events like this one, but it was still big enough to hold at least a few thousand people.

When we hit the floor, the energy in the room buzzed around me, reminding me of the other shows I'd been to, but this time, there was curiosity in the air as the crowd speculated on what they might see tonight.

I found myself wondering the same thing as Holly led us to our section, which was indeed just a gated-off square down in front, giving us a perfect view of the stage that sat a good ten feet away.

"He's about to go on," Holly warned us, igniting whispers behind our group, as the people around us heard her statement. She ignored them as we locked eyes. "Phoenix…I just have to say that I am *so* fucking glad you're here. Happy Birthday, babe."

Warmth, once again, spread through my chest as I grabbed her hand and squeezed. "Fuck my birthday, thank you for taking a chance on him."

With a single nod, she stated, "Turns out, he's worth the risk."

Damn right he is.

As soon as she left, I heard my name spread through the crowd as people started to realize I was in attendance, and it had Ricco moving to stand behind me.

"You good?" he asked, running both hands down my exposed arms.

Goosebumps spread as I replied, "Sure am."

"You ready for this?"

I turned my head to look up at him, grateful as fuck for the friendship he provided and the support that never ran out. "I honestly don't even know."

"Well, you better get ready," he nodded toward the stage as the crowd began to scream. "Look."

I turned back as quickly as I could, but just as I did, the lights went out.

And the last thing I saw was TheColt, standing ten feet away.

JUDAH

THE SCREEN behind me lit the room and the sound of the media hit my ears.

"We just got word that TheColt has overdosed."

"Breaking news here in LA today—Judah Colt, otherwise known as TheColt was rushed to the hospital this morning after being found on the floor of his bedroom. An overdose is suspected."

"We knew this was coming, but TheColt has fallen."

"It's a sad story we've come to report today…"

"His condition at the moment is unknown," the last layer of the voices became the clearest one, the most impactful, "but we are left to wonder…will TheColt ever return to the stage?"

The last woman's voice faded into nothing as the screen went blank and that monster in my soul, the one that fueled the rage behind the music, stepped front and center. Pharaoh's sticks tapped against the cymbals, creating a low, rushing sound effect as a spotlight lit me up from the ceiling above.

Gripping the mic in my hand, I kept my head down and told the waiting crowd a story.

Little pink pills
Hard to find veins

Smoke in my lungs
Please come kill me either way

Higher than the clouds
I surrendered to my fate
Met the devil
Let him hit it

No more hiding
No more running
No more scheming
No more gunning
For the finish line

So with acid on my tongue
As that lean slid down my throat
I popped two more and called it good
'that'll hold me over'
'that'll get me through the day'
'that'll push me through anxiety
That I cannot escape'

Fuck depression
Fuck it all
Fuck it up
Fuck right off

Fuck you mommy, daddy too
All that rage and the abuse
Led me straight into the hole I'm in
Yet somehow it's not you
It's not your fault
It's my own
Now that's a pill I cannot swallow

EVEN IF WE FIGHT

I heard six figures bought you tickets
"it's a magnificent event"
So I stole one off the table
And threw myself inside the den

Little pink pills
Hard to find veins
Smoke in my lungs
Please come kill me either way

I'm a cautionary tale
So don't go followin' the leader
Or you'll see what happens
When Hollywood nightmares come to life
Together we play with rope
Create a noose
Decide on different ways to die.
We fall in love with social homicide.

I tried to do the job for you,
emptied the entire fuckin' bottle
Went to hell and met my maker,
Turns out The Devil didn't want me either.

So when you think about how much you hate it
How you wish I had succeeded
You can choke on all that hatred.

See TheColt needed a reinvention
And a kiss with death would do it.

Now that cup you hold so tightly
Might be poisoned so be careful
Wouldn't want you to end up like me

Not sure you could survive it.

As soon as Pharaoh crashed the cymbals, ending the song, the crowd went *wild*. It wasn't like it would have been if the venue was full of my own fans—rather than influencers that had been invited just to spread the word—but the reaction was there nonetheless. And even though I was done with that first song, I was nowhere near done with the job I needed to do that night.

Nerves felt like screws in my stomach as I wiped my forehead and listened to the waves of praise coming my way, but because I wanted to get it over with, wanted to just lay it all on the line, I took a deep breath and started my speech.

"Fuck is up, Los Angeles?" I addressed the crowd, earning another round of cheering as camera flashes turned on once again. "I think by now I can be honest enough to say I'm really fuckin' bad at this so I'm just going to jump right in, yeah?"

I was hit with chuckles, as they all simmered, waiting for me to say what I came to say.

"At the end of last year, I attempted to take my life." I swallowed thickly, noticing that while it was moving toward quiet before, it was damn near silent now. "I can't say that it was selfish in the way that some might, but I now believe that it would have been a mistake if I had received the outcome I desired."

"Got that right!" Someone yelled, making me reach up to scratch a non-existent itch on my temple.

I was uncomfortable to say the least.

"I believe that I'm only standing in front of you because God, the Universe—whatever higher power sits in the sky and watches all of us idiots screw up the planet—decided to save me from my own actions."

"Why'd you do it?!" Someone screamed toward me, and the question felt like a bullet.

Anxiety crept in as vulnerability suffocated me, reminding me that every word I said would be blasted to the public in real-time.

"Yeah! Why?!"

Fuck.

I snapped. "I did it because I hated it here. I hated my life, my past. I hated the industry and all the ruthless motherfuckers out there that live to tear others down just for the publicity. Just because they can. Just because they don't think about what that person might be going through or why they choose to say what they say in their music." My words were fast, to the point. "I hated that I had to bury myself in my issues in order to handle the pressure, and that I was too weak to find any other way to survive. But fact was, I had no guard, no sense of self, and no love for the talent I was given."

No one called out again, but flashes were still blaring in my direction as people video taped my whole rant.

Fuck my life.

"But while I was in rehab—after spending weeks refusing to talk, barely eating, and falling right back into the same depressive state I was attempting to block out with drugs and alcohol—I found myself at a crossroads. And people talk about that all the time, you know? Whether you're an addict, going through a breakup, grieving the loss of a loved one, or considering suicide, it all includes pain, it all comes from a *place* of pain, and there always comes a time where you meet that fork in the road." My heart rate slowed to a manageable beat as I continued, "The one that screams 'stay where you are or push yourself to find happiness again.' Except for me, my journey would lead me to happiness for the *first* time."

One of our hired crew members brought out a stool, placing it behind me as I spoke, so I took a seat and got a little more comfortable in order to get out the next part of my story.

"In my eyes, before my overdose, happiness was fleeting.

It lasted a handful of seconds, for a single moment, and then it vanished, and I always felt like that small blip in time was never worth it because when it was gone, the fall back into depression was so much worse than it was before I knew what it felt like to be happy. So, naturally, I was terrified. I didn't believe I was meant to feel happiness, didn't think I could ever achieve a high that was that pure, rather than synthetic and capable of killing."

The truth wrapped around my vocal cords.

"But eventually, after my therapist—shout out Dr. B—finally broke through my bullshit, I recognized that while the land of happiness was extremely foreign to me, it was still a place I could visit and eventually build a home in. I just had to be willing to go all in."

"What was it like?!" Someone yelled, while another person backed him up. "Yeah, what was rehab like for you?!"

"Basically torture," I called out, then swallowed, trying to clear my throat. "It sucked—as I'm sure you guys could imagine—because submitting to getting sober meant going back in time. And for months, I did exactly that. I revisited my childhood memories, my parents, my suffering, and learned what made me who I was back then. I figured out how I became an addict and why, I discovered why I thought everything I touched turned to ash, and why my insecurities were not only debilitating but all-consuming. I touched every trigger, pressed every red button, and got lost in all the things I tried to bury under my addiction."

As I took a deep breath, I glanced down at the crowd—starting from the left side—and stared into camera lenses, glanced past faces displaying pity or curiosity, until I landed on a pair of shining brown eyes.

I would recognize those eyes anywhere, at any time of the day, in this lifetime and the next.

Phoenix was looking right at me, her expression showcasing pride and worry all wrapped together in a twisted bow, but now that I found her in the crowd, I relaxed even further, settled into myself and my truth.

I spoke only to her as I said, "But then I started to write."

A handful of people cheered, but rather than reacting, I remained entirely focused on P.

"As I spent three months in that facility, I wrote every morning, afternoon, even in the middle of the night, until I found myself with enough songs to create an entire album." P's only reaction was a slight tilt of her head as questions swirled in the space between us. "Of course, I had no label, no bandmates, no one to help me turn it into anything, but by the time I finished…I had hope. I had begun to formulate a plan in my head, started to think about all of the people I needed to apologize to, the challenges I'd face, and the fact that I would have to start from scratch, but for once, I didn't want to give up or hide because I had fifteen stories to tell. Fifteen truths to reveal. And I genuinely believed that not only did I need to do this for myself, but the world also needed to hear them."

Those brown eyes swam in moisture, leaving me feeling choked up, more vulnerable than before, and yet somehow alone in a room with the one person I cared about the most. It was just her and I. But I needed her closer, needed to touch her, when I told the last part of this story, even though that wasn't the original plan.

Standing from my seat, I spoke as I walked to the edge of the stage. "So, when I got out, I made it a goal of mine to prove my worth, my sobriety, and my growth to the people I let down. I made it my mission to get back to the original dream, the one where I wasn't the highest one in the room, picking fights and throwing fits. But rather the one that changed the tide of this industry and made a true impact on the people that heard our sound."

When there was no more stage in front of me, I sat down

and broke eye contact with Phoenix to address the crowd. "I thank my lucky stars every fucking day that my bandmates chose to take a chance on me again. Vale, Pierce, Pharaoh, even my adoring, brutal assistant Holly came back and joined me on my mission to reinvent TheColt and bring him back to life."

Fear ignited in my chest, sending hot flashes of nerves into my system as I looked back down at Phoenix again, finding her watching me as if the distance was too much for her as well. Still, she stood where she was, with Ricco's hands on her shoulders and Frankie's fingers interlaced with her own, as they supported her while she supported me.

I was overcome with a wave of intense gratitude for my group of friends because if they hadn't kept P standing, hadn't made sure she made it through my downfall, I wouldn't have gotten back up.

It was all because of her.

I lowered the mic, exhaled, then fell into the honeyed brown depths of her stare.

"But there was one person in my life that I knew I didn't deserve forgiveness from," I began again, making sure Phoenix knew I was talking about her, "and I would be a lying son of a bitch if I said I wasn't sure what I was going to do if I didn't receive it anyways."

Tears pricked my own eyes then, as I felt the weight of that statement.

"When I began to write in rehab, I found that most of the songs featured her presence, her strength, even though I didn't feel any of it yet. I wrote openly and honestly because she told me I could. I dreamed because she told me to, and I believed because *she* believed in me."

Phoenix shook her head, as if in awed disbelief.

"So, when I finished—when those fifteen songs were written—I knew what the title of my new album would be almost instantly. It was the last song I wrote that became the title track, but this album was also the first secret I kept from her when I got out of rehab, and it was the only one I held onto until this very moment."

The crowd had figured out I was talking about Phoenix just a few sentences after I sat down and the whispering had gotten louder, rapidly moving into excitement as they realized there was more going on here than just a listening party.

Smiling only a little, I stated, "And while I am well aware of the fact that this event is not a proper birthday present, I knew that if my girl could forgive me after all of the shit I put her through, still find a way to put her trust in me, and show up every day to support me, she'd see why this present is one I couldn't put money on. She'd understand the gift I was giving her."

I hopped down from the stage, then, and moved toward her while Phoenix lifted a hand to her mouth, trying to hold in a sob I knew would break through eventually.

"You've seen her face in the tabloids, heard her name around the city, and watched her tangle and untangle herself from my toxicity over the last year. She's got these bright, haunting brown eyes and a smile that could heal the sick. Pretty lips, high cheekbones, and her right ear is just a little bit bigger than her left."

The crown gave a collective chuckle as I stopped in front of Phoenix.

"And *she* is the reason I'm standing in front of you today—whether she wants to be or not. Her strength was a model for my own, her light is what I followed through the darkest tunnel, and her growth is what my demons hated. Yet, they never tore her down. She faced the devil in me head-on, she met him blow for blow, and…she never left. Even when we fought. She stayed with me in that rehab facility, she was a nightmare and daydream all at once, and she was my muse for this entire album. She's the headliner in this next phase of my life."

"Judah, what are you doing?" Phoenix whispered as I nodded at Ricco, signaling that he was good to step back. I winked at Frankie, who smiled as she let go of P's hand, leaving room for me to step in and replace it. "Oh my god, you aren't."

I was.

"Judah!"

I nodded at Silas, signaling that he follow us as I pulled Phoenix toward the stage.

I stated into the mic, "I was supposed to do one more song before this one, but fuck it, I make the rules, yeah?"

The crowd exploded, proving their readiness for the next part of the event.

"All right, good," I smiled into the mic before I let go of P's hand and hopped up on stage again, leaving her with Silas, who whispered the plan in her ear. "Glad we're in agreement. So, Phoenix Royal…" At the mention of her name, the crowd cheered louder while I glanced down, finding her on Silas' shoulders, making her the perfect height to climb on stage without getting hurt. "Will you join me for a song?"

There was a reluctant smile on her face as she shook her head, but when we locked eyes, she rolled her eyes and nodded.

I couldn't hide my joy as Silas walked forward and bent so she could place her feet on the edge. I held her hand until she was steady and standing next to me, wearing a stark white sleeveless dress, ripped in all the right places, showcasing that tan skin, with designer combat boots on her feet.

Holding the mic away from my face, I told her, "Take a seat on the stool."

"I'm going to make you pay for this," she whispered, meeting my eyes with a dangerous smile on her face.

"You can get your revenge on our flight to Costa Rica," I smirked. "We have a whole jet to ourselves and plenty of time for you to get back at me—though I think our little visit with the rabid wild monkeys you insist on spending time with will be punishment enough."

"Judah!" She yelled as quietly as she could. "What the hell?"

She was still smiling so I took that as a good sign as I said, "We leave after this. And yes, Kenji knows. He's been secretly booking all of your appointments for the next two weeks on his schedule rather than yours."

"Ohhhhh we have so much to talk about," she warned, yet sat down on the stool anyway.

Loving the banter and the feel of her on stage with me, I winked. "Fully prepared."

As the crowd gave off waves of anticipation, I glanced behind me, making sure the guys were ready for the switch in song. Pharaoh shot me a thumbs-up as the other two nodded, so I knew they were set to go.

Those nerves made a U-turn, coming back around to torture me once again, but I shut them down and stepped behind Phoenix, addressing the crowd once again, asking, "Y'all recognize her?"

The screams were nearly blinding, proving that damn near everyone sided with the little bird over me in our catastrophe, but how could I blame them?

"Good," I nodded, bending to kiss the top of P's head, before grabbing my guitar from one of the crew members that rushed out to hand it to me, "because today is her birthday, her patience saved my life, and this one is for her."

The crowd screamed as I revealed, "Here is the title track of my upcoming album…On The Wings of a Bird."

CHAPTER 50
Phoenix

I WAS able to wipe my face clean of tears before Judah pulled me on stage, but they started right back up again when I heard the title of his album.

On the Wings of a Bird.

I should have been mad, I should have felt that constricting suffocation I used to feel whenever Judah made me the object of his obsession, but this time was different. It *felt* different.

It felt like Judah had grown into a healthier state of being and was now able to see me as a form of motivation and inspiration, and yet he'd made sure to prove over the last few months that he was capable of living his own life, of thriving without me being a constant crutch, while also leaning on me when necessary. He was finally giving as much to our relationship as I was and it felt balanced, it felt equal, but this praise? This gift?

It felt like love.

It felt like strength.

It felt like the goddamn truth.

I *was* his light, I'd impacted him on such a level that we both couldn't look away from the fact that without my influence, without my faith in him, he probably wouldn't have had a reason to get clean. He wouldn't have had a reason to hope or dream or take life by the balls and twist until he got exactly what the fuck he wanted. If it weren't for my growth, he never would have hit such a low bottom and although that bottom threatened to kill him, it didn't. He survived. And for once, I was okay with the way he loved me because this time, it didn't feel like pressure, it felt like gratitude.

But when Judah began to play, standing next to me with his guitar, I couldn't hold in the emotion, but rather fell victim to the sadness floating within the chords of his melody. There was longing, memories, pain, but when he began to sing, I lost all coherent thought and was forced to surrender to the timber of his voice and the story he wished to tell with it.

I'm still not sure if it was a dream
Or my memory made it feel like one
But in the midnight hour of a random weekday
A little bird met me on the roof

A party raged below, full of everything I hated
Of everything I loved
Booze, drugs, and neon lights,
Started and ended in a fight.
I was pissed and feeling sick
Dancing with demons, smoking cigarettes
One by one and back to back,
Hoping one day it would all go black

But then she was there
That little bird
Shining brightly in my living hell
And even then I had a feeling it wouldn't end well
I didn't care, there were no fucks given
Because she was the perfect victim
She'd hop on my ride and chase me to the bottom

EVEN IF WE FIGHT

Where we'd sit surrounded in fire
Burning together for the rest of forever

I saw it in her eyes, I swear it was there
She was just like me
Sick of bullshit, sick of people
Sick of fear and endless depression
Full of hatred, full of noise
Relentless suicide and doubt
We'd be perfect, flawless, frozen
We'd fly high then plummet straight
To hell

But she was clueless to my wishes
She didn't know my sick intent
I was broken, fucking useless
Demonic and alone
She was magic
She was truth
She was everything I wasn't

Still she loved me for who I was,
Who I am and who I'll be
Without her kindness, that endless patience
I wouldn't be the man you see

On the wings of a bird
I learned to fly
On my own without a parachute
Just me inside my mind
Because of her I learned to love
Because of her I learned the truth
Because of her I am the man you see right here in front of you.

There was no traditional bridge or chorus, just a song written like a letter, and I was left sobbing on that stage as Judah stood before me and took my hand, laying his heart on the line in front of thousands of people.

And now I promise,
For the rest of our lives

I'll hold you down, I'll lift you up
For worse or better, we'll fly together
Sober, clean, and true
I give my all
But because I know you better than any others do
I'll keep your heart safe
Store it deep inside myself
And hold us both steady.
Keep us grounded
Keep us healthy.
Keep us shining, keep us thriving
What I failed to do before.
From now until our next lifetime
I'll give my all and even more.

As the song ended and the crowd screamed, Judah bent to kiss me. Faces wet, hearts pounding, he sealed the deal for the entire venue to see while I couldn't feel anything but awe.

He said I inspired him, that I was the source of his motivation, but there, on that stage, he had *me* inspired. He had me motivated, dreaming, believing.

I dreamed of a future where he could tour and I could tattoo on the road. It had me formulating ideas, thinking of ways we could both do what we loved without the brutal separation. If I could get with local shops in whatever city he was performing in and book appointments around the world, I wouldn't have to leave him. We could do it all together—both his dreams and mine—because for the first time, I felt comfortable intertwining our lives in that way.

Giving him my everything didn't sound so scary anymore.

In fact, it was already done.

The realization hit me slowly but then finished in a blast as our kiss came to an end. Judah had stolen my heart on that rooftop, and I'd known it even then. It was what scared me, what made me run, but I couldn't get far because that was never in the cards.

Fate had different ideas.

Destiny was a twisted bitch.

Judah Colt was made for me, and I for him, but before we could be truly together, we had to fall apart and while it was hard and I wasn't even sure we could come back from it, I almost hated myself for ever doubting.

Just before Judah finally pulled away, I found a smile on his face, igniting a mirrored one on my own.

"I'm so proud of you," I choked out, feeling the truth all the way to my toes as more tears stung my eyes. "I'm so fucking proud."

He closed his eyes for only a moment, then those blue orbs seemed to shine brighter as he said, "I love you, baby bird."

The name had all new meaning as the album title rang in my ears.

I lifted a hand to his face to wipe the tears that still lingered, and replied, "I love you more, skyscraper."

※ ❋ ※

I LEFT the stage and joined our group once again after my song was over, but watched with just as much amazement as

Judah performed a final, all-new, completely feral track, reintroducing himself to the industry.

And from what I gathered in the whispers of conversation around us as we left the building, the feedback was brilliant. Though there were a still few people bitching about TheColt's new sound, talking about how he was better when he was high, and the comments had my blood boiling, but I reminded myself that Judah would need my strength, not my anger.

I knew he wasn't perfect, knew that at the end of the day the criticism would still get to him, so I had already begun to mentally prepare myself for what may or may not be said in the days following the event, but luckily, it seemed Judah had taken care of that.

"Are you fucking kidding me?" I rolled my eyes, even though my smile wouldn't go away.

"Not even a little," Judah laughed, holding my hand as we got out of the limo and walked toward a private jet parked in the same airport I'd left him at before his tour. "You wanted to play with monkeys—and while that is a fucking ridiculous thing to want—it's perfect for a birthday present and the timing works for everyone. We get to go away while people talk shit about my performance tonight and enjoy a tropical vacation for just the two of us."

Because I was an asshole and still in shock, I replied, "You know two weeks won't be enough for people to stop talking, right? You said the album would come out in August and you have two singles coming out between now and then. You're going to be in the spotlight for months."

Judah squeezed my hand, "Okay, fine, you win that round. But at least *this* way we have two weeks to mentally prepare ourselves for the next two months. How's *that* for a loophole?"

Glancing up at him, I smirked, "You don't actually need an excuse to take me on vacation, I'm just being a dick."

"I know," he replied, shrugging his shoulders, "but the banter is fun."

"True," I laughed. "So…does this jet have a bed?"

Judah clicked his tongue and tugged me into his side where he dropped my hand and draped his long arm over my shoulder instead. "Of course it has a fucking bed, who do you think I am?"

Anticipation blew heat through my body at the thought of fucking him in the air.

"We've never been on a plane together before," I pointed out, but my voice was a dead giveaway as far as my thoughts went.

"We sure haven't," he responded in a tone matching mine. But when he looked down at me, fire burned in those blue eyes, and I nearly tripped over the need to be surrounded by his scent, his taste. "And I plan to make a memory out of it."

I had to remind myself to breathe. "One that we can try and top on our way to backpack around Europe for *your* birthday?"

His grin was megawatt. "I like the way you think, woman!"

As I chuckled, a thought hit me, so I mused out loud, "Do you plan to tour again? With this new album?"

Judah sighed as we walked, changing the energy of our conversation as he admitted, "I'm not sure. It will depend on how people respond and how well received the album is. I don't really want to not after the disaster of the last tour—because it still feels triggering right now, but I might change my mind if my fans ask for it."

I remembered the thought I had at the concert, and decided to tell him my little dream, thinking that it might help ease some of his worries. "I was thinking that if you did, I could create my own kind of tattoo tour…I could link up with Holly and figure out which cities you'd play in, then find shops in the same city and see if they would let me guest tattoo while I'm there."

Judah stopped walking, halting our forward movement with shock written all over his face. "Holy...shit. Phoenix!"

"What?" I laughed.

"I had the same thought months ago, but wasn't sure what you'd think of it."

I smirked at his excitement and shrugged, explaining, "Your fans could get tattoos the next day if they wanted to. I'd only be able to do a few in one day but we could make sure every stop on your tour was a 3-day thing."

"Fuck yeah!" he shouted again, grabbing both sides of my face as emotional excitement took over. "You...you—you're fucking brilliant."

I grinned full and wide. "We can make it work without having to be apart for months on end. This way, we both get to live out our dreams."

"Okay, but wait," Judah requested, stepping back and shaking out his hands, "this gives me the confidence to ask you what I've wanted to ask for a while, but couldn't because you didn't know about the album and all that. But...since you mentioned tattooing, I have a thought and a request."

"...okaaay?" I muttered, wondering why he was so nervous.

"I was thinking maybe you could create a specific flash sheet—one that matches the album—and my fans could make appointments to get one of the designs tattooed after a show if they wanted to." Judah's offer had me dumbfounded as ideas began to whip through my mind. Adrenaline pumping through my veins, as he continued with, "but in that same thought... I've been wondering if maybe you'd be willing to draw up the album cover for On the Wings of a Bird."

Before I could say a word, he rushed out, "I'd pay you of course, but I was just thinking that since the album is inspired by our last year together and my past and all that, not to mention the fact that I don't have a designer right now…I mean, I could find one if you said n—"

I closed the space between us and kissed him, shutting him up, knowing that if I didn't, that run-on sentence would run on for *way* too long.

His nerves were adorable but completely unnecessary.

When I pulled back, I lowered my feet back to the ground and said, "I already have two solid ideas, and I'll start drawing them *after* you fuck me to sleep. Sound good?"

The smile that bloomed on his face was blinding, full of gratitude, awe, and everything I felt when I watched him on that stage tonight.

And it was then that I realized that for the rest of our lives, we could take turns making each other proud.

The two of us would never truly stop struggling. We both knew that every day would be a fight, every moment would provide a choice, and every second was another second closer to death. But we'd chosen to live this life together, and as long as we continued to fight, stayed open with each other, and remained honest about our fears and our issues? We'd make it through.

Because together, we were solid gold.

"You never fail to amaze me," Judah whispered as he lifted me off the ground. I wrapped my legs around his waist and looked down at him as he stated once again, "Happy Birthday, Baby Bird."

My only response was to press my lips to his and pour my gratitude, along with my excitement into his energy. Telling him without words that I couldn't *wait* to see what was next for us.

After all, this was just the beginning.

EPILOGUE
Frankie

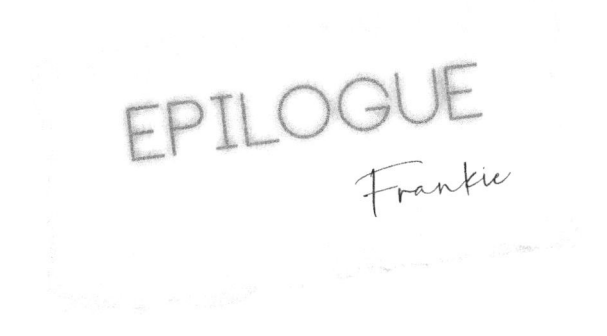

Three Months Later

"SORRY, CAN YOU REPEAT THAT?" I asked Julia as I slid to the floor of my bedroom with my back against the door. My heart beat wildly in my chest as I finished with, "I don't think I heard you properly."

My agent sighed and stated simply, "You heard me, Frankie. The same network that created the dating show Raelynn was on last year, is back with season two and they want you on it. But they're switching up the cast list this time around and rather than pulling in random people, this season is for established, single, influencers, looking to find love. Now, you know these things are generally bullshit and most of the relationships don't work out, but that doesn't matter because it's geared to make everyone money."

"Except, I'm not single," I replied numbly, as dread, fear, and a myriad of other negative emotions bled through my system.

"Well, I suggest you fix that," she replied as if it were that easy. "This is a big deal, and it will get you *other* big deals. With this much public recognition you could do whatever you wanted when you're done. Sponsorships will be through the roof and opportunities will be endless."

She wasn't wrong. I knew it in my fucking bones.

But there was the tiny little fact that I'd be going on a TV show to find love when I was already dating Silas, and I seriously doubted there was an influencer on that cast list that would be any better than him.

Do you really care though?

It's not like you even want *to find love, and this is a solid excuse to break it off with Silas. You've wanted to for months. You knew you were going to hurt him, and this way, you have a business opportunity you just* have *to take.*

How could he blame you?

Shaking my head to shut off the shitty thoughts, I asked, "When?"

"Three months until filming," she answered immediately. "It's filmed in Mexico."

Of course, it is.

"I have to go, I'll call you tomorrow with an answer," I told Julia in a rushed tone, feeling panic creeping up.

Which was only made worse as she replied, "Make it tomorrow morning, they need an answer ASAP."

Fucking hell. "Fine, bye."

After hanging up and before I could stop myself, I threw my phone across the room, watching it smash against the wall.

The screen would be shattered—if it even worked at all—but I couldn't seem to care.

My head dropped into my hands as my hardened resolve broke and I fell into a fit of sobs that matched the many breakdowns I'd had over the last few months.

My entire life was changing.

Phoenix and Judah were finally in a solid place and my best friend spent more time at his house than she did here. I didn't blame her—not even one bit—especially because she still made time for me and the guys, making sure we all spent Sunday mornings together getting brunch or shopping, and leaving Sunday night's for family dinners at our house, but I still knew what was coming. She would eventually get sick of driving back and forth to Thousand Oaks and would just move in with Judah, instead. She'd merge her life with his, as she should, and get on with crafting their future together. Which was great for her. A welcome step forward. But that meant that I would be alone and *fuck my life*, I…didn't know what to do with that.

It gave me very real, very visceral anxiety to think about my life without Phoenix living here.

And Silas?

He was a damn good fucking guy, but I knew deep down, he wasn't *my* guy.

I'd been fighting it for way too long, wasting his time, leading him on, and all because I couldn't get my shit together.

Truth was, I was no closer to figuring out what I wanted than I was back in January. Nothing had changed, it had only gotten worse.

"What the hell am I going to do?" I cried into my hands, fearing my future, wondering if this damn opportunity was a good one or a stupid one.

How would this help?

How would I—

There was a knock on my door just before P's voice hit my ears, "Hey, you in here?"

Shit. Shit. Shit.

"Mhm," I replied, trying to wipe my face, even though it wouldn't matter because Phoenix would see right through it.

"What the hell?" *Yup, immediately.* "Frankie, what's wrong?"

Giving up on trying to hide my breakdown, I told Phoenix about Julia's phone call and the whole reality TV thing, then ended with, "But how in the hell is this a good idea? It will only bring more drama!"

"Okay, just breathe for a second," Phoenix replied with a sigh. "This is a lot to take in and we are gonna need to make a *serious* pros and cons list, but my first thought is—Julia isn't wrong. This *would* open up a helluva lot of opportunities for you and you know reality TV stars end up building businesses with the money they make, and those businesses take off because they get sponsorships, just like Julia said. You wanted to get into interior design or even event planning. This could be the starting point as long as you don't lose your mind and make yourself a hated contestant."

"Jesus Christ," I muttered, dropping my head back into my hands. "This is *not* how I expected today to go."

"Uh…yeah," Phoenix responded, sounding sheepish, which made me look at her.

"What?" I asked. "What's wrong, now?"

"It's not bad," Phoenix rushed to say, then cringed, "but Judah is on his way with an offer for you. He wouldn't tell me what it is, but he said it's pretty big…"

"Fucking hell!" I groaned. "I can't handle this."

"You can just tell him that!" P soothed, running a hand down my back. "He will understand, Franks."

"Ugh," I stood up, abandoning Phoenix, not feeling like being consoled, just wanting it all to go away. "I need to clean my face up and then I need a fucking shot. Or six. *Then* I'll hear him out."

"Frankie, seriously," Phoenix tried to stop me, but I was already walking away. "I can tell him to call you later!"

"Nope!" I yelled back from the bathroom. "Let's see if his offer is better than Julia's."

I doubted it would be, but I was holding onto hope anyways.

AFTER TWO SHOTS of vodka and a full can of Truly, I was onto my second, when the front door flew open and Judah announced, "I brought friends, so please don't kill me, but this is important."

Phoenix and I glanced at each other with identical curiosity, and I was suddenly grateful for the slight buzz in my system because it wiped my anxiety pretty much clean.

When Judah stepped into the kitchen, he was flanked by a guy and a girl, both appearing younger than him, but rather than introducing them, he stopped when he saw me.

"What's wrong?" he asked immediately, looking as concerned as he sounded, and—not for the first time—I found myself hating the fact that we'd become close enough for him to see through my mask. "What happened?"

I shook my head, "Nothing."

"You're a fucking liar," he shot back. "What's wrong, Franks?"

"J," Phoenix interrupted, and when he looked at her, she shook her head, signaling that now wasn't the time.

Still, Judah glanced back at me—not one to take no for an answer—so I caved and said, "Fucking hell, I'll tell you later, just get on with it."

He studied me for a moment longer before saying, "Fine," but then wrapped his arms around both of his guests and said to Phoenix and I, "Here we have Cassie and Brian, my two friends from rehab."

There was only a quick second of silence before Phoenix jumped up from her seat at the island and ran toward them. "Oh my god, hi!"

She hugged Cassie first—a pretty pale faced girl with

orange hair and blue eyes—then wrapped her arms around Brian—a blond kid with glasses and a baby face.

I was being a bit rude, making them sound so young, when they clearly appeared to be in their early twenties, but my mood was shit and I was having a hard time faking it.

I zoned out as Phoenix talked to the two of them for a few minutes, while Judah got everyone glasses of water and pulled a package of Oreo's from our pantry, before signaling that we all sit around the island.

Judah got straight into his explanation.

"So, the three of us got to talking over dinner last night, and we've decided that we want to start a foundation for Addiction Recovery and Suicide Prevention."

Whoa.

Holy shit...

I straightened my shoulders, understanding this wasn't a topic I could brush off.

"We are working on a name, but we thought that we could throw a gala to raise start-up money for the foundation. Howeverrrr..." Judah drew out the word, then looked directly at me, staring at me with those damn humble puppy dog eyes, all full of excitement and faith in me, "we need someone to plan it, and there isn't a single person on this planet I'd rather have do it."

Shocked, still annoyed, and feeling completely unlike myself, I uttered, "Me?"

All three of them nodded, but it was Cassie that spoke next, "I saw what you did to Judah's house, and I've been following you for a while now. We all agreed that we'd trust you to plan it. If—I-if you'd be willing of course."

I must have looked like a total bitch because the girl was nervous, but I brushed it off and glanced at Phoenix, who was looking at Judah with stars in her eyes, no doubt feeling all types of ways about the fact that he wanted to start a whole foundation around addiction and suicide.

Again, I couldn't blame her, but I was fucking jealous of what she had.

Her strength, the way she'd grown. She looked so goddamn content and I was *sick* of feeling lost.

But at the end of the day, one thing I knew for sure was that the only time I *didn't* feel lost was when I was creating. When I was using my brain, utilizing my preference for all things designer, and turning ordinary things into extraordinary.

I cleared my throat and glanced back at Judah. "When would you like to host the gala?"

Would I even be here for it? Would it clash with the reality show filming?

Did I care?

Ugh.

"End of November."

Fuck.

One month before I'd have to leave.

That meant the gala would be my last big move before filming if I decided to take Julia's offer, and while I wasn't sure about the reality show, I was positive that I loved event planning.

Doing this gala for Judah and his friends would mean more content for my portfolio, more experience under my belt, and getting to work with him again…

As much as I complained about the man, I loved spending time with Judah and our friendship was one that I cherished. I could feel the excitement he held toward this new idea, and I couldn't help but feel like I would be an idiot to say no.

I couldn't let my bad mood and questionable life choices get in the way of the opportunity to do something *good* in this city. Los Angeles needed this, as did Judah, and all the people who would benefit from this foundation becoming established.

I could figure out the rest later on.

"I'll do it," I told them, tacking on a semi-fake smile. "I'd be happy to."

"Ahhh!!!!" Phoenix yelled, jumping from her chair to wrap me in a hug, one that I needed desperately, before giving the same affection to Cassie and Brian. "I'm so fucking excited for you guys!"

And Judah? Well, he wrapped me in those long arms and planted a kiss on the top of my head. One that overwhelmed me, one that made me hold him tighter because for some reason, I understood him better now that I was in such mental turmoil.

"We're having a conversation later," he warned me, speaking against the top of my head.

"I know," I responded into his chest, feeling the tears already pricking my eyes.

"But thank you, Franks," he stated. "I know you're gonna crush it."

I was. I would.

But I couldn't be bothered with much more celebration, and Phoenix understood when I left the room, telling everyone that I had some work to get done.

There was nothing to get done, only things to think about.

I had less than twenty-four hours to decide if I was going to expose myself to the television industry for my own personal gain, while simultaneously breaking Silas' heart, or if I was going to say "fuck the opportunity" and make a name for myself all on my own.

Not easy.

Not ideal.

But unfortunately…necessary.

THE END

ACKNOWLEDGMENTS

PHEWWWWWWWWWWWWWW.

I am a messy mess right now. Anyone else?

The Love Kills series has officially come to an end and our little bird and her skyscraper are officially free.

This has been the most insane journey. From listening to "In These Walls" by Machine Gun Kelly, and thinking "this is a twin flame relationship" (yes, I believe in twins) to meeting Judah and Phoenix immediately after. I tried to push them away, told them I had another series to complete before diving head first into the craziness the two of them would bring me, but they weren't having it.

I couldn't escape them, much like they couldn't escape each other, and before I knew it, I was knee deep in a world full of broken people searching desperately for love. It wasn't easy, it wasn't pretty, it was sometimes fun, but maaaaaan, I can honestly say I never expected the amount of growth that took place by the end of this story.

I'm so fucking proud of Judah for taking his healing by the balls and owning that shit. I'm in awe of Phoenix and her tenacity, her ability to withstand the harshest of truths in order to get to the bottom of the issue. Frankie, Pharaoh, Silas, Kav and Ricco…my god. They're family. They're real to me. And their stories are coming.

Now. Onto my "thank you"s.

Brittany BeeBee Elizondo. You absolute fucking queen. I love you more than words can describe. You're my life partner, my rock, my backbone, my sounding board, my everything. These last two years have been the best of my life because you're in it. I love you to fucking mars.

Dee. My absolute dude. Thank you for being who you are, for never forgetting about me when I left you to heal. For trusting our friendship, even when you struggled. Without you, I wouldn't have gotten through half the shit I went through this year and it goes far beyond books. It goes beyond marketing and covers and teasers. Our friendship is soul deep and I can't even express how much it means to me. You're one of the strongest people I know and I love you to fucking pieces. Your support is unmatched, your talent is out of this world, and you're stuck with me for life.

Summer. Um, hi. Where the hell did you even come from? I swear, you dropped out of the sky and slammed into my life with so much passion and excitement that it lit me back up. Before you made space for yourself in my life, I was a goddamn mess. I didn't know how I was going to get it all done, but you just showed up and did it. And you did it with love and dedication. People like you are fucking rare and you, my lil cancer darling, are a blessing. I love you I love you I love you. Thank you for every single thing you do for me. Here's to many more years of friendship.

My mom. Debbie muuuuhfuckin' Harris. You the wholeass shit, you know that? Of course you do, because you're Debbie. You're my rock, my best friend, my number one fan, and you never fail to keep me standing up right (except when you don't answer my 40th phone call of the day. How dare you.) I'm so lucky to have a mother like you and for fuck's sake, never doubt that. I love you so big.

Caitlin, Tia, Zoe, Kelli…thank you for reading this huge ass book in tiny little chunks and putting up with my unorganized, crazy ass for the last three months. We've put in WORK on this book and without you, it wouldn't be what it is today.

I'm so lucky to have a beta team like this one and I am forever grateful for everything you do. Thank you thank you thank you. Love you all to pieces.

To my street team. HEY YOU GUUUUUUUUUUUYS. You're so valued, so loved, and so fucking appreciated. Your shares, your hype, your dedication, none of it goes unnoticed and I am so lucky to have a team like you. Thank you thank you thank you.

And finally, to you guys, my misfits. You took a chance on me, as a new author with absolutely zero idea what the hell I was doing and you showed UP. You believed in me, you rode with me, and your support has not gone unnoticed. It's because of you that I get to do what I love to do every day and I can't express how much it means to me. I love you.

Alright, that's it. I'm done.

We're done.

But we're also not.

Drumroll

While the Love Kills series has ended, Dear Industry is about to begin. That's right, Frankie, Pharaoh, Silas, Kav AND Ricco, are all getting their own books under the umbrella of Dear Industry, which is set to begin in 2022 with none other than Frankie fuckin' Skyes.

I can't wait to see where we go from here.

Love you guys so hard.

ABOUT BRIANNA

Brianna Jean is a book loving, donut eating, vodka drinking, kind of human. Born and raised in Buffalo, NY, she thinks pizza and chicken wings are a food group and the Buffalo Bills are a way of life (even if they lose).

She has a daughter named Harley, two fur babies, and more plants than she knows what to do with. She writes modern dark romance, set in both fantasy and contemporary worlds, and lives everyday with characters wreaking havoc in her brain. Writing is her passion, books are her favorite pastime, and music soothes her soul.

Loud, sassy, and a little embarrassing, Brianna lives to love herself and those around her. Being an author was the dream, and now that dream is coming true—one book at a time.

Join the Misfits: https://bit.ly/2N4yjpl

ALSO BY BRIANNA

LOVE KILLS

Why Are You Here? (Book 1)

https://books2read.com/WAYH

ANGELUS

The Rise of Monsters (Book 1)

books2read.com/u/banvLL

Printed in Great Britain
by Amazon